Daydream

Content Warning:

Daydream *is intended for mature readers only*

It contains complex themes and sexually explicit content.

Also by Hannah Grace

Icebreaker

Wildfire

Daydream

HANNAH GRACE

**SIMON &
SCHUSTER**

London · New York · Sydney · Toronto · New Delhi

First published in Great Britain by Simon & Schuster Ltd, 2024
First published in the United States by Atria Paperback,
an imprint of Simon & Schuster, LLC, 2024

1 3 5 7 9 10 8 6 4 2

Simon & Schuster UK Ltd
1st Floor
222 Gray's Inn Road
London WC1X 8HB

Simon & Schuster: Celebrating 100 Years of Publishing in 2024

Simon & Schuster Australia, Sydney
Simon & Schuster India, New Delhi

www.simonandschuster.co.uk
www.simonandschuster.com.au
www.simonandschuster.co.in

A CIP catalogue record for this book
is available from the British Library

Paperback ISBN: 978-1-3985-2574-0
eBook ISBN: 978-1-3985-2575-7
Audio ISBN: 978-1-3985-2576-4

Printed and Bound in the UK using 100% Renewable
Electricity at CPI Group (UK) Ltd

MIX
Paper | Supporting
responsible forestry
FSC
www.fsc.org
FSC® C171272

For the eldest daughters in my life
I see you
I appreciate you
and most important
I love you for who you are and not what you do for everyone

Playlist

ART | TYLA	2:29
DAYDREAMIN' | ARIANA GRANDE	3:31
HOSTAGE | BILLIE EILISH	3:49
LET ME GO | GIVĒON	2:57
WHAT MAKES YOU BEAUTIFUL | ONE DIRECTION	3:20
END OF AN ERA | DUA LIPA	3:16
MARJORIE | TAYLOR SWIFT	4:18
VALENTINE | LAUFEY	2:49
NEVER KNOCK | KEVIN GARRETT	4:36
WE CAN'T BE FRIENDS (WAIT FOR YOUR LOVE) | ARIANA GRANDE	3:49
GIRL I'VE ALWAYS BEEN | OLIVIA RODRIGO	2:01
DON'T | BRYSON TILLER	3:18
WANNABE | SPICE GIRLS	2:53
KARMA | TAYLOR SWIFT	3:25
LITTLE THOUGHTS | PRIYANA	1:12
I MISS YOU | BEYONCÉ	2:59
HOW DOES IT MAKE YOU FEEL | VICTORIA MONÉT	3:36
TEENAGE DREAM | KATY PERRY	3:48
POV | ARIANA GRANDE	3:22
DANDELIONS | RUTH B.	3:54

"But a Book is only the Heart's Portrait—
every Page a Pulse."

—Emily Dickinson

A Letter from Hannah

Dearest reader,

I know you're eager to get started, but I just want to set the stage before you dive into Henry and Halle's love story. I said this would be a "quick note," but as I sit here and work out what I want to say, I can tell it isn't going to be, so buckle up.

Since I first published *Icebreaker*, I've received so many messages asking if Henry will receive a diagnosis to explain the traits that I've always called "neurodivergent coded." The short answer is no, he doesn't.

Some of you might be thinking, okay? Cool? I could have read the book to find that out . . . but I know many of you feel represented by Henry, or might be on a journey of your own, and knowing this ahead of time might be important to you.

I've always said I wouldn't write a diagnosis storyline, so this shouldn't be a shock to the ones who have followed me for a while. There are so many reasons why, but aside from the real-life obstacles Henry might face in the health-care system, the main reason is people live fulfilled lives every day without an explanation for why they feel different.

It doesn't make anyone, their wants, or their needs less valid to not have a medical diagnosis.

Henry and his actions have always been loosely based on my own and it's taken thirty years to receive my AuDHD diagnosis, something I did not have when I started writing Henry. When I was twenty like Henry, frustrated and upset because it felt like my brain just would *not* work properly and I was suffocating, at no point did anybody think it could be something more than the anxiety and depression I was diagnosed with.

I've been very honest that this book was difficult for me to write. I wanted to get it right for you all, and more important, I wanted to get it right for Henry.

I put a bit of myself in every character I create: Anastasia's anxiety, Nate's self-sacrifice, Aurora's need to be wanted, Halle's loneliness, and the internal scars Russ has because of his father's gambling addiction. I've spent a lot of time worrying about people understanding Henry for the parts of him—parts of me—that shut down or need to be alone. The part of me that exhausts herself mirroring those around her and soaking up their characteristics like a sponge. The part of me that tries so hard and still gets things so, so wrong.

Ironically, the pressure I put on myself to not let you all down was possibly the most Henry thing I could do.

I believe Henry is the character who has changed the most since I created him, but that's because *I've* changed so much since I gave you all Nate and Stassie.

I hope you read this story and see a man who *loves* the people around him, and when it comes to conflict, you watch through a lens knowing not everyone thinks the same way.

I truly hope *Daydream* was worth waiting for.

Get comfortable, she's a long one.

All my love,
xo, Hannah

Chapter One

HALLE

"I THINK WE SHOULD BREAK up, Halle."

Will's somber expression looks ridiculous against the backdrop of my kitchen. The frills and florals once picked by my nana, always too sentimental and nostalgic for me to replace. Lemon-yellow cabinets, a DIY project undertaken after she learned to mix dry martinis at home with Mrs. Astor from next door. Joy, the Ragdoll cat Nana bought to celebrate me moving in, snoozing on the breakfast bar surrounded by crochet fish. The smell of the second batch of croissants, because I always ruin the first.

It's all too domestic. Too unserious. Too normal to warrant his rigidness.

His eyes follow my every move as I remove the This Is Me Baking apron he bought for my birthday, like he's waiting for me to have some kind of dramatic outburst. The tightness in his jaw accentuates the sharp angles of his face, and he looks nothing like the laid-back guy I've dated for the past year, and even less like my friend of ten years. No, this Will looks very much like a man on the edge.

After hanging my apron on the hook beside the stove, I pull a stool toward me so we can sit opposite each other at the breakfast bar. When I rest my face on my palm, I'm not sure if I'm intentionally mirroring him or if this is the result of knowing each other so long.

He reaches across the counter and takes my hand in his, giving it a tight squeeze, an encouragement. "Say something, Hals. I still want to be your friend."

I need to say something. What I lack in experience, I make up for in common sense, so I'm fairly confident that breakups are a two-way conversation. I squeeze his hand back so I at least *appear* to be engaging with him. "Okay."

This isn't how I imagined my first breakup would go. I never expected to feel . . . nothing? I thought I'd physically feel my heart crack in my chest. That the birds would stop singing and the skies would turn gray, and while there is the emptiness I once imagined, it's somehow not the same. I'm not necessarily sure it's normal to imagine your first heartbreak, but I thought mine would be the tiniest bit interesting at least. But sadly, in line with my love life as a whole, this is bland. Nothing shatters and the sky is the same blue it always is here in Los Angeles.

"You don't need to hold back, Hals. You can be honest about how you feel."

His encouragement to speak my mind almost makes this whole thing worse. Taking my hand from his, I press my palms into my thighs and weigh the best way to tackle this. "I'm not. You're right; I don't think we're supposed to be more than friends."

Will blinks twice, hard. "You agree? You're not upset?"

I get the overwhelming sense that Will wants me to be upset, and I can't say I blame him. I'd be happy to be upset because at least if I was, I could believe that I'm capable of falling in love.

Because I really, really wanted to fall in love with him.

I'm not a person who struggles with words, but right now you wouldn't be able to tell that about me. I have no desire to hurt Will, which is why it's so hard to find the right thing to say. I'm honestly beginning to regret not faking an emotional outburst.

"It's not that I'm not upset; I just don't think we should drag things out if we're not working. I love you, Will. I don't want to compromise our friendship trying to have a relationship." *More than we already have*, is what I don't say.

"But you're not in love with me," he adds, the bitterness clear in his tone. "Are you?"

If I could kick myself, I would. "Does that even matter when you're in the middle of breaking up with me?"

It's like I kicked *him*. "It matters to me. Saying you love me and being in love with me isn't the same thing. But you're not, are you? You never have been, and that's why you're happy."

I can't believe he thinks that this is me happy. Does he know me at all?

To everyone but the two of us, Will Ellington and I were inevitable.

When my parents split up and my mom married my stepdad, Paul, we relocated from New York to Arizona for Paul's job. The Ellingtons lived next door and our parents quickly became best friends. I've lost track of the number of holidays and vacations we've spent together over the past decade, meaning Will and I had little choice when it came to spending time together.

However, there was never tension between us. No will-they-won't-they rumors, no lingering hands or secret moments. Just Halle and Will, neighbors who were good friends.

We survived high school together, and I watched him date everyone in our class without a "You Belong with Me" moment in sight. Then a year ago, when we were both home from college for the summer, Will invited me to be his date to a wedding. I'm pretty confident he had a first choice, and it wasn't me, but my invitation came in the form of pressure from his parents.

Ever the *traditionalists*, they didn't think it was healthy for a woman to spend her summer reading and writing, because I'd "never find a boyfriend hunched over a book." Even when my teenage sister,

Gigi, told them the 1800s called and wanted their mindset back, they still insisted I accept the invitation.

It was at the wedding, after too many gulps from a wine bottle we'd stolen from one of the tables, that we had the kiss that sparked this whole mess.

It was exciting at first, and those two weeks before we went back to school, I saw our relationship in a whole new way. Will had always been popular, and as much as I despise admitting it now, I felt special that he wanted to date me.

He was the captain of our high school hockey team, a future NHL star according to those in the know. He'd always been handsome and charismatic; he could get himself out of any situation with that charming smile of his. College had only increased his confidence, and during my visits throughout our freshman year, it was clear he was as well liked there as he had been back home.

So, all things considered, why wouldn't I want to date him when everyone else did? He was my only friend. It made sense, right?

I was captain of nothing, with no need to get myself out of any situation because I wasn't doing anything of interest. There isn't a long list of complimentary adjectives that follow when people talk about me. So yeah, I was a little flattered.

Our parents were elated, naturally. Their dreams of wedding planning and shared grandchildren felt that much closer, and it didn't matter that I was going to be in Maple Hills and he was going to be in San Diego. It's only two hours away, and they were certain we'd be totally fine because I could arrange my schedule around Will's hockey commitments.

No. Big. Deal.

Their confidence gave me confidence, which was something I desperately craved after that initial buzz wore off the first time Will asked me to have sex with him. I told him I wasn't ready, and he said I was intimidated by all of the girls he'd slept with, but that I didn't need to worry. I, through a horrified grimace and the strongest urge to vacate the building, told him I didn't care about who he'd been with before and his sex life had no bearing on us taking that step or not.

I wanted butterflies and the unexplainable need to pop my foot up delicately when we kissed, but I got wasps. Nasty, uncomfortable things that stung me every time Will would slip his hand beneath my T-shirt. My gut told me something was wrong, but my heart told me I just needed to give it time. My head told me I already had all the answers, but I was just too much of a chicken to listen to them.

"Halle? Will you get out of your head for long enough to have a fucking conversation with me? Jesus," Will says harshly, raising his voice enough to wake Joy. She saunters across the table, brushing her tail along my chin before lying back down in front of me. The oven timer beeps, and Will mutters expletives under his breath while I turn it off and take out the croissants I now have no desire to eat.

"Nothing about this makes me feel happy. I feel like you're annoyed at me for saying okay instead of what? Screaming at you? Sobbing?"

He scoffs, bringing his coffee mug to his lips, smothering whatever he muttered. I've always hated the muttering. "I'm annoyed about all the shit I'm going to get for being the one to break up with you, when you're just too much of a fucking people pleaser to do it yourself.

"I'm going to be the world's biggest asshole for doing something you've been too much of a coward to do. It isn't fair. I want you but you don't want me, so I have to be the bad guy."

I was wrong. There are adjectives that follow when someone talks about me. Just not complimentary ones, I guess.

"I'm not being a people pleaser. I was trying to give us a chance to work things out. It's not like I wanted to suck at this."

"I wish you wanted to suck. Maybe that'd solve our problems," he mutters just loud enough for me to hear.

It's like he's poking a tender bruise. A metaphorical one that's there because of him in the first place. I want to roll my eyes and tell him how childish and pathetic he's being, but in reality, he's finally found something in this awful conversation that makes me hurt.

I don't know why my sexual urges disappear as soon as he's in the equation, and I *really* wish I did. I don't want to give him the satisfaction of letting him know he's gotten to me, so I sigh and cock my head. "You're being an asshole."

He folds his arms across his chest as he sinks into his chair to shrink himself. Pinching the bridge of his nose between his thumb and forefinger, he lets out a noise that's somewhere between a sigh and a groan. "Sorry, that was low. I just"—he sits up straight again, his restlessness a contrast to his normal easygoing nature—"can't help but think things would be better if it actually felt like an adult relationship. I don't know how you can know you hate sex if you won't even try. I've been so patient with you, Halle, haven't I? More patient than another guy would be."

His need to break up with me right *now* suddenly makes more sense, given I said I still wasn't ready to have sex with him last night. If patient means stopping when I say stop, then yes, Will has been patient. If patient means repeatedly bringing up sex and interrogating me about my thoughts and feelings but becoming moody when I once again say I'm not ready, then sure, he's been patient.

I'm pretty sure neither of those things could be construed as patience, but I don't have the energy to delve into my mostly solo sex life during breakfast.

"We're two adults in a relationship—that's what makes it an adult relationship." As I've said a million times before. "And oh my God, for the last time, I never said I hate sex. I've only said I'm not ready and we compromised, I did the other stu—"

"Oh, because calling it a compromise makes me feel really great. Thanks."

I want to bash my head on the table. "Look, we're getting off topic. We can tell our parents it was a mutual decision. No bad person, mutual."

He shoots me a disbelieving look. "Like they'll buy that. What about Thanksgiving? Christmas? The vacation at spring break? You're naïve to think they'll drop it."

I can't pretend it's a stretch for him to be worried about how our parents might take the news. It's the thing I've been worrying about, too. Maybe he's right; maybe I am a coward and too much of a people pleaser, and I've forced his hand to save myself.

The summer we just shared back home made it very clear that without our hobbies or our family commitments to fill our time, we've outgrown each other. Will wants adventure with his friends until he starts his professional career, and I want to be a published author by the time I'm twenty-five. We're both driven, we're just driving in different directions. When you add the tension caused by my unwillingness to drop my panties on demand, this breakup was the only thing inevitable about us.

If I had any friends that I didn't share with Will, I'm sure they'd wonder why we were together in the first place. It's something I've thought about a lot over the past year, and the answer didn't paint me in a very good light.

I bounced between everything from being a people pleaser like I'm so commonly called, to having a late rebellion phase against my older brother, Grayson. He always hated Will, claiming he was too arrogant and our friendship was too one-sided. I was too well behaved to rebel about anything else going on, so not listening to my brother was as rebellious as I got. Even then, my rationale felt a little far-fetched.

In the end, I couldn't escape the truth: loneliness. Because if we split, who would I have?

Sure, our relationship wasn't perfect, but he called me every day and he wanted me around.

"I'll say I have the strongest urge to spend Christmas with Dad and Shannon. I think my brother will be there so I can use him to make it more believable. By the time we're both home in March for the spring break trip, everyone will be over our split."

"You sure?" he asks. I just offered him the best get-out-of-jail-free card in existence and he can't even hide the happiness. God, this is nauseating.

"I'm totally sure."

I watch as he relaxes. "If you're not coming home, I also don't think you should come to my games anymore."

Albeit not unexpected, I wish he'd broken up with me *before* I decided to give up my book club and rearranged my class schedule to give me time to visit for his games.

I say *decided*, but since we're not together now I guess I don't need to spin things to make Will look better anymore. I can admit that Will begged me to all summer, even though I repeatedly said I didn't want to, until I finally gave up arguing after he said that all the other girlfriends make the effort. I did it as soon as the school year restarted. I hated letting the bookstore down on such short notice, but they were so sweet about it, and one of their booksellers is excited to take over.

"Yeah, that's fine. I don't want to make our friends feel like they need to pick a side, and me not being there will probably make that easier."

If I didn't know Will as well as I do, I might have missed the way his eyebrows pinched together and he started to pout, but it *was* definitely there. That look of incredulity. "Ha, yeah." He scratches at his jaw. "Everyone's been telling me to end things for a while, so I don't know how they'd be if you were there. Awkward, probably."

For the first time since he uttered, "I think we should break up," I feel like crying. Even though to me it was obvious that something wasn't right between us, the idea that all his college friends have been weighing in and collectively decided he should end things makes my stomach twist.

I've always made an effort to go to the games I could drive to, even before we were a couple. I wore his jersey, sat with the other girlfriends, cheered him on. I looked up their interests, tried my hardest to fit in while they talked about people from their college I didn't know, because my friends have always been Will's friends. Even as kids, he was always introducing me to someone new.

His words are still stinging as I watch him finally finish the rest of his coffee. He looks so unbothered, yet I'm fighting the desire to find the nearest field and bury myself in it. "Not my friends anymore, got it."

"They were never really your friends in the first place when you think about it." He's staring at me, waiting for me to say something, like he didn't just throw my biggest insecurity in my face as casually as asking for the weather. "Do you ever wonder if you'd have your own friends if you didn't live in a fantasy world?"

"God, you sound like your parents right now. People can enjoy reading and still maintain a healthy attachment to reality, Will," I drawl. "I'm not a social pariah because I like fiction. Nobody has ostracized me from the Maple Hills social calendar because I read romance novels. Maybe if I spent more time in Maple Hills instead of following you around, I'd have my own friend group here."

He snorts, and he's one more arrogant action away from getting a croissant launched at his head. "Maybe if you were as invested in our relationship as you are in ones that aren't real, I wouldn't have just wasted a year of my life."

It's incredible how one conversation can change how someone looks to you. "I think you should head home now."

"Don't be so sensitive, Hals." He stands from his seat and walks to my side. The arm that drops onto my shoulder feels ten times heavier than it should, and his kiss to the crown of my head burns like acid. "I'm just putting myself first. Doing things for me, y'know. It's a fresh year and I deserve a fresh start. Hockey is get—"

His voice rumbles on in the background, but I can't bring myself to listen properly because it's taking every shred of my self-control not to launch into a rant about how I *do* know, because I've also been putting him first for as long as I can remember. Putting everyone first, in fact.

I've spent my entire life being encumbered by the tasks and responsibilities other people don't want. I make sacrifices without question because that's what I've always done, and at this point, it's hard to know if it's a true desire to help or just habit.

As my family blended and grew through my parents divorcing and remarrying other people, my list of people to help grew, too. Even though Grayson is the oldest, everything has fallen to me. For as long as I can remember, all I've heard is, "Oh, Halle won't mind helping," and not once, "Halle, do you mind?" or, "Halle, do you have time?"

I don't remember opting in, and I'm tired.

I'd love to say my issues with people pleasing are limited to the people I love, but I know they're not. Whether it's Will, his friends, his parents, neighbors . . . strangers . . .

It feels like every single person who has ever come into contact with my life has somehow wriggled their way above me on my list of priorities, and look where it's gotten me.

Single, no friends, no hobbies, and a schedule perfect for being the ideal hockey girlfriend but little else given I now have nothing to fill that time with.

I'm tired of being a passenger in my own life. So if Will is going to spend junior year doing things for himself, so am I.

Chapter Two

HENRY

IF TIME TRAVEL WERE REAL, I'd use it to go back and convince Neil Faulkner to turn down the opportunity to coach college hockey.

Despite my best intentions, and twenty long years of practice, I'm not always on the pulse when it comes to understanding people's motivations. I am, however, usually on the pulse of not getting on Coach's bad side. Which is why a knot of anxiety appears in my stomach the second I hear my name being yelled in Faulkner's gruff bark.

"*Ooooooooo*." Bobby's best attempt at sounding like a cartoon ghost causes a wave of laughter to rip through the half-full locker room. He misses the glare I shoot at him as he pulls his Titans T-shirt over his head. "Someone's in trouble. Whatcha done, Cap?"

"No idea," I mutter back as I pull my sweats up my legs. "Play hockey. Breathe. Exist. The possibilities are endless."

"It's been nice knowing ya, brother," Mattie says, patting me on the back as he passes in the direction of the showers. "Don't tell the others, but you were always my favorite."

"Am I a joke to you?" Kris shouts, launching what looks like a dirty sock at him. It bounces off the back of Mattie's head, ruffling his jet-black hair, and rolls beneath a bench.

And just like that, my tolerance for my teammates has reached its limit for the day.

"I'm sure it's fine." Russ attempts to reassure me, rubbing his towel against his wet hair. "If you're not back when I'm ready to go, I'll wait for you at my truck."

We're only a few weeks into the new school year and I already feel like what I imagine being run over is like. During the summer I spent a lot of time googling what makes a good captain, and while I don't feel like I have the exact answer, I'm trying to put into practice the few points I picked up. I'm the first one here and the last to leave. I've been making the effort to encourage the new, less confident players. I'm trying to be positive, which means not always saying the first thing that comes to mind. Being open to trying new things when it's in my nature to stick to what I know. I've been doing my full workout instead of letting myself get distracted by the perfect playlist. I don't spend practice daydreaming.

I'm doing a lot of things that go against my natural instincts, basically.

I didn't even drink at Anastasia and Lola's joint birthday dinner because I fell down an information wormhole about the ties between sports performance and alcohol consumption.

So the fact that Faulkner is angry with me about something when I'm trying really hard to do a good job makes me more than a little nauseated. My fist knocking against Coach's office door seems to echo around the room. "Come in," he yells. "Take a seat, Turner."

He points toward one of the worn mesh fabric seats opposite him and I do as I'm told. It's through me trying my hardest to pay attention to this man that I can clearly identify his three main states of being:

1. Irrationally angry and loud.

2. Irritated by a life surrounded by hockey players.

3. Whatever the word is to describe the way he's looking at me right now.

He taps his pen against the desk repeatedly, the plastic making a sharp clicking noise against the wood. It takes everything in me not to lean across and take it away from him to stop the noise. "Do you know why I called you in here?"

"No, Coach."

He thankfully puts the pen down and pulls his computer keyboard toward him. "I just received an email requesting a phone call to discuss you, because you failed your paper in Professor Thornton's class, and instead of going to Thornton to find a way to fix it, you went to your academic adviser to try and get out of his class. Do you have anything to say for yourself before I dial this number?"

Every single word I've ever learned evaporates from my head other than *oh shit*.

"No, Coach."

He runs his hand across the top of his head like he's brushing back a mane of hair. I've always wanted to ask why, considering he's bald, and according to the game tapes we've watched, has been bald for the past twenty-five years. Despite encouragement from some of the guys, Nate told me not to ask him that unless I wanted a world of misery, which I don't. But the question plagues me every time I watch him brush away his nonexistent hair. "Okay, then."

His chubby fingers practically poke a hole through the handset as he punches in the number and rests the phone between his ear and shoulder. I have no choice but to listen while he introduces himself then ums and ahs through the call. Nate always told us that Faulkner can smell fear, so you should never show him your weaknesses. Admitting I fucked up the semester before I've properly started it feels a lot like weakness.

He puts the phone down and stares at me so intensely it feels like he's staring at my soul.

"Ms. Guzman said she reminded you three times to schedule your appointment to register for your classes—"

"That's true."

"—and by the time you tried to register, the class you wanted was full. So you picked Thornton's class thinking you could get on the waiting list for something else and drop him during swap week."

"Yes."

"But you didn't add yourself to the waiting list and you didn't try to drop it during swap week."

I intended to. I truly did, but I've been so busy worrying about following Nate and being a good captain that everything else took a mental backseat. Every obstacle let me push things off, and I kept telling myself I'd fix it until it was eventually too late.

"Also true."

"So, you mean to tell me," he says, then pauses to take a long sip from his coffee mug just to make me extra miserable. "That despite ample opportunity to rectify the situation yourself, you didn't, and now you're here, disturbing the few sweet hours in a day where I don't have to look at your face, expecting me to help you?"

I want to point out that he invited me in here and I went to the adviser who is specifically employed to support student athletes for help, but I suspect he'd take that as well as he's taking me failing one assignment. "I guess."

"What's your grievance with Thornton?"

I think back to what Anastasia and I workshopped ahead of my visiting Ms. Guzman. I repeat her words like a parrot. "His teaching style and my learning style are incompatible."

"You're going to have to give me more than that, Turner." Faulkner sighs, leaning back in his chair. He clicks his mouse and stares at his computer. "You're excelling in everything else, and I know you're a hard worker. So what is it with this class that makes you think you need to quit?"

I'm trying to remember how I explained it to Anastasia and Aurora the day I came home from my first session with Thornton. I ranted for five minutes and then had to lie on the floor and stare at the ceiling for an hour. "I need to take a writing intensive class to meet the requirements of my major. Professor Thornton's syllabus is known for being a lot of reading and researching—it's why nobody wants to do it. He essentially teaches world history; it's barely even about the art. I struggle to focus on the material because there's so much that's irrelevant to what he wants . . . I think.

"And I don't love reading things I'm not interested in. I struggle to stay focused. I also don't understand what he wants most of the time. I've found myself in information black holes to only end up in the wrong place anyway, and then of course, failing."

Faulkner sighs again. I wonder if he does it at home or if it's something he reserves for this office. I wonder if it gives his family the same sinking feeling it gives me. "It says here you have a similar kind of class with Professor Jolly and you're not trying to drop that."

Jolly is a borderline hippie and believes the history of art should be something you learn about and feel in your soul. She hates the idea of grading people on how they interpret and enjoy learning about art, so her class is final exam only, and that's just because the department makes her. It's impossible to fail as long as you show up, and she doesn't have a class cap, meaning I could get in even though I signed up for classes later than everyone.

I love Professor Jolly's class not only because it's *actually* interesting, but because I understand what she wants from me. What I learn helps me with my practical work, and I don't leave her class feeling unprepared and lacking direction like I do with Thornton. It would have been the perfect solution, but it doesn't meet the requirement. "I work better under the pressure of an exam."

Faulkner starts tapping his pen again. "Have you talked to Professor Thornton?"

Professor Thornton is even less interested than you are, I want to say. "He was unwilling to hear me out."

"It's out of my hands," he says, giving me an uninterested shrug. "Should have come to me sooner so I could have helped you."

Be more organized. Come to me sooner. I don't know how to explain to someone who doesn't live inside my head that they could have physically carried me to the office or glued a laptop down in front of me and I'd have still found a way to avoid the task. "What happens when I fail the class?"

I'm not even worried about my GPA because I dominate at things I enjoy, and I love everything else on my schedule for the rest of the year—assuming I register for the rest of my classes in time. It's just *this* class and Faulkner's obsession with team captain academic perfectionism.

After his professional career was cut short by an accident that left him unable to play, he's obsessed with us having a backup plan. Yes, as student athletes we're tied to achieving a certain grade point average to be able to keep that title, but what Faulkner wants is next level. I know there's no point in fighting it, because no person who ever fought it before me won.

"We're not talking about that. You're the leader of this team, Turner. You don't get to fail your classes and keep your title. Partner with a classmate, join a study group, use your academic adviser for something other than quitting . . . I don't fucking care. You do whatever it takes to make it work. I don't expect to hear about any more bad grades."

Nate made it all look *so* easy, and I'm kind of mad at him for downplaying how much of a hard-ass Faulkner is in private. I've been told so many times that being captain is an honor, but as I drag my feet out of Faulkner's office, it feels more like a weight around my neck. Leadership doesn't come naturally to me; I've always been happier in solitude, but I'm trying as hard as I can. I don't want to let my teammates down, or Nate and Robbie, who convinced Coach I deserved it.

Being captain is a lot like Thornton's class. I'm expected to know so much that nobody has ever explained to me, and yet I'm supposed to just smile through it. It's why I said no when I was originally offered the position. I expected it to be given to someone else and I could carry on living my life. But that didn't happen, Nate and Robbie continued to reason with me.

They tried everything from comparing me to everyone I suggested would be a better captain to saying I'd be the first Black hockey captain at Maple Hills. They dropped the latter when I said it was a damning snapshot of opportunities for people of color in hockey and not the win they were making it out to be.

The more my teammates pushed, the more others started. My moms, Anastasia . . . so many people told me they thought it was amazing, and how excited they would be to see what I could do. In the end, even though I still had my doubts, I accepted.

I don't give in to peer pressure, but this is the one time I did, and look where it's gotten me. Not only do I need to stress about letting the entire team down, but I also need to worry about letting down everyone not on the team, who, through no fault of my own, believes in me. It's so hard having supportive friends and family who don't immediately assume the worst.

"ANY SUCCESS?" RUSS ASKS AS I climb into his truck in the now-deserted parking lot.

"I'm fucked."

"I'm sure it's not that ba—"

"He told me I don't get to quit or fail my classes and to find a solution."

Russ sighs as he navigates us out of the empty lot. "Helpful. Look, it might not be as bad as you think the more practice you get. I'll help you as much as I can, and so will Aurora. Next time, we can get our codes to register for classes together."

I rest my head against the window as we pull up to a red light and wonder how I can possibly put into words that don't make me seem unhinged that, short of a perfect set of circumstances all aligning to allow me to feel excited about the prospect of organizing my schedule, I'll probably be in this mess again in January. "Thanks."

"Don't mention it. Rory is at the house with Robbie waiting to hang out, but if you need peace, we can go to her place," he says softly as we turn onto Maple Avenue. "I don't mind."

I like living with Russ because he always seems to interpret a person's mood without many words. I think it's a skill born from the constant state of fear he was in when growing up with a dad who wasn't nice to live with, but I don't think it would be okay to ask him if he agrees with me outright. Especially since his dad is trying to be better and Russ is trying to give him a chance to prove himself.

"You don't need to go anywhere. I like Aurora."

I lift my head from the window in time to catch the small smile on his face. "She likes you, too."

Russ changed a lot this summer when he was working at a sleep-away camp. He met his girlfriend, challenged his dad's gambling addiction, and, while I don't think he's ever going to be the loudest person in the room, he's more confident than he was.

As for Aurora, she's not who I was expecting for Russ, but I think that's a good thing. Russ likes her because she's generous and kind, and he spent a long time feeling second best before he met her. He's her number one, which isn't me making assumptions: she says he's her number one to literally anyone who will listen. There's no room for doubt in his head that he is important to Aurora because she tells him, and boy is she loud.

I don't like to compare my friends because they're all different, but she's the only one who doesn't talk to me about hockey, which puts her pretty high up on my list given it feels like the only thing people ever want to ask me about now.

Trying to remember the last time someone asked me about one of my other interests makes the trip home quick. Before I realize where we are, Russ is pulling into the drive beside his girlfriend's car.

Aurora looks up when I open the front door, but her eyes travel straight past me and the widest grin spreads across her face when she spots Russ. I feel like we just shipped one lot of girlfriends out, and immediately gained more.

She's conventionally attractive—average height and build, sun-tanned white skin with green eyes and blond hair—but I don't think she'd be very interesting to draw.

Russ is obviously very attracted to her, but they make an effort not to be loud about it, which I appreciate. I loved when Anastasia was living here, but she should have been charged with disturbing the peace.

"Are you okay, Henry?" Aurora asks as I drop into the recliner opposite her. "You look extra pensive today. Brooding, like the tortured artist you are."

"Coach found out I got an F on that French Revolution essay," I say as Russ leans in to kiss her temple.

"That blows, I'm sorry. Did you try to charm him?" she asks.

"I don't know how to charm people on purpose, and even if I did, he'd be immune just to punish me. He thinks I should have academic superpowers because I picked up a hockey stick fifteen years ago."

"I think you're incredibly charming," she says.

"Who has superpowers?" Robbie asks as he rounds the corner from his bedroom. He stops his wheelchair in the space between the couch and recliner, looking right at me. "Faulkner called. Apparently it's my fault you didn't sign up for your classes. Because *appar-*

ently I'm psychic and I'm to blame for you fucking your way through California all summer instead of prioritizing your education. Even though I was busy graduating and, y'know, being in a different state."

Living with my friends is great. Living with my friend who is also the assistant coach is occasionally not as great. Occasionally being now, when I can't even escape Faulkner in my own home because all he has to do is call Robbie.

"That's dramatic," I grumble as Robbie lifts himself into the recliner beside mine. I stayed local and I never told Coach about my summer. It wasn't even intentional. I think I might have felt a little lonely while everyone was home or working.

I hadn't thought of it that way until Anastasia asked me about it, and I realized I was keeping myself busy until my friends got back. I like my own company, prefer it even, but this summer I found that there's a limit.

Plus, women like me a lot and I like having fun without commitment.

Robbie shakes his head, pinching the bridge of his nose. "Do me a favor, Casanova. Concentrate on not getting my ass beat this year instead of getting laid. You're the supreme leader after all and you must lead the way in morality and dignity and all the other shit."

I don't think he's being serious. Robbie always laughs right before he says something sarcastic that he doesn't mean, but it still causes an uncomfortable prickle at the nape of my neck. "The only thing I know is I don't know how to be a leader."

Russ leans forward in his seat, looking right at me. "You're doing a damn good job for someone who claims he doesn't know what he's doing. You're good at everything, Hen."

"Except revolutions," Aurora interrupts.

"It's fucking annoying if you wanna get into it. I'd be obnoxious as hell if I was good at everything the first time I try it," Robbie adds. "Stay focused and you'll kill it."

"Who told you you aren't obnoxious?" Russ says, quickly blocking the cushion that flies in his and Aurora's direction.

"Why don't we get you some books on leadership?" Aurora says, shuffling to the edge of the couch just like Russ is. It makes me want to move my chair back just to increase the space between us again. "I'm skipping book club this week because it's only an icebreaker meeting and Halle has a boner for Austen that I can't get on board with, but I still haven't checked out Enchanted and it'd be nice to drop by to say hi . . . Why are you looking at me like that?"

Russ chuckles beside her, but I continue to stare at her blankly. "I don't understand anything you just said."

"Enchanted," she repeats, like somehow it'll clear this whole thing up. "The bookstore that just opened near Kenny's? Next to that creepy bar Russ used to work in that's turned into a wine bar."

She may as well be speaking French. "No idea."

Aurora immediately gets more flustered, her voice pitching up. "We literally drove past it two days ago and I said *look how busy Enchanted is!*"

"You say a lot, Aurora. I don't always listen to you," I admit. "I find it hard to concentrate when you're driving. Fearing for my life takes up a lot of mental space."

She huffs, and the guys laugh, but I'm not joking. "Halle. The girl who used to run the book club at The Next Chapter. She's starting a new romance-only book club at Enchanted—the new bookstore we drove past. I'm not going because I don't like what they're reading and it's an introduction session for people who have never been to a book club before. But I want to go say hi to her and check out the store."

"What does all this have to do with me failing and having to change my identity to hide from Neil Faulkner?"

"This conversation is massively reducing my quality of life," Robbie groans. "Can you two wrap it up, please? It's like watching aliens from different planets try to communicate with each other."

Aurora looks up at the ceiling, muttering something under her breath before turning to Robbie and giving him the finger. She turns her attention back to me and brushes the stray strands of hair from her face. "Henry, do you want to come with me to a bookstore and buy books that will help you learn about leadership? And thus help you be a better captain?"

"No."

Robbie and Russ burst out laughing, and I'm not sure exactly what was funny about that fact.

"But why? Emilia is at dance and Poppy is busy and I don't want to go on my own."

"Have you been paying attention? I need to work out how to pull off a miracle. Take Russ."

She lightly bops Russ in the ribs and his laughing immediately stops. "Russ is having dinner with his parents tonight. This might help! If you come with me and give it a chance, I will buy you a milkshake."

"No, thank you."

"And chili fries."

"Fine," I say, but only because I want to be a good friend to her, not because I actually want to go. "But I'm not getting the fake meat this time. And I'm counting down until you can pull away from stop signs. In fact, scratch that. I'm driving. Let's get this over with."

Chapter Three

HALLE

THERE'S A STRONG POSSIBILITY THAT I could be hallucinating, because there's an alarmingly attractive man eating my welcome cookies.

After placing half of the chairs in a circle, I went into the storage room for approximately ten seconds to get the rest, and when I came back out, there he was.

Is. Maybe? Possibly, depending on the hallucination thing.

Starting a brand-new book club has had my nerves out of control all day, not to mention I've had an excessive amount of caffeine. I'd originally said no when the owner of Enchanted asked me to run her book club last term, because I thought running two would be too much work. However, in a slightly frantic *I'll show you, Will Ellington!*–type moment, when I saw her at the store's opening night, I told her my schedule had opened up. Meaning the two weeks since Will and I split have involved me zooming around to try to ensure this venture isn't a flop.

The "real" first session is next week, but when I started posting about the club, many of the prospective members asked for a welcome session to get a feel for what to expect. I picked a book that most people said they'd already read to give us something to talk about.

So, under the circumstances, hallucination is not quite as unbelievable as it may have originally sounded. I will admit, though, if I am hallucinating, my imagination has certainly stepped it up.

When he takes a seat and picks up a book from the pile beside his chair, I decide, albeit not confidently, that he's real. Which brings me to my next predicament: introducing myself.

Introductions have always been my least favorite part of book club. I've spent my life relying on Grayson, or, as a teen, Will, to make introductions for me. Even Gigi and Maisie, my younger sisters, are better at it than I am.

This has always been the one place they haven't been able to pick up the slack socially. It's not that I don't know how to have a conversation with people; I just don't know where to start. Once I have started, I spend the conversation worrying if I'm making a good first impression. I wouldn't call myself shy; I've just spent my life around louder, more dominant personalities, which has never allowed me to properly challenge myself to get confident in these scenarios.

However, books are a great equalizer, and I just need to remember that everyone comes here with the same purpose.

Thankfully he's so engrossed in reading the back of his book that he hasn't noticed my minor confidence crisis in the corner of the room. The more I stare—to work out what to say, not to be a creep—the more I'm beginning to feel like I know him from somewhere.

Right on cue, he leans back in his chair to stretch for another cookie from the table, and the hem of his T-shirt rises enough to reveal a sliver of light brown skin covering his solid, muscular stomach.

I know he isn't one of my neighbors, given that I'm surrounded by senior citizens.

And he isn't in my major, because I would *not* forget him.

I don't go to parties, so I can rule that out.

He isn't here with anyone, so he doesn't appear to be someone's boyfriend.

Maybe he's a model and I've seen him on a billboard. He has the bone structure for it, *my God*. Sharp and yet soft at the same time, an oxymoron I know, but it makes sense with his face, I swear. Reddish-brown curls cut short. Dark lashes line his brown eyes, fanning against his cheek as he watches me. Full lips settled in a relaxed smile. Wait, as he watches me.

As. He. Watches. Me.

It could be my imagination and/or the coffee again, but I swear he smirks. I've never broken eye contact so quickly in my life.

"Hi!" I choke out as I speed across the hardwood floor toward him. "Welcome to book club!"

My God, he's even prettier up close. I'm firmly backing my billboard theory. I make the split-second decision as I reach him not to shake his hand, because not only would it mean I had to do it to every other person who comes in here, it's also really weird. What I'm slowly realizing is my brain is coming out of a deep slumber and it's just remembering that other men exist, and some of them look like models. I give him my most welcoming smile, and God, I really feel like I know him from somewhere. "Hi, I'm Halle."

"Henry."

"Hi." *You've said that.* "Have we met?"

"No. I'd remember you," he says. Ironic, because I'd definitely say the same thing about him, but I still can't place him. "Do you want some help with the chairs?"

"I'm well practiced doing it by myself, don't worry." Henry ignores me and stands to start repositioning the chairs anyway, so I copy, even though it was my task in the first place. It's so quiet up here and I feel like this might be the worst I've ever been at welcoming someone to group. *Say something, Halle.* "So, big fan of romance?"

"Are you asking me out?" he asks, and the chair I'm holding slips out of my hand and crashes to the floor.

"What? No!" I say, my voice rising a few octaves.

"That's a shame." If I wasn't already blushing, I *definitely* am now. "Kinda sounded like you were hitting on me."

There are tomatoes that will never be as red as me right now. "Oh shit, I'm sorry. I was just asking about your reading preferences."

He heads toward the storage room to get more chairs and looks back at me over his shoulder. "I don't really have any. I'm more of a hands-on person."

"Oh, so you're hoping to get into reading romance?"

"No," he says, dragging a stack of chairs like they weigh absolutely nothing.

"I see." I don't see actually. This is probably the least I've seen, ever. I take a seat on the chair he vacated and pick up the hardback on the top of the pile beside the chair leg. It's a book about leadership. "If you're joining book club to talk about nonfiction, I'm really sorry, but this one is specifically for romance fiction. You could join the club at The Next Chapter; I don't run that one anymore, but they rotate different genres and themes there. The new person who runs it is really nice."

"I'm not joining a book club. My roommate's girlfriend convinced me to come here with her to buy books on how to be a better leader. She thinks it'll solve all my problems. I don't think she's right, but she says things in a way that makes you believe her. I just wanted somewhere to sit until she's done."

No wonder he thought I was hitting on him. "It seems I've massively misunderstood, sorry. It's a new club and we're doing an icebreaker session and I, uh, assumed."

"Icebreakers are one of my least favorite things." He takes the seat beside me, and I concentrate on the shiny dust jacket of his book. "But you don't need to apologize."

"What are you supposed to be leading?" I ask, picking up the next book from his stack. "To be a better leader for?"

I recognize this memoir because Will has the same one in his bedroom. I look up at Henry and everything clicks into place. "Hockey," we both say at the same time.

His brow creases, the smallest lines forming between his eyebrows. I put the book back on the pile, shaking off the uncomfortable feeling plaguing me as I try to force out words. "Sorry, I just realized I recognize you from watching hockey. My boyfr—ex-boyfriend has played against you before. That's why I thought we'd met."

"Who's your ex-boyfriend?"

My stomach sinks, because how in the hell have I managed to make this about Will? "Is it bad taste for me to talk about an ex? Sorry, I'm new to the whole ex-girlfriend thing."

"I wouldn't know. Dating isn't my thing," he says casually.

"Will Ellington," I respond. "He goes to a school in S—"

"San Diego. I know him." My stomach sinks again. What if he tells Will I'm talking about him? Will it make me look bitter or something? This is what happens when I have to socialize unsupervised. "He's not as good at hockey as he thinks he is."

I snort. Literally. My body clearly didn't know what to do with the shock of that statement. "Sorry!"

"You apologize a lot when you don't need to."

"Force of habit . . . I don't think I've made that sound before. It's just Will and I have known each other since we were kids, and all I've heard for a decade is how amazing he is and how he'll be the star of the NHL in a few years."

Henry's eyes widen, disbelief shadowing his very handsome face. "He plays with the ego of a guy who's been told that his whole life. I've played him. It's not true."

I don't quite know how to react. I've never heard anyone other than Grayson be critical of Will, and I always put that down to him being a protective older brother. Will has always been the golden boy. Since we agreed to stay friends after our breakup, I shouldn't feel happy hearing someone talk about him so negatively, but I do. I suppose given how our conversation ended, I'm entitled not to feel super friendly toward him at the moment. "Good to know."

"You should come watch me play. I'm much better than your ex."

Before I can answer, not that I had an answer prepared, we're interrupted by the sound of footsteps on the stairs. "Didn't have you down as a *Pride and Prejudice* lover," she says as she approaches us. I'm about to throw out a loud *huh* before I realize she isn't talking to me.

Aurora Roberts looks like someone bought Malibu Barbie and brought her to life. She's gorgeous, confident, and funny. We have some very drastic differences in opinion on books, but she's a total sweetheart the rest of the time. We've had practically the same class schedule since freshman year, and even though I only see her outside of class at book club, she always makes the effort to be kind to me.

She sent me a nice message when I posted that I wouldn't be continuing with The Next Chapter book club, and an even nicer message when I posted that I was starting a romance-only book club here at Enchanted. I've always thought that maybe we could be friends, but Will said rich girls like her want rich friends who can afford to do the things they do.

"Hey, Halle," she says cheerfully before putting her hands on her hips and staring at Henry. "I genuinely thought you'd just left me here. I thought I was going to have to call Russ and tell him to come get me."

"How do you lose someone who tells you their location?"

"I, apparently incorrectly, assumed you wouldn't be waiting for book club. I've been calling you. Have you bought your books already?"

I quickly realize that Aurora is the roommate's girlfriend Henry referred to earlier.

"Not yet," he says, grabbing the remaining books on the floor. He rests his arms on top of the pile and smiles as I hand the two in my lap back to him. "Do you want to hang out with us? Aurora bribed me with chili fries and milkshakes, so we're heading to Blaise's diner."

It takes everything in me to not ask him to repeat himself. Blaise's diner is popular with students because it's cheap, the food is great, and it's fairly close to campus. Will and I went there for lunch sometimes when he visited, and it's usually full of big groups of friends hanging out. This is my third year at Maple Hills, and not once has someone asked me to hang out within an hour of meeting. I don't think anyone's asked me to hang out, period.

"That's really sweet of you, but I sort of have to host a welcome meeting in fifteen minutes."

He tsks. "Oh yeah. After?"

"After book club I'm starting a new job." I need someone to remind me why I'm starting a new job, pronto. "Sorry."

"New book club and new job in the same day?" Aurora says. "I don't know where you find the time. You're like Superwoman."

"Yeah, my schedule opened up," I explain coyly, hoping she doesn't make me delve in deeper.

Henry doesn't look happy or sad at my refusal, just neutral. "Another time."

"Bye, Halle," Aurora says as they both turn to leave. "See you in class. And good luck! I promise I'll be here when you do a romance book that's *actually* a romance book."

"You survived!" Inayah shouts as I descend the stairs to the main store. "How did it go? I wanted to come up, but I got an influx of moms who just dropped their kids off at Simone's for ice skating lessons. They're going to come to the meeting next week. As soon as I said 'social media influencer and farmer reconnect after a one-night stand,' they all bought the book immediately! How cool? I didn't even think about the rink for potential members!"

Even though the past few weeks have been a rush of recruiting members, planning my life, getting back into the swing of college, and resisting the urge to check my phone for messages from Will ten million times a day, it's truly worth it to be a part of someone living their dream.

When the Enchanted page first followed me and I saw it was going to be opening in Maple Hills, I immediately messaged to share my excitement. Inayah introduced herself and told me it was a lifelong goal of hers to open her own bookstore. This building had sat empty for a couple of years, probably because of the fights that used to happen outside the bar next door before it was shut down.

It's full of charm, with high ceilings and tons of light, and now that the building next door is being renovated, Inayah thought that this store would be the perfect place for her. When I came for the grand opening, I fell in love immediately when I walked through the soft lilac painted door.

In reality, even without Will taking up my time, I don't *really* have the time for a book club. Junior year is for sure going to kick my ass, but I'm the eldest daughter and nobody taught me how to say no. Not technically true in this specific scenario, because I did say no at first, but I felt bad about it, that's for sure, and here we are.

I'm supposed to be doing things for myself, and I really like Inayah. Plus, romance is my favorite genre, so when she said she wanted to try a romance-focused book club, it felt like fate.

"Good, I think." She accepts the storage room keys from me and puts them in the drawer beneath the counter. "It was a really good turnout for an intro session at a brand-new club, and everyone was enthusiastic. Only a few of them had watched the adaptation instead of reading the book."

She leans against the counter, resting her chin on her fist. "Firth or MacFadyen?"

"MacFadyen."

Inayah nods with approval. "I, too, am a twenty-seven-year-old frightened burden to my parents. How did they react to your final question?"

"Really well, and I have about fifteen more people in my Team Romance camp. I'm happy I started with *Pride and Prejudice*, because asking people if it's *actually* a romance book started some really interesting conversations."

"I'm so grateful you changed your mind, Halle. I know you have to get to your new job, so I won't keep you chatting all afternoon."

"I'm grateful you still wanted me! Do you have those fliers you mentioned earlier? I'll put them up around college."

Sliding off her stool, she dips behind the desk, only the top of her glossy black hair visible as she rummages around before reappearing with a stack of fliers and pot of pins. She begins to separate them into piles, dashing beneath the desk again when she realizes she's missing some. "Do you want one about the writing competition?"

I feel like a dog that was just told she's going on a walk. My ears all but prick up. "Writing competition?"

"Yeah," she says, putting an extra flier on the pile. "Calliope Publishing is hosting it; their indie team reached out to me about advertising to customers. You have to submit a novel of at least seventy thousand words, and the winner gets a place in some fancy creative writing course in New York City during the summer. I think the deadline is around spring break, but double-check the flier. It sounds cool, but with the exception of some questionable fan fiction when I was fifteen, I'm definitely not author material."

I feel like my eyes are about to pop out of my head like a cartoon character as I skim the glossy paper. This couldn't be more perfect, and I have no shortage of ideas, and I have all this free time now, and . . . I need to go to work. "I'll take a look. Thanks, Inayah. I should get going."

"Good luck!"

The drive to the hotel takes half the time I'd planned, and I spend fifteen minutes sitting in the parking lot debating with myself if it's rude or conscientious to arrive thirty minutes early. In my defense, I'd imagined every possible thing that could go wrong and planned for it. It's not my fault that I returned to my car in the parking lot of Enchanted and still had all four of my tires.

The writing competition flier is staring at me from my passenger seat, but I've already read it ten times to confirm that yes, I am 100 percent going to submit something. If I were dating Will, he'd tell me it isn't enough time or that the competition is too tough. He'd convince me that it was selfish to spend time I could be with him working on something I'm excited about, since I already have *so* many commitments.

But I'm not dating Will, and I want this for myself. I refuse to feel guilty about it, and even if I don't win, I'll have finally put myself first and completed a goal that I'm excited about.

The impatient part of me wishes I could head home and start working on it straight away, but the responsible Halle that I'm so good at being decides to put it in the back of my head and concentrate on my current task: working at The Huntington hotel.

I originally interviewed for a summer job at The Huntington back in May, when I was trying not to have to go back to Phoenix for three months. I love my family, but spending my time off being used as free childcare for my two younger sisters is not my idea of a productive summer. At least a job would pay me for my labor, and looking after a fifteen-year-old and an eight-year-old *is* labor. I'm still recovering from the constant tears, arguing, and door slamming.

I'm also still trying to remember a time when Grayson was expected to put aside his summer to play third parent and look after us, even before he started playing football professionally in the NFL and moved to the East Coast.

It might take me until next summer to come up with an answer to that one.

I obviously didn't get the job I interviewed for; they had a member of staff transfer from a different hotel, but Pete, the manager, said he was impressed with my interview and he'd call if there was ever a vacancy.

True to his word, Pete called last week to say there was a position at reception that could be mine if I wanted it, and I'd need to come in today to do the paperwork and online training before picking up shifts from next week. The hours he wants me to work overlap with the time I was supposed to be visiting Will, which feels like another instance of fate intervening.

The Huntington hotel is one of those chains you can't escape. Their hotels and country clubs are all over the world, catering to rich and famous clientele. That's why it's so wild to me that Maple Hills students are some of the brains behind this particular hotel's operations. Jokes aside, this hotel has excellent reviews, so they're doing something right.

Pete is friendly but quick to give me the rundown on the day-to-day of the hotel. I feel like I'm on a Huntington-themed roller coaster as he flies through information I'm supposed to remember. My head feels like it's going to explode when he finally introduces me to the woman I'll be working alongside on most of my shifts.

"Halle Jacobs, meet Campbell Walker. Campbell, Halle," he says quickly. "I have a meeting to go to, but if you can let Halle shadow you, maybe introduce her to the computer system if you get any periods of quiet. I've given Halle West's old pass and locker. Could you track down his old training folder because it might have some guides I can repurpose? I'll be back in an hour."

I feel a little like I've been dropped off at day care and my parent is leaving me to fend for myself as Pete walks away. I immediately forget what to do with my hands. Letting them hang at my sides feels unnatural, but folding my arms feels standoffish.

"I don't bite, I swear," Campbell says gently. "Unless you're into that." She gestures to the chair beside her and smiles. "And *please*, call me Cami. It'll be quiet for the next hour or so, so don't stress too much. As for West, the man has never taken a legible note in his life, so let's not bother trying to track down his stuff."

"Is West the guy I'm replacing?"

Her smile fades a little, like she's remembering something she'd rather not. "Yup. He graduated and decided to get as far away from this place as he could. He was useless anyway. Always goofing around and being annoying and . . ." Her voice trails off. "Anyway, tell me about yourself, Halle Jacobs. What brought you here?"

It's a second-long decision on whether to sugarcoat it or be totally honest. Will broke up with me, and all the friends we shared removed me from our various group chats, leaving my phone practically silent. I'm avoiding my mom's calls so she can't ask me about him, while simultaneously telling myself that having sex with him to keep him around would not have been better than the loneliness I'm feeling because he hasn't checked in.

In summary, I don't have a lot to lose and even less to gain from lying to her.

"My boyfriend broke up with me and the people I called my friends shut me out, which wasn't surprising because I knew they were his friends deep down, but it was surprising how much it hurt me. So now I'm doing things for myself, but equally filling my time so the whole experience doesn't have a chance to hit me in the face one day."

Cami is quiet at least three seconds longer than I'd like her to be. Then she smiles. "We are going to get along really, really great."

Chapter Four

HALLE

I FEEL LIKE I'M AT a One Direction concert and not in a good way.

My stepsister has a whole host of talents: gymnastics, bringing back a plant from the brink of death, and weirdly, being able to hustle anyone out of their money during a game of pool, but I can confidently say singing is not one of them. The smooth vocals of Zayn are being replaced by the out-of-tune and out-of-time screeching emitting from my laptop speaker. "Gigi," I say with a groan, turning down the volume.

She can't hear me over the sound of "What Makes You Beautiful" being brutally murdered, or more likely, she's ignoring me. "Gi!" I repeat, louder this time as my eyes scan the same line for the third time. "Gianna Scott! Could you please shut the hell up?"

The music stops abruptly, and I watch as she focuses back on our video call. "Did you say something?"

"I can't concentrate on your essay when you sound like Joy when she's hungry." I don't even think she's old enough to remember One Direction being a band, but Mom found all my old CDs while cleaning out the garage, and now they're Gigi's latest fixation.

"What if I wanted to be a singer? What if you just crushed my dreams and became my villain origin story?" She sits up in her desk chair to fold her arms across her chest, a symbol of defiance, I guess. Her thick brown curls are secured in braids down each side of her face, tied with pink ribbons that sit right above the logo on her swea—

"Oh my God, that's my sweatshirt! What did I say about going through my things when I'm at college? It isn't even your size!"

"How's my essay?" she asks, deflecting entirely the way only a fifteen-year-old with no fear can.

"I haven't finished it yet because I can't focus through your performance. Just be quiet for five minutes and then I'll be done, and you can get back to your concert." Gigi pinches her thumb and forefinger together, sliding them across her lips like a zipper, and I get back to reading about Orwell's *1984*. "Thank you."

I get two lines in before her fingers drum against the desk as she hums what sounds like the tune of "Best Song Ever."

Sighing dramatically so she knows how annoying she is, I mute her.

Getting Gigi to listen to the audiobook this summer was practically a full-time job, so I'm quietly proud of her for finishing her essay on time. I've been helping her with her schoolwork since our parents got married when she was five. I was the one who originally suspected she was dyslexic and had ADHD, and the one who worked with her for hours practicing dictation until she mastered it.

Now I'm her unqualified tutor because, according to my mom and Paul, her dad, I'm the only person Gigi listens to. Which, as I unmute her and immediately hear her blasting "Midnight Memories," I can confirm is a lie.

They claim she needs academic reassurance. As well as all the assurances I give when they call me begging for me to "talk some sense into her." Paul has full-time custody of Gigi because Lucia, Gigi's mom, gets posted overseas often and it isn't guaranteed Gigi would get the academic support she needs if she moved to different schools. As nice as he is, Paul has no idea how to handle a teenage girl and my mom wants an easy life, which teen-me gave her, so it's easier for her to send Gigi in my direction. Maisie, our shared half sister, is too quiet to be any kind of threat to Mom's peace. Grayson was a nightmare teenager, always fighting and getting into trouble, but my mom looks back on it with rose-tinted glasses because he's her golden boy.

"It's great, Gi. Good job! *Gianna*." Of all the things I need to do in a week, getting through this video call with a child who clearly is less interested in it than I am is the most stressful. "Gianna, for God's sake!"

The music stops again. "You're very stressy today, Hallebear. What ever happened to gentle parenting?"

"Well, I'm not your parent, for starters, and you may find this surprising, but reading about how Orwell's vision of a dystopian future written in 1949 stands against the reality of today is not my idea of a fun Wednesday night."

"Why?" she asks, spinning around on her desk chair. "What other options do you have? I saw Will pregaming a party on his story, so I know he's not with you."

The casual mentioning of my ex knocks me for a moment, and it's a sad reminder that I haven't had the courage to tell my family we broke up yet. I love my sister, and ordinarily I'd share my life with her, but I know as soon as she needs to divert my mom's attention she'll throw my breakup to her like throwing a dog a bone.

It might seem foolish to assume any parent of a college-age child would be that invested in their love life, or loveless life in my case, but my mom sends me pictures of wedding dresses for fun.

In the theme of keeping secrets, I also haven't told Gigi about the writing competition. That's less about her snitching to my mom, though, and more about the fact I have no freaking clue where to start. All I've ever wanted to be is an author, and I can't even decide on what story to write for the competition. I have so many ideas that I genuinely thought it would be easy, but nothing feels right. It doesn't exactly fill me full of hope about my chances of winning a place in that course. Every single resource I've looked at says write what you know, and, as it turns out, I happen to know very little.

"I was invited to a party." I don't know why it sounds like I'm lying when I'm not, but there's a hint of *I can't quite believe it* in my voice. It's enough to stop Gigi's incessant chair spinning and for her to dramatically plant her hands on her desk, and drop her jaw in shock. "And I think I'm going to go."

"Since when do *you* go to parties without Will?" She picks up her laptop and carries it with her as she drops onto her bed, tilting it onto its side as she lies against her pillows. "Who are you going with? Where are you going? Is it a book club thing?"

"Cami—the girl I work with—invited me. It isn't a book club thing; I think it's the basketball team or something. I can't remember." Can't remember being code for the fact Cami said the name of the guy who's throwing the party and I have no idea who it is, so I'm guessing from the basketball emoji she sent. "So, yeah. More interesting than high school English homework."

Her surprise isn't even that insulting because it's very un-me. "What are you going to wear?"

This is the thing I love about Gigi—she doesn't dwell on things. Once she's processed it, she rushes on to the next thing. The next thing being telling me I can't wear what I wanted to wear because it makes me look like an elementary school teacher.

"Maybe I want to look like an elementary school teacher." *I do not.*

"And maybe you watched *Matilda* too much in your formative years. Can you borrow something from your friend?"

"I don't really know if she's my friend, so I don't know if it's okay to ask to share her stuff. Plus, she's really slim, so realistically no."

One of Gigi's eyebrows creeps up to allude to her confusion. "What do you mean you don't know if she's your friend? She invited you to a party."

How am I supposed to explain to a fifteen-year-old—who once called our mailman her friend because she sees him every day and, to her, that's friendship—that making friends is not easy for every person? Especially as an adult when it's difficult as hell? That there are new categories that spring up with no instructions? That it's a directionless minefield that I've been failing to navigate since birth?

Cami is great, but is she a work colleague? Is she a work friend? Is she a friend that I also work with?

I could obsess over this for hours. I *have* obsessed over this for hours before. "Why couldn't you have just let me live in ignorance?" I ask, not entirely talking about my outfit given how my friendship status is the main thing on my mind.

"What kind of sister would I be if I let you go to a party looking like Miss Honey's socially inept twin?" she says playfully.

"A good one, because I don't think I have an alternative. And hey! I'm not socially inept. I'm just out of practice."

Out of practice feels like an understatement. I used to go to parties with Will at his college, and he'd encourage me to get ready with the girlfriends of his teammates. I'd go, I'd try, and no matter how hard I did try, I'd never had a good time. I just didn't fit into his college life as his girlfriend the way I'd fit into his high school life as his friend. I don't know exactly what I did wrong, but Will eventually stopped encouraging me to get ready with them. Or they stopped inviting me, I don't know.

Sighing, Gigi rolls onto her back and balances her laptop against her knees, giving me the perfect view of the top of her head and a poster for a K-pop band I've never heard of on the wall above her bed. "Okay, well, I'm going to go, because watching you spiral is bumming me out and I have math homework to do."

"Drop a bomb and leave why don't you."

"You'll be fine. Love you. Bye, Hallebear. Make good choices."

The top of Gigi's head disappears as she ends the video call and I sit for five minutes working out the best thing to do. I finally admit defeat and pull out my phone to text Cami.

CAMI WALKER

> Hey. Thanks for the invite but I don't have anything to wear

> My sister says I look like Miss Honey

miss honey was my ex's bisexual awakening and i only have enough energy to think about one person who doesn't want me anymore currently

ava (one of my roommates) said she has stuff you can wear

> Oh, thanks! What size?

i'd say she's a couple of sizes bigger than you, but she literally has every size bc she's a fashion student/long-term clothes hoarder

> Are you sure she doesn't mind?

i don't know her SUPER well yet bc i've only lived with her since last month, but she's so chill and she said she's excited to dress you up

so anyway let me know when you're outside bc our building can be a pain to get into

Location Shared

also don't be alarmed but i dyed my hair red and it's the patchiest thing you've ever seen in your life

i've been dyeing it blond since i was 14 but i have a salon appointment to fix it in the morning.

feel free to come and keep me company

My trust issues have me sprinting to see which Avas Cami follows because I've been stung by the "oh, you're basically the same size" so many times in my life, and it's always by someone significantly smaller than I am. Thankfully, the first picture on her page is with a girl called Ava Jones, and one minute of scrolling through her page soothes all my worries.

CAMI WALKER

I'll let you know when I'm on my way

Cami hearts my message and I drag myself from the sofa to get ready. Joy is following me around, confused probably, because I never do anything this late. She's easily distracted by the food in her dish, and I use the freedom from her weaving around my feet to check every closet for an emergency outfit *just* in case Ava doesn't have anything I like.

When I come up with nothing, I admit that maybe something new might be a good thing.

ON THE DRIVE TO THE party there was a split second, honestly just a tiny blip, where I had the urge to call Will.

It caught me off guard more than anything because I've done my best to push him to the back of my mind since I had my "new starts" last week at book club and work. Rationalizing, with some encouragement from Cami, that if he wants to say we can still be friends, he needs to put the effort in to be my friend. As it goes, I haven't heard from him at all, and I've adjusted to not reaching for my phone to text him when I wake up.

In that blip, I think I wanted his reassurance that I was going to have fun. As the car moved through familiar-looking streets and

Cami talked about people I don't know with her roommates, I began to feel like I did going to all those parties in San Diego.

It's funny that with a different house, different people, different school entirely, I still managed to feel like the outsider.

Until we stepped out of the car and Cami linked her arm with mine, reassuring me that she wouldn't leave my side unless I decided to make some poor life choices with someone from the basketball team. She said it was a shame we only met now, because her favorite player just graduated.

Her intuitiveness about how I'm feeling soothes me. Earlier, when Ava suggested I wear something that was so far from what I'd normally wear, Cami sensed my hesitation and was the one to suggest something different.

Having a group of women to get ready with—ones who seem to want me there in the first place—is what I've always wanted. Maybe I watched too much TV growing up, but it always seemed like the pinnacle of girlhood, and I've always felt like I've missed out.

The party is like others I've been to. Hot, overcrowded, and full of drunk college students. Kaia and Poppy, Cami's other roommates, put themselves in charge of "drinks and fun" the second we walked through the door—which roughly translates to more liquor than is smart and games that make me laugh so hard my sides hurt.

"Three, two, one . . . drink!"

Poppy blinks rapidly and grimaces as she struggles to swallow the contents of her cup for failing to find a basketball quicker than Ava.

"Halle and Cami," Kaia says, scanning the room. "Your quest is . . ."

"Oh, so they're quests now?" Cami says, pushing her—sort of blond but sort of red?—hair over her shoulder as she laughs.

"I mean, quest sounds more noble and honorable than calling it a dare," Kaia argues. "Roll with it! Your quest . . . is go get someone's phone number. Three, two, one, go go go."

I'm taking a sip of my drink when Cami immediately runs into the crowd of people. "Shit," is the only thing I manage to say as I run off in a different direction. It's not until I take a second to take in the guys in the room that I realize what I'm doing.

I've literally never asked for a guy's number in my life.

And that's when I spot him. Henry. Staring at his phone in the corner of the room alone. Considering he's the only other person at this party whose name I know, I suspect it'll be so much easier to explain to him why I need his number.

But as I'm about to head over, a girl approaches and hands him a Solo cup. She's much shorter than my five-foot-ten height, I'd guess half a foot smaller. She has long brown hair and a gorgeous smile. He leans in to whisper something into her ear and she laughs, and for some unknown reason, I feel a *tiny* bit put out.

"Hi. You look lost." Turning to my left, I immediately spot the guy talking to me. Much taller than me, probably about the same difference as Henry and the girl he's with. "I'm Mason."

I don't know whether it's the alcohol . . . No. That's a lie. It's definitely the alcohol that gives me the confidence. "Can I have your number?" I ask.

He holds out his hand. "Sure. Do I get your name before I give you my number?"

"It's Halle."

"Pretty name," he says as he types his digits into my cell phone. The fact that he saves his name with both a basketball and an eggplant emoji tells me everything I need to know about this guy, but who am I to judge, I guess.

"Thanks," I say over my shoulder as I'm running back to the girls. Cami joins the others a second before me and I don't even wait to be encouraged to take the shot. I'm not someone who's ever partied, which means every drink feels like five. Even in high school, if someone threw a party when their parents were out of town, I'd be Will's designated driver.

"Gimme your phone," Cami says seriously. I don't question it as I hand it over and she navigates to my contacts. She taps on Mason's recently saved number and hovers over the delete contact button with her thumb. "Do you like toxic men?"

"Huh?"

Kaia laughs and nods in the direction of Mason across the room talking to someone else. "Toxic men. Do you like them? Is your life being ruined by a fuck boy something that you want to experience in college?"

It isn't something I've ever had to consider. "Uh, I don't think so. No, no I don't want anyone toxic. Why?"

Cami's thumb taps the screen to delete the number and hands me back my phone. "Then I just saved your life. One of the housekeepers at the hotel has a sister who dated him, and let's just say he isn't for the weak hearted."

Of course I picked out the guy in a room full of guys who is likely to ruin my life. Not that I would have called him, but it's good to know that my natural instinct for self-preservation is zero. "Thank you?"

"You are so welcome!" Cami says happily.

I take another huge sip and Poppy wraps her arm around my shoulders. "This is why I don't date men."

"And this is why I hate them," Kaia adds, sighing dramatically. "But I do date them . . . unfortunately. It's my main character flaw, but nobody is perfect."

I don't know whether it's the buzz from the drinks or the high from being surrounded by fun people who seem to be genuinely happy I'm here, but my brain doesn't stop me when Henry walks toward the stairs alone in my line of vision. "What do you think of that guy?"

"Who?" Poppy asks. "Henry Turner?"

Oh crap. "Do you guys know *everyone*?"

They all look into their cups. Cami is the first person to break. "I don't *know* him, know him. But I know *of* him. And his reputation. A very positive one, nothing like Mason, but well earned if rumors are to be believed. He's . . . popular on campus. With women."

"I think he's nice," Ava says, interrupting Cami. "I had a class with him last year. He's quiet. Sweet."

"I think he's hot," Kaia says. "Like really, unreasonably hot."

"My friend is dating his roommate, Russ. Do you want me to find out about him?" Poppy asks.

It's in that moment that I realize how entangled the Maple Hills web is. I don't mention to Poppy that I know Aurora, too, or that Henry was talking to someone earlier anyway. I just down the rest of my drink and put the cup on the counter. "What's my next quest?"

Chapter Five

HENRY

WHEN ANASTASIA USED A BASKETBALL party last night to back me into a corner and tell me she was going to come around today to make sure I study and stay on track academically, I thought she was kidding.

I thought it was weird when she showed up to the party, particularly because I was there to avoid her coming over to try to help me. The woman doesn't know how to accept the word *no*.

But as I listen to her sigh for the twelfth time, while not breaking her typing speed, I realize she wasn't kidding, and I'm somehow in a study group with the least productive people I know. "It's not a valid source, Kris," she says when her long sigh ends.

Kris is still spinning his pen around his finger, like he has been for ten minutes. "What do you mean it isn't a valid source? It's Wikipedia. It's *the* source."

Anastasia finally takes her eyes off her laptop to glare at him across the dining room table. "Stop being antagonizing or I'm banishing you from study group. You freaking know it isn't a source, Kris. You've been writing essays for as long as I have. Work or leave. They're your options."

I wish she'd banish me from study group. I love her; she's my best friend, but she doesn't understand that forcing me to try to do something makes me not want to do it. Plus, she'd have to banish my teammates from far more than study group for them to stop antagonizing me.

"You're grumpy today, Allen," Mattie says, probably not as carefully as I would have given the scowl on her face. "You need a hug?"

She looks down at her laptop again, shaking her head. "Not from you. Just study, okay? I need to head to the rink in literally two minutes and I only have two more paragraphs to write."

The guys look to me like somehow I'll know what's wrong with her. I want to ask her if she means a hug from me, because it's not really something we do, so I'm not sure what the signs are. Before I can speak, Russ nudges me with his foot and my cell phone lights up on the table beside my textbook.

RUSS

She misses Nate.

I miss Nate, too. Definitely not in the way she misses him, but it's been an adjustment without Nate, JJ, and Joe around. I'm grateful that she'd find time for me in her busy schedule, but maybe she needs to study with me more than I need to study with her.

I was going to tell her this isn't helpful to me, but now I don't think I will, because I don't want to upset her. Anastasia cries a lot, and usually Nate would handle it, but I already took over the captaincy from him. I don't have the energy to be someone's pseudo-boyfriend as well, no matter how much I like them.

There's an unusual silence in the den as we all sit around the dining room table, mostly pretending to work. Even though he's angled his laptop away from me, I can still see that Bobby is playing Tetris. Russ's cell phone starts vibrating against the table, and he immediately looks embarrassed when the guys start booing him.

"Sorry, sorry," he mutters, standing quickly to take the call outside on the patio.

His interruption is a welcome distraction from the line of this book I've read four times. Professor Thornton's class continues to be as terrible as I originally determined.

The French doors open and Russ reenters, pushing his cell phone into his pocket. "Rory is coming to study with us, if that's all right with everyone."

"You know you live here and we don't, right?" Bobby asks, looking up from his game. "You don't need our permission for your girlfriend to come over."

"I thought she was going to book club," I say, wishing I'd asked her to get me some cookies.

"Halle texted everyone to say a pipe burst and they've had to close the store to repair the damage, so it's been canceled."

It was frustrating when I met Halle a couple of weeks ago and on the way to get food Aurora could tell me basically nothing about her. When I suggested she was a lousy friend, she argued that Halle keeps to herself and she'd love to know more about her, which makes two of us.

"Tell her to bring everyone here. They can set up in the garden, just get everyone to bring a picnic blanket or something," I say, closing my textbook, officially giving up for now.

Mattie shuts his laptop. "I support this vision."

Anastasia scoffs. "You'd support anything that gave you a five-to-one ratio of women."

"It's actually more if you consider Russ has a girlfriend and Robbie is both taken and not here."

"Are you sure?" Russ asks, reaching for his phone. "Is having a houseful of strangers not very distracting and counterproductive to finishing your essay?"

"Does this have anything to do with you having a crush on the book club girl?" Anastasia asks, causing overdramatic gasps from my friends.

I roll my eyes at how childish they all are. "I don't have a crush on her."

"Rory said you were flirting with her," she counters, shutting her own laptop and tucking it into her bag.

Kris leans forward to get a better look at Anastasia. "Did Aurora say exactly how he was flirting? Because I've been trying to get eyes and ears on that situation for over two years now."

"I wasn't flirting. I was talking to her."

She's hot, so I would have flirted with her, but she was flustered and it sounded like she'd just gone through a breakup. Didn't seem like the right time.

"Ah," Mattie groans. "A conversation first. That's where I'm going wrong."

"Aurora said they're going to head over now." When we look at Russ, the tips of his ears have gone pink. "She also says thank you."

"Looks like she said more than thank you, you big ol' beet," Kris teases. "Right, what was the book they read this week? Time to google the shit out of it until they get here so I can look educated and appealing."

Anastasia's eyebrow rises as she stands from her chair and slings her bag over her shoulder. "You're going to be a doctor . . ."

Kris nods. "With a shitload of college loans. I need to find a wife while I still have this body."

Anastasia gives one last sigh. "Goodbye."

MY BEDROOM WINDOW IS CRACKED slightly, which is letting me listen to the laughter outside while I once again attempt to concentrate on my work.

As soon as Aurora turned up with her arms full of blankets, I retreated to the safety of my bedroom to stay out of everyone's way. The noise outside eventually dies down, and I hear the front door open and close, signaling the end of the meeting.

Five minutes pass and there's a light tapping at my door. When I pull it open, I'm pleased to find it's who I thought it was going to be. "You cut your hair off," I say.

"What?" Halle responds, instinctively running her hand down the now-shorter length of her brown hair. "Oh yeah. The girl I work with encouraged me to when I went to the salon with her this morning. Nicely, not forcefully or anything. I've just wanted to cut my hair for a long time and my e—someone stopped me doing it."

The blunt ends sit right on her collarbone, dragging my focus across the area and up the column of her neck before I meet her eyes again. "I like it. You look really good."

She's flustered instantly, but I don't think I said anything weird. It was just a compliment; a tame one at that. I step out of the doorway, holding out an arm to usher her in. She complies immediately, sitting on the bottom corner of my bed when I throw myself down onto my normal spot.

Maybe she's not used to hearing compliments. Although that seems unlikely, because she's beautiful. Maybe Will Ellington is as shit at being a boyfriend as he is at playing hockey. "Thank you," she eventually chokes out. "That's sweet of you to say. And sweet of you to let us use your house. I brought you something to say thank you. I made double in case you happened to show up again, then the pipe happened, and well. Here."

She holds out a glass container lined with paper towels, and when I open the lid, the smell of fresh cookies fills my room. I take a bite, and they're just as good as I remember. I'm glad she brought them up here so I don't have to share with the guys. "Thank you. Want one?"

She holds up her hand in protest. "No, thank you. I'm a little sick."

Now that she's mentioned it, her skin is a little paler than the last time I saw her during the day and there's clearly makeup under her eyes trying to cover dark bags. "What's wrong?"

"I went to a party last night and I'm not that experienced when it comes to drinking, so I feel like I've been hit by a car."

"I know, I saw you. If you spend more time with Aurora that might happen. She nearly reversed into me yesterday. Have you taken Advil?"

"You saw me?" she says, her voice missing its normal airy tone.

"Yeah," I say, wiping a cookie crumb from the corner of my mouth. "You were asking Mason Wright for his number. I don't recommend you call him."

"Why not?"

"He's a dickhead."

She snorts as she laughs abruptly. Cute. "I don't know why I keep snorting in front of you, sorry. The girls I was with already deleted his number. I didn't realize you saw that."

"You looked like you were having fun with your friends, so I didn't want to approach you. I didn't know if you'd remember me and I didn't want to ruin your night by bothering you."

"Of course I'd remember you," she says softly. "You can always approach me at a party. It would've been nice to see a familiar face, last night was . . . a lot of new faces."

"Have you taken medicine, Halle?"

She shakes her head, so I swing my legs off my bed and head to my bathroom to grab the box of stuff I keep for emergencies. It's mainly full of skin care items, socks, hair ties, etc., but I do have painkillers and things in here, too. She watches as I dig around for the Advil I keep handy for hangovers.

I've never known a woman to look so out of place in my bedroom. She seems nervous for some reason and looks like she's thinking far too hard. Sometimes I struggle with conversations because human beings, especially the women in my life, naturally want to fill silences with something. I watch Anastasia and Aurora do it all the time; it's like they've appointed themselves as guardians of the conversation flow and natural silences are counterproductive to their work. I don't think Lola's had a quiet moment in her life, but lately it seems to be because of arguments she has with Robbie. I don't think they know I know they're fighting a lot, but my room is directly above his.

I love the silence, but judging by the look on her face, Halle does not. "Is this your girlfriend's stuff?"

"Someone stayed the night once and the next day got really sick. I didn't have anything to look after her with and I felt really bad. Since then, I've kept stuff in my bathroom just in case," I explain. "I don't have a girlfriend."

"I wasn't sure, because I saw you with someone last night and . . ." Her voice trails off. "Yeah. Anyway."

"Anastasia. My friend's girlfriend." I can't help but smirk. "Were you jealous?"

My question finally adds a little color to her white skin as her cheeks flush pink. "No, of course not! I just . . . God, I am so hungover."

"Of course not," I repeat, holding out the Advil to her.

"This is a pretty cool thing to do," she says, shaking two pills onto her palm. She digs into her bag and pulls out a water bottle, throwing back the pills quickly. "Thank you."

The silence returns. Leaning forward, she swipes a book from my nightstand. It's the same one I bought last week at the store. The same one I've hardly touched. "How's your leadership reading list going?"

"I read two chapters and gave up. It's about his whole life, which I guess is fair for an autobiography, but who has that much to say about their family?"

"Not a family guy?" she says, flipping the book over to read the back. "Sorry, that's so personal! Ignore me, I didn't think."

"It's fine. I love my family. My moms are the best people I've ever met, but I could cover it in half a chapter. Max."

She laughs, and it's exactly like I thought it would be. Light, pretty, musical. Everything about her is soft. "I have to stop myself from writing super long chapters all the time. So unfortunately, I can relate to"—she flips the book over—"four-time Stanley Cup winner Harold Oscar. I'm sure what he has to say is far more interesting, though."

"You're an author?"

"I'm trying to be, but there's something not clicking right now. I think I'm still trying to find my style or something. There's a competition I want to enter but I can't decide what to write about. I'm, I don't know, seriously lacking in inspiration I guess. Weirdly, a song came on at the party last night that clearly wasn't supposed to be part of the playlist and I thought about a plot, but I don't know if it'll go anywhere. All my other ideas and drafts don't feel good enough, so maybe something new is a better idea."

"I get that. Sometimes I feel like that about a painting if it's a new subject or technique I'm trying. Stuff we create is personal. You're probably overthinking it."

She smiles and rubs her fingers against her temple. "You're probably right. But anyway, you're an artist? That's so cool, I didn't know that." She looks around my bare room. "Where's your work?"

Good question. I shrug. "Never made anything I've wanted to stare at every day. I move on quickly."

"Wish I could relate. I feel like I've been dragging around the same ideas for years. It's a good thing I'm a better reader than I am author; I think I'd lose my mind."

"I'm a much better artist than reader." She laughs again. "I can't concentrate on a book I'm not interested in long enough to get to the interesting stuff. I try really hard and before I know it, I zone back in and I've been pointlessly scrolling for twenty minutes. But I don't even remember picking up my cell phone. It's infuriating."

Halle doesn't give me the weird look people give me when I try to explain how frustrating I find some things other people find easy. She just nods. "My younger sister has the same problem. We found it's because she has ADHD. I help her a lot with her English homework because it's her least favorite subject, and if she doesn't want to read the book it's a battle."

Battle feels like the right word for how I feel sometimes. "It's weird, because I can google something and accidentally end up tangled up researching a different thing but read everything that's ever been said about it no problem. But the one thing I *need* to do is impossible."

Halle chuckles, but I don't feel like she's laughing at me. I like how easy she is to talk to. "Yep, Gianna is the same. Getting her diagnosis has given her more resources and support, but I dread to think what school would be like for her if we hadn't pushed her doctors. I spent a lot of time looking up ADHD, and some people go their whole lives not knowing that they're neurodivergent. Sorry, oversharing."

"It's good your sister has support now. I'm going to spend the rest of the day looking up these cookies," I admit, taking another one from the container. "They're too damn good."

"My nana once visited for an entire summer to look after me while my parents were at work and my brother was at football camp. She monitored every step of the process to make sure I perfected it. She said I couldn't give out shit cookies and then tell people it's her recipe."

"Please pass my thank-you on to your nana."

"Oh, she passed a few years ago. I live in her house, so I have all her personal recipe books and things. I think the cookies are the only thing I don't completely ruin."

"She'd be happy with her cookie reputation," I reassure her, taking another bite. "You're doing a great job. It's cool you live there, though, and have her stuff. My grandma was a fancy restaurant kind of lady, so I don't have recipes, but I do have a list of approved places to eat across the world."

My mama stopped talking to her parents thirty years ago when their "strict, conservative values" meant they couldn't accept she was gay, so even though they're still alive I haven't met them.

My mom's parents were both career-focused people who didn't have her until later in life and they both passed away before I was fifteen. They did everything to make my mama feel loved and included in their family since she'd lost her own. One of my grandma's favorite things to do was to take us all to eat at her top-ranked places and show off her family.

"Oh, I love that! Also I'm not sure anyone has ever described me being a college junior and living alone in my nana's house as cool. But I'll accept the baking praise," she says, pulling at the sleeve of her cardigan. "Thank you."

"Why don't you live with your friends?" I ask, and judging by the way her face sinks, I think that was one of those things I'm not supposed to ask.

"That's a good question. A really good question, um . . ." I'm stuck between her telling me it's a good question and her visible discomfort. I'm about to say she can just ignore it when she finally answers. "I don't have any friends, really. Ones I kinda had don't go to UCMH, but everyone dropped me when I split up with my boyfriend anyway."

She looks embarrassed, but only a couple of years ago I didn't have friends, either. Now, if anything, I might have too many. They're hard to keep track of, but I think adding one more won't hurt. "I'm your friend."

Her eyebrow tweaks up. It's an expression I'm used to. It means I've caught her off guard. I seem to be forever catching people off guard. "You're not."

"Yeah, I am," I say a little harder.

"That's not how people make friends," she insists.

"How would you know? You just said you don't have any." The way she visibly flinches guts me. I move on quickly. "We're friends, Halle. Friends do nice things together. I let you use my house for a book club and you brought me food. I'm not saying you should live with me or anything, but you're not friendless."

"Okay, we can be friends then," she says, her shoulders dropping an inch as she relaxes a little. I don't want her to be uncomfortable around me, and I *do* want to be her friend.

"Good. This weekend is our annual preseason party that my roommate said he was too old and mature to throw, so it's obviously happening anyway. You should come, so I know you mean it when you say we can be friends."

I think Russ and I are the only people not alarmed about Robbie wanting to party less. The rest of the team, however, particularly the ones who Nate wouldn't let in and are now older, all feel like they're missing out on some kind of rite of passage. Robbie didn't say he'd never throw another party; he said he wants to focus on showing Faulkner what he's capable of and being more responsible. But obviously nobody listens to anything properly, as I discover every practice, and they just heard "less parties."

Before Nate and JJ moved out, Robbie viewed multiple places to live on his own this year. He said he wanted to create some distance between Robbie our friend, and Robbie the man hoping to get a faculty position once he's finished his studies.

Robbie said the only reason he didn't move out when he wanted was because none of the places that were available were built with disabled people in mind. He said the stress he would have experienced trying to get a landlord to do the bare minimum like improve the building accessibility and safety wasn't worth it, and he'd look again in a year.

Halle rolls her eyes at my offer, tucking Harold Oscar's book under her arm as she stands from my bed. "I don't think so. It'd be weird to go to a party alone, and I have stuff to do. Assignments, my writing project, book club stuff, y'know."

"You won't be alone. I'll be there."

"You'll be busy with your friends."

"We just established you're my friend."

She sighs, but it's different from when Anastasia sighed earlier. "Are you always this . . . persistent? Convincing? Dare I say, slightly stubborn?"

"I don't know," I admit honestly. "I never need to work this hard usually. Most women want to be my friend."

"I'm sure they do, Henry. I'm going to go, I have work soon, but I'm going to borrow this book, if that's okay?"

I shrug. "Sure. I'm not reading it anyway."

"Thanks again for the garden."

"Thanks again for the cookies."

She turns to leave, and right before the door closes, I call her. "Halle?"

Her face peeks through the small gap. "Yes?"

"I really do like your hair."

Chapter Six

HALLE

"FOUND ANYTHING?"

I look up from my tablet screen and give Cami an unenthusiastic thumbs-down. "Sadly, they don't seem to stock *happy, healthy kids* or *to live long enough to see my children get married* online. Maybe a fruit basket?"

"Fruit basket is good. It'll help with the long-life thing," Cami says, taking the seat beside me in the break room. She leans over to look at the options on the fifth department store "gifts for her" section I've scoured since my brother texted our sibling group chat asking what *we* were getting Mom for her birthday next week. "Could you maybe promise to take her to a spa when you go home for Thanksgiving?"

I decide to avoid explaining how, in a misguided attempt to negotiate with my ex-boyfriend, I committed to not going home for the holidays this year. "That's a great idea, but I'm kind of in charge of making sure my siblings have something to give her, too."

"I thought your brother was older than you," she says, and I can't help but sigh in Eldest Daughter.

"He is, but, like my stepdad, he's incompetent. Which means if I don't arrange a gift, Mom won't be getting a gift on her birthday. It's totally fine. I'm used to being the family manager."

I know that Cami is the youngest sibling, so she probably has no idea what I mean when I call myself the family manager. Ironically, it's a title Grayson gave me when we were younger to fully signify his less-than-enthusiastic contributions to any and all family responsibilities.

Cami locks my screen and slides the device away from me slowly. "Y'know what will help you decide . . . alcohol. I make all my best decisions drunk."

I haven't decided if I like drinking yet. I like being invited to things and I like the confidence I get when I'm buzzed, but I despise being hungover. It makes me anxious and tearful and a little oversensitive, but I'm not sure if those invites will stop if I'm not as fun.

"Weren't you drinking when you decided to home dye your hair?"

Cami's previously blond hair is now a deep auburn shade, but only after we spent hours in the hair salon, while fighting my first hangover I should add, getting it fixed. "Okay, so maybe my execution was bad, but try and tell me that red is not my color. Four different people have told me I look like Jessica Rabbit. Do you know what it's doing to my ego? If only I had her titties. I'd be even more unbearable."

"You don't want the back pain, trust me." I instinctively push my shoulders back a little to fix my posture and the space between my shoulder blades crunches. "And you do look like Jessica Rabbit. You should buy the Halloween costume now."

During our trip to the salon, I learned that Cami had a situationship with West, the guy whose job I got. She thinks it's silly to be upset since they weren't even a couple and she kind of hated him anyway, but she is and she's dealing with it in the only way she says she knows how. Partying as much as possible.

Cami is two years older than me, but she changed majors and didn't have enough classes to graduate with her own year group. All her friends, and she clarified she definitely wasn't calling West a friend, moved away for grad school or job opportunities. She said our circumstances are different, but not that dissimilar, and that's why it's so easy for us to be friends.

Seeing her so cut up over West made me feel bad accepting any form of sympathy from her about Will. I immediately felt like I was deceiving her, so I tried to clarify that, apart from the occasional blip, I'm fine being single.

She said she was going to pretend I hadn't said it because it makes her feel less like a lonely loser to have a friend experiencing the same kind of heartache. She laughed, clarifying she was kidding, and told me that if the blips become less bliplike and more dye-my-hair-red-like, she'd be there for me.

Box dye in hand.

I don't know whether it was the hangover or the general emotions that come with seeing your life change in such a short space of time, but in that moment—literally just a few hours of my entire life—I felt sad for past Halle who didn't have this.

"You're right, and I love my little pancakes anyway," she says as she pats her chest affectionately. "I should wear something that shows them off when we go to a party later. Don't you agree?"

Part of me wants to say no, I'm staying home to finally start working on my entry to the writing competition. That tonight the planning and the mood boarding and the mind changing finally becomes a work in progress.

But a bigger, louder, and more persuasive part of me is going to say let's go, because it doesn't know how to say to no to people, and it's arguing that isn't this what I've always wanted? My own friends who invite me to things because of me, not because of a man? Isn't this what I'm supposed to be doing post-Will? Putting myself first and also having fun? How am I going to decide if I like partying if I don't try it out properly?

I fold my arms across my chest and sit back in my chair in a fake display of defiance, but in reality, I feel a little giddy, because among all the unknowns, I *want* to learn about myself. "Which party?"

Cami claps her hands excitedly, and staff I can't remember the names of yet at the next table look up from their phones. "Oh, you're going to love it. Robbie's parties are the best."

"Who's Robbie?"

THE HOCKEY HOUSE HAS AN entirely different atmosphere at night compared to when I was here for book club.

Even though Henry invited me before Cami's intervention, I still feel a little weird about being here. I haven't seen him once, which isn't surprising, since from the moment we walked in here several drinks ago, the place has been overflowing with people. What is surprising is how much I've been looking out for him.

A mixture of liquor and soda bottles have taken over the kitchen island, and every other surface in the large living room is covered in red cups and beer bottles. Music is blasting from every corner of the space, making it hard for me to hear my own thoughts, never mind the guy everyone seems to hate trying to talk to me while we dance.

I think under normal circumstances I'd have backed away from Mason slowly and found an excuse to run away, but these aren't normal circumstances, because I am heavily under the influence of whatever is in the very large punch bowl.

Punch Bowl Halle isn't worried that she can't dance or talk to men, never mind the fact that this one might ruin her life. Punch Bowl Halle is having fun because that's what she's supposed to do at college parties. She also opted to let Mason press his very large body against hers and put his hands on her waist instead of answering his question about why he hadn't received a text.

I wish Cami was here to save me, but she went outside to call her roommate seconds before Mason found me. Apparently Sober Halle and Punch Bowl Halle have one very clear similarity: they're both cowards.

"You look really hot," he yells. His mouth lingers near my ear, his breath warming the sensitive spot on my neck. These are the experiences I've read about in romance books. The hot bad boy showing interest in the—let's face it—inexperienced, sheltered virgin. We're a cliché, and drunk me finds it funny, but I suspect sober me would be embarrassed as hell.

The worst part is as his hands tighten on my hips, I've been waiting for my body to react in some way. My skin to prickle, heart to speed up, something to indicate that my lack of desire was to do with Will. That I'm not entirely sexually dead in the face of a good-looking man. Because that's how this cliché goes, right? Immediate and unmistakable sexual prowess, but alas, nothing.

I know that I'm still young, and I know that my worth is not associated with what happens between my legs, but I just want to understand myself.

I *want* to want someone, and it's beginning to make me a little frustrated.

"Thanks," I say back, finally responding to Mason's compliment. "Uh, so do you."

I can feel my cheeks heating as I hear what I said in my head, and that honestly wasn't the kind of bodily reaction I was looking for. It sounded flustered and ungenuine. Like when someone wishes you happy birthday and you respond with, "You, too." Immediately followed by cursing yourself for saying something so silly.

I reluctantly lean backward to assess how embarrassed I should be, and I'm surprised to find he's looking at me like he wants to eat me.

"Do you want to find somewhere quieter?" he shouts. "More private?"

"No, she doesn't."

I don't need to turn around to check who just spoke on my behalf, because even with the loud drum from the speakers, I recognize his deep voice. My heart rate picks up. Looking up, I see Mason's face has turned sour.

"Didn't realize you'd started bodyguarding, Turner," he snaps.

"Surprised you have the time, Captain."

"C'mon, Halle," Henry says, placing both of his hands on my shoulders and guiding me backward, slipping out of a now irritated Mason's grasp. "Have the night you deserve, Wright."

I'm basically a puppet. I put up zero resistance as Henry takes my hand in his, tucking me close to him as he navigates us through the crowd toward the back of the house. *I really would be easy to kidnap* is the recurring thought running through my head as we approach the den.

Henry still hasn't said anything, and as we head toward a beer pong table my survival instincts finally kick in. "Wait!" I say a little more enthusiastically than is necessary, grinding to a halt. "What the hell was that?"

He turns to face me, the same neutral expression he normally wears painting his face. "I was saving you from your terrible taste in men."

Ouch. It's like a sobering slap to the face. "That felt personal."

"I already told you Mason Wright is a douche bag," he says calmly. "If you want a rebound, he isn't the place to go."

Sober Halle would drop it immediately, too embarrassed at her dance partner faux pas to ask more questions. Punch Bowl Halle doesn't have the same reservations. "Do you always interfere in the activities of your party guests?"

"What happened to always approaching you at parties?" Henry's smirking, and I feel like I'm missing something until I remember he's using my own words against me. "I interfere in the activities of my friends, if needed. If you want to hook up with someone, there are better options than him," he says, and Punch Bowl Halle loses the small amount of drunk defiance she had. "I know him. He went to my high school. He's angry and irresponsible and not good enough for you."

"I wasn't trying to hook up with him. He didn't try anything," I explain, like somehow I need to justify myself. "Sorry."

"You're beautiful, Halle. Of course he was trying something. You don't need to apologize."

My mouth opens to immediately offer something more but closes when his words register. Beautiful. I push it to the back of my brain to mull over tomorrow when he isn't watching my every reaction.

"I just wanted to get drunk and dance with a guy at a party. Have the experience or whatever. It's silly."

"Nothing you say is silly. You're starting to look sad, and I think I've caused it when I didn't mean to. Can we start again?"

I nod, grateful for the chance to start over. "Hi."

He smiles. "Hi. I'm happy you're here."

"I'm happy you invited me."

"It's my turn to apologize to you," he says, moving to my right to walk beside me toward where his friends are now waiting. "I'm about to make you play beer pong against Aurora, and she's really annoying and competitive. And she's going to spend the rest of the night telling you how much she hates Mason, too, because she's the one who spotted you."

I feel a little like I'm walking into the lion's den as we reach the table, and I would really benefit from more punch right now. Henry picks up the ball and bounces it against the table once, catching it in his palm and holding it out to me. Tucking my concerning lack of coordination in the back of my mind, I scoop the ball from his hand.

"I've spent the last two years hearing about how much Aurora hates poetry. This will be easy."

More of Henry's friends appear from the garden, including Aurora, who immediately beelines for me and traps me in a tight hug. "I'm so happy you're hereeeee. Are you with me?" she asks, looking between me and Henry.

"She's mine," he says. "Find your own teammate."

Before I have a chance to speak for myself, I'm beaten to it by one of Henry's friends walking through the doors dragging a chair behind him. "There was a minor incident," he says. Mattie, Kris, or Bobby, he's called. From height and build to ethnicity and hair color, they all look totally different, as well as having accents clearly from different states. But when I first met them at book club, they introduced themselves almost at the same time and now I can't remember who is who.

"I can see that," Henry drawls as we look at the crushed camping chair on the ground.

"We were trying to play musical chairs and the indestructible chair was apparently destructible when jumped on. My bad," Mattie, Kris, or Bobby says. "Hi, Halle!"

It takes a second to realize he's talking directly to me, and now everyone is looking at me. Henry is crouching on the floor, looking to see if the chair is salvageable, but stands up quickly when he also hears my name. "Hi—" *Oh my God, what's his name?* "—there."

"You can't remember my name. I'm hurt. After we enjoyed that book together," he says, tutting dramatically. "Hen, you clearly don't talk about me enough."

That book we read together is a very creative way of saying the book he googled before book club started. As much as I love a trip to Inglewild, if he read it before my impromptu book club meeting in this very house and wasn't just trying to impress the members, I'll give him my next paycheck.

"I never talk about you, Kris." Henry shrugs in the nonchalant way he does. "It's only important that she remembers my name."

My God.

Concentrate, Halle. Six-foot, dark-haired white guy with a sort of hybrid accent that I can't place. Big shoulders and back. Huge, in fact. Kris. Kris, Kris, Kris. Only two more to remember. Uh, plus all his other friends who also still seem to be looking at me.

"Do you hear yourself?" Aurora asks Henry.

"Usually. I can only drown one of us out at a time and I always pick you. Are we playing?"

Aurora bursts out laughing and gives him the finger, but I get what she means. There's something about what he says and how he delivers it that's just . . . hard to pinpoint why it sounds so good.

She bumps him in the arm playfully. "I see you've been taking notes from my dad. Emilia and Poppy will be here in, like, one minute. Can we just wait for them to arrive?"

"Sure." He turns to me. "Are you good at beer pong?"

Oh boy. "Do you want the truth that will make you feel bad now or a lie that might make you feel good in the short term, but bad when you discover it's a lie?"

"I always want you to tell me the truth."

"I know the rules but I've never played, so I'm probably terrible."

"I can fix terrible," he says with a smile. He guides me forward until my back is to his front and takes my right hand that's holding the Ping-Pong ball he gave me earlier. He leans in until I can feel his soft breathing tickling my neck, and his hand guides mine up into a throwing position. His voice is low and deep as he speaks just to me. "Does this feel comfortable?"

He smells like expensive aftershave, and his other hand is on my waist to gently move me into the right stance, and I'm having a really hard time concentrating, and . . . "Halle?"

My cheeks flush when a shiver shoots down my spine. "Yup. Comfortable."

"It's all in the wrist. Don't overthink it," he says as he guides my hand to throw the ball toward the cups on the other side of the table. I'm essentially a puppet again, for the second time tonight. "Perfect. You're a natural."

I'm vaguely aware of Cami returning with Poppy and who I assume is Emilia, but I'm focused on Henry. "Or you're just a good leader after all."

"See if you still think that in ten minutes. Because we are not losing to Aurora. I need you to bring your A game, okay?"

Someone starts filling all the cups with alcohol and I'm laughing to myself before I even speak. "Yes, Captain."

Chapter Seven

HENRY

I DON'T THINK I'VE EVER worked through a book this quickly in my life.

Flipping to the next tab, I read the parts that Halle has highlighted for me in blue, ignoring all the parts she hasn't. When her redhead friend was leaving last night, and Halle drunkenly slurred she had something for me in her purse, I wasn't sure what to expect.

When she returned, she handed me the book she'd borrowed, explaining she'd read it and highlighted all the parts I might find interesting or relevant.

I'm already halfway through the book when she finally wakes up, jolting up in bed, clutching the duvet to her chest. I watch as a dozen questions hit her all at once. Her eyes widen, teeth nibbling at her bottom lip as she considers what to ask first.

"Hello," I say, breaking the silence between us.

She swallows hard and I nod toward the bottle of water and painkillers I left next to her. With one hand keeping the duvet pressed to her body, she collects the pills and drink, quickly taking them. When half the water is gone, she replaces the lid and stares right at me. "Did we have sex last night?"

I double fold the tab for the page I'm on and put the book down in front of me. Pointing to the half-deflated air mattress below me, I meet her stare. "No."

"Do you promise?"

"I'm on an air mattress that definitely has a slow puncture, Halle. Why would I have sex with you then not sleep beside you?"

"That isn't an answer, Henry," she says.

"Yes, I promise we didn't have sex last night," I say. Her shoulders relax. The tension in her face begins to disappear. "I don't have sex with women who have more alcohol in their system than any other fluid."

"If we didn't have sex"—she clears her throat—"then why am I naked in your bed?"

"You didn't want to leave with your friends and I was worried about you not being able to look after yourself, since I know you live alone. I wanted to put you in the empty room next door but Mattie took someone in there," I explain. "So I found my air mattress and brought you in here."

She takes another drink from the water bottle. "Yes, but why am I *naked*?"

"I don't know. I went back downstairs because you left your purse in the den, and when I came back upstairs your clothes were gone. I offered you something to sleep in and you told me no."

Her eyes widen again, and while she has whatever internal crisis she's having, I recap what I just said to work out what was the thing that triggered it. Finally, long after I've given up recapping, she speaks again. "You saw me naked."

Oh, there we go. "I've seen a lot of people naked."

"You saw me naked," she repeats, but I don't think she's talking *to* me.

"Friends sometimes see friends naked. It's not a big deal."

"It's a big deal to me that you saw me naked. People don't see me naked."

She has no reason to feel insecure. "People are missing out then." I wanted the joke to boost her confidence, but it doesn't land. At all. Her cheeks flush pink and she goes back to looking unhappy. I don't want her to feel bad, but sometimes when I open my mouth I just make things worse. "Do you want to see me naked to even things out?"

She laughs at that one, but that one wasn't a joke. "As glorious as I'm sure it is, I'll pass. God, you must think I'm so embarrassing. I'm so sorry. Drinking is a new thing for me and I think I overdid it. Again."

"Can you stop apologizing for everything? It's really unnecessary. I don't think you're embarrassing."

"I bet the place is a mess after last night. I can totally help you clean up if you want me to, or I could get everyone breakfast. No, that's silly. I can just get out of your hair so people don't know I was here."

"You don't have to do anything. You're not in my hair. People already know you're here. Aurora checked to see if we wanted breakfast but you were asleep and I didn't want to wake you. Plus, it's lunchtime now and I think everyone went out."

"It's lunchtime? Oh my God, I never sleep in this late. I'm so sorry." I watch as she starts to spiral and I'm beginning to think maybe she's never woken up in someone's bed before, so I don't point out that she just apologized to me, *again*.

"This is a bigger deal to you than it is to me," I say before she can say sorry for anything else. "I like that you're here and I'm happy you came to the party. You're not the first naked drunk person I've looked after, Halle. You're not even the first naked drunk person this week. You really don't need to feel embarrassed. It isn't embarrassing."

"I think I'll just grab my clothes and get out of your way. I really appreciate you for being so cool about this."

"We're friends," I say. "Have a shower. It will help you feel better. The box of stuff is under my sink and clean towels are on the rack."

She nods but doesn't move. When nothing happens, she smiles properly for the first time since she woke up. "Could you maybe, um, cover your eyes or something? I know you've already seen it, but I might die if I have to do this sober."

Oh shit. "Yeah." I lean back against my near-empty mattress and press the pillow to my face. As soon as I hear the shower turn on, I get back to my book.

"Henry?"

"Yeah?"

"Could you pass me my dress, please?"

"Do you want to wear something of mine? You seem to be pretty against nudity, and your dress doesn't do much to combat that."

I'm not exaggerating. I nearly choked on my drink when I saw her and her tiny, shimmery minidress. I'm used to the floral dresses and the cardigans. I overheard her tell Aurora that she borrowed it from Cami's roommate. It seems like she's made more friends recently, which makes me happy. Judging from the groan that comes from the bathroom, I think she's embarrassed again.

"I'm a big fan of the dress and you in it," I add. "You just might be more comfortable in my clothes."

She goes quiet for a moment. "If that's okay . . ." I grab her some sweatpants and a T-shirt from my clean laundry basket and pass them through the gap in the door. "Thank you."

When she finally reappears, fiddling with the band of my sweatpants, she looks much better than she did when she woke up. "Let me help," I say, waving her over to where I'm sitting on the bed. Putting my feet on the floor, I move her between my legs, taking the sweatpants string and attempting to unknot it. She's patting the ends of her hair with a microfiber towel, and the whole scene feels unusually domestic. "You smell really good."

She chuckles. "Thanks. You're incredibly prepared. I've only ever slept over at Will's house, and even he didn't have toiletries for when I visited."

"Bad hockey player. Bad boyfriend. Figures," I say, finally getting the last knot. I pull it tight so the waistband clings to her hips and tie a bow to keep it in place.

"He wasn't a bad boyfriend, he was just—"

"I have no interest in hearing you list the redeeming qualities of your mediocre ex." She snorts, a sound I've grown fond of. "I thought you hadn't made that sound before. You're well practiced at it."

I shuffle back on the bed, resting against the headboard on the opposite side from where she slept last night. I pat the area beside me, indicating for her to sit down, which she does. "It isn't a noise normally in my repertoire. I'm just not used to hearing people talk about Will with such . . . dislike. I think the only exception is my brother, Grayson. But I don't think he really likes anyone."

"Get used to it. Everyone on the team thinks he's a dick."

She looks to me at her left, lips curved slightly. "Noted." Her eyes flick down between us. "Oh my God, you're reading it?"

"Yeah. I'm just reading the bits you highlighted in blue. It's really helping keep my attention. I liked the part where you drew the hockey stick, although maybe you should leave the drawing to me." Her small smile has developed into a full grin. She's beaming at me and I don't know why. "Why are you looking at me like that?"

"I'm just so happy it's helping you." She tucks her knees to her chest and rests her head against them. "I wasn't sure if it would work, but it's one of the things we've done over the years to help with Gigi's concentration. We found that when the irrelevant bits were stripped away she was able to process the important ones a lot better. She prefers using audio now, but I thought this might help you. Gigi is my fifteen-year-old stepsister, by the way."

"I remember. And got it," I say, taking the book back and running my fingers across the colored tabs poking out the side. She left a Post-it note on the first page with a key to her tabs: yellow for his struggles and mistakes; pink for his victories; orange for things he'd do differently if he had time again; and green for advice he'd give to players of the future.

"Not everything in the book was about hockey, not unexpected given it was an autobiography. He talked a lot about his family and things he's done since he retired that I guess wouldn't interest you."

"I wish all the stuff I don't want to read was filtered like this. Maybe then I'd be able to pass Thornton's class this semester."

"Oh, I love Professor Thornton! I was supposed to be taking How History Shaped Art with him, but Will asked me to change my class schedule to free up my Fridays for hockey and I couldn't get Thornton's class to fit." I'm so confused and I guess it shows on my face, because she adds, "I've done at least one with him since freshman year."

"I don't know what's wilder to me. You being asked to change your education for *hockey,* or the fact that you like Professor Thornton. Or that if you hadn't changed your schedule we'd have met a month earlier because that's the one I'm in."

"I like the idea that we might have still become friends in another reality," she says quietly. "I can see why you're struggling with him if you're not a fan of reading widely. His classes are super intense on the front, but honestly he's a teddy bear. He acts mean, but once you know how to write the way he likes, and which academic sources he favors, he's easy. I'm going to take Sex and Sensuality in the Eighteenth Century with him in spring. How have your essays gone so far?"

"I've only submitted one. He said it lacked proper research and attention to detail."

She frowns, and two faint lines appear between her eyebrows. "That's harsh for your first essay. Did you talk to him about it?"

"Yes. I didn't have much of a defense. I wrote about the wrong revolution."

She lets her knees drop into a cross-legged position, and her fingers play with the bottom of my sweatpants that are too long for her legs. It's weird seeing a woman wearing my clothes, but in a comfortable kind of way. "You just need to know what to look for with Thornton. When's your next assignment due?"

Tuesday. "Two days."

"How many words do you have so far?"

"Fourteen. My name and the title."

She buries her head in her hands and laughs before looking at me again. "You don't make it easy for yourself, do you?"

"I'm only like this for this class, I swear. I'm anxious I'll get it wrong, so I don't know where to start."

"Let me help you. You're struggling with the research material, right? I can just highlight the relevant parts and you can reference them."

"Won't that be really boring for you?" I ask. I know I want to take her up on her offer immediately. I'm so lost with this work and I'm not being dramatic when I say I don't know where to start. I was planning to let the panic fuel me tomorrow after I get home from the gym. "And do you even have the time to help me?"

Halle shrugs. "I don't mind. I don't have anything else to do today. I was just going to work on my novel, but that isn't urgent."

"How is your novel going? Have you found your style yet?" I feel bad for not asking her that yesterday. That's something I should have remembered.

"It's going about as well as your essay, except your word count is higher. I was supposed to work on it last night, but, well, I was talked into coming here by Cami. But as embarrassed as I feel today—"

"Stop feeling embarrassed."

"—it actually makes me feel super inspired. I want to write about people who have all these experiences and are a bit messy, but I think I can't start because I don't *actually* have any experience of my own. I never do anything," she explains. "But maybe by doing stuff it'll clear the creative rubble. Even if I did expose myself to you and also dance with your enemy, which I'm still very sorry for."

"There are other ways to get experiences than putting yourself in Mason's path. And we can have a friendship ground rule that means you're allowed to get naked in front of me whenever you like, if that helps with your misplaced guilt."

There are worse ground rules to have with someone who looks like Halle.

Her cheeks flush pink but she doesn't look uncomfortable like she did earlier. "Do you have a tablet?"

"Yes, why?"

She climbs off my bed, my sweatpants hanging low on her hips. "Because you're delaying us starting your essay by distracting me. I'm going to use the bathroom, you get your tablet, and we'll start, okay?"

"Yes, Captain."

I ordered lunch while Halle read my outline, and by the time the food arrived, she'd already downloaded a dozen PDFs and had started highlighting relevant sections for me to work with.

She's lying on her stomach beside me, feet crossed in the air behind her, leaning against her hand speed-reading each thing she's downloaded while I type on my laptop. She makes me stop writing after twenty-five minutes and take a five-minute break. At first I didn't understand and thought maybe she was bored and wanted to chat, but she happily lets me sit in silence if I want to.

I don't want to. I've been using my five minutes to ask her more about the book she's writing. I won't be reading it—unless she highlights the important bits for me—but I really like listening to her talk about stuff. Maybe I will join her book club.

It takes us a couple of hours to find the right rhythm, but when we do, everything becomes so much easier. She's intelligent and knowledgeable, and the questions she asks me make me think harder before I answer her. Then she makes me write it all down before I lose my train of thought.

When I finally shut my laptop, I feel like a weight has been lifted off my shoulders. "Thank you. I couldn't have done it without you. You're amazing."

"You did the work. I just highlighted stuff. I'm happy I could help you. I really should stop overstaying my welcome now and head home."

"You're not overstaying your welcome," I argue. "I'd tell you if you were."

"You would?"

"I would tell you to leave if I didn't want you here. You're not a prisoner and you can go if you want to, but if you want to watch a movie with me you should stay."

Halle sits up on the bed to sit opposite me and I can't tell if she's about to move beside me to settle or run for the door. "What kind of movie?" she eventually asks.

"Horror. My friend JJ's mom texted me a new recommendation last week. I was going to watch that."

"Not a rom-com then?"

I sigh. "You're just like the others. When my friends' girlfriends lived here last year they were relentless. I watched so many shit movies."

"How about we rock-paper-scissors for it?" she suggests, holding out her fist. "I win we watch *How to Lose a Guy in Ten Days*, but if you win, we watch JJ's mom's suggestion and we both pretend that I'm not crying the entire time. Ready?"

I hold out my own fist, shaking it three times and choosing paper, knowing statistically she'll choose rock, which she does. My hand wraps around her fist and she pouts up at me. "Best of three?"

"No, sorry, we didn't agree on that ahead of time." I reach for the remotes to roll down my blackout blinds and turn on my TV.

"Are you really not going to play me again?" She's still a little pouty. Cute. Distracting. "That isn't very sportsmanlike."

"No. You snooze, you lose. Do you need extra pillows? Blankets? Protective weapon?"

"We're good on the pillow front and no weapon needed," she says, slipping farther into the bed. "I'll use you as a human shield."

I scoff as I press play on the movie, fluffing up the pillows behind her head to make her more comfortable. I slide down, too, relieved not to be on that damn air mattress, and pretend not to notice when she shuffles an inch closer to me. "Not if I use you as one first."

Chapter Eight

HALLE

THERE'S A LARGE MAN EATING my cookies again.

"You know I'll just make them for you if you ask me to," I tell Henry as I approach him next to the snack table in Enchanted. Inayah has her first local author event and I promised to bake some treats and help set up while she serves customers in the store downstairs. I used to do it for The Next Chapter sometimes, so I didn't mind offering. "You don't need to sneak in here and steal them."

"I don't have your number, otherwise I would have," he says through a mouthful of chocolate chip cookie. "Why don't I have your number?"

"I don't know why you don't have my number. Why don't I have your number?"

"Because you haven't asked for it. Why haven't you asked for it?" There's something extra cheerful about him today, playful really.

I cross my arms as he smirks up at me from his seat. "Why haven't you gone out of your way to give it to me?"

"Excellent question." His finger hooks through the loop of my jeans, pulling me a few steps closer so I'm standing between his legs. He's not even touching me and I feel flustered. Henry carefully pinches the top of my cell phone peeking from my cardigan pocket and pulls it up. "What's your passcode?"

I pluck it from his hands, swiping up when the face ID unlocks. "I'm not telling you my passcode."

I look anywhere but him as he taps away on the screen. "That's wise. I'd definitely do something you don't approve of."

When I hear his cell phone start to vibrate, I finally look at him again. "Are you here to buy more leadership books?"

He looks at me like I've just asked him the wildest question. "No, I was looking for you. I saw you were here on your story."

The idea of Henry Turner looking at my page that is mostly just unhinged book reviews makes me feel perceived in a way I've never felt before. Changing the subject quickly, I say, "You're in a good mood today. Is that what my baking does to you or . . . ?" He locks the screen and pushes the phone back into my pocket.

"I'd love to say it's just your food, but it's actually because Thornton loved my essay." Henry leans back in his chair to look up at me. "Well, love is extreme. I'm not sure he's capable of an emotion that strong. I wasn't expecting anything back so quickly, but I think maybe Coach made an inquiry about how I was doing. Anyway, he liked it. I came by to say thank you for your help and bring you something."

He reaches beneath his chair and produces a bouquet of daisies.

"Oh my goodness."

Standing from his seat, he tilts it in my direction, gesturing for me to take it, which I do. Henry pushes his hands into his pockets and shrugs. "I didn't know what you like. Anastasia said sunflowers and Aurora said peonies, but I remembered you have a pink dress with tiny daisies on it so I thought they might be your favorite." I might start crying. He senses it. "You're giving me the look. Please don't start crying. I deal with crying women *so* much more than I ever expected to and I'm still never sure how to react."

"You're the first person to ever buy me flowers, Henry," I admit reluctantly. "They're happy nearly-tears. I promise."

He sits in his chair again, eyebrows pinched. "I'm sorry."

I lift my nose from the bouquet. "What for?"

"For being the first person to buy you flowers."

"That's okay . . . Hey, what did we say about apologizing unnecessarily?" He pins me with a look that suggests I shouldn't use his own words against him. It really is okay. Will thought they were pointless because they die. Which I suppose they are, really, but I still have a weird weightless feeling in my stomach. "And you were right, daisies are my favorite."

"It isn't okay, but I'm glad you like them."

I've somehow managed to make the sweetest gesture awkward by revealing that I was in a relationship with someone who clearly wasn't invested. Is that harsh? To assume someone isn't invested just because they don't take you on dates or buy you flowers? Maybe.

"I really like them. And I'm proud of you for getting on Thornton's good side."

"For now. He's already given the next assignment."

I can't help but laugh at the unimpressed expression decorating his face. "You look enthralled already." He huffs and sits back in his chair, reaching across to pull the one next to him closer, gesturing for me to sit. "Do you want me to help you again? No flowers required if you pass."

I take a seat, resting the bouquet between my knees while he considers my offer. "Do you have the time?"

The honest answer is no, probably not, but I'm not going to tell him that. Especially since he's maybe the first person to ever ask me if I have the time. Everyone else just assumes; my nana used to say it was a tale as old as time. She understood because she was also the oldest girl. She knew what it was like to be labeled the helpful one.

The reliable one. The third parent. It's the reason she was the only person who put Grayson in his place for not helping more.

This goes above that. Henry's my friend and I do *want* to help him; I just need to reshuffle some of my other commitments. He looks so unabashedly happy right now. During the time we've spent together recently, I haven't seen him act like that before. It might be my favorite. "Of course I have the time to help you. When do you want to start?"

"My instincts are telling me to put it off until the very last minute, but judging by that very judgmental look on your face right now that is not the right thing to do."

"I do not have a judgmental look on my face. I am judgment-free, *always*."

"If you say so. Tonight?"

"Um—"

"You are allowed to say no, Halle," Henry insists. "You do not need to change your plans if you're busy."

"It's not that. I just need to bake a cake. One of the girls I work with has a birthday tomorrow and she forgot to take a vacation day. I normally work tonight but they convinced me to switch to tomorrow so we could have a little birthday party in the break room. I said I'd bake the cake."

Behind Henry, customers for the event start to appear from the staircase. I recognize them from book club. Whatever they think about Henry and me sitting close together talking, they don't say anything as they take a seat in the front row and give me a small wave.

"So tonight is a pass and you're working tomorrow. What about Saturday?"

"Surely the captain of the hockey team has something better to do on a Saturday night than study?" I tease. I know their first game of the season isn't until next week, so this is his last weekend of sort-of-but-also-not-really freedom.

"I'm sure there will be something loud and busy happening. It'll happen whether I'm there or not. I honestly kind of hate the parties sometimes. It takes me a long time to recover from all the noise and socializing."

"Saturday it is then. Do you want to come to my place? It'll be quiet and I promise I won't make you do a keg stand. You don't even need to talk to me if you don't want to."

"I like talking to you more than I like talking to almost anyone. Yes, that'd be good. I'll text you when I'm done at the gym? I can pick up dinner."

Far too many seconds pass without me saying anything. More people begin to filter in and take their seat and I'm almost certain my cheeks are bright pink. I offer Henry a nod, swallowing hard. "Sounds good. I think I should probably greet people now instead of giving you all my attention. Do you want to stay and watch the panel? It's a very interesting book about a serial killer."

"Tempting, but you're the only person I like listening to talk about books. And I have hockey practice in fifteen minutes."

"Oh my God, go!" I squeak. "You can't be late!"

He stands slowly, clearly in no rush. "Yes, Captain. Talk to you later."

I whisper a "bye" as I watch him steal one final cookie and stroll away just as Aurora appears at the top of the stairs with her friends Emilia and Poppy. I watch her eyes narrow as she watches him walk past her, telling me she didn't know he was going to be here. When her eyes leave him and land on me, immediately spotting the flowers still in my hands, her face breaks into the biggest smile.

I have a feeling she isn't going to want to talk about serial killers today.

I'm LOSING MY THIRD FIGHT with eggshell fragments in my bowl when my cell phone lights up on the counter. Henry's face stares back at me, because when he added his number he also took a selfie and changed my background. Wiping my hands on my apron, I swipe at the notification to open it.

HENRY TURNER

Ate too many cookies and nearly threw up on the ice.

> Offended that you're blaming my baking.

> Have you considered you might just be out of shape?

No. I can show you if you like.

> I'm good. I'll take your word for it.

How's your cake?

> Being victimized by eggshells but otherwise okay so far.

Want help?

> Do you know how to make a cake?

I don't know how to do a lot of things.

Doesn't mean I'm not good at it.

> That's the most confident nonanswer ever.

> Are you not tired from hockey?

Exhausted. What's your address?

I stare at my screen for at least forty-five seconds before typing out my address for him. As soon as I hit send I immediately start to panic, scanning the chaos I've created in the kitchen and mentally recapping the mess in the rest of the house. It was fine when he was coming over in two days because I had two days to make this place look presentable, and now I have, what? Fifteen minutes at most?

It's not a total disaster, but I'm not confident there isn't a bra or pair of panties somewhere they shouldn't be. It takes me seven minutes to sprint around the house scanning for stray items, and a further four to clear up the random Tupperware littering my counters. It would have taken me less, but Joy followed me into every single room.

I don't blame her; she's probably never seen me move so quickly. When Henry knocks on the door a minute later, I'm still wondering if I've done enough. He looks me up and down lazily as I pull the door open. "You're very sweaty," is the only thing he says.

I want to tell him it's because I've been running around my house like a woman possessed, trying to ensure he isn't going to be hit by an errant piece of lace when he walks into a room while also trying not to fall over a cat, but I don't.

"The kitchen is hot with the oven on," I say. "Come in."

I notice the sketchbook tucked under his arm before I notice the gray sweatpants, and for that, I feel like I deserve some sort of praise. I follow him through the doorway and he takes a seat at the breakfast bar opposite where I've set out all of the ingredients. Joy looks up from her bed in the kitchen and immediately makes a beeline for Henry. "You're not allergic to cats, are you?" I ask, instantly relieved when he shakes his head. "Good, because she loves affection."

She looks so tiny when he picks her up and she rests her head against his chest. I watch as he takes in the room, eyes scanning shelves and surfaces as he strokes her. "I'm glad I knew your grandmother lived here before you, otherwise I'd be seriously questioning your interior design skills," he says casually, turning his attention back to me.

"Oh."

I don't mean to say it out loud, but his tone just caught me off guard. I've always known the house is dated, so it shouldn't be a surprise, but I guess I'm not used to having new visitors. My mom brings it up every time she visits, but I'm reluctant to erase Nana's choices.

"That was rude," Henry says quickly, rubbing the palm of his hand not cradling Joy against his jaw. He clears his throat. "I'm sorry. I shouldn't have said that."

"It's totally fine," I say instantly, slipping my apron back over my head, double wrapping it around my waist and tying it extra tight— like somehow that'll help squeeze out the knot in my stomach at the thought of this house not feeling like hers anymore. "You're right. I should definitely decorate."

"You don't have to tell me it's fine, Halle." He stands and walks around to my side of the counter, reaching for the bow tied at my side and tugging the loose end until it unravels and the apron strings fall. "I try really hard not to say things I shouldn't, but sometimes, like when I'm tired, it's harder to keep up with thinking about what I should say, not what my brain automatically wants to come out with."

The apron molds to me as he pulls the strings to the base of my spine, not too loose and not too tight, and ties it into a bow. "You don't have to filter yourself for me. I know you're not being mean. You just say what you think."

"It can be exhausting," he admits, returning to the spot in front of me. "But so is seeing the look on . . . my friends' face when my words hurt them."

"They didn't *hurt* me, I just . . . you are right about it. It's kind of a weird long-winded situation."

He returns to his seat and Joy tries to climb onto his shoulder. "Give me the speedy version."

I start mixing the ingredients again, concentrating on my hands. "Hmm. Speedy version, okay. It was my dream to go to college in New York. Senior year of high school, Nana had a fall, which scared the shit out of Mom. Nana was old and stubborn, wouldn't move closer or accept hired support. Mom was terrified every day, and I wanted to help, so I offered to move in with Nana to look after her and go to UCMH. I had already applied anyway as a safety choice. I got in. Nana bought Joy"—I nod toward the cat asleep on him, then look back at my hands—"to celebrate us being roomies and keep her company until I moved in. She got really sick and died right before I graduated high school."

"That's sad, Halle. Why didn't you go to New York if it was your dream?"

I shrug, wondering how I can avoid mentioning that there was a part of me that wanted to stay closer to Will. Henry doesn't like it when I bring up Will, which is fair because neither do I. I think it would be weird and complicated to try to explain how grief made me rely on him emotionally more than I ever had before.

"I was grieving and didn't have it in me to change my plans again. My mom inherited this house and said I could still live here and redecorate it however I want. At first I was hurting too much from to grief to want to change anything, and as time has moved on, I don't really have the time or the resources to redecorate a house by myself. There are a few things I definitely would change, but I kind of like living among all her weird mismatched things. Makes it feel like she's still here."

"I'm sorry I was rude," he says. "And I wish you didn't have to put everyone before yourself. If you ever decide you want to change those few things, I'll help you. I'm very good at painting."

"I don't think you were rude . . . I don't put everyone before myself. She was probably my best friend. Living with her would have been fun, although at the time I did worry about her wanting to go to frat parties. Would have absolutely annihilated everyone at beer pong, I bet. I just miss her, Henry. I'm not sad because of what you said. Promise."

He nods and is quiet for a little while. The silence of the kitchen feels peaceful, not awkward, and I almost jump when he talks again. "Do you have an apron for me?"

The idea of watching Henry putter around my kitchen in a floral apron edged with frills immediately replaces all other thoughts in my head. "On the back of the door. And wash your hands, please."

The corners of his mouth tug up. "Yes, Cap."

He kicks his sneakers off and places them neatly next to the back door before returning Joy to her cat bed. After he's washed his hands, he grabs the apron. I divert my attention from watching him to scanning the recipe book in front of me. My nana's familiar cursive sweeps from left to right, and out of all the things in this house, this old, falling-apart recipe book is my favorite.

"I think it's only fair I tell you I've never baked anything before," Henry says, leaning against the counter beside me. "But I'm confident that my ability to be good at most things will also apply here."

"Most things? What are you bad at?"

"I'm not telling you that," he says instantly. "Mainly because I can't think of anything. I was trying to be humble."

"I appreciate the honesty, but I don't think we can mess this up. We just need to stick to the rules and follow the recipe and all should be well."

He scoops some buttercream I've mixed with his thumb, licking it off slowly. "Following rules might be on the list of things I'm not great at."

"Well, you're lucky I'm a habitual rule keeper."

He sighs, but he's smiling at me. I'm smiling back, trying not to start laughing, and I don't even know why. "Weird use of the word *lucky*."

Chapter Nine

HENRY

"TURNER, MY OFFICE!" COACH YELLS into the locker room.

There's a chorus of "ooooooooos" from my teammates, which I ignore as I walk past them all in the direction of Faulkner's office.

"Take a seat," he says, not looking up from whatever he's writing. I watch his untidy scribble mark the page over and over before he eventually stops and sits back in his seat to look at me. That's the thing with Faulkner: he couldn't make it clearer that he does not give a shit about anyone's time but his own.

"How do you think things are going?" he asks casually.

"I think I wish JJ and Joe were still here," I say honestly. "But I think we're in a much better place than we were. Matthews and Garcia are working hard—I've talked to both of them. I think we'll be okay next week."

"Okay or great? Because I need you to be great, Turner."

I want to let out a loud, tired groan, but I don't. I hate this side of things. Of course I want us to be great; the entire team wants us to be great. It's almost like if I don't hit the buzzwords then I'm not doing things right. Why does it matter if I say okay or great? I want us to win and so does everyone else.

"I think we will be great," I say back, apparently hitting whatever benchmark of enthusiasm I'm supposed to.

"Happy to hear it. How are you getting on with your classes?"

Did Nate have to answer these questions? Probably not. I doubt Nate's ever failed a class in his life. He made balancing hockey, studying, and having a relationship all at the same time look easy.

"Great," I respond, remembering that "okay" doesn't cut it. "Rocky start, but I listened when you said to do whatever it takes, and someone is helping me now. That's what I'm doing tomorrow after I do my workout; I have an assignment due on Tuesday."

He runs his hand through his nonexistent hair, not picking up on my hint that I want to leave. "You're paying a tutor?"

I think Halle would make a great tutor. She's so patient and soft-spoken. I can't imagine her ever getting irritated when someone can't work something out. "Not quite. She's a friend."

"From your class?"

I've seen her doodles. I'm not sure she'd make it through a fine art BA. "No. She studies English."

"I'm confused." *You and me both, big guy.* "How can she help you?"

"She's done Professor Thornton's classes before, so she knows what he's looking for. And she makes the research material more accessible for me. Making it less overwhelming to face," I explain, repeating how Halle worded it to me when we talked about it again while making the cake.

"And what are you doing for her?" Faulkner asks. I don't know what he means, and whatever expression my face has twisted into is telling him that. "If she's doing all this work for you, and she isn't a paid tutor, what are you doing for her?"

I think about it for a little while before finally answering him. "Nothing. I bought her flowers to say thank you when I received good feedback on my essay. We're friends. She's a nice person."

"Hmm," he says, and that little noise maybe guts me more than him barking my name. It's the noise people make when they're about to say something I haven't considered. Then I spend the rest of my day mad that I didn't consider it. "Make sure you're not abusing her kindness. You don't want to lose your friend. You don't need distractions this year. That's all, Turner. Enjoy your weekend."

Abusing her kindness plays on a loop in my head as I exit Faulkner's office. The locker room has emptied out now, my teammates eager to get their Friday started. Russ is waiting for me in the lobby, smiling at his cell phone. I think maybe I need to use my savings to buy myself a car instead of relying on him. Am I abusing his kindness by getting him to give me rides everywhere? I give him gas money.

"You okay, man?" Russ asks as I approach.

"Do I give you enough gas money?"

Russ slow-blinks twice, nodding his head. Surprise, maybe. "Yeah, why?"

"I don't want to abuse your kindness."

He stands from the bench, his eyes narrowed as he stares at me. "You're not, at all. Where's this coming from?"

"Faulkner. Do you think I'm abusing Halle's kindness by letting her help me and doing nothing for her in return?"

"Uh." He rubs the back of his neck awkwardly. "I honestly don't, since she offered to help you. She seems like that type of girl, y'know? Rory has been borrowing her notes for years apparently, and she runs the book club and other stuff. I think she's just one of those people who is generous with their time. She's your friend, right? Friends help each other. You're still doing ninety-nine percent of the work, dude. I don't see how it's any different from if you joined a study group and you guys shared stuff. Don't let Faulkner get in your head."

"She is my friend. I really like her. I just don't want to take advantage of her. I hadn't even thought about it until he mentioned that she was getting nothing in return."

I should have thought more about her when she offered. I was just so relieved to have one less thing to worry about this year that I didn't take the time to think about it.

We climb into Russ's truck and he rolls his eyes at me as he slips the key into the ignition. "I *really* don't think you need to take advice about friendship from Faulkner. Try talking to her when you get there. Maybe there is something you can help her with, and then you both win."

"I just want to be a good friend to her," I admit.

"You like her? As more than a friend?" Russ asks carefully.

"I like being around her." There's something about her that I'm drawn to. Something about her that makes sense to me. "She's so calm. Being with her doesn't drain me. Does that make sense?"

Russ nods, pulling out of the parking lot. "It does. Talk to her. At least she'll know you're thinking about her, even if there isn't anything she wants from you."

I rehearse what I'm going to say in my head for the rest of the drive.

IT'S NOT UNTIL I'M STANDING at Halle's front door with a bag filled with Chinese food that I forget everything I've been rehearsing since I saw Faulkner yesterday.

"Hi," she says softly as she pulls the door open. "That smells good."

I immediately notice something is off about her as I follow her into the living room, dropping the bag of food onto the coffee table and putting my tablet, sketchbook, and laptop next to it.

She looks the same as usual. Glossy lips, thick dark eyelashes lined with black, a glow to her cheeks. Loose blue jeans, a white camisole with buttons up the middle, the lace of her bra peeking out at the top, finished with the thick, oversized cream knitted cardigan with stars on the elbows I've seen her wear a few times. The cow slippers are new, but still feel oddly appropriate for her.

But there's something not right.

Halle knocks her laptop closed as she passes it, throwing herself onto the couch on the opposite side of the room. The device snaps as the lid closes, making her cat jump up and move to circle my feet. I catch Halle force a smile when she spots me watching her. "That was aggressive," I say, taking the seat beside her, trying not to fall over Joy.

"I'm so—wait," she says, interrupting herself. "I'm not apologizing. It was aggressive, you're right. It wasn't intentional."

I don't believe that it wasn't intentional. "Are you hangry? I didn't mean to be so long. I've been trying to actually complete my workouts this year instead of goofing off at the gym."

She twists on the couch to look at me, pulling her knees to her chest with her head resting against the cushion. "That's okay. I'm not hangry, but maybe we should eat before we start working. That way it doesn't go cold."

Halle is good at diverting conversations like Russ is. Which is why I think there is actually something wrong. "I'd like it if you told me what's wrong with you. Something is clearly bothering you."

"It's silly," she whispers.

"I don't think anything you say is silly," I whisper back.

She rests her head on the top of her knees. "Do you have siblings?"

I shake my head. "Only child."

"You're lucky. No, no, I don't mean that. I *love* my family, but sometimes." She tugs at the sleeves of her cardigan and shuts her eyes. "*Sometimes* they make me feel like I'm losing my mind. It's like nothing can happen without my intervention, and it's so fucking tiring. I thought it'd change when I moved out, but if anything, I feel like they're worse . . . Like how is that possible? And they don't care what I'm doing when they call, or even consider that I might be busy and doing something for *me*."

When her eyes reopen and she looks right at me, I don't know what to say to make her feel better. "Keep going."

"It's just boring drama, Henry. We should eat."

"Tell me."

"When Will broke up with me, I promised myself I was going to do things for myself. This writing competition was supposed to be that thing, and I was so excited. And I feel like a broken record, but I'm not getting anywhere with it, and it's making me frustrated. Because all I've ever wanted to do is write books, and I can't even do something for an amateur competition.

"I'm going around in circles and then my stepsister calls because she's had a fight with my mom, then my mom calls to tell me her side of it, then my youngest sister calls because she's upset that everyone is fighting. When I'm finally done being mediator, I can't remember what plot idea I was developing in the first place. Not that it matters, because it's all weak and it's impossible to make strong because the ideas aren't the problem, *I'm* the problem."

She looks like she's about to burst into tears and is doing everything to hold it in. I hate it. "How are you the problem?"

Five words that cause her face to sink. "Because I haven't lived, Henry."

"Oh."

"I want to write about a relationship and experiences that I've never had and it *shows*. I have these moments of clarity and it's like the sun finally poking through the clouds after a storm, and I feel unstoppable. I write something, then I get to something simple that shouldn't be hard and it's like I don't even speak English anymore and I delete it all. I stare at my screen and *nothing* happens because *nothing* happens in my life."

Experiences. Halle talked about having the experience when I interrupted her with Mason, but I didn't think much of it. "But Will . . ."

She huffs and I regret saying his name instantly. "Our relationship made sense on paper but not in reality. I was never in love with him. We didn't even go on a date in the whole year we were together. We just hung out with his friends or our families. Our relationship changed in title, but it never felt like anything progressed romantically."

"I'll take you on a date."

"Henry, no," she says, panic seeping into her voice. "I wasn't hinting that I wanted you to take me on a date. I was just venting, ignore me. I'll get through it! Honestly, it's totally fine."

"Let me take you on a date. You need the experience to write it in your book, right?" I say calmly. "Let me help."

"I can't ask that of you," she says quietly.

"Technically I'm asking," I argue. "You want experiences, and I want to pass Thornton's class, so let's help each other. I don't want to take advantage of your kindness, Halle. Let's make things even."

"You're not taking advantage. I like helping you," she argues back.

"And I'm going to like taking you on a date." I've been on a few dates before and I've never had the strong desire to go on more, but something tells me that this will be different.

The pink flush of her cheeks returns. "What will people think?"

I want to say that I'm sure my friends already have bets running on what's happening, but I don't, because I don't think she'd take it very well. She feels embarrassed about the smallest things and I think that would be one of them. I'm trying really hard to think before I say something that might make her feel that way.

"I don't care what people think. It's none of their business."

"But your friends—"

"Will be jealous they didn't ask you out first."

She chews on her lip. Thinking hard. "What if they think we're dating?"

"Do you always worry about what other people think about things that have nothing to do with them?"

"Yeah, I sort of do, actually."

"Is people thinking we're dating worse than not achieving your goal?"

Her eyes widen and she shakes her head frantically. "Oh my God, I'm not worried about *me*. I'm thinking about *you*. I don't want to, like, I don't know, mess things up for you. You have a lot on your plate."

"You don't need to worry. Go on a date with me, Halle. Live."

Her bottom lip juts out while she considers it and I just watch her. The slow way her eyelashes brush against her skin when she blinks. How shiny her hair is when she tucks it behind her ear. Her big brown eyes staring at me. The way she's actually smiling even as her mouth moves. *Her mouth is moving.* "Sorry, run that by me again."

"I don't want to be a burden. If you don't have the time, we stop, promise?"

"Yes, Cap."

She rolls her eyes, but I sense her begin to relax. She lets go of the death grip she's had on her legs and removes her chin from her knees, letting her legs cross in front of her. I slide a little closer as she pulls out her phone, tilting it so I can see her open a notes app. I fight the urge to point out that she hasn't changed her phone background from the picture of me in the bookstore. I watch her type "RULE BOOK" in bold letters along the top. "Okay, what do I need to write down?"

"Nothing. We don't need a rule book."

"Of course we do. Number one: you have to be honest with me if you're too busy. Hockey and school are more important than inspiration for my silly book."

I take the phone from her hands and huff. "New number one: we have to be honest with each other about how busy we are, and you have to stop belittling things that are important to you by calling them silly." She reaches to take the phone out of my hand but I move it out of the way. "And number two: you have to stop being embarrassed around me. You won't be able to tell me what you need for inspiration if you're embarrassed about everything. I've seen four of my friends naked since you, by the way."

This time she snatches the phone out of my hand, typing frantically. "Number two continued: we are not allowed to talk about the fact you've seen me naked ever again." I try to take the phone back but she holds it in the air out of my reach. "Number three: if you want to date someone and our arrangement is uncomfortable for them—we can end it straightaway. I don't want to ruin your chances with someone."

"Delete number three," I say before she's even finished typing. "People who don't understand our friendship don't get to stick around. I have the same rule for people who have an issue with my other friends, so you can't argue."

"New number three: since this is for my benefit, I pay for everything," she says, squeaking when I snatch the phone from her hands.

"Delete," I grumble, tapping at the delete key aggressively. Halle moves onto her knees, leaning across, mumbling my name in a disgruntled fashion. My arms are longer than hers so all her attempts fail. "New new number three," I say as she admits defeat and sits back on her legs. "Finance is reviewed on a case-by-case basis. I'm paying for our dates and other stuff, but if one of your experiences is that you want to go to Bora Bora on a private jet you can pay for that."

"What if we fly coach?" A grin spreads across her face and I know she's kidding.

"I can fly you coach to anywhere in the surrounding states."

She laughs and it's a sound I've grown to really like. "If you whisk me away to Reno, I may simply fall in love."

"There's rule number four," I say, adding the number to our rule book. "You can't fall in love with me. You're going to want to. Anastasia tells me I'm very lovable, and the more time you spend with me the harder it'll be."

Now she's really laughing, and I feel so relieved that I've managed to improve the sour mood she was in when I arrived. "I couldn't fall in love with my actual boyfriend so I'm pretty sure I'm incapable of it anyway."

"Yes, but he's a dick. I'm not." She pins me with a look that I can't decipher. She looks both annoyed and amused. As bad as Will Ellington is, I bet it's hard for him to know she never loved him. "Like I said, very lovable."

"Okay, Mr. Very Lovable," she sighs, gently taking the phone out of my hand. She maneuvers onto her butt, her body pressed up against mine as we sit side by side. I watch her fingers as she types number five. "Our final rule: Henry must break Halle's heart if she falls in love with him. Hey, it'll even double as a new experience! Give me plenty to write about."

"You sound unusually happy at the prospect of heartbreak."

"And you sound unusually confident that you're going to be able to melt my ice cold heart," she says, locking her cell phone now that our rule book is complete.

"There isn't anything about you that isn't warm, Halle."

She doesn't say anything at first. She just watches me, her face ten inches from mine and her body still pressed against my arm, taking slow and steady breaths.

"You know what isn't warm anymore?" she says, quickly standing from the couch. "Our food. I'm going to go and heat it up for us."

And with that, she disappears into the kitchen, takeout bag in hand, leaving me to wonder what exactly it was about Will that she couldn't love.

Chapter Ten

HALLE

It takes one Google search to confirm with certainty that misogyny is alive and well in the world.

My first date—experiment? Experience?—with Henry will be starting any minute, and it suddenly occurred to me as I waited in my living room, possibly looking like Miss Honey, that I don't have any idea how to go on a date.

After Henry and I confirmed today would be the first day of our—partnership? Scheming? Shenanigans? Whatever we're doing—I made the choice not to tell anyone. I do honestly feel like that's the right decision, but it's forced me to consult the internet for advice rather than a person like Cami or Aurora. So when I typed "how to not mess up a first date," links to articles by self-declared alpha bros wanting to share their "wisdom" were the first to appear.

Thankfully, I don't have concerns about being a "low-value woman," so I was able to swiftly move on to slightly less toxic results. I'm reading an article about how to keep the conversation flowing when Henry texts me that he's on his way.

His looming arrival is enough to make me panic more than the alpha bros ever could, and I'm suddenly reevaluating all my choices.

HENRY TURNER

Ten-minute warning. Leaving my
house now.

>Not too late if you want to change your
>mind about this!

I know. I haven't.

>What are you wearing?

I think you're supposed to save the
questions for the date.

>I just don't want to be overdressed.

Impossible.

>This conversation is very unhelpful.

I'll make it up to you later.

There's a ridiculous grin on my face when I lock my phone and catch my reflection in the screen. My phone buzzes again and I swipe up automatically, not realizing it isn't Henry until I read the message.

WILL ELLINGTON

Have fun on your date

I choke on air so loudly that Joy jumps. I haven't heard from Will since we broke up a month ago, and this is not the first message I was expecting to get from him. I mentally run through all the options, from psychic abilities to phone cloning, before eventually realizing the answer is my mom.

When she called earlier to talk to me about Thanksgiving next month, I was desperate to get her off the phone so I didn't have to tell her I wouldn't be coming home. I wasn't exactly lying when I said I had to go because I was getting ready for a date.

Given my cowardice, and honestly, my desire not to have to manage other people's feelings and reactions about my own breakup, I still haven't told them.

WILL ELLINGTON

Have fun on your date

> I will, thanks!

Not even curious about how I know?

> Nope

Your mom told mine that we're going on a date

Can't believe you still haven't told them about our breakup

If I think about it too hard, I'll be upset that the first time I've heard from Will in weeks is because I'm going out with someone else. He hasn't once checked in to see how I'm handling things, and even now, his attitude is weird. I shouldn't engage . . . but I do.

WILL ELLINGTON

> Neither have you if your mom called.

You can tell them when you introduce them to the guy that isn't me lol

Can't wait to meet him! ☺

I *really* shouldn't engage.

WILL ELLINGTON

> You already have ☺

I put my cell phone on do not disturb so I can't be jolted by Will's name flashing and throw it into my purse. By the time Henry is knocking on my door there's no telling where the weird nerves in my belly came from.

It takes all my powers not to let my jaw drop when I open the front door and spot Henry standing there in a suit and white shirt. Holy shit, he looks really good.

"You're staring at me," he says calmly. "Really intensely."

"I haven't seen you in a suit before. You look really good," I admit.

He doesn't respond to my blatant ogling and reaches into his inner suit pocket, pulling out a folded piece of paper. "I was going to buy you flowers but I already did that last week, so I brought you this instead."

The last thing I'm expecting when I unfold the piece of paper is a drawing of me. I'm in my kitchen, smiling as I lean against the counter, surrounded by mixing bowls. "Henry! When did you do this?"

"I sketched it while I could see you, but I didn't finish it properly until today."

Henry was doing what I thought was doodling while we waited for the birthday cake to bake, but this is *not* a doodle. "You are so unbelievably talented. I love it. Thank you."

"You're welcome. And you look really good, too. Ready?"

"Let's do it."

IF HENRY NOTICED MY RESTLESSNESS on the drive to the restaurant, he didn't mention it. Which makes me think he didn't notice because I definitely feel like he would mention it.

The second I saw the suit I realized we weren't going to somewhere like Blaise's diner, and I was right, because I can't even pronounce the name of the restaurant we're in. My heart stopped a little, and it took every bit of courage to quietly whisper to him while we waited to be seated that somewhere like this is probably super outside of my budget.

In true Henry fashion, he shrugged and said, "It's a good thing the rules say you're not allowed to pay then, isn't it?"

I've been staring at the menu for far longer than is necessary, the luxurious paper a barrier between me and the man in front of me. I've never been short of words before, but maybe Date Halle is quiet and mysterious, or boring, depending on which way you look at it.

After another few minutes of me staring at the sea bass description, Henry clears his throat. "I'll happily sit in silence all night, but I don't think that'd be a good date experience for you. Are you okay?"

I lower the menu slowly and reluctantly. "I think I might be nervous."

Henry doesn't look nervous at all. He looks even more calm than normal, like he's comfortable in a setting like this. I feel scared to touch anything in case I break it, but I'd bet that he's accustomed to going to fancy restaurants from his grandma's list. He takes a sip of his water and leans back in his chair. "Does Joy miss me?"

Easy answer. "Of course she does."

"I asked could we get a cat. Turns out Robbie is allergic."

"Devastating news. You can visit her anytime, she's a big fan of yours." I'm not even exaggerating. Ragdolls are clingy and affectionate anyway, but she has really stepped it up for Henry.

"I get that a lot."

"I'm sure you do. Even more now that you're captain, I'd bet."

He shakes his head and picks up a roll from the basket. "We're not talking about hockey. Tell me about your book. Did you finally pick a plot?"

"I did! Finally. I wrote a whopping three hundred words before I had to shower for our date."

He looks genuinely happy. "Tell me about it."

"Are you sure?" He nods enthusiastically. "Okay. It's a dual time-line book where the present is a guy watching a woman walk down the aisle from the front of the church, and the past is watching them meet for the first time, and the relationship that follows. It's a really up-and-down relationship, but they just keep being drawn back to each other, probably across several years. It'll show all their best and worst moments until in the present she reaches the front of the church."

"And what?" he asks. "The book ends with them getting married?"

We're interrupted by the waiter taking our order, and the fact that I'm eager for him to disappear again so I can tell Henry the end of the story is how I know I've picked the right one to work on. "No, it doesn't. That's my big twist. The whole time he's watching her walk down the aisle to get married to someone else."

Henry is quiet for a moment, tearing off pieces of bread and looking pensive. Until he eventually talks again. "Anastasia and Lola are going to lose their shit if there isn't a happy ending."

Henry talked about his friends' girlfriends and their love of rom-coms when we watched the horror movie together. I can't help but laugh, because losing their shit is the reaction of most readers I know. "It's only a fiction competition, so it doesn't need a happy ending. I want to write something that has romantic elements, but I also want it to stand out. I think having a bit of a twist at the end will set it apart from other entries. I think it's realistic that two people in love might not get their happy ending."

"I'm surprised you think that. You give hopeless romantic energy," he says.

"I think I always had myself down as a hopeless romantic. The things I read, the music I listen to, the movies I watch, etcetera. I guess who we think we are and who we are can be different."

"I don't understand the point."

"Of love? Is this the part where the handsome playboy reveals he doesn't believe in love? Are we that cliché?"

Henry smiles, and it really invokes a feeling in me I haven't quite gotten used to yet. "You think I'm handsome? Are you flirting with me?"

"I'm not even sure I know how to flirt, so no."

"You can practice on me."

"How generous of you. C'mon. Playboy who doesn't believe in love, tell me more." I laugh, but the heat is creeping up my neck. Nobody needs to witness me attempting to flirt, especially not him.

Henry rolls his eyes but he's still smiling. "You watch too many movies and I'm not a playboy. And no, I do believe in love. I just don't value it over other types of love. There are people in my life I love. I love art. I love my parents. I watch my friends love each other. I just don't see what the big deal is about romantic love. Everything seems more complicated when people fall in love with each other."

"Sometimes complicated is exciting, I guess. I imagine, at least."

"People value romantic love over platonic love or familial love every day," he says. "I didn't really understand platonic love until I met Anastasia, and now I think I'd rather have that with someone. I look at the art people have created on the basis of being in love with someone and it's never the emotion I feel."

I can't think of anyone I platonically love anymore. "What do you mean?"

"If you made a piece of art—a picture—I'd look at your choice of medium, the colors you chose, your personal style, your skill level. I'd *see* a landscape, or a person, an event, or whatever you wanted to create, but I'd *feel* something else.

"People paint people they're in love with and I feel the lust, the longing, the joy, the sadness. It's a physical manifestation of someone going, *Look! Look at how in love I am.* But I don't believe people can look at a painting and *see* love. I can see friendship, though. It's hard to explain."

"Remind me not to paint you anything. I have a feeling you're a harsh critic."

Our food arrives and we fill the silence with a mix of questions about my book, life, and family while we eat. By the time our desserts—plural because Henry ordered multiple when we couldn't decide—arrive, I realize all I've done is talk about myself.

"Are you avoiding talking about yourself on purpose or . . ." I ask, taking my first bite of cheesecake.

He leans over with his fork, stealing the top corner. "I like listening to you talk."

"Well, I like listening to *you* talk. Where are you from? Where did you go to high school? When did you realize you could draw? Did you have any pets growing up? What's your favorite color? Where would you have studied if you didn't choose UCMH? I don't know. Tell me something, mystery man."

At no point in any of the articles I looked at did it say *start interrogating your date at the dinner table*, but I feel totally self-absorbed right now so we're going off script.

"I grew up in Maple Hills and I went to Maple Hills Academy from kindergarten to senior year. I don't know exactly, but I'm told my kindergarten finger paintings rivaled Picasso. My parents put me in a creative kids program after school. We did different things and I learned I liked basically everything. No pets because my nanny was allergic to almost everything. I don't have a favorite color."

I'm trying not to visually react to the idea of Henry in a Maple Hills Academy uniform. It's a private school not far from the hotel, and I see the kids after school sometimes when I'm driving to work. Little Henry in a blazer and tie sounds *adorable*.

"I don't believe you don't have a favorite color. You're an artist, for God's sake."

"Adults don't have favorite colors, Halle," he says, stealing another piece of my cheesecake. I push the plate slightly closer to him, but he pushes it back and stands up. Saying nothing, he moves his chair beside me and sits back down, moving the plate between us. "And Parsons, but everyone told me I'd regret not playing hockey if

I didn't go to UCMH. I wouldn't have, but I was scared of moving to the other side of the country and trying to make friends."

"But you make friends so easily!" I wish I'd said it in a calm, normal way. Especially since he's close enough to me that his leg is resting against mine. But no, it comes out all high and scratchy. "Sorry. I just mean you have so many people around you now. And you befriended me."

"I had no friends freshman year, and I didn't have close friends in high school. People were nice to me and I had acquaintances and teammates, but I preferred to be by myself. I sometimes mirror new people by accident, but I can't maintain it." He pushes the final bite of cheesecake toward me on the plate. "Being around so many new people is overwhelming. I stayed with my parents a lot because the guy I shared a dorm room with used to watch his TV, laptop, and phone at the same time. There would be different sounds blasting constantly and I felt like I was going to lose my mind."

"What changed?"

"Nate and Robbie. They're like an old married couple and they treat everyone like they're their children. They grew up together, and Robbie had a serious accident and Nate's mom died, so I think they trauma bonded. Now they act like they're everyone's dads. They let me live with them and it gave me space to adjust and learn how to process college." He reaches for the next dessert. "And JJ, too, but I guess he's more like an irresponsible uncle than a dad."

"That's really nice, Henry. I'm happy you found your feet."

He pushes the strawberry on top of the torte to my side of the plate, a gesture born from me telling him strawberries are my favorite fruit. "I told you, platonic love is more effective."

My fork sinks into the strawberry. "I think you might be right."

The car ride home is the same comfortable quiet as the one there. He tells me he's thinking about getting his own car so he doesn't abuse Russ's or Aurora's kindness by borrowing one of theirs. I tell him I doubt they would ever think that about him.

When I'm finally home, Henry hovers close behind me as I rummage around in my clutch for my keys. When I finally find them, unlock the door, and take a step inside, he doesn't move. "Are you not coming in?"

He shakes his head. "I'm being a gentleman."

"Do you not want to be a gentleman inside?"

"I want to, but you should send the guy home at the end of a first date."

"A date *and* advice. I'm getting the full Henry Turner treatment tonight."

Henry looks like he's about to say something but stops himself. "Not quite."

He leans forward and my heart stops. His lips press against my cheek gently, and I'm not confident I'm breathing fully. He moves back, the hot sear still present on my skin. "Good night, Halle."

"Good night," I say as he walks away, but it once again comes out as a whisper.

When he's climbed back into the car and driven off, I lock the door behind me and take a look at the drawing of me propped against a photo frame in the hallway as I pass it.

After getting ready for bed, I climb under the duvet with my laptop. With *The Great British Baking Show* playing on my TV, I create a new chapter and start typing.

Chapter Eleven

HENRY

WHEN THE FIRST THING I saw this morning was Lola in my kitchen wearing a hockey jersey inside out, I thought it was a bad omen.

I've never understood athletes and sports fans with their superstitions. Maybe it's because I was raised by people who don't believe in them. I've always raised an eyebrow at the team's various habits: specific underwear, only certain playlists, the need to drive a precise way to the rink, to name a few.

But when Lola stood in front of me pouring coffee into two mugs, not even aware I was at the bottom of the stairs, I thought, *Oh fuck. We're going to lose today.*

The thought made me want to be sick, and I realized quite how nervous I'd been pretending I wasn't for our first game of the season. Hearing the words "Captain Debut" had quickly become my biggest pet peeve in the run-up to this game, but it was the moment I thought we were going to lose that I realized how responsible I feel for the success of this team.

That feeling doesn't go away for one second of the day. I'm so hyperaware it makes me nauseous. We smash it, but the need to throw up only very slightly subsides. I expect a switch to flick on, to feel like I can do this, to become different somehow as I step off the ice with my teammates to celebrate in our locker room together, but I don't.

I think about tomorrow, and next week, and the week after. I think about the shots we missed and . . . I think about everything far too much and it's like I'm sinking beneath my own worries.

Nobody else is affected.

Nobody else is sinking.

Nobody else will understand because we still won, and for now, that's all that matters.

I match their energy to their faces and smile, mirroring back exactly what they give me. I tell them we can do this again, and again, and again. I don't want to become one of those superstitious people, but the last thing I'm going to do before I go to sleep is tell Lola to pour her morning coffee with her jersey inside out.

WHY IS IT ALWAYS WHEN I need some privacy that nobody wants to leave me alone?

Faulkner is nowhere to be found when I approach his office, so I let myself in and close the door behind me, pulling up Nate's name on my phone.

"Hey, bud. Congrats on another win!" he says as soon as he answers. "I'm driving. Can you hear me properly?"

"Have you always said *bud* or has it only been since you moved to Vancouver? I can hear you."

He's quiet for a few seconds. "I honestly don't know. I can't remember . . . anyway. What's up?"

"How did you do it?"

"Do what, Hen?"

I don't know what I'm trying to say. I just know that despite the fact we won yesterday and today, I still feel like there's so much more

I should have done or need to do. Did I support the team enough? Did I answer questions well enough? How did I perform in comparison to last year? And how the hell am I going to keep it all together to do this repeatedly. How do I not fail my friends?

Before I can find a way to articulate that to Nate the office door opens and Faulkner walks in eating a muffin, looking somewhere between surprised and disgusted to find me in his office. "Doesn't matter, got to go," I say quickly, ending the call.

"Two wins does not give you the right to use my office, Turner," he says. "What're you doing in here?"

"Sorry, Coach. I was trying to find somewhere quiet to make a phone call. Bye."

I speed past him before he has a chance to probe further. The locker room has emptied out, and once I've grabbed my bag, I head out, too. The adrenaline hasn't quite worn off yet, and I feel oversensitive to every sound and light. I'm relieved when I see Russ in the hallway waiting with only Aurora, but I haven't even reached him when our phones simultaneous ding.

PRETTY BEST FRIENDS

MATTIE
Honeypot for a belated birthday
celebration?

KRIS
Yessssss. I feel like spending my monthly
food allowance on two drinks.

LOLA
Go off, Budget King!!

LOLA
Count me out, shit to do

BOBBY
It's your boyfriend's birthday how can we
count you out?

ROBBIE
Yeah count me out, too. I have work to do

ANASTASIA
Not for me. I have an early start
tomorrow and I want to video call Nate
tonight. But congrats on the wins, guys!

MATTIE
I can't believe my eyes right now.

"What's happening?" Aurora asks, watching us read the messages as they roll in. "You guys go to The Honeypot after your wins? Campus bar too good for the hockey team?"

"It's Nate and Robbie's favorite place to drink," Russ explains. "Nate was friends with a girl who worked there and would get tables and stuff for really cheap. I don't think I've ever been."

The honest answer is I don't really like The Honeypot. I don't really like nightclubs, but Nate went through so much effort to make sure I could go with them last year even though I'm underage that I didn't know how to say I was fine hanging out at home alone. I've been there so many times that now I don't know how to tell the people who love it that I don't have a great time.

"It's fine I guess," I say. I knew either way people would want to party tonight, and I'd need to be there, but I was secretly hoping that maybe this weekend would be the one where everyone collectively decided to go home. I don't often give in to pressure, but I feel like I need to be there to celebrate with the team. "I was going to see if Halle wanted to hang out."

"You could probably catch her," Aurora says, nodding to the exit. "She was shuffling toward the parking lot in the crowd when I came in here. She was with Cami Walker and Ava Jones. I'd suspect they're still outside somewhere."

"Wait, she's here?"

Aurora nods slowly. "Yeah. Did she not mention it?"

"No."

"Did you ask?" she says, looking at me knowingly.

I was going to ask her yesterday if she would be coming, but she said she might be helping out at Enchanted while the owners were at an event, so I didn't. I intended to text her back and ask if she could come today, but I was so stressed by the Lola/jersey situation that I got distracted by Russ putting on a brand-new pair of socks and forgot.

"Text her," Russ says. "Maybe don't tell her you forgot about her."

HALLE 🌐

Where are you?

Hey!! I'm on my way home
You were great!!

Are you drunk?

She doesn't send me an answer, just a picture of Joy. Which, as far as I'm aware, means yes.

HALLE 🌐

What are you doing tonight?
Going to that new bar next to Enchanted
that just opened
I'm not 21 yet but Ava says it'll be fine

"Halle's going to the new bar that has replaced the place Russ worked at. She said she isn't twenty-one yet." I've gone from not wanting to be anywhere near a busy, crowded place to wanting to check out the new bar.

"Tell her she can use Emilia's fake ID," Aurora says. "They look similar enough. No one will care if Halle's boobs are on show."

I bring up the chat with my friends and see the conversation has continued in the form of a debate about what to do tonight.

PRETTY BEST FRIENDS

HENRY
What about the replacement sketchy
bar?

HENRY
Halle is going with her friends and is
going to use Emilia's ID

LOLA
Uh how?

RUSS
Aurora said they look similar enough and
"no one will care if Halle's boobs are on
show"

BOBBY
No one say anything. Muffin is setting up
a trap

MATTIE
I didn't even know she had any, Hen.
Promise

ANASTASIA
WHY are you guys like this?

LOLA
Let's hope they don't pay too much
attention to height lol

KRIS
It'll be fine. What's 7 inches between
friends

JAIDEN
That's what Henry said to her last night

JAIDEN
Boom

JAIDEN
Good evening

JAIDEN
Who's Halle?

LOLA
Jumpscare. Yuck

JAIDEN
Now that isn't very nice is it

BOBBY
Halle is Henry's new "friend" who he
wants to spend all his time with but
"definitely isn't hooking up with"

MATTIE
I'm down to give sketchy bar 2.0 a
chance.

KRIS
Same

ANASTASIA
It's gorgeous there isn't anything sketchy
about it now

Russ is trying to hide his laugh at the same time as hiding his
phone from Aurora. I switch back to Halle.

HALLE 🌑

We're going, too. Aurora is bringing you
a fake ID.

Thank you!! See you later

I—incredibly reluctantly—switch back to my friends.

PRETTY BEST FRIENDS

ANASTASIA
Of course they can be friends and not
hook up JJ

KRIS
Are you really the person to champion
that as a possibility?

LOLA
She's so gorgeous I sort of want to bow
at her feet

ROBBIE
I'd like to see how she'd react if you did
that

MATTIE
No I get what you mean in a very
platonic and not at all triggering to
Henry way

RUSS
I think she's a nice person

BOBBY
That's the spirit, muffin

                                                    HENRY
                                Please don't be weird to her. She's my
                                                        friend.

KRIS
We're just playing, Cap. She's great and
we'll stop

BOBBY
Message received mon capitaine

ROBBIE
Fuck it maybe one drink

MATTIE
Normality at last

I THINK EVERY SINGLE PERSON in LA decided to try to come to this bar tonight and I haven't even seen Halle yet.

Four people have hit on me according to the guys, who take great enjoyment in keeping count, but I hadn't noticed. I don't know how many times I've checked my cell phone, but I now receive punches to the arm every time I tap my screen. I keep looking at the time, but I can't actually remember what time it is.

It's too hot. It's too busy. It's too loud. My clothes feel too tight and scratchy and it's like I can feel my hair too much, but I need to be here for the team. And I do really want to see Halle. We were lucky to grab a few tables next to the wall when another big group left as we arrived, but even with more privacy than standing at the bar, it still feels too busy.

I didn't notice Aurora was gone until she reappears, tailed by Halle and her friends. Halle immediately makes a beeline for me, grinning broadly. As she gets closer to where I'm sitting, her smile dulls and eyebrows pucker. "What's wrong?"

How do you tell another person that you can feel parts of your body too much? And if whoever is in control of music puts on one more squeaky, repetitive, poorly remixed track that you might scream. "Not a fan of the noise."

She nods and puts her purse down on the table beside my phone. "Can I touch your head? Just your ears and temples?"

Anyone else I'd have immediately said no, but I nod. She steps closer, positioning herself between my legs. The bar stool I'm sitting on puts us face to face and she really is even more beautiful up close.

Halle's palms flatten over my ears, and she applies pressure gently. Her thumbs find my temples, and to anyone else she probably looks like she's about to kiss me, but she's muffling the noise. Leaning in toward my left ear, she lifts the pressure of her hand slightly. "Should we leave? You've had a big weekend. Nobody would blame you if you needed to rest."

Her hair tickles against my cheek. I tuck it behind her ear, placing my mouth next to her ear so she can hear me. "You only just got here. Your friends . . ."

"We've been together for hours and they won't mind. Let's go!"

Before I can object she's picking up her bag and walking toward Cami and Ava. She leans in and they both nod and smile, seemingly unbothered that I'm stealing her away. The guys all give me a look as I let them know I'm leaving, and I don't have it in me to argue that we're not leaving together in the way they think. Halle slides her hand into mine as we navigate out of the bar, and as soon as the fresh air hits me the tightness in my chest slowly begins to ease a little.

"Sorry for ruining your night," I say as I summon a car on my phone.

"Has anyone ever told you you apologize a lot?"

"Never." I slide off my jacket and place it over her shoulders. "Here, you're not wearing a lot and you might get cold."

"Thank you. I've sobered up a lot after the game and I'm not as protected from my own, well, Ava's, outfit choices." She pulls it tighter. "You haven't ruined my night, by the way. You could never."

"I'm sorry I didn't invite you to the game. I meant to, I just got in my head about something else. I'm happy you were there."

"I did feel a little weird going at first. But Cami convinced me it wasn't a big deal because it's a sports game. I guess it's just I would only go to Will's games *because* I was invited, so I didn't want you to think I was . . . I don't even know. But you don't need to be sorry."

"We talk about Will far more than I'd like."

She bursts out laughing, and the soft sound only helps to soothe me. "He responded to my story earlier. I posted a picture in a Maple Hills jersey and he said 'jersey chaser lol.' I think I stared at my phone for like forty-five seconds and then I got the giggles and couldn't stop."

I know Will texted her before our date, so it doesn't surprise me. "Important question. Whose name was on your jersey?"

"It doesn't have a name. It wasn't actually mine, I borrowed it from Ava."

The car pulls up to the curb and I hold the door open for her to climb in. "Yeah, we're fixing that on Monday."

Chapter Twelve

HALLE

TODAY HAS BEEN ONE OF my busiest days in a long time.

I went to my classes, had lunch with Aurora, went to the library, put some new fliers up for Enchanted, delivered some groceries for Mrs. Astor next door, helped Gigi with her Shakespeare essay, started my own essay, and now I'm letting two imaginary people called Harriet and Wyn tear my heart up via an audiobook on 2X speed while making cookies. I'm exhausted and somehow still falling behind, but that's an issue for another day.

And yet, despite all of those things to keep my mind very, very busy . . .

I can't stop thinking about the fact I had a sex dream about the man sitting on my couch.

When we got home on Saturday after the club, Henry was clearly overstimulated mentally and physically. I put a blanket and pillows in the middle of my living room, and we lay down and watched my baking show in silence. Joy nestled between us, asleep, and at some point between the technical and showstopper of the first episode, I drifted off. When I woke up again, I was in my bed and Henry was asleep beside me.

Three times this week we've repeated that process, each time waking up closer together.

Except last night, when I slept alone, and the offending dream happened.

Now I'm keeping myself as busy as I can so I don't have to look at him, because my imagination has seen things it can't unsee, and I feel like I cannot make eye contact with him without blushing intensely.

This month's book club read is playing loudly through my headphones, which means I don't hear Henry approach or realize he's behind me until his hand reaches past me to take one of the hot cookies from the baking sheet.

He gently pulls the headphones from my head. "You're jumpy. Are you okay?"

I don't realize how close he is until I turn around and we're almost nose to nose. He takes a step back and uses one hand to cup under the cookie as he takes a bite.

He moans.

Of course he moans.

"Did these get better or is it just because I haven't had one in a few days?" I shrug and look away as he sucks the melted chocolate chips from his fingers. "You're being weird."

"I'm not." I so, so am.

Henry washes his hands at the sink and turns, leaning against the surface as he dries them on a towel. "Watching you zoom around is tiring. Sit down with me and Joy?"

"Oh, it's you and Joy now, is it?"

He is smiling in a way that feels illegal to enjoy as much as I do. He walks back toward me, stopping the same distance away as earlier. A normal distance that would not even be an issue if he hadn't done an endless number of filthy things to me in my subconscious last night. "Jealous?"

"You wish." I, reluctantly and with *so* much resistance, let Henry take my hand and walk me to the living room couch. "We need to finish the research for your essay soon. This is the only time this week I'll have time to help you."

"Shhhhh," he says, pulling me down onto the couch beside him. "Let's nap instead."

"Don't shush me to get out of working. I have my own essay to do, too, so it's happening whether you like it or not."

"I've already finished it, Halle."

I sit up immediately and look at him properly for the first time. "What?"

"I finished it earlier. It was on something I already knew a lot about. I went through a phase. I just stuck to the structure you showed me and it was easy. So you need to find something else to boss me around over, Cap."

"I'm not bos—"

"I *like* you bossing me around, Halle," he says softly. "You're allowed to be assertive. You don't always have to do what other people want. Except for now, open your laptop and write your essay. I'll supervise."

I'm pretty sure my jaw is hanging open. Standing from the couch, I walk across the room to grab my laptop from the last place I used it. Henry is showing Joy a fish video on his phone when I sit back beside them. "Unbelievable," I mutter as I tuck my feet under my butt and open the screen.

"No distractions, please," he says. "I'm very busy."

After twenty minutes of writing, I feel a hand on my ankle. When Henry lifts it onto his lap I have no choice but to drop to my elbow. When he grabs the other one and repeats I'm basically lying down on my side, making it impossible to work on my laptop. "Can I help you with something, Henry?"

"No."

I roll onto my stomach from my side for comfort, placing my

laptop in front of me to attempt to continue to work. He uses my complacency to stretch my leg out across his lap and push my jeans up to my knee. That's when I feel something tickle against my foot. Looking back at him over my shoulder, I eye him suspiciously. "Are you drawing on me?"

"I was raised not to tell lies," he says.

When I turn back to my laptop I feel the tickling again. It continues, progressing over my ankle and up my calf. I'm convinced it takes twice as long to finish my work because I might be strong, but I'm not strong enough to be able to block out Henry's soft touch against my skin. This is the worst possible timing after my dream last night.

After what feels like forever, I finally shut my laptop and climb off the couch. There's a chorus of disapproving mumbles as I disturb Joy from her sleeping spot and interrupt whatever Henry has been doing.

"It isn't finished," he says as I pull up the leg of my jeans to investigate further.

My head twists and I try to bend my foot at an angle it's not supposed to go. "What is it?"

He looks at me like I'm ridiculous not to immediately be able to tell upside down. "Cats in a meadow."

It's actually very cute. If only it was somewhere I could keep, instead of decorating my skin. "I would have shaved my legs if I'd known you were about to pay extra attention to them."

His eyebrows pinch together a little. "It isn't surprising for me to find hair in a place where hair grows, Halle. You haven't shattered any illusions for me that women are smooth and hairless."

The inner feminist in me is screaming at myself because he's right. What he said to me is exactly what I'd say to my sisters, because I don't want them to grow up scrutinizing and changing themselves, and yet I don't say it to myself. "Sorry, you're right. It's not a big deal."

"Don't apologize. It's not your fault; you've been brainwashed by the cosmetics industry and men with porn addictions." A laugh chokes its way out of me. He's right, again, but it's the flat, matter-of-fact way he delivers it that shocks me, because he isn't like anyone I've ever met. Then I remember he was raised by women and he isn't doing it for some kind of brownie point or praise. He immediately moves on before I can even weigh in. "What do you want to do now?"

"I need to finish the book I'm reading for book club and I kind of want some fresh air. I'm also hungry. I'm also tired and want to lie down. I also need to write."

Henry nods along until I'm done listing. "Okay. Go change into some sweatpants, please. We're going on a date."

I have so many questions. So, *so* many. Instead of asking them, I nod in agreement and disappear upstairs.

THE EXCITEMENT OF THE UNKNOWN is the thing keeping me quiet as we drive uphill in Russ's truck.

Heat from the pizza box on my lap is keeping me warm, and the sliding and scraping sound echoing from the truck bed makes me curious. Henry told me it was a surprise, so I'm not asking questions, and frankly, there's something about watching him drive a truck that is giving me a lot to think about.

I can't work out if I had the dream because I'm attracted to him, or if I'm attracted to him because of the dream. Of course I've always known he's attractive—I have eyes—but there's definitely a difference between knowing something and actually being attracted to that something. Either way, I feel guilty about feeling hot and flustered over someone who's done nothing but be a good friend to me.

When we finally stop ascending, Henry reverses into a parking spot and climbs out quickly to walk around to my side. He takes the pizza box with one hand and my hand with his other and helps me slide out. "What are we doing here?"

The view looks out across the whole city, thousands of tiny lights shimmering across the skyline. "Dating. I told you." He hands me the pizza as he gets to work at the back. When I look over the truck side, there's an air mattress and blankets as well as a speaker and a cooler box. "Food and fresh air, and we can play your audiobook while you lie down. If you feel like it after, you can write. Can I have your phone to get the audio up? Can you grab the drinks from the front so I can put them in the cooler?"

I swipe up on my screen to unlock and hand it over. "Henry, this is amazing. Seriously."

Tucking the drink bottles under my arm, I close the passenger-side door with my hip. As I approach the back of the truck, that's when I hear it, and all the bottles slip out of my grip.

The sound of moaning and skin slapping against skin is unmistakable.

"Oh my God!" It comes out as a screech at the same time the stranger in my phone moans the same three words in a much more erotic way.

The slapping slows, and the stranger talks again as I scramble onto the bed in the most unflattering way possible and crawl across the air mattress to snatch my phone from Henry's hand. "*Put it back in, put it back in,*" she begs as I press pause.

Henry says nothing as I look up from my phone. "Wrong app," I say breathlessly.

My entire body feels hot. Not in a sexy way, in a "I might pass away from embarrassment" way. He's wearing the biggest smile. "So that isn't your book?"

"That isn't my book," I say, sitting down properly. Not even the dark could hide how flushed I am right now.

"What is it?" he says, a hint of curiosity in his voice. The look on his face tells me that he knows what it is. In his defense, I'm, like, 99 percent sure I left the app running in the background by accident after I used it this morning. That damn dream is the problem that keeps on probleming.

"It's an, um. Oh God. It's an audio erotica app called Whimper."

"Why are you so red?"

That's an excellent question. Why am I so red? I lie down flat on the bed and stare at the sky so I don't have to look at him. "Just a little embarrassed."

"Why? Because now I know you like to listen to people having sex to get off?" he says calmly.

"I'd rather you kill me than try to have this conversation with me."

Henry laughs, and even the sound doesn't soothe me. He lies on the spot next to me on his side, propped up by his hand. "I've seen you naked and now I know your sexual preferences. We're getting super close."

My jaw drops as I turn to look at him. "You broke a rule!"

"So did you by being embarrassed."

"And it isn't a sexual preference as such. I just like audios—of lots of things, not just people having sex. Jesus Christ, can we revisit the killing me idea?"

"I lived between Nate's and JJ's rooms for a year. I'm accustomed to knowing the intimate details of my friends' sex lives. JJ wasn't too bad because I never saw anyone again, but I have to look at Anastasia regularly. You like audio. I bet I'd like audio, too. There's nothing you can tell me you've done that I haven't *heard* them do. But we don't have to talk about anything if it makes you uncomfortable."

"There's nothing to tell," I admit sheepishly. "I'm a virgin."

Henry doesn't say anything straight away, giving me the perfect amount of time to consider my escape route. People care about my lack of sex life more than I do, so I don't dread their reactions because I think there's something wrong. I dread their reactions because I end up having to convince them nothing's wrong.

"Virginity is a social construct," he says. "It's good I didn't let you leave with Mason. Would have been the worst forty-five seconds of your life. I'm a good friend."

I can always rely on Henry to surprise me. "How did you manage to make my sexual inexperience about you?"

Henry's mouth tugs up at the corners in that way that makes my insides go weird. "I can make everything about me if you give me enough time. Including your sex life."

"I . . ." have no response. "Our pizza is probably cold, and I think we should put the book on now. Maybe let me do it, y'know, to prevent any other audio mistakes."

"That's a shame. I was looking forward to seeing if he finally put it back i—"

Rolling onto my side at a speed I didn't know I was capable of, I press my palm to Henry's mouth. "Stop talking. I'm adding this to our rule book under things we're not allowed to talk about."

His hand closes around my wrist, lifting my hand from his mouth. He kisses my palm gently and puts it on the air mattress between our chests. "Good luck getting it signed off by the board."

"The board for our rule book?" He nods. "And who's on the board?"

"Me and you. And I'm not putting it on the list."

"You're unbelievable, do you know that?"

"So I've heard."

Chapter Thirteen

HENRY

NATE HAWKINS IS SITTING ON the living room couch. I blink once, twice. Desperately try to remember if I've hit my head today.

"At least pretend to be happy to see me, bud," he says when the surprise of him being there stops me in my tracks in the doorway.

"Do you say *bud* now because you're a fake Canadian?" Robbie asks him. They're both sipping from their favorite mugs, and a nostalgic wave drags me under when I realize how familiar the sight of Robbie and Nate gossiping in the living room drinking coffee feels.

"How about I stick my foot up your ass and you can tell me how fake that feels," he snaps back. "Hen asked me the same thing a few weeks ago."

"Are you going into the house?" Russ asks from behind me. I drop my bag at the end of the couch and sit beside Nate, resisting the urge to poke him to check that he's real.

"So," he says, turning in his seat to face me. "How's it going, Captain? How's Faulkner?"

Robbie and Russ both loudly groan, but before I can respond Russ holds up his cell phone. "JJ is video calling me. Did you tell him you were coming?"

Nate shakes his head as Russ accepts the call. "I sensed something was happening," JJ says immediately. "Having a reunion without me, are you? Selfish bastards."

"Aren't you playing in Florida tonight?" Nate asks him. "Sensed something was happening, my ass. You saw it on my close friends."

"Why do you have a Canadian accent?" JJ says, screwing up his nose.

"Thank you!" Robbie shouts, making me jump, and Nate mutters something under his breath. "I said that when he got here and he said I was making it up."

JJ's smile is huge. I suspect it's the success of annoying Nate from the other side of the country. "There is definitely something distinctly moosey about you these days, Nathan. Very off-putting. So what are we gossiping about? What's the 411? Or *the tea* as the youth say."

"When you say 'as the youth say,' are you talking about when you said that, like, two months ago?" Robbie asks. "Nate was asking Hen how being captain is when you called."

JJ makes the same groan Russ and Robbie did a few minutes ago, and I feel like my friends have conveyed my feelings without me even needing to say a word. "Why the fuck does everyone keep groaning at me?" Nate says, looking confused.

I should step in and explain how I feel, but in all honesty, I'm too tired. Me talking about my feelings leads to my friends offering mountains of advice to make me feel different, but it doesn't work. I can't escape the constant worry that everything is going to go wrong and it's going to be my fault.

"I'm just tired of Faulkner's incessant need to talk to me about hockey," I say, opting to go with my easiest annoyance. "I don't want to see him as much as I do."

"Henry takes everything too personally," Robbie says to Nate. "He's internalizing every mistake and holding himself responsible for them, even though we've all told him it doesn't work like that."

This starts a conversation I can largely sit back from while everyone, as predicted, weighs in. Robbie explains how he's trying to mediate between me and Faulkner, Russ talks positively about how the season is going, and Nate gives a speech about teamwork.

JJ clears his throat. "Is no one going to point out how our faithful leader fucked off to play in tights for several months last year? Hen, as long as you actually play in games you're gonna be better than Nate. Don't even sweat it."

I can hardly tell what anyone else is saying over the sound of JJ laughing at his own joke, while Nate lists every single thing he covered JJ's ass for in the four years they lived and played together. By the time they're done, I feel like my head might explode from all the advice they've given me. I successfully zone out, only mentally rejoining them when Nate starts giving Russ's phone the finger. "Friends are allowed to have different opinions on how to handle things, Jaiden. I don't have to agree with you because I know you're wrong."

JJ immediately fires back, but I've already stopped listening again.

"Are you coming to the gig tonight?" Russ asks Nate when it quiets down again.

Russ's brother's band, Take Back December, is in town tonight, and Russ got everyone tickets. I said I didn't want to go because I don't like their music, and more relevantly, I think Russ's brother is a jackass.

"No. I'm only here for twenty-four hours—I don't even think it's that. I need to leave soon to watch Stas at the rink and then I'm taking her to a bookstore. She's really stressed out at the moment. Well, I guess you guys will have noticed. Plus she's struggling with the distance." Nobody says anything. "Shit, we both are. It fucking sucks, but I'm going to give her my full attention while I'm here. She's in a meeting with her professor right now so I had time to stop by."

I didn't know Anastasia was stressed out because I haven't

checked. She's always busy, and since I started studying with Halle and didn't need her study group, I've barely seen her. It was easy when she lived here because I saw her every day. It's easy to make sure the other guys are okay because they turn up at my house almost daily. It's made me realize that I'm not good at maintaining friendships that don't appear in front of me, and that I need to add checking in on her to my priority list.

When Nathan says goodbye and leaves, Robbie is the first person to say something. "We need to keep a closer eye on Stassie. I'll speak to Lola. I don't know why she hasn't mentioned it. She's pretty busy, too; maybe she hasn't noticed."

"I feel really bad," Russ admits. "I knew she missed Nate, but I thought she was okay otherwise."

"I didn't know," I say. "I haven't asked her how she is."

"Well, I knew," JJ says, and I had kind of forgotten he was there. "Guess I'm just better than you all."

"Goodbye, Jaiden," Robbie drawls. "Go and do your job."

"Bye, friends. It's been a pleasure as always."

When it's just the three of us again, I lie down on the couch. "I might go to bed."

"Are you sure you don't want to come tonight? Aurora asked me to put Halle's name on the list."

I was supposed to see Halle last night, but I had to go to the studio to finish up a project, so came home instead. "Why didn't she ask me to put her name on the list?"

Russ shrugs. "Dunno. Are you coming then? Since she's going? Should I put your name on the list? It'd be cool if you came. No pressure, though, or anything. But it's no problem if you want me to add your name."

I still don't want to go, but I do want to see Halle, and Russ is being kind of weird. Also, Robbie's giving me the look I've seen him give Nathan a thousand times. JJ would joke that it was them communicating telepathically, but I'm getting nothing. I hate when people give me weird looks and expect me to know what the fuck they're trying to say.

Everyone is being weird today.

"Sure, I'll come. I'm going to nap here, though, before I get ready. I'm too tired for the stairs."

My roommates both put their recliners up, nodding in agreement, and Robbie turns on *Judge Judy*. "I'll set an alarm. Oh, this is a good episode."

"WHY DO YOU LOOK SO mysterious and brooding?" Kris asks, holding his hand up to get the attention of the bartender.

"Thinking." *Trying to drown out the music by dissociating.* "Not brooding."

"Well, not to interrupt whatever plan you're cooking up in that beautiful brain of yours, but Halle just walked in with her friends," he says, nodding toward where our group is. "God, I'd let Cami Walker ruin my life."

As excited as I am to see her, there's something about Kris saying Halle is with her friends that makes me feel good. I think it's because not that long ago Halle was saying she didn't have any.

"Ask her out then."

Kris scoffs. "I did. Last year at Robbie's birthday party, and she told me she wouldn't date someone younger than her. It's a curse liking older women."

Kris carries on talking about his recent unlucky spell with women, but I've stopped fully paying attention. I'm not sure one year counts as liking older women, but I don't have the energy to debate it with him.

Halle's taken the spare spot between Jimmy and Brody, two new guys from the team who love the band and were offered tickets by

Russ. I don't like either of them. I wish Russ had thought more about his generosity. They're good at hockey, but they took the douchey athlete stereotype and ran with it.

Maybe it's because I was raised by two moms or maybe it's because I *actually* respect women, but I'm not a fan of how some of my teammates act.

"You might want to go and save her from Tweedledee and Tweedle Douche Bag," Kris adds. "I'll wait for the rest of the drinks."

Brody is already hitting on Halle by the time I get over to them, which means I get to do the only good thing about dealing with men who respect bullshit hierarchy and misogyny more than they do human beings. "Leave."

I feel like I'm pretending to be someone else when the harshness comes out of my mouth, but I do really want them to leave. Leave the venue, ideally.

"Sorry, Cap," Brody says, hitting Jimmy on the shoulder to get his attention. "Didn't realize she's yours."

She's yours says everything anyone would ever need to know about these two, and I'm embarrassed to know them as they shuffle away to bother someone else.

I can tell Halle is buzzed as soon as she giggles and leans in to hug me. "My hero. I'm so happy I'm *yours*." Her laughter is so loud I can hear it over the instrumental being played from the speakers while we wait for the band. "Sorry, that was straight out of, like, *90210* or some old teen show or something. '*Leave*.' Oh my goodness, I don't think I've ever seen you actually look intimidating before."

Her laughter instantly makes me feel better. "I'm very intimidating when I need to be."

"I'm happy to be your damsel in distress if you're going to be Mr. Serious." She pinches my chin and shakes my head a little, pouting, and that's when I realize she's more than just buzzed.

"How drunk are you?" I ask, tucking a strand of hair behind her ear while she rummages around her purse for something. "Do you need help?"

"I am very drunk. I brought you a present but I can't freaking find it." She huffs dramatically as she continues to dig through her purse that is not big enough to warrant this amount of effort. I don't think I've ever seen her so flustered. Eventually she pulls out a tiny drawstring bag and drops it into the palm of my hand. "Open it."

I don't know what I'm expecting to find in the bag. "Is it seeds?"

"I love that I hand you a small mystery bag at a concert and you go to seeds before drugs. Just open the bag, Henry."

She watches closely as I empty two black loops onto my hand. "Thank you, but I don't have my ears pierced."

Halle starts laughing again and takes each of the loops from my palm, poking them into my ears. The noise around us dulls instantly. "They're noise reducers. It's so I can divide my time between dancing with Aurora like I promised her and cupping your ears. Working two jobs tonight, Turner. You gotta share me."

I can hear everything but it's like someone turned down the volume. It doesn't feel like someone is hacking at my head anymore. Her arms wrap around me as I pull her into a hug, truly grateful. "Thank you."

She smiles up at me and I kiss her forehead, catching us both by surprise. "You're welcome."

Right on cue, the lights dim and everyone starts screaming. Halle spins toward the stage but she doesn't step out of my grasp. My hands land in a comfortable spot around her waist and she leans back into me.

Maybe the band isn't that bad after all.

Chapter Fourteen

HENRY

"Hey, daydreamer," Halle whispers as she nudges my knee with hers to get my attention since I'd definitely zoned out. "I need the bathroom."

She's staring at me like I'm supposed to be reading her mind right now, but I can't. After I don't say anything, she nods toward the door. "Will you help me find it?"

Two of the band members—I can't remember their names—are talking about Russ when he was a little kid and they used to rehearse in the Callaghans' garage. Aurora is eating it up, but I've been ready to leave for twenty minutes; Russ is waiting for his brother to appear. I don't understand why since they don't seem to like each other, but I'm an only child so I don't presume to understand sibling behavior.

"I'm going to pee my pants if we don't go right now," Halle whispers.

"You're not wearing any pants," I whisper back.

It takes two minutes to find the door labeled Restroom, and I'd argue that Halle didn't need my help. I'm about to point that out when she pushes the door open and reveals Ethan, Russ's brother, snorting a line of white powder from the edge of the sink with a woman.

There are various other clear plastic bags around them with powders and pills, and a half-drunk bottle of vodka. Ethan doesn't pay any attention to either of us as Halle rushes into one of the stalls. It's taking everything in me to not ask him what the fuck he thinks he's doing.

I frankly don't care about what irresponsible act he wants to do, but I'm angry for my friend. Russ deserves better.

"Close the fucking door, man," he yells in my direction, not even bothering to look at me.

I reluctantly step into the bathroom, letting the door shut behind me. I don't want to be anywhere near this, but I don't want to leave Halle in here alone. I know Russ suspects there's something going on with his brother because he confided in me about it over the summer.

He said it would be typical for his family to find something new to fall out over now that his dad is doing so well in his gambling addiction program. Russ thought maybe Ethan was using sleeping pills to help with traveling with the band, and that's why he looked so strung out when they saw each other over the summer. I don't think he suspected this, and I really don't want to be the one to tell him he has another family problem to worry about.

Halle's stall opens, and now that she's turned toward me, I can see the horrified look on her face. I don't think this is the experience she was looking for tonight. She doesn't look at Ethan or his friend as she washes her hands beside them.

"What the fuck?" she says, having stormed out of the bathroom.

Halle doesn't know about Russ's family, other than what everyone who came here tonight knows: that Russ has issues with his brother but he's supportive of him. I haven't told her, and I know Aurora won't have.

"Yeah, wild," I respond, not knowing what else to say. This entire day has been a drain, and when I'm tired things come out wrong, and I *need* not to say things wrong right now.

I don't want to betray Russ's trust.

"Does Russ know?" she asks. I shrug. "You should go and tell him. I'm not being a narc, but, like, that doesn't look recreational. Did you see the counter? There was *so* much."

"Russ doesn't need this. Ethan is an adult."

"I should tell Aurora then," she says, and my stomach sinks. "She's being so nice to me, we're friends now I guess, and this is so dangerous. What if he overdoses and we didn't tell anyone? She can decide what Russ needs to know, but at least we said something."

"No." I don't know how to deal with this. "We need to mind our business. It's nothing to do with us. If Ethan goes out there looking like that Russ will probably work it out himself anyway."

"But what if h—"

"Halle, *no*. I know them better than you do. You're drunk and you're not listening to me. Now isn't the time."

I watch her face sink and hate myself. "Okay. You're right, they're your friends, you know what's best."

It's like watching a balloon deflate as all the confidence she's gained in the past few weeks leaves her. "They're *our* friends," I say, but it's pointless. I've already upset her.

She shuffles awkwardly. "I think I'm going to find Cami and get an Uber home. I'm pretty tired and I dunno. I don't think hanging out with the band and seeing everything that happens is my thing. I guess I'm really sheltered because I feel really weird and uncomfortable."

"I don't like it, either. I'll come with you."

Cami doesn't want to leave when we find her hanging out in the bar next door with some of her friends. Neither of us says anything on the ride back to Halle's place. I'm grateful for the quiet, and our driver doesn't seem to want to be the one to start the conversation. The car pulls up in front of her house and she starts to get out. When I don't move, the little line between her eyebrows appears. "Are you not staying over?"

"Not tonight. I want to go home and sleep." If I can get my brain to shut off quickly, I'll even sleep through everyone coming home later. "But I'll walk you to your door."

"No, I'm fine, stay here. Goodbye then," she says with a weird edge to her voice. "Thanks for everything."

She's closed the door before I have a chance to respond to her strange goodbye, and that's when the driver looks at me in his mirror. "Jeez. What did you do, man?"

I don't bother answering him and make a mental note to rate him only four stars.

Fuck Ethan Callaghan.

I NEED TO TELL RUSS what happened last night, but I don't want to.

Halle was right. Russ needs to know, and if he finds out I knew and didn't tell him I think he might be upset. But, like I said, I don't want to have that conversation with him. I don't trust myself not to deliver the news in a way that will make it worse, but I know Halle can't help me.

Maybe that's why I feel like not even the fire alarm could get me out of my room right now.

"Henry?" Russ calls my name as he knocks on my bedroom door. "Are you in there?"

Anastasia would say this is the universe intervening.

"Yeah, come in."

Russ's head pokes through my door, his cell phone pressed to his ear. "She's not here," Russ says into his phone. "Okay, give me a chance to ask him, Ror. You took Halle home last night, right?"

"Yes. Why?"

"He did, Ror. Stop panicking. She's probably just hungover. No, no, I'll tell him. It'll be fine, sweetheart. Yes, he'll call you. Okay, love you, too." When he disconnects the call he comes into my room and sits at the end of my bed. "She's freaking out because some people got roofied last night, and Halle didn't show up to class this morning. One of them was Poppy, and Rory is really upset over it. She's fine, nothing happened, thank God."

Russ carries on talking as I go into autopilot to get dressed. He gives me a ride to Halle's place, and it's only when I knock on her front door and see her that I finally feel like I can exhale.

"What are you doing here?" she asks, wiping her eyes with the sleeve of her cardigan. Stepping through the door, I immediately wrap my arms around her and rest my face against the crown of her head. "Henry, you're freaking me out. Did someone die?"

Taking a step back I look her up and down, and aside from her red eyes, she looks un-Halle-like in a way I can't pinpoint. "Are you okay? You look terrible."

"I'm fine," she whispers, bottom lip wobbling as she forces herself into a smile. "So, so fine."

"Halle, why are you crying?"

"I'm not," she says as she begins to fully sob. "Everything is fine."

I guide her into the living room, and she's compliant as I take a seat on the couch and pull her onto my lap. "Why are you crying? Did something happen?"

"I thought you wouldn't want to be my friend anymore," she blurts out. "I thought you were mad at me."

This is not what I expected her to be upset over. "Why wouldn't I want to be your friend anymore?"

I wipe the tears rolling down her reddened cheeks with my thumbs. She looks so sad. "I was pushy and weird last night. I tried to interfere with you and your friends. I know I overstepped, Henry."

"No, you were right. I should have said something to Russ; he has a complicated situation with his family, and I don't know how to handle it sometimes. Usually, I just listen to him rant, and I don't need to give advice. I'm going to talk to him about it. You didn't overstep." New tears form and I watch her carefully while she avoids looking at me. Gripping her chin lightly, I tilt her face in my direction. "What's wrong?"

"I don't know. Our friendship is so new, and you were right, you know your friends better than I do, and the thought of losing everyone and having no friends agai—"

"Friends are allowed to have different opinions on how to handle things, Halle. It doesn't make me not want to talk to you anymore, and even if something did happen, people don't want to be your friend because of me. They like you as you are all on your own."

I hold my arm up, and after a moment of deliberation she leans into my body, letting me wrap my arm around her. Her head fits perfectly in the crook of my neck.

"I don't know why I'm crying so much," she mumbles. "I just woke up feeling so depressed and anxious, and now you're here and it just won't stop."

"You're being dramatic because you have a hangover, Halle."

"I'm not being dramatic," she immediately replies before I feel her body start to shake gently. Shit. "Not on purpose."

Stroking her hair gently, I hold her tight with my other arm. "Alcohol is a depressant. It's why you feel so shit when you're hungover. Does this happen every time you drink?"

She shakes her head; the smell of her shampoo radiates from her hair. She smells like vanilla. "Only if I drink a lot. I don't think I like it."

"Then why do you do it?" I know she's crying again before I hear it from the way her body moves. I hate it. "Shh. You'll feel better once it's out of your system. Just stop crying."

Sniffing, she wipes her eyes with her cardigan sleeves. "I don't want people to think I'm boring and stop inviting me to things. I never drank at parties when I was with Will, and they definitely thought I was boring. And it makes me feel more confident, and I like it for the first couple of drinks, but then if I go further, I end up feeling like this the next day. I worry everyone hates me while I also feel like death."

"You really skipped those peer-pressure talks in high school, huh? Let's not talk about Will, because then *I'll* feel like death and won't be able to take care of you." I finally get a short laugh out of her, and the relief is immense. "Halle, nobody with more than two brain cells thinks anybody is boring for not drinking when they don't want to. Don't do something you don't like for other people."

"I know. Nobody is pressuring me. It's just in my head, and logically I know I'm being ridiculous."

"Sometimes you can't trust your head to think the right thing, especially when you drown it in tequila. People like *you*, sober you, not the extra-confident version when you're buzzed you. Getting a new group of friends all at once is a lot, but you don't need to change for them."

"Oh," she says. We sit in silence, and there's thankfully no more crying. I rub my hand up and down her outer thigh and try to remember when being this close started to feel so natural. Minutes of quiet continue, and I think she's fallen asleep until she speaks quietly. "Can I ask you a question?"

"Of course you can."

She sits up to look at me, her butt sliding off my knee into the gap between my thigh and the couch end. Her legs stay draped over mine and my hands settle on her shin. "If you aren't mad at me, why didn't you stay over last night?"

"When I'm overwhelmed, I need to be on my own to process everything and sleep it off. I'm sorry, I could have explained that to you. I will next time."

She nods. "That makes sense. Sorry for asking, and for being needy or whatever. It was just when you didn't want to stay, and you hadn't actually invited me, so I thought that maybe you hadn't wanted me there, and the girls sa—it doesn't matter. Thank you for explaining."

"I didn't invite you because I wasn't going. I only went because I wanted to see you." I chuckle when her eyes widen a little. "I don't even like Take Back December. And Russ's brother is a dick, as you now know. What did your friends say?"

She leans back into me, burying her face in my chest like it's the most instinctual thing for her. She mumbles into my T-shirt, "Ifyou-wantedtoyouwouldbutisaidwe'renotlikethat."

"Huh?"

She looks up so I can see her face and her cheeks are flushed again. "That if you wanted to you would. But I said we're not like that. And now I know you weren't even going so I feel silly."

"What does that mean?"

"It's like when guys don't make an effort for stuff people say oh, if they wanted to they would. Because people always remember to do the things for people that are important to them. So if they don't make the effort, it's just not a high priority for them. It's just because you said you forgot to invite me to your game, then you didn't invite me to this and, I don't know. It isn't a big deal, they were just talking while we were getting ready."

"I always want to and I always will, but I have to be honest, sometimes I don't know I should. I need you to talk to me if you feel like I'm not stepping up, because I will. I'll do anything for you, Halle. I just don't always know it because sometimes that isn't how I think. I get wrapped up in things and then I don't focus on the outside things I want to focus on. You are a high priority to me."

"This was a really deep conversation to have while simultaneously feeling like I might throw up at any moment. Maybe I am dramatic," she says as she rests her head against me again. I don't think she needs me to confirm to her that she is. I'm willing to give her a pass because being hungover clearly isn't for her. I listen to the pattern of her breathing while twirling a piece of her hair between my fingers. "How did you know to look for me here?"

"Aurora was worried about you because you didn't show up for class. Some people had their drinks spiked last night and she panicked when she couldn't reach you. I should text her."

"I don't know where my cell phone is. I'm sorry, I didn't mean to frighten anyone. That's so scary." I don't tell her about Poppy because I'm not sure if I'm supposed to, and I don't want to make her cry again. "Let her know I'm okay, please."

Pulling out my cell phone, I bring up Aurora's name.

AURORA

> She's fine. Just hungover.

Omg. I can stop stressing now. Tell her she can have my notes

Thanks Prince Charming

> Need to talk to you about an Ethan thing later. Don't know how to bring it up with Russ.

 ??

> Yeah.

Russ already knows. It blew up after you left last night.

He'd suspected something was up since summer so it wasn't a surprise

Will talk to you about it later. I'm meeting my professor now

"Why do you have over four hundred unread messages? Do you not have, like, intense anxiety when you don't open your messages, or is that just me?"

"It's just you. It's mainly group chats, Kenny's offers, and women looking to hook up late at night when they're bored and horny. Nothing important."

She scoffs. "Yeah, my messages are definitely the same."

I sit up a little straighter. "People looking to hook up?"

"Tons of them. It's always the bored and the horny. My inbox is actually overflowing with that particular type of message. What an inconvenience, amiright?"

"Guys I know?" I think she's kidding. Emphasis on think.

She gives me a pointed look, but I don't know what it means. "Be serious. Literally nobody is texting me to hook up."

I feel relieved and I'm not sure why. I know I'm not supposed to feel relieved considering she's just a friend. "Is that something you want? That experience?"

"It depends what you're asking. There's a lot of things I'll do for the writing competition, but hooking up with someone random for more inspiration isn't one of them. But would I like the experience of hooking up with someone I care about? Yeah."

"That makes sense."

It's a natural end to the conversation. Halle is still curled up on my lap, and any sign she's attempting to move makes me hold her that much tighter until she relaxes again. Joy joined the equation, taking her place on Halle's lap, and the whole image is unusually domestic for me. I like how calm I feel, and it's making me consider skipping my afternoon classes and staying here. Well, until I remember that I'd have to face Faulkner if I did.

"I need to google why being around you makes me want to fall asleep," she says after a long stretch of quiet.

"Oxytocin."

"I don't know what that is."

"Neither do I. I was googling why I couldn't fall asleep as well as I do when you're there, but I got distracted by a pregnancy pillow ad. It arrives on Monday."

"You can stay here whenever you like, Henry," she says gently. "You're always welcome and I like the company. It's really nice having friends. Even if maybe I panic I'm going to lose them all every single day and have dramatic embarrassing outbursts when I'm hungover."

"You're not embarrassing. You are dramatic, though. But if it makes you feel better, you're not even in the top three of the most dramatic people I'm friends with," I say, squeezing her side playfully. "You broke a rule, though; please stop feeling embarrassed around me. Maybe your friendships will feel less delicate if you get to know people better. We need to give you a new experience anyway. Have you ever been on a group date?"

"I sort of have, actually. It was horrible and I felt like an alien the entire time."

"Good, it's better that you've done it before. That way I won't have to feel bad about stealing you away the minute we get there. We're playing away this weekend, but we're going to the beach on Sunday when we get home."

Halle laughs, her body vibrating against mine. "So not a group date then. Just a date with witnesses."

"Annoying witnesses."

When she frees herself from being curled up against me, she looks happier than she did when I got here, and I'm thankful I haven't somehow made this worse. "Annoying witnesses? What could possibly go wrong?"

Chapter Fifteen

HENRY

OF ALL THE BORING THINGS I'm required to do this week, watching Anastasia weigh cooked rice is the most boring.

I lean against the palm of my hand on the other side of her kitchen island, observing her move the glass container from the counter to the scale and back, over and over. By the time she moves on to chicken breast I'm half asleep. She occasionally turns around to stir the sauce she's concocted for all of this food prep, but other than that, she's a cooking robot, hardly saying anything.

"Santa Monica will be more fun than this," I say, hoping that will be enough to convince her. The reality is anything would be more fun than this.

"I don't have fun scheduled in my planner, so like I said, I'm going to have to pass."

"All you do is skate and study. You need a break."

"That's not true. I also eat seventeen thousand times a day like a fucking shrew." She abandons adding broccoli to her meals and leans against the counter. I don't think she knows how tired she looks. "Did Nathan put you up to this?"

"No." She stares at me in the way she does that makes me feel like I'm being disciplined by a parent. "He didn't. He said you were stressed and it made me realize I hardly check in on you. I haven't intentionally neglected you."

"You haven't neglected me at all, Hen. I know you have a lot going on with school and hockey, and you're spending a lot of time with Halle"—a borderline unhinged smile spreads across her face—"who I want to hear all about, by the way. I had to find out you were dating from Mattie, and I spent our entire lecture stunned. Didn't learn a thing."

"We're not dating. We're friends."

It's annoying how smug she looks right now. "I'm your friend and you've never kissed my forehead or held my hand."

Fucking Mattie. "That's your own fault. Grow six inches and then we can talk about it. I'm not bending over to be nice to you."

She flips me off and huffs. "I'm just saying. Special rules for special friends and all that. I would *love* for you to have a girlfriend. I worry about you when you're being slutty."

"I haven't even kissed anyone in more than a month, so you can stop worrying. Were you worried about yourself when you were being slutty?"

I don't know why I haven't kissed anyone, so I don't have an answer if Anastasia asks. I could come up with tons of excuses about stress and hockey. I wouldn't admit to her that I'd feel weird kissing someone in front of Halle, and we're together a lot. I don't even want to kiss someone. Maybe I overdid it in the summer, and now I'm in a different phase. Maybe I like the idea of kissing the same person. I don't know.

She rolls her eyes and plucks a grape from the bag in front of her, waving it about as she talks. "I dispute I've ever been slutty, but the point is, sex is fun—"

"I know you think that. I've heard you do it tons of times."

She launches the grape at me. "—and if you're doing it because it's fun, great. But you start running through women when you're lonely."

"I wish I hadn't told you that."

"Well, suck it up because you did. It would just make me really happy if you could have both. The companionship as well as the other stuff. You like her, right? Even if you're not officially dating."

"I like her, but I don't know how to or want to date someone. What if it ruins how good things are?" It's something I've thought about a lot since Halle's emotional outburst. All I wanted to do was hold her and look after her. I hated having to leave because I had other commitments. I've also thought a lot about how the idea of her hooking up with someone makes me unhappy, even though she was joking. And how I want to watch her have friends and be confident that she'll keep them.

Anastasia plucks another grape and pops it into her mouth. "How would you feel if she dated someone else?"

"Don't know . . . I do know. I'd feel unhappy. I don't understand why, though."

Anastasia raises her shoulders and smirks at me, like she's somehow just easily unraveled a great mystery. She hasn't; I've already considered all of this. "Because you like her, Hen. Which is amazing, but I get why it's hard to process if you haven't liked anyone before. If the idea of her being with someone else makes you unhappy, make a move before someone else does."

"You're not being as helpful as you think you are," I groan.

"I *am* helpful, you're just stubborn. Don't fucking procrastinate with your feelings, Henry. If she's so great that you want to be around her all the time, someone else is going to think she's so great and want to be around her all the time."

"You should come to Santa Monica today and meet her," I say, not bothering to answer the stuff she said. "Make your assessment in person."

"Nice deflection, but no. The pier sounds like a nice place for a first kiss, though. Very romantic."

"Definitely more romantic than pressed up against a door."

This time a handful of grapes fly in my direction.

"DEEP BREATH. YOU'RE FREE," HALLE says to me quietly as we wait for everyone to get out of their various cars in the parking lot.

"I don't feel free." She nudges me with her hip and shushes me, so I lower my voice. "They're not riding with us on the way home."

Kris and Bobby said a group date was discrimination toward single people, i.e., them, and demanded to be invited. Mattie said he was happy to be discriminated against because his fear of seagulls makes him strongly anti-pier. I also think he's seeing his ex again. To balance things out, because apparently that's a thing we need to do, Halle invited her work friend, Cami, and Cami's roommate, Ava.

Bobby and Ava are both from California, so on that basis alone, despite the fact they're from totally different places in California, Aurora and Halle assumed they'd be a good match. They're not. I've just had to listen to the two of them arguing about sports teams for the entire ride here.

"I still think they're a good match. All that rage toward each other has got to go into something."

"That's like saying they're a good match because they're both blond. It makes no sense."

"Love doesn't have to make sense."

"The only thing Bobby loves is happy hour and free food."

Halle nudges me again with her shoulder, but she's suppressing a laugh. We watch the pair of them continue their argument, now on basketball instead of baseball, and I clearly don't see what Halle sees. By contrast, Cami isn't talking to Kris at all, instead choosing to talk to Emilia and Poppy.

"I assume you're ditching us," Robbie says as soon as he joins us with Lola.

"That would be correct," I say, unsurprised when I'm met with an eye roll.

"Only you could get away with inviting us all to an event then leaving us," Lola says. "It's like you don't want me and Halle to be friends."

"I don't. Halle is the nicest person I know, and you are the most terrifying. I don't want to mix those two personalities."

Lola bursts out laughing, but when I look at Halle she appears shocked. "You can't say that," she mouths, but I know Lola well enough to know what I can and can't say. She likes it, which I don't understand, but I try not to ask too many questions.

After some negotiations, we—well, Halle—agree to meet up later after spending some time doing our own thing. The others mostly want to go to the beach anyway, whereas I've promised Halle to help her win a prize.

"I haven't been here since I was a kid," she says as I slip my hand into hers and we walk along the pier.

She looks down at our joined hands then up at me. "I love how committed to the date experience you are."

It takes me a second to realize what she means. I truly don't remember the moment I decided to reach for her hand. "I forgot this was supposed to be an experience. I just like it. We don't have to . . ."

She holds my hand tighter as I start to unweave my fingers from hers. "No, I like it, too."

"Good. Games or funnel cake first?" I ask as we approach the entrance to Pacific Park, the amusement park element of the pier. She considers my offer, eyes bouncing between the various counters then back to me.

"Games, then tacos, then funnel cake, maybe? I feel like it's only fair to tell you how bad I am at anything that requires hand-eye co-ordination."

"This is a great opportunity for me to tell you I'm great at everything."

"Again. Tell me that you're great at everything, *again*. Your humility is my favorite thing about you, by the way. I've literally never won a teddy at these things—not even the shit tiny ones."

I wrap my arm across her shoulders and tug her closer to my body, kissing the top of her head as we walk toward the first game. "I'll help you win the biggest one."

WHEN I WAS GROWING UP, my parents taught me that it's more valuable to be the person who helps someone achieve their goals than to be the person who achieves it for them.

I've always understood that mindset, and my moms reminded me of it often to help me fight my natural instinct to just do things myself because it was quicker and easier. However, as I watch Halle fail for the fifth time, it's getting harder and harder to remember that I should be helping her achieve her goal of winning, and not winning for her.

"I see you weren't exaggerating," I say carefully.

Halle looks at me over her shoulder, scowling, before she proceeds to launch the ball at the target again. When the ball goes through the center of the two clown faces she's supposed to be knocking down, she curses loudly. This is the fourth game where we've had this very specific problem: Halle's athleticism.

"These games are rigged, y'know," she mumbles, stomping in my direction and resting her forehead against the center of my chest. "Not even you can beat a rigged system."

"I don't think your ball is getting close enough to anything to claim you're being conned. Do you want me to have a go?"

I cup the sides of her neck with my hands and she looks up at me. "I don't want to give them any more money. They're scamming us. Let's go get scammed by someone else."

When I let go of her neck, her hand slides into mine like it's the most natural thing in the world, and I think back to what Anastasia said about never holding her hand. She's right, but I think the main difference between Halle and Anastasia is that I've never been attracted to Anastasia. And now I know Halle likes it, too.

We stop in front of a ring toss game and I can immediately tell that this isn't going to go well. I can't watch this. "Let me help," I say as I place myself behind her. "You need to throw it like this."

I rearrange her positioning until she's at least close to having a chance. "I really want that massive duck."

I blink hard because I definitely thought she said something else.

On the wall is a stuffed duck the size of an average child and I can't escape the thought of it sitting in the corner of Halle's room while we sleep at night. Thankfully, Halle isn't good at this game, either. When her turn is over, she looks disappointed. More than when she was bad at any of the other games. Why do I care so much?

"Can we go again, please?" I ask the guy.

"But I'm so bad," Halle groans.

"You're fucking terrible. You're in carnival time-out—stand to the side."

It isn't even hard, and the more rings that land on the bottles, the more excited she gets, which results in her cheering me on.

"Please stop shouting."

"Sorry, sorry. Go, Henry," she whispers. "You can do it."

She's right and I do, leading me to say something I never thought I'd ever have to say. "We'll have the massive duck, please."

"My hero." She accepts the duck and can only just fit her arm around it. "I'm going to call him Henry."

"Please don't." She looks so happy it makes me ache. "What else do you want?"

We retrace our steps, going back to every counter we walked away from empty-handed. I shoot hoops, guns, balls, beanbags, and kick soccer balls until you can't see Halle under the pile of stuffed animals. Halle's staring at me like I personally made them for her.

There's a massive cow tucked under my arm and two bears in my hands as we find a bench at the end of the pier. I take a seat and Halle unloads her haul beside me to find herself seatless. "Didn't think this through," she mutters, trying to stack them to make room.

I hand her the bears and pat my lap, indicating for her to sit. She looks at her pile of prizes then back at me and opts to sit on my knee. "This is my favorite day since I moved to LA. I can't decide if that's sweet or sad. I think I'm edging toward sweet. Thank you, Henry."

"Thank you for not making me watch you continue to lose."

Her arm rests across my shoulders and she looks straight at me. Her face is close to mine and I concentrate on her mouth as she talks. "Look, I know hockey is your thing or whatever, but . . . have you ever considered a professional career in carnival games? Because you're really annoyingly good. And don't tell me you're good at everything, because not every guy can just walk up to a game and win it."

My eyes meet hers. "If he wanted to, he would."

"That's what the word on the street is."

I rest one of my hands on her thigh and she leans in to me as we listen to the ocean beneath the pier. The one thing about dates with Halle versus every other date I've been on is I don't want them to end. With everyone else, I've looked forward to going home—alone or to hook up. With Halle, even though it's not strictly a real date, I want it to keep going.

"You're being very quiet," she whispers.

"It's my brand."

"What're you daydreaming about?"

You. Always you. "Telling Bobby that he has to give up his seat in your car because of your massive duck and it's friends."

She starts laughing, and it's the only sound I'd choose over quiet. "I'll let him name them. Is it maybe time to join the group aspect of our group date?"

"What if I said I enjoy not having to share you?"

She swivels in my lap to look at me properly, and her ass pressed against me reminds me how long it's been since I had sex. "I'd say share me now and have me to yourself again later. I need to write but you can stay tonight . . . if you want to, that is."

I'm not always great at reading facial expressions, but I feel like I can read Halle pretty well. She looks hopeful, and I know it's everything to do with wanting to get to know people better. Halle thinks she's an introvert, but she isn't. I'm an introvert. Sure, she likes doing things like reading and writing, which are solitary activities, but she's her happiest surrounded by people.

I can only imagine how difficult the past few years have been for her. Desperately craving connection only to be left alone or unappreciated by people who don't get her.

"I want to stay," I say. "Let's go hang out with other people then. But just know, I'm only doing it to further your romantic experiences."

"I think there are definitely other things we could be doing to further my romantic experiences besides hanging out with Kris and Bobby, but I'll take it."

The breeze is blowing her hair, sun bouncing off the high points of her face. I reach out slowly, using my finger to tuck the strands dancing across her cheek behind her ear. She looks so beautiful; I wish I could capture her right now, but even with a paintbrush or pencil in my hand, I fear I wouldn't do her justice. I wonder if she'd believe me if I told her.

She should be told. She should hear it every single day, but would she like it if I was the one saying it to her?

"There are," I say. "I could give you a list." My eyes flit to her lips. Anastasia's voice plays in my head, repeating that the pier would be a romantic place for a first kiss. Does Halle want to be kissed? I've never been so unsure before. "You look beautiful right now. Is that okay for me to say?"

The hand of the arm around me cradles the side of my neck. She shifts slightly in my lap. "Do you really mean that?" I nod. "Then it's okay for you to say."

I wonder how many other complimentary things it would be okay for me to say. We're so close our noses could touch if we leaned forward slightly. She smells like cotton candy and the vanilla of her hair products. I inch closer *slightly*. "Halle . . ."

"Henry," she says quietly in the only way I want to hear her say my name from now on. I cup her cheek and her free hand covers mine. Her eyes look past me. "We have an audience."

Whipping around to check where she's looking, I see our friends standing with ice cream cones thirty feet from where we're sitting. As soon as they realize we've noticed them they start walking toward us, when all I want to do is to yell at them to disappear.

Halle removes her arm and puts her hand in her lap with the other. I want to disown my friends. Bobby takes a long, unbothered lick from his ice cream as he stops in front of the bench. "Tell me that duck is not sitting next to me in the car."

Chapter Sixteen

HALLE

WHEN HENRY ASKED IF I wanted to grab lunch with him after class, it didn't occur to me that I wouldn't feel cool enough walking through the art building.

The same way Grayson stole all the athletic genes, Mom saved all the artistic genes for Maisie. Sure, I can string a sentence together—sometimes—and read a five-hundred-page romantasy book in a day, but as I take in the creations around me, it doesn't quite feel the same.

Following the directions Henry gave me, I find the sculpture studio easily, and as much as I hate to admit it, I'm slightly disappointed to find him already sitting there with his bag ready to go. He looks up from his cell phone as I approach, smiling in a way that makes me believe he's truly happy to see me.

"I was hoping you were still with your professor so I could find your work," I say, pouting playfully as he stands, throwing his bag over his shoulder.

He puts his arm across my shoulder in the super friendly way we are with each other. That super friendly way that doesn't make me question my entire existence one bit. "You're sixty seconds too late, Cap. I just finished."

He's using his arm to guide me toward the exit. "Are you really not going to let me look? I'm mad that you won't show me your work."

"Aw," he says, but there's nothing sympathetic about his tone. "You're going to have a really tough time being mad forever, huh?"

I'm still being guided away like the puppet I am when it comes to this man's hands. "I've never wanted to see something so bad in my life."

"I draw for you all the time."

"You draw *on* me all the time. Or draw *me* all the time. It isn't the same—I already know what I look like."

He sighs, but again, there's nothing about his tone or demeanor that makes me think he's not finding this really fun. "Art is personal to me. I don't show anyone voluntarily, so it isn't you. But if you want to fight about it, I don't see you offering to let me read your book."

Damn it. He's smiling so big because he knows he's got me right where he wants me. "That's because it's less book and more chaotic ramblings of a woman who daydreams too much and spends her time finding the perfect playlist when she should be writing. Anyway, don't distract me when we're talking about you."

"But I love distracting you." Henry holds the door to the hallway open for me, and walking through it feels like defeat. I do it anyway, but only because I'm considering the potential implications of me breaking into the sculpture studio later. "Stop scheming, Halle."

"I'm not!"

"You are. You get pouty when you're plotting. You do it when you're working on your book. Where do you want to go for lunch?" he asks, pressing the button for the elevator.

"I'm not talking to you until you agree to tell me what you're working on."

"You underestimate how much I like the quiet." My mouth opens to argue back, but I've got nothing. Pressing the button for the ground floor, Henry pushes my mouth closed with his knuckle. "My project is to re-create a popular sculpture in my own style using influences from a different art period. My piece is a reimagined Renaissance sculpture, using influences from Harlem Renaissance artists like Augusta Savage. My version is much smaller than the original and I'm using clay. Happy now?"

"If your goal was to make me want to see it even more, you won. Is that all the detail I'm getting? Not even which sculpture you're reimagining?"

"Not even. I don't trust you not to go looking for it. And I always win, Halle." The elevator doors open and he ushers me out, wise, since I really want to go back upstairs. "Now what do you want for lunch?"

The idea of Henry creating something so special and me never getting to see it makes me sad, but I understand not wanting people to see something you've created. He's waiting for my answer, and all I can think of is him tirelessly working to make something beautiful.

"Something I can use my hands on. You've inspired me."

"I have a suggestion, but it will need both hands." He holds the door to the courtyard open and I duck under his arm. Looking back at him over my shoulder, I watch as the door closes behind him. His expression slips into something slightly scandalized, but mainly amused. I love how happy he is after time in the studio versus a classroom. "Burgers, Halle. I know that look; get your mind out of the gutter. Let's go to Blaise's."

"My mind wasn't in the gutter." It *so* was, and the butterflies in my stomach agree. "Fine, let's go. But you can't judge me if it doesn't fit in my mouth."

For the first time in the two months we've been friends, I've caught him off guard. The look on his face is . . . enjoyable.

"Touché."

WHEN WE ARRIVED AT BLAISE'S earlier, it was closed for maintenance, so we went to a different place close to school.

Fifteen minutes into a debate with Aurora about the book we were analyzing for our class, my phone started buzzing with messages from Henry about him feeling sick. The messages continued throughout the afternoon with increasing levels of self-pity until he finished at hockey practice, went home for his overnight bag, and turned up on my doorstep.

I haven't seen Henry sick before, but I'm quickly discovering that it turns him into a massive baby. Looking over to where he's sprawled across the length of my couch, I see Joy is happily purring on his lap as he scratches behind her ears. The two of them have become the best of friends, and it's getting increasingly more difficult not to be jealous.

"Do you need anything? I'm helping Gigi with her homework soon." The last thing I need is for him to walk shirtless behind my laptop.

"Attention. Sympathy. A cure," he says, his deep voice monotone as he lists his requirements. "A do-over where I didn't eat a suspicious-smelling hamburger."

"Feeling real good about the chicken burger you called boring right about now. I can offer you freezer homemade chicken soup and at best a half-sympathetic pat on the back." He scowls at me. "No, seriously. I'm sorry you don't feel great. I promise to give you all the attention and sympathy when I'm done."

"Thanks. I'm good. I had chicken soup already and yours won't be as good as mine."

"Where did you get chicken soup?" I ask, powering up my laptop and not even bothering to defend the integrity of my soup. Henry stretches his arms up; the ripped muscles of his stomach flex as he reaches above his head. He twists, fluffing up the cushions before rolling onto his side and repositioning Joy next to his chest on the couch so they're both looking at me.

"My mom dropped it off on her way to work when I called her looking for attention, sympathy, and a cure."

"You are so spoiled." He smiles like he knows it. "What does your mom do? What's her name? So I don't confuse your moms."

"Yasmine. She's a surgeon at Cedars-Sinai, but she volunteers at a nonprofit in her free time, so she was heading there to do a few hours at the clinic when she dropped off my soup."

I want to know every little thing about him, and I don't think he realizes how much. "What does the nonprofit do?"

"Advocate for Black women who need medical support. They're disproportionately impacted by medical negligence or insufficient care, and are more likely to go undiagnosed because of institutional racism."

He looks like he's about to stop explaining, but I imagine it's the information-hungry look on my face that encourages him to continue.

"She volunteers in the clinic for people who aren't being listened to by their own doctor or because they don't have access to a doctor. And sometimes she does talks about racial bias in the medical industry at hospital events. Mama is also a doctor and she used to volunteer at the clinic with her, but not that much now that she's teaching."

"She sounds amazing, Henry. They both do. Where does your mama teach? What's she called?"

He looks at me like I just asked him for the winning lottery numbers. "Maple Hills. She's called Maria. Do you not already know this?"

"Clearly not," I say, rolling my eyes playfully. "What made her start teaching?"

He yawns, covering his mouth with the back of his hand, and I swear he's doing it because he knows how interested I am. "College was rough for her at first because her parents stopped talking to her. She says she had no queer professors that proved to her success was waiting. She wants the people who need that to be able to get it from her. Great career, wife, kid, etcetera."

"Were you ever tempted to follow in their footsteps and go into medicine, too? Or was it always art for you?"

"Mom went to med school because both of my grandparents were doctors, and it was important to her to carry on their legacy by helping her community. Her parents had her when they were older so she's an only child, too. Mama went to med school because she wanted a job that paid her enough to never have to ask her homophobic parents for financial support, and she wanted to help people. I never had those kinds of pressures, so I've always followed my passions, which are sports and art."

"I love hearing about your family," I admit honestly. "I could listen to you talk about yourself all day."

He smiles but buries his head into Joy to hide it. Lifting his head, he brushes her white hair off the bridge of his nose and leans against his hand. "Did you have to wait until I'm sick before quizzing me on my life?"

"I need you incapacitated so you sit still long enough to quiz you. One last question because Gigi is going to call me any minute. Why art? I know you're talented, but why not a sports major or something?"

Henry's quiet while he thinks, and I say a tiny prayer that Gigi doesn't call before I get my answer. "It's always been a way to say the things I didn't know how to. Especially when I was younger and I wasn't as talkative as I am now. Don't raise your eyebrow at me; this is my version of talkative. Art tells a story; it can change people's minds or reaffirm their beliefs. I've spent my life worrying about saying the wrong thing. I can't get art wrong."

The video call ringtone starts to sound out of my laptop and I've never had the urge to throw it at a wall quite like I do now. "I lied! I have so many questions," I say, how frantic I suddenly feel clear in my tone.

"You ran out of time, Cap," he says, lying back on the cushions. "And I'm very sick, so I'm going to take a nap until you're done."

"This isn't over," I say, pushing my hair behind my ears and positioning my laptop on the arm of my chair.

"I look forward to round two," he says, shutting his eyes.

I click accept, and Gigi fills my screen. "You took your time."

"Hello to you, too," I say back, watching her move through our house. "You're giving me motion sickness. What's happening?"

The framed pictures lining the staircase come into view as she descends the stairs. "Your mom wants to talk to you. Can you convince her to let me get a belly button piercing?"

"Uh, no. Is that even legal?"

Gigi sits down on the stairs, leaning into the laptop camera. "With consent from a legal guardian. Please, Halle. I *really* want one. All my friends have them, it isn't fair."

"There's no way in hell she's going to give you permission. You should get your mom to take you when she gets home."

Gi sighs dramatically in the calculated way she does to try to make me feel bad about not helping with her latest scheme. "I already asked her when she called, and she said no."

This child. "And you think my mom is going to go against your mom why, exactly?"

"Because you're so persuasive, Hallebear. If you really wanted to you would help me!" Grayson is so lucky that I never put him through this. "Please, please, please. I'll never ask you for anything ever again."

"Aren't you supposed to be delivering me to my mom for something?"

Gigi rolls her eyes, standing from the stairs again, and even through the unsophisticated laptop speaker, I can hear how hard she's stomping. I can hear the TV and Maisie talking to her dad as Gigi walks through the house before I'm shoved into my unsuspecting mother's path while she appears to be in the kitchen.

"Oof," she says. "I'll bring it up to you when I'm done, Gi."

I don't even get a *see you later* before she—I imagine—storms off. "Hi, Mom."

Mom puts Gigi's laptop on the kitchen table and there's a stab of longing when I realize I'm not going to be home for a while. "Hi, honey. Can you believe that girl wants me to go against Lucia and take her to get her belly button pierced?"

"I can believe that, yeah. What's up? I have a lot to do tonight and I haven't looked at her homework yet."

Mom launches into a recap of Maisie's dance recital, which apparently is not the thing she wanted to speak to me about, before moving on to how nice it would be if Grayson was traded to a West Coast team. She keeps going and going, so much so that she doesn't even hear Henry's loud yawn. "Anyway, Gianna has decided she *does* want to go to college, and she wants to go on some college tours with her friends. Can you find some time to go with her? She said she wants a college in California since that's where her mom will be settling when she gets home. A girls' trip sounds fun! Right?"

When Grayson and I both went off to college, Gianna always said she wasn't going, even as a little kid. She said she wanted to learn how to look after plants, so our conversations switched to trade schools whenever she'd ask. Everything was good until we realized she hated school because she didn't have the support she needed, and she incorrectly thought working with plants wouldn't need much studying.

"It's far too early for her to be doing college tours, Mom. She's barely a sophomore. Why can't she wait until next year?" I say.

"I know, honey. But I don't want to discourage her. Her new friends are talking about college and it's got her excited, and if that's what she wants, I don't want her to think we're not supporting her."

I feel bad for my mom because she's trying her best to be a good stepparent. I know she worries a lot about doing the wrong thing, and about Lucia thinking that she treats Gigi different from her own children or is less supportive of her goals. "I can, but could we have this talk again after spring break? I could talk to her while we're on vacation and we can go from there."

"Sure! Thank you, Hallebear. I'll let you get back to your study session."

When I'm back in the familiar surroundings of Gigi's bedroom, she appears to have gotten over her earlier tantrum. "Well? Did you get her to change her mind?"

Why she's so intent on piercing herself I'll never know. "I'm working on it, kid."

"You are such a bad liar," she says, rolling her eyes.

When I finally close my laptop, both my own work and Gigi's work now complete, my head feels like it's melting. Henry, still claiming to be unwell but also claiming to be hungry, gives me a long list of things he wants when I place an order for takeout to be delivered.

"Do you need attention, sympathy, and a cure?" Henry asks, peeping at me from beneath the forearm he lays across his eyes.

Rubbing my tired eyes with my palms, I nod. "Yes."

"Come join our pity party," he says, putting Joy on his chest and shuffling to the edge to create a gap between him and the back couch cushions.

There's no graceful way for me to get into that space, and when I try, Henry pulls me down onto him so I'm half in the gap and half on him. I'm forever wondering when this level of contact became the norm for us, but I'm scared that if I ask him it'll stop.

"Why is Joy in the pity party?" I ask, reaching to run my hand down her back.

"She's an empath," he says.

"Is that so? I've had an empath cat this whole time and didn't know."

"Uh-huh. The fact you didn't know is another reason she should live with me," he mumbles, resting his chin on the top of my head.

My mouth opens to argue back, but he quickly interrupts. "I don't want to hear about Robbie's *alleged* allergy."

"Why do you like her so much? I mean, I love her because she's my cat, but why do you like her so much?"

"Question time is over," he says, tucking a stray strand of my hair behind my ear.

"Please, Henry. One more. You promised me round two."

The three of us lie together on the couch in the quiet of my house. I begin to think maybe he's ignoring me, or he's fallen asleep, but then he holds Joy to his chest as he rolls onto his side so we're almost face to face.

She hates her new spot between us and runs off, settling in her seat on the back of the couch cushions, leaving the two of us stomach to stomach, my nose level with his chin. He looks down as I look up, watching his mouth as he wets his bottom lip with his tongue. "Because she's sweet, and I like her funny little personality. I love when she's affectionate, and I love that she lets me hold her as much as I want to. She makes me feel calm and I like that she likes me, too."

"She's a very good cat like that," I whisper, because talking loud feels like too much with how close we are.

"She is," he whispers back.

There's a moment when our breathing synchronizes and our eyes meet that I think maybe Henry Turner would be an experience I wouldn't survive. That having him talk about me the way he talks about Joy could devastate me beyond repair.

But then the doorbell rings, letting us know our food has arrived. And I remember that there's never been a long list of complimentary adjectives that follow when people talk about me anyway.

Chapter Seventeen

HALLE

THE ENTIRE ROOM ERUPTS INTO cheers when the Titans clinch the win in the last ten seconds.

I've been going to hockey games for years, but there's nothing like seeing this kind of result, *knowing* how relieved Henry will be. Aurora is jumping up and down, too, and honestly you'd think *we'd* personally done something.

Henry told me they'd win if I wore the present he'd gotten me—the present being his jersey. I always feel like I'm comparing, but having fun today with Aurora really feels so different from when I sat with other girlfriends at Will's games.

We've been chatting—okay, borderline debating about which is the better sport—with the guys sitting next to us all game. I have a football family because of Grayson, Aurora's is obviously motor-sport, and the guy who's name I never quite caught has a brother who's a baseball player. Thankfully we had hockey to unite us, and as silly as it was, it was fun to interact with new people and not stress about it.

As we pick up our cups from the floor and grab our purses to leave, the nameless guy stops me. "Hey, would I be able to get your number? Kinda wanna debate the whole football-versus-baseball thing a bit more. You seem cool."

I'm so confused. I look to Aurora, who just gives me a look that says, well?

"Oh, sorry. Uh, um. No? Sorry, that's rude. I just kinda—" I have no idea where I'm going with this.

"She's pining for someone else," Aurora says with a smile, putting me out of this particular misery, but very firmly into another one.

"Got it," he says. "Was good to meet y'all."

"Really?" I say when he's out of earshot.

Aurora shrugs. "Tell me you wanted to give him your number, and then I'll apologize."

I huff. "Touché."

As soon as I reach my car, I pull out my phone to text Henry.

HENRY TURNER

> Still campaigning for you to switch to carnival games, but I guess that was a pretty spectacular win.

Thanks Cap

Where are you?

> Cami is sick. I'm taking her a care package.

Where was my care package when I was sick?

> I gave you dim sum and didn't complain when you threw it all up.

Fair.

Can I make it up to you later?

> Yup. I'll text you when I'm leaving Cami's.

The massive duck has to go in a different room.

> Quack Efron lives there and you don't.

I hate Bobby so, so much.

Hurry. I miss Joy.

There are women in Maple Hills who would give an organ to have Henry talk about them the way he talks about my cat.

After a quick visit to the grocery store, I pull into the parking lot of Cami's building as Will's name flashes up on my caller ID. I nearly crash my car into one of the bushes lining the concrete. After the initial shock subsides, it's the easiest rejection of my life. He probably played today, too, and he probably saw my story from the game. I have zero desire to argue with someone who only wants to speak to me when he's—jealous? I don't even know—calling to try to make me feel bad about something.

By the time I reach Cami's front door, I've talked myself in and out of calling him back. In because what if something has happened to him or his family, then out, because my mom isn't also calling me. In because what if he wants to fix our friendship, then out, because if that was the case he'd start by text.

Cami's door opens and she looks like a deer in headlights. Her red hair is braided over her shoulder and she's wearing her pajamas. There's been something off about her recently at work and I haven't been able to put my finger on why. She's quieter, I think. Her normal confident demeanor almost feels like it's been muted.

My biggest sign that something is up with her is that she's started being on time for work. She's *never* on time for anything. And when a guest yelled at her, she didn't argue back even a little bit. I hold up the paper bag. "I brought you chicken noodle soup and some other healthy-looking things."

"Oh, Halle," she says gently. "Come in and sit down."

I know her roommates are all out because I was just with them, and it was Ava who told me she was sick. Ava agreed with me that she doesn't seem herself recently, but when I asked if she knew why, she changed the subject. I think there's a small part of me that's worried I've done something and nobody wants to tell me.

"How are you feeling?" I ask, taking a spot on the couch.

She sits across from me and pulls her legs up against her chest, hugging them. "I've been better. Thank you for bringing me food."

"Have I done something to upset you?" I ask. I hate how desperate it sounds as it leaves my lips. I hate how desperate it makes me feel. "I want to apologize if I have."

There's a visible change to shock on Cami's face. "What? No, oh my God. Of course you haven't done something to upset me."

"I can take it if I have. I'm kind of inexperienced in the whole friend department, as you know. And, well, I just don't want to be that friend that doesn't apologize when they need to apologize."

"Halle, you have nothing to apologize for. It's me. It's my head. It's all fucked up. I, ugh." She wipes her hands against her face. "Someone put something in my drink at the Take Back December gig, and, no, no, don't look panicked, nothing happened. Poppy was spiked, too, and Ava realized something was up immediately and took us to the ER. We were lucky."

"There's nothing lucky about having your drink spiked. I'm so, so sorry that happened to you. I swear I didn't know or I wouldn't have come here and made it about me."

"You haven't! And I didn't want anyone to know because, well, I've been roofied before. Senior year of high school. I wasn't as lucky that time," she says, and my stomach sinks. "I really don't want to talk about it if I'm being honest. It's just shaken me a little and I'll get through it. I just don't want you thinking you've done something, Hals. You haven't. I just need to be by myself to process and then I'll be back to normal, I swear. I'm going to skip tomorrow, though. I don't think a Halloween party is where I should be with the way I'm feeling, but I swear I'll be back to normal soon."

There's a million different emotions I'm experiencing finding out something like this happened. Not one of them is bigger than rage for my friend. "You don't need to be back to normal; I just want you to be okay. Is there anything I can do to help you? I can hang out with you tomorrow night so you're not alone."

She shakes her head. "I really do process better alone, but thank you. I'm a good compartmentalizer."

"Is that a good or bad thing?"

She laughs, but I still see the pain in her eyes. "I dunno, but we'll find out."

"Do you want to hang out on Sunday? We could go for breakfast or go shopping, maybe? I hear what you're saying about processing better alone, I really do, but I also feel like you shouldn't do this alone, and I know your best friends don't live around here anymore, and I'm not them but—" I'm rambling. I'm rambling *so* bad. She lived with Summer and Briar for four years before they graduated, and I don't want her to think I think I'm equal to that level of trust and friendship. "I just feel like—"

"Halle," she says, laughing as she interrupts me. "Breakfast would be fun. Blaise's diner? What time is too early for you if you're going to The Honeypot? I sleep through my alarm when I'm hung-over."

"Anytime works for me. I'm not going to get drunk." She doesn't gasp in horror or do anything other than look through the grocery bag I gave her, pulling out snacks. "I've learned I'm a really anxious and emotional hungover person. Hopefully I won't be boring and people will still want to hang out with me."

She stops rummaging through the bag and looks at me. "Summer didn't get drunk for the exact same reason. Me and Briar actually convinced her to stop because we couldn't deal with her thinking the world was going to end every time she had more than two glasses of wine. It doesn't make you boring."

"I know that logically. Like, seriously, I know I'm being ridiculous and peer pressure should not be something I'm thinking about when I'm a literal adult. But—"

"But you're worried that if you don't want to do what everyone else does, that they won't invite you and you'll be alone," she says, plucking the words from my head. "I get it. That ex and his friends really did a number on your self-worth, huh?"

Oh. That was an unexpected twist. "I guess. I don't know, I haven't really thought of it like that. The self-worth thing: they definitely thought I was boring when I look back."

"Just because they didn't appreciate how great you are to be around doesn't mean the rest of us don't. Also, soda is statistically less roofied than alcoholic drinks, so, a win is a win." The shock must show on my face because she frowns. "What? How else am I supposed to cope if I can't make jokes about it?"

"Campbell, do you need a hug?" I ask.

"Oh God, you full-named me." She's laughing, but I watch as my words settle, and she nods. "Yeah. I sort of do."

I move to the space beside her that isn't covered in healthy snacks and wrap my arms around her shoulders. She hugs me back, and we sit there quietly until she speaks. "Your boobs are really comfy."

"Thanks."

"You should go before I fall asleep on you."

"You sure? I can stay. I'll just need to text Henry to let him know I'm busy."

"No, you're good. Need to get back to my compartmentalizing anyway. Breakfast at ten?"

"Yup. See you there."

I'M STILL THINKING ABOUT CAMI and the other people who had their lives impacted in the worst way that night as I pull up outside my house.

Henry is sitting on my porch, and like a bad fucking omen, Will's name comes up on my caller ID again. Henry stands with his sketch pad and overnight bag, mouthing, "Are you okay?" when I don't get out of the car.

Reluctantly, I press answer, rationalizing I'd rather get it over with now instead of having him potentially call all night. "Hey. What's up?"

"Since when does it take calling you six times to get you to answer?"

"Since when do you call me?"

"Your sister is here," he says flatly.

That gets my attention. "What do you mean *your sister is here*? Where? Where are you?"

"You sure forgot my schedule quickly, Hallebear," he says, and if I could reach through the phone and shake him I would.

"What the hell would Gigi be doing in San Diego on a Friday night? Are you trying to stress me out on purpose or are you just that oblivious?"

"I wouldn't call me oblivious when one of us knows why your sister is in the wrong state and one of us doesn't."

I hate him. I hate him so much. "Will, put Gigi on, please."

"She doesn't know I'm calling you. She specifically asked me not to call you, actually. She didn't think you'd be chill about it, and I'm inclined to agree with her. She's safe, though. I'm looking after her."

"I feel like you think I won't drive to San Diego and murder you, but I will. Explain, now."

He laughs, and the urge to get on the road increases dramatically. "I like you when you're feisty. Gianna lied to your parents and said she was going on a campus tour with a friend and friend's parents. Clearly nobody followed up with anyone's parents because the friend is older than Gi and can drive, and they were actually visiting the friend's older sister. Gi and her friend had an argument about sneaking into a party and the friend said bye-bye. I got a call after my game—won by the way, thanks for asking—from your sister, asking if you were here, then when I said no, she asked for a place to crash. And because I'm a good guy, I said yes."

Gianna's sudden interest in college tours now makes sense.

"Where is she now?" I ask Will.

"She's downstairs watching TV with the guys."

"You left my baby sister alone with your roommates? For fuck's sake, Will. Go get her! My mom is going to flip."

"I think you should come down. We can work out a plan to return her and probably avoid telling your mom altogether."

Henry's looking really concerned by my front door as I look between him and my windshield. "Fine. I'll leave in a second. Do not let her out of your sight. I mean it, Will. Make sure everyone knows she's a minor. If I get there and they're so much as looking in her direction, I will burn down your house."

"Whoa. Jesus, Hals," he says, and I've shocked myself as much as I've shocked him. I think I'm still reeling from finding out my friends had their drinks spiked, and I've never liked Will's roommates. As not funny as this situation is, it's funny to think that if Gigi had turned up on Henry's doorstep, I'd have no worries about leaving her in the care of his friends. "I'll make them all wear blindfolds if it makes you happy. Just get here."

As soon as I climb out of my car Henry walks toward me. "I need to go to San Diego. It's a long story, can I call you from the car to explain?"

"Do you need me to come?" Henry asks.

"No, no. It's just little sister stuff, and you have a game tomorrow. Would you be able to feed Joy for me and hang out with her for a little while? If you can't, I can ask Mrs. Astor to take her until I'm back."

"Cat duty. Got it," he says. His hands cup my neck and I instinctively gravitate toward him, his lips press against the crown of my head. I want him to do it a million more times. "Call me if you need me. I'm pretty sure Aurora can charter a helicopter or a jet."

I still haven't determined when Henry's touch became soothing to me, but I sink into him, resting my cheek against his chest. "I'll call you from the road, promise."

THE ONLY POSITIVE THING ABOUT the drive to Will's is getting a chance to catch up on my audiobook for book club. Literally the *only* positive.

When I called Henry to explain, his first question was how could a kid leave the state and her parents have no idea she was lying to them. My mom and stepdad aren't negligent, although I accept that this isn't their greatest work. I would've never even considered doing this at Gigi's age, and Grayson had no reason to sneak around because he got away with everything anyway. They're just inexperienced.

Henry's second point was she's lucky she was at a college where she knew someone, but the alternative is not something I can stomach right now.

There's an unmistakable unsettled feeling in my gut as I pull up in front of Will's place. I've been here so many times, and yet a little time away and a new group of friends have made me realize how not unwelcome, but not welcome I was. The reception I receive when I go to Henry or Cami's house compared to here is so different. But I truly didn't realize at the time.

Knocking on the door hard, I can hear laughter on the other side, and see Gigi and Will's roommates when he finally opens the door. "Hi, baby," he says, leaning in to kiss me. I don't think he's ever called me "baby" before.

I dodge him like he's a bullet. "What are you doing?"

He pulls me closer to him by the waist, leaning in again slower this time to kiss my cheek. He lowers his voice. "You didn't tell her we broke up. So pretend that you love me. Shouldn't be hard for you."

His face lingers near mine, but having him so close makes me uneasy. I can't remember if I used to feel like this, or if I was just better at suppressing it.

I step around him and focus on Gigi on the couch looking guilty. "What the hell are you playing at?"

"It isn't my fault," she says immediately.

"It's never your fault, Gianna. Stuff just happens to you and you're never to blame. That's how this goes, right?"

Will's roommates immediately stand and shuffle toward the backyard.

"You're not my mom, Halle. You don't get to talk to me like this. I'm not a child!"

"I know I'm not your mom. Do you think I want to parent you? Do you think I want to cancel my Friday night plans to drive here to argue with you?"

"You love telling me what to do, so maybe this is your idea of a good time."

"Do you know how lucky you are that Will goes here? Do you have any idea what happens to girls alone at night in this country? To them in the middle of the day? You're irresponsible, Gianna, and actually, you are a child. You are literally a child, and the fact you think I'm going to put up with your attitude when you're in the wrong freaking state is *wild*. How could you be so reckless with your safety? What if Will was at an away game? What would you have done?"

"Okay, okay . . ." Will says, stepping closer to me. He stands behind me and rubs his hands up and down my arms. "I think maybe you're escalating things that don't need to be escalated, Hals. Let's not terrify the poor girl. She made a mistake and she's sorry."

"I already talked to my friend. She said she'll drive me home with her in the morning like we planned, but she wants tonight to cool off from our fight. You didn't even need to come. It isn't a big deal."

I immediately spin to face Will. He holds up both hands defensively. "I don't want an unsupervised minor in my house any more than you want her here. She didn't tell me it was fixed until you were already on the road, and I didn't want to distract you when you were driving. Stop looking at me like you're going to rip my head off, Hals."

"Oh no, you have to see your boyfriend unexpectedly," Gigi mumbles, and it just shows how out of touch she is with how mad at her I am. "Poor Halle."

"We broke up, Gi. Two months ago," I say flatly, getting a twisted sense of satisfaction at the way her eyes widen in shock. Not because it's an enjoyable topic, but just because her attitude sucks. "I had no desire to come here unexpectedly."

For the first time in the ten years Gianna has been my sister, she's speechless.

"I'm happy to see you even if you're not happy to see me," Will says as he takes a seat beside Gigi on the couch. I purposely walk to a chair on the other side of the room. Out of all the people in the world I'm mad at, they're the top two. "It's like old times—the three of us hanging out together. You telling Halle she isn't your mom. Halle blowing things out of proportion. It feels nostalgic. You two can take my bed and I'll sleep in one of the other rooms."

"We're not staying," I say quickly, looking at Will and not Gigi, whose attitude has definitely softened in the past thirty seconds. The arms folded defiantly across her chest are now tucked in as she picks at her nails on her lap. Her head is hanging lower, with lips pressed into a hard line.

"Halle, look. I know you're mad and I get it. She's like my little sister, too, but just stay. You're not going to be able to get a hotel and you can't drive back to Maple Hills to come back with her in the morning. So just stay. I miss hanging out with both of you."

"Fine. Gi, go upstairs, please. I'll be up in a minute," I say to her, and thankfully she goes without any argument. I turn to Will. "Do you have something to wear to bed, please? I'm going to need to go straight to work in the morning, so I don't want to sleep in my clothes."

He's looking at me like he just won, and I don't know why. "A clean load of laundry just finished. I'll get you a T-shirt. If you don't want to sleep next to her, you can share with me."

I ignore him. I don't even have an answer for that. Pulling out my phone when he disappears in the direction of the utility room, I see Henry sent me a video. It starts on the TV with my baking show, and pans around to him, shirtless, with Joy asleep in the center of his chest.

HENRY TURNER

Video message

We miss you.

How's it going there?

> I'm going to stay over with Gigi, then drive back in the morning.

> Wish I was with you guys. I called Mrs. Astor on my way here and said you'd drop Joy by when you leave.

Wish I'd come with you.

> I'm not sure how well not turning up for your game would rank on the being a good leader scale.

> Heading to bed. Good luck for tomorrow

> 🖤

Night, Cap. Lock your door.

"That the new guy?" Will says as he reappears holding a T-shirt with his college's crest on it.

I lock my screen quickly, but it's pointless given my background is also Henry, since I didn't change it after Henry set it himself. I don't think he saw more than a glimpse, so I quickly move on before he starts asking. "Thank you for calling me, Will. I appreciate it."

"Why are you being so formal with me?" he asks. "You've never been this formal with me."

Honestly, it's because I don't feel like I know him anymore. I'm uncomfortable and awkward around him, and I'm struggling to remember that at one time he was my closest friend. "I'm sorry. I'm just tired from the drive, and school and—"

"Yeah," he says, interrupting me. "I want to talk more, Hals. I mean it. I don't like this distance between us and there's no reason for it. We should do something, just me and you, when we're home for Thanksgiving. Dinner and a movie, maybe."

I don't know if it's the surprise or the stress of the evening, but it takes four times as long for me to blink. "But I'm not going home for Thanksgiving . . . We agreed months ago."

He shrugs nonchalantly, and for some reason, it enrages me. "I think we were being dramatic."

Disbelief. Pure disbelief. "But I've already agreed to work . . . You couldn't have mentioned that you thought we were being dramatic before now?"

"I didn't realize you thought it was such a big deal. Just switch your shift with someone."

"I can't just switch my shift. Everyone has plans for the holidays. I haven't even told my mom yet because I know she's going to be mad. I can't believe you've just changed your mind and didn't tell me."

"Baby . . ."

"Why are you calling me that?" I snap, standing from my seat. I take the T-shirt and head toward the stairs. "Thank you for helping with my sister. I'm going to bed."

I ignore him calling after me as I climb the stairs, and when I enter his room with Gigi already in bed, I do lock the door like Henry said.

"I'm sorry," Gigi says quietly.

"I know."

"I won't be irresponsible again," she says after I change and climb into the bed beside her.

"You will."

"I'm sorry you and Will broke up."

I turn off the beside lamp and pull the covers over us both. "I'm not."

Chapter Eighteen

HENRY

"THIS IS NOT WHAT WE agreed," Bobby snaps, looking Russ up and down.

"What happened to team spirit?" Mattie adds, planting his hands on his hips. "What happened to flavortown?"

Aurora scoffs as she repositions her ear headband. "Yeah, sorry guys. I'm not making out with Guy Fieri tonight. I have a boyfriend for the first time in my life. I'm doing cute couple shit on Halloween."

"Your whiskers are smudged," I point out to her. Russ blushes the way he does about everything, so I don't bother telling him that he has whisker residue on his face. It doesn't take a genius to work out why they're late. "Why are you a mouse in a chef's hat?" I ask Aurora.

"I'm Remy!" She looks offended, like she expects me to have any idea what she's talking about. I think she recognizes the blank expression that's no doubt on my face because she clarifies. "From *Ratatouille*! Russ is Linguini. And I'm a rat, not a mouse."

"If I knew there were options outside of this I'd have taken them."

"Where's your bunny?" Aurora asks, looking around the group dressed in black flamed shirts, blond-spiked wigs, goatees, and sunglasses.

"Over there taking a call," I say, nodding toward the wall outside The Honeypot, where Halle is flanked by Poppy and Emilia. Aurora has Halle's new fake ID that is apparently indistinguishable from a real ID, so we've been waiting for her to turn up before heading in. "Her mom called because she missed the video call from her little sister in her trick-or-treat costume by accident earlier. I think she's being yelled at."

"How's her outfit?" Aurora asks.

"We're not talking about the outfit," Kris answers before I can, stroking the fake facial hair stuck to his face like a Bond villain. "It's the safest option for everyone involved."

"That good?" Aurora blows out a breath. "You know I had to talk her out of being a clown."

That good is the understatement of the century. I've never had a thing for fictional characters, but Halle as *Space Jam* Lola Bunny might have unlocked something in me. When she told me what she was wearing I assumed she'd wear a rabbit onesie similar to the Minion one I wore last year, maybe with a basketball uniform over the top.

I was only half right, and it wasn't about the rabbit onesie.

Basketball uniform is also a stretch, since what she's wearing is tiny shorts, a bunny tail, thigh-high socks, and a matching top.

Work and hockey interfered with us being able to catch up today after she got home from her ex's place. The desperation to know what happened while she was with him for the first time in two months, coupled with how fucking good she looks right now, is not helping me make sense of my feelings about our friendship.

The fact that I haven't gotten laid in forever also doesn't help my judgment when I'm going to have to look at Halle's curves and ass all night. God, I miss sex.

It's not even that she looks fine; seeing how confident she got when everyone told her how great she looks makes me so proud of her. She thrives in a group setting, and I'm so relieved my friends have accepted her without question.

"Earth to Henry," Aurora says, waving her hand in front of my face. "My God, those bunny ears are really doing a number on you. When are you going to accept that you have feelings for her and ask her out?"

Who did I piss off to end up with two interfering women in my life? "You know rats can't speak, right?"

"Squeak squeak, bestie. Someone's going to beat you to it."

"Do you and Anastasia pass the torch between you for who gets to interfere in my life the most?" I ask, lowering my voice as I spot the girls approaching us. Anastasia and Lola were at our game earlier, and the first thing Anastasia asked me was where Halle was. Not *sorry it was a tie not a win* or *wow, you're so great at hockey*. Thankfully, Lola admitted she didn't make her morning coffee with a jersey on inside out and it allowed me to get the conversation off Halle.

"Yes." Aurora grins, immediately turning to greet Halle, Emilia, and Poppy. She holds out the card to Halle. "I bring gifts."

"Yeah, late," Emilia grumbles, flicking her best friend on the forehead. "I've seen how many watches you own; why are you like this?"

"Would blaming a man be a suitable response?" she asks. "Because I'm totally down to blame Russ."

Mattie comes up behind me, draping his arm across my shoulders as he looks Emilia and Poppy up and down. He uses the temple of his sunglasses to lift a strand of Emilia's blond wig. "What are you two supposed to be?"

"They're Dionne and Cher from *Clueless*," I say, looking between the plaid-skirt-and-blazer combos. "I hate that I know that."

"It's like trying to herd cats," Bobby groans, repositioning his sunglasses on the back of his head. He's done nothing but brag about not needing to wear a wig since his hair is already blond. Between all our outfits, I think we've created a blond wig shortage in LA. "Okay, team Fieri and friends, we are moving *toward* the entrance. It's going to be November before I get a fucking drink at this rate."

I don't know why I feel so nervous every time I go to The Honeypot when I know I get in every time. Daisy, Briar's younger sister, took over the job when Briar graduated. We hooked up once and we're cool when we see each other in the studio. Like her sister, she's happy to let us in on the basis we don't cause any scenes.

I'm doing this for the team. A good leader is there for the wins and losses, and ties in this case. I'm doing this for the team, even though I really don't want to. Everything I've read said I need to make the best of a bad situation, to find the good in the not so good, so that's what I'll try to do tonight when I'd rather be at home.

Aurora booked the table so she goes first into the booth and the rest of us follow. The DJ is playing R&B and not the repetitive techno stuff that makes my head feel like it's going to explode, so that's a good in the bad. I might even be able to enjoy tonight if the music doesn't change.

Daisy stops right in front of me on her way out of the booth, tilting her headset mouthpiece up. She moves onto her tiptoes to bring her mouth to my ear. "I like the shirt. If you're still here at closing, find me."

She's gone before I even have a chance to think of a response, a flash of blond hair and long legs as I watch her head back to her post at the entrance. When I look back at the booth, Halle's watching me with Poppy. Halle gives me a tight smile, then immediately looks away. Poppy doesn't look away, and it's in this accidental staring match that I realize how much she reminds me of my mom sometimes.

It could be how sweet-natured she is, with similar shades of the same kind, hazel eyes. Or that they have a similar rich brown skin tone and long micro-braided dark hair. It's probably that they glare at me in the exact same way when I've done something wrong, though.

I'm not interested in Daisy, but maybe that isn't obvious to people who aren't me. I smile at Poppy, but it seems like the charm everyone claims I have doesn't work on people who don't like men, given she whispers something to Emilia and I see her roll her eyes.

"I don't understand women," I shout to Robbie over the music as I drop myself into the seat beside him out of everyone's line of sight.

"I'd be more worried for you if you thought you did," he responds, rolling himself to the edge of the table, making his drink then pouring me a soda before maneuvering back to the spot beside me. I know Halle is worried people will think she's boring for not getting drunk. They won't, but if they do, they can think I'm boring, too. "You have two goals this year. Pass your classes and don't get on Faulkner's bad side. The rest you can worry about some other time."

I'm listening to Robbie drunkenly explain how we're definitely going to win next week when Aurora reappears at the entrance to the booth with someone I wasn't expecting to see tonight.

"What's Ryan Rothwell doing here?" Robbie asks, looking at me in confusion.

Aurora immediately waves Russ over, and by the fact they do that friendly but borderline awkward handshake Ryan and Nate do, I'd bet that Ryan knows Aurora in the way he seems to know every other woman in the United States. I look a few booths down and recognize some players from the LA Rockets, the NBA team Ryan plays for, with Kitty Vincent and some people I don't know.

I shrug in response to Robbie's question. "Looks like he knows Aurora."

Aurora waves Halle over, and as soon as she's close enough Ryan starts talking to her.

Halle starts laughing, and I've never experienced jealousy so quickly in my life. Robbie is watching just as closely as I am. "Does he know Halle?"

I'm confident as I say, "Halle doesn't know anyone."

Why is everyone laughing? What's so funny that's making every-one so happy? I'm about to get up and walk over, but then Aurora moves out of my line of vision, and I realize that Ryan's dressed as *Space Jam* Bugs Bunny and has the outfit to match Halle's.

Robbie takes a long sip from his drink in my peripheral vision. "It looks like he's trying to get to know Halle. They're basically wear-ing a couple's costume."

"What do I do?" I ask him. I've never needed advice with women before, but I've never cared about who someone talks to before or after me.

"That depends on if you want to sit back and let Ryan take your girl or do something about it. He's capable of it. The guy must have a magic dick."

"She isn't my girl. She's my friend."

"I don't get you," Robbie says, leaning closer so I can hear him better. "I'd get it if you said you wanted to hook up with other people so you don't want to start something with her, but I haven't seen you bring anyone home in—fuck, I don't know. Have you brought some-one home this year?"

"How do you know the difference between liking someone as a friend but being attracted to them, and them being someone you want to have a relationship with? How do you even know when you're ready for a relationship with *anyone*?"

"Oh boy. Where's Jaiden when you need him? You've just gotta take the chance, I guess. Look, I'm not good at this kind of stuff. Uh, imagine your friendship with her stays the same, you still spend time together as much as you do now, but Ryan goes home with her to-night. Next week it might be someone else taking her out on a date, but at the same time, you're still doing whatever the fuck it is that you two do that makes you wanna be with each other every minute of your spare time. How would you feel?"

"Jealous."

"Or the not as nice side of that is she doesn't have as much time for you anymore."

"She wouldn't do that," I argue. I feel like I know Halle. She wouldn't drop me for a guy.

"How much time do you spend with Stas now that you're friends with Halle? I'm not trying to make you feel bad, man, but relationships change things for people. Do you know someone asked Halle for her number yesterday? And she spent last night at her ex's house. What's it going to take for you to step up and do something about your feelings?"

He says it like it's so obvious, but in reality I didn't realize I had feelings for her until very recently, and I'm still working to get my head around it. Robbie is right, though, even though I might not like his delivery.

When I look back over to Halle, she's taking a photograph with Ryan, and they look really good together. I hate how good they look together. I hate the idea of her getting experiences from other people. I don't want her to look at other people the way she looked at me when I won her that fucking ridiculous duck at the pier. Or any of the other shit I won for her.

Ryan drapes his arm across Halle's shoulders while they pose as Aurora takes another picture of them, and it's the nudge I need to do something about it.

"Whatsup, man. Love the costume," Ryan says as I approach them. He pats me on the back in the friendly way I'm accustomed to. "Stassie not with you?"

"Not tonight. Her parents are in town for the weekend."

The worst thing about Ryan Rothwell is how nice he is. Nate always said it and I never understood how the worst thing about someone could be how nice they are. Now I get it. He isn't doing anything wrong and I want to get Daisy to throw him out. It'd be a more tempting option if I thought speaking to Daisy wouldn't result in Halle's friends trying to kick my ass.

Halle takes the spot at my side and looks up, her bunny ears slipping backward. "You okay?"

"Want to dance?" I ask her.

Her eyebrow quirks. I'm as surprised as she is. "Uh, sure." Halle takes my hand and leads me through the crowd to a less crowded spot out of the view of our friends. "Spill it."

"Spill what?"

"What's got you all agitated? You definitely don't voluntarily dance. Do you have your noise reducer things in?"

"It isn't that. I—" She's looking up at me, patiently waiting for me to say something. "Have you been to a Halloween party before?"

"Not since I was a kid. And I've never been in a nightclub before."

Of course she hasn't. "So this is a new experience for you?"

She nods, her bunny ears wiggling. "It's kind of perfect, because I'm writing a chapter that starts in a nightclub."

"What do you need to help you write? What are your imaginary friends up to in this part?"

This is what I'm supposed to be doing. Helping her in return for all the help she's given me. Not thinking about who she is or isn't talking to. I don't ask her about her book as much as I should. She brushes me off all the time if I bring it up.

"They're not imaginary friends! Okay, well, maybe they're imaginary, but anyway. Nothing. I just need to try to write it I guess. My characters—not friends—get into a big fight, and she storms off. He follows her, tells her she's stubborn and awkward, and makes him feel like he's losing his mind. They kiss. It's kind of hard to visualize that while we're dressed like this, though. Maybe we could just dance? And you can tell me what's making you act weird? C'mon."

I don't know how to dance so I follow Halle as she leads me from the quieter edge of the dance floor to the center. Her hands link at the back of my neck, her body pressing into mine so we can still talk with other people behind us. Her heels put us at a closer height.

"Is this okay? If I touch you here?" I ask her when my hands grip her waist gently, feeling her move to the rhythm of the song seamlessly.

She nods, mouth skimming my ear when she leans in so I can hear her. "You don't need to ask me."

"I do. I should. Men should." *How have I steered this conversation in the direction of Halle considering that other men should touch her?* "You deserve only good experiences."

"You're not just men, though, you're you. I like when you touch me. I only get good experiences with you. Henry?"

"Yeah?"

"I know you're dressed up for the occasion, but can we lose the spikes?" she says, nodding toward my hair. "I kinda like the shirt, but I can't concentrate when you look at me."

Music to my fucking ears. Hanging the sunglasses from the button on my shirt, I *joyously* rip that plastic crap the guys got from the Halloween store from my head. "You like the shirt?"

"Mmm." Even though her mouth is next to my ear, I can tell she's smiling. Her body feels so good against mine. She smells so good. Every single thing about her is so good.

"I like your costume, too. A lot." If she presses against me any harder, she'll feel how much I like her costume. How much I like her.

"Did you see my tail?"

"I saw your tail. And your socks. And the heels. And the ears. I always pay attention to what you're wearing, but you made it impossible not to tonight."

"I hoped you'd like it," is all she says.

And those five words give me something to think about for the rest of the night.

I CAN STILL HEAR MY friends drunkenly singing a song about karma in the Uber as it drives away from Halle's house.

"They're going to get me in trouble with Mrs. Astor. I swear her hearing aids pick up sound two streets away," Halle says, walking up her driveway with her heels in hand.

I'm close behind her, trying not to concentrate on her bunny tail or the curve of her waist where my hands spent the night. "Mrs. Astor loves me. I'll protect you from her."

She digs in her purse for her keys, and the second we're through the door she drops her shoes and purse on the floor and table beside the door. "Is there anyone you can't charm?"

"Professor Thornton." I kick my shoes off beside hers. "You."

"You think you haven't charmed me? You're in my house, Henry. You're about to sleep in my bed." I move closer to her and watch the way her eyes take me in. Leaning around her, I drop my sunglasses onto the table next to her purse. I swear I hear her breath catch. "I'm pretty sure you've charmed me real good."

She doesn't move when I stand straight, close enough to her that I can see every dark lash when her eyes close. Every barely there freckle on her nose. Every tiny movement of her chest as she tries to control her breathing. "I haven't tried to charm you, Halle."

"What would you do? If you wanted to charm me?"

"I'd tell you how fucking beautiful you are. That when you laugh I want to listen to it forever. I'd tell you that when I daydream, I think of us. And all the things I want us to do. And all the things I want to do to you."

Her big brown eyes are fixed on me. "I think that would definitely work."

It's unmistakable the way her eyes trace my lips. I push the bunny headband from her crown and throw it onto the floor behind me. "This isn't for experience, Halle," I say gently, trailing my thumb along her jaw. "This is because I want to, and I only want to if you want to."

I lean in slowly, slower than I've ever moved, because if I'm wrong, if everyone is wrong, then I ruin this. My heart is thumping dramatically in my chest and I'm more nervous than I've ever been to kiss someone. And then she whispers, "I want to."

And I finally kiss her.

Chapter Nineteen

HALLE

I'M NOT ASHAMED TO ADMIT that I've wondered what it would be like if Henry Turner ever kissed me.

My subconscious was kind enough to give me a more X-rated sneak peek a few weeks ago, but now that I have the real thing, I can confidently report that my subconscious doesn't know what it's doing.

Both of my hands are gripping his shirt, clinging to him like if I don't, he'll disappear into a breeze. His hands are cupping my face, mouth working to leave me breathless and hot and pulsing between my thighs. This is what it's supposed to feel like, I quickly decide.

The longing, the desperation, the desire to do something—*anything*—to ease the aching.

The voice in my head saying, no, *screaming* that this feels right, me and him.

"Halle," he murmurs as he pulls back and rests his forehead on mine. The smooth way my name rolls off his tongue should be illegal. "Let's go to bed."

"Let's."

"To sleep," he adds.

Henry never needs to worry about not giving me enough new experiences because they happen all the time. Like right now, while I'm *disappointed* that he doesn't want to go to bed and take this further. I can guarantee this has never happened before.

"Oh. Are you not . . ." *Where was I going when I started this question?* "Into it? Wait, you don't need to answer that. I wa—"

Moving his hands to my waist, Henry keeps me close to him as he walks me backward for the few steps it takes for my ass to hit the table. He presses his hips into me, and I get my answer. Feeling how hard he is and knowing I'm the reason makes me feel drunk.

"I'm into it," he says, kissing me gently. "But we don't need to rush anything."

I nod in agreement, even though I'm not sure I do agree.

Taking his hand when he steps away, I let him lead me up to my bedroom. Every step reduces the lust-driven haze sitting like a cloud over my head, until we finally reach the top of the staircase and the logical Halle is back in control. For now.

"You need a box of stuff for your bathroom," Henry says as I crouch beneath my sink, trying to find the toiletries he used the first time he stayed over unexpectedly. I put them somewhere safe in case he wanted to stay again, and now I can't find the safe place. I've never needed them, because he brings an overnight bag now, but with work, and Will, and . . . He's taking off his pants. "Halle?"

"Yeah?"

"Why do you look so shocked?"

Great question. He folds them over his arm, then again until they're in the perfect little square, and then drops them onto the lid of my laundry basket. His fingers start on the shirt button and I get back to exploring under my sink. "I'm not."

"Do you not want me to sleep in my underwear? I could sleep in my pa—"

"No! You're good. Underwear is fine. Underwear is *great*. I don't want you to be uncomfortable." The first time Henry stayed, when I fell asleep downstairs and he carried me to bed, when I woke up he was sleeping on top of the covers fully dressed. "There's no dress code."

"Is it seeing my thighs that's making you act weird or is it because we kissed?"

Henry does have very nice thighs. Arguably the nicest I've ever seen. After finally finding what I'm looking for, I stand with his toothbrush and washcloth, putting them on his side of the unit. "It might be both."

We look at each other through the bathroom mirror. Well, I watch as he strips off his shirt and he watches me watch him with a smirk. Walking up behind me, he wraps his arms around my shoulders and kisses the sensitive point between my neck and shoulder. "Have a shower and process. Then come to bed with me."

"Okay. Good idea."

After kissing my temple, Henry collects his things and heads to the other bathroom, leaving me alone to "process" and shower. Choosing what I'm going to wear to bed takes longer than it should, but then the time it takes to deglitter myself does help and I'm glad I listened to him. Although even after dousing myself in cold water, the swollen and sensitive feeling between my legs remains.

"I grabbed you a bottle of water. And thanks for getting silk pillowcases," Henry says as I exit my bathroom. He looks up from his phone as I close the door behind me. "Feel better?"

"Mm-hmm."

He starts to say something then stops. I climb into bed beside him, putting my phone on the bedside table. He leans over me when I lie down, his bare chest inches from mine, and puts his phone next to mine. "Good night, Halle."

As he hovers over me, and I don't know where I find the confidence, I angle my body toward him and reach until my hands meet at the nape of his neck. My mouth angles up as his comes down. I feel less stunned this time around, more in the moment as his tongue moves against mine perfectly. Every single inch of my skin feels like it's glowing as I spread my legs and he climbs between them.

His body is made up of masses of hard muscles and defined lines, but he holds himself above me like I'm too precious to touch, when all I want is to feel the weight of him between my legs. My hand traces down his back from his neck, and when my finger brushes along his spine gently he flinches. "Firm touches," he says, kissing my cheek. One by one, he takes my hands and puts them next to my head, weaving his fingers through mine to pin them there. "I don't like being tickled or touched lightly."

I nod to reassure him. "Got it." With our hands intertwined, his body lowers onto mine. The pressure of him settled between my thighs does nothing but make the ache worse when I realize how hard he is again. My hips move against him of their own volition; he moves against me until we're rocking against each other, the thin fabrics separating us doing very little to dull the sensation.

"I haven't felt like this with another person before," I say when his mouth travels along my jaw and down my throat. It comes out more of a whimper, but it makes him pause.

"In a good way? Or do you want to stop?"

"A good way. I like you touching me. I'm not ready to go all the way, though."

His hips stop moving but he stays on top of me. "Can you tell me what you've done before? Was it only with him?"

"Yeah, only him. I let him finger me twice and I gave him head a handful of times."

"And did you enjoy it?" My face must do something weird because he kisses my cheek. "Be honest."

"I didn't like giving head, but it sort of wasn't sexy when I'd been begged for it, and he was a bit rough. I'd try it again if you promised to be more patient, and gentle, I guess. I didn't like him touching me, either, but I think I'm one of those people who can only get themselves off."

"He never made you come?"

While anyone else's body on top of mine would make me feel trapped, having Henry so close to me while we have such an intimate conversation makes me feel safe. "No, but like I said, I think it's me. I can do the same thing to myself and orgasm, but with him it wasn't even close."

"Is that what you do to yourself when you listen to people fucking on that app on your phone?"

There's a satisfied glint in his eyes when my lips part. "Yes."

"Can I make you come, Halle?"

I nod. "But don't feel bad if you can't."

Kissing me again, he rocks his hips one last time, and it sends a lightning bolt up my spine. "I'm pretty confident about my chances. We'll work it out together. Might take a little bit of time for us to get there, but we will."

Henry unlocks our hands and climbs off me, lying on his side next to me. I groan quietly in protest, but he silences it with a searing kiss. "Give me your cell phone," he says.

I pass it to him without objection. "Why?"

"So you have something better than strangers getting off to listen to when you think about this." After I unlock my screen, he clicks on the voice recorder app and places the phone on my stomach. "Show me how you want me to touch you, Halle."

All the heat in my body rushes to my cheeks. Those ten words are enough for me to delete the Whimper app. "What about you?"

"Always thinking of others." He smiles and leans toward me to kiss me slowly, reassuringly almost, but it's not enough to stop the nerves vibrating through my system. "I want to watch you get what you want. Without distraction."

Pushing my shorts down over my butt, Henry uses his free hand to help pull them off, tossing them over the side of the bed. I'm grateful he convinced me to shower, otherwise he'd be admiring the pumpkin-themed panties I was wearing, instead of see-through lace ones.

My breathing feels so loud and it's like my heartbeat is thumping in every bit of my body. "I'm nervous," I whisper, laughing slightly because I want it so badly at the same time.

"If you change your mind or you don't like it, just say stop," he whispers back, running his hand along my thigh. "I only want to make you feel good."

"I know. I trust you." Taking his hand, I guide him beneath the lace. My breath hitches, my stomach tenses as his fingers brush against my clit. With my fingers over his, I apply the smallest amount of pressure and rub gently. "I like this."

"What else do you like?" he murmurs, not taking his eyes off me.

If the man wants me to give him some kind of coherent answer, he's really going to need to stop looking at me like that. And touching me like that. And existing in the same universe as me, because he's too distracting and my head is filled with nothing but heart eyes and cupids on clouds. But, like, the explicit version.

"I don't know. I'll know when you try it."

Henry kisses me, his tongue moving against mine at the same time his finger rubs in the perfect rhythm. I take my hand away because he doesn't need me to guide him. Every whimper, every heavy breath, every movement of my legs, he notices. My hands cup his face, his neck, his body. Anywhere I can touch to feel closer to him.

His hand dips lower as my back arches, my hips desperately trying to follow. He waits until I nod before he slips a finger inside of me. "You're so wet, Halle. You're soaking my hand."

It's amazing how something so personal would embarrass me normally, and yet with Henry, he makes it sound like praise. There's a tightness building; everything feels so swollen and wet, and I can hear how wet as much as I can hear Henry telling me how pretty I look with my head thrown back. My body bucks against his hand, moans echo, eyes snap shut.

"You're going to make me come," I whimper through fire sparking across my skin.

And, in the most Henry Turner way, he says four words. "I know. Do it."

My thighs clamp shut around has hand as my orgasm rips through me. Shocking me as much as it overpowers me. I can't believe I spent a year thinking only I could do this for myself. His mouth meets mine, taking in every moan of his name, never changing his rhythm until I'm too spent and too oversensitive and he stops, gently removing his hand.

He repositions my panties and pulls me in to his chest, kissing my forehead tenderly. "Was that charming enough for you?"

I nod. "Yeah, think you got the charm thing covered."

"FAKE YOUR OWN DEATH."

I roll my eyes for the millionth time. "You sound like Aurora."

"That's a really cruel thing to say after I made you come last night. You should apologize by not going."

"Can I add you bringing that up as a bargaining tool to our rule book?" I say, pulling my cardigan over my shoulders.

He pushes himself up to sit against my headboard, covers bunched around his waist like he's on the cover of a romance book. "The board said no, sorry. Come here, Cap."

"You need to get up and go back to your own house. I don't trust you here alone, you'll throw Quack Efron in the trash."

"Halle," he says again, holding out his hand. When I'm foolish enough to take it, he pulls me onto the bed, laughing.

"Was that necessary? You could have just asked."

"Halle, will you please sit on my lap so I can look at you?" he says far too politely. I push myself up, and he navigates my leg across him until I'm straddling him. He pushes my hair from my face then rests his hands on my hips. "How do you feel?"

"Stressed that I'm going to be late to meet Cami and Aurora for breakfast because you wouldn't let me get out of bed." I tried really hard, honestly. But Henry climbed on top of me and kissed me and I just like the feeling of him on top of me. Then he apologized for being hard all the time and I asked if he wanted me to do something about it, but he questioned if I was offering because I felt like it was only fair or if I wanted to.

When I said I felt bad that I got off and he didn't, he climbed off me and explained in detail about why that was bullshit, and that sex isn't for exchanging favors. I told him he sounded very wise, and he said he'd read it online. He followed it up with how he didn't know why some men were so clueless when everything you need to know about sex is on the internet.

"You could have tried harder to get out of bed. And we both know Aurora and Cami won't be on time." His hands squeeze my hips and I do everything I can to stay still. "Are you okay after last night?"

I nod, probably a little too enthusiastically. "Very much okay. Are you okay?"

"Need to jerk off as soon as I get home, but yes, I'm good," he says, lifting his hips up for me to feel how good he is. "You should password-protect that recording."

I know I'm blushing. "Do you want me to send it to you? It might help with your morning plans."

His hands rub up and down the front of my thighs. I truly believe that with a bit more effort on his part, he could convince me to stay. "Yes, but don't. Only you should have it. I have the memory of you squeezing and riding my hand, so I'll be fine."

"I was about to say this is a very formal chat about something very informal, and then you talk," I say, shaking my head. I feel like I'm in a meeting debrief, but I appreciate Henry checking. It's more than Will ever did. Will couldn't make me come, and now I realize he was never truly trying, so he shouldn't be part of the conversation anyway. "But thank you for caring if I'm okay."

"I'm down to show you how much I care anytime. I have multiple ideas of things you might like."

Leaning forward slowly, I kiss him gently. "I'll make space on my phone for the files."

BY THE TIME I'M WALKING into Blaise's diner, I've created at least three different excuses for why I'm late.

Aurora and Cami are both sitting on the same side of the table, arms folded in the same way looking equally unimpressed. I wouldn't have invited Aurora to breakfast if I'd known I was going to be ganged up on.

I slide into the red leather booth, poised to plead my innocence and offer some half-assed excuse when Cami gasps. "You got laid last night!"

"What?" I say, voice squeaking. "No, I didn't!"

"Then why are you glowing?" Aurora says, leaning in to look at me.

"Maybe it's the body shimmer stuff from yesterday. Maybe I didn't wash it all off," I say as they inspect me like I'm a zoo animal.

"Liar. You had that *I had an amazing orgasm* walk when you came in here. Is that why you're late?" Cami says. "Was it Henry?"

"Of course it was Henry," Aurora says, sporting the widest grin I've ever seen. "Look at those pink cheeks. I want to know all the details, but also, it's Henry, so I kind of don't want to know all the details. Can you kinda filter the details specifically for me?"

"I want all the details. No filter, please," Cami adds.

I shrug, because what else am I supposed to do? "There isn't anything to tell."

"Having integrity is no fun, Halle," Aurora says, pouring me a glass of water and nudging it in my direction. "Can you at least tell us if you're happy?"

"I'm happy."

Cami fans me with her menu, which normally I'd question, but I can practically feel the heat radiating from my face. "And were you safe?"

"I honestly didn't have sex last night, guys," I say, lowering my voice so as not to disturb the other Blaise's patrons with my recently established not-solo sex life. "I haven't had sex ever, actually. But I'm happy, and I guess I do feel a little like I'm glowing."

Aurora looks like I just won some kind of competition. "I'm so happy for you, but also, kind of grossed out because it's Henry and it feels a bit like finding out my brother is doing it with my friend. But really happy for you! I bet he was sweet, right? He likes you so much. No wait, don't tell me if he was sweet. I don't want to know."

"Ignore her, tell me if he was sweet," Cami adds, leaning on her hand.

I know I'm blushing, but I also feel really good. "He was *really* sweet, and patient, and told me we didn't need to rush because he knows I'm a virgin. You guys are honestly not acting how I thought you would to that news, by the way."

"What news? You saying you haven't had sex before?" Cami asks, putting her menu fan down. I nod. "Why would we? It isn't a big deal. And penetrative sex being considered your first time is a heteronormative thing. My first sexual experience was with a woman. Plus I believe in science and, not to get too deep on you over breakfast, virginity isn't a medical concept."

It's the second time I've been told something similar recently. Aurora is nodding along with her until she finishes speaking. "That, but also, Will sounds like he was a dick, so I wouldn't have wanted to fuck him, either."

"This conversation is enlightening," I say, taking a sip from the water glass in front of me. "So many people have made me feel weird about it. The girlfriend of someone on Will's team once said to me, *Aren't you worried about him cheating on you if you're not keeping him satisfied?* Ironically, her boyfriend cheated on her."

Aurora's eyes widen. "Why do people care so much about what's happening between other people's legs? It's so fucking weird. Like, yes, I'm your friend and I want to know all the things going on with you, but, *Jesus*, I'm not going to try to tell you what to do with your own genitals."

"Please don't say genitals so early on a Sunday morning," I plead.

"Did Will make you feel weird about it?" Cami asks. "I'm totally down to do something I won't verbalize to make sure he never has a professional hockey career or, like, any happiness in his life, if he did."

"I feel like if I answer that honestly I'm going to end up being an accessory to a crime."

"You can only be an accessory if I tell you what I'm planning," Cami says with a wink. "I'm sorry he was so bad to you, Hals. I hope you know there isn't some kind of deadline for this stuff. Without sounding like a bumper sticker that I'd definitely buy if I had a car, bodily autonomy includes the things you don't want to do as well as the things you do want to do. I'm so happy Henry is a good guy and he's experienced, too, which will help make it easier for you."

I'm happy Henry is a good guy, too. For some reason every time he comes up, I want to bury my head in my hands and kick my feet excitedly. Never occurred to me that him being experienced would be a benefit. "He is. I do want to have sex with him. I just don't want to rush into everything all at once, y'know? I'm nervous."

"Not to sound like your mom, but did someone give you the

birds and the bees talk? Do you know how to be safe?" Aurora asks, and honestly, it feels a little like I'm being quizzed by my parents right now. "And y'know, arranging tests and things? Do you take birth control?"

She looks so genuine, but it's hard not to laugh. This is not how I imagined breakfast going. "Yes, someone gave me the birds and the bees talk. I'm not on birth control because I worried that Will would see it as a green light before I was ready. I should probably look into it before we start, right?"

"Maybe to just decide if it's something you're interested in? Not everyone takes it. If you need help navigating them, I've literally tried them all. I have killer periods, so I've been on it since I was fourteen," Cami says.

"And if you decide you want to get some, I can go to your doctor with you," Aurora adds. "I once had to try to get the morning-after pill in some random-ass village in Switzerland in broken Italian so no conversation about contraception fazes me now."

"I—" I'm so confused. "I have so many questions. What were you doing in a random Swiss village?"

"I lived a *life* before Russ turned me into the responsible and refined woman you see sitting before you." Cami looks as confused as I feel. Aurora's pre-Russ life is well documented online, so it's not hard to imagine. "Okay, I still literally have no idea how it happened. I was supposed to be in Italy. There was a guy from my dad's work that I liked to get into trouble with. It's a story for another time. Anyway . . . we're talking about Halle and Henry. I hope we've made you feel okay with what we've said."

It's affirming to hear them say the things I knew but had never been told before. Will made me feel like I was somehow lagging behind, that there's something wrong with me. Looking back with fresh eyes, it's kind of clear that aside from our relationship, I'm not sure he was a good friend. Cami and Aurora are good friends. "Thank you both. Seriously."

"You look like you're having a moment, so I'm going to talk about myself to give you a free pass to process," Aurora says, leaning against her palm. "No more conquest tales, though. My birthday is coming up and I have no plans. I told Russ I didn't want to organize anything because he's so stressed out with his asshole brother, but I kind of do, but I don't know what to do. My mom will pay for anything I want, I just need to decide quickly, but I'm fussy."

Our breakfast orders are taken, and while we workshop ideas and after I've eaten half of my pancakes, we've settled that we don't have enough time to organize a music festival.

"What about a sleepover?" I say, holding out my plate for Cami to give me her strawberries. "Like a movie night sleepover? We could do it at the hotel. If it's a weeknight the penthouse will probably be free."

"Yeah, if your mom waves her Black card at the event planner, they will move heaven and earth to pull something together. They're actually really good, you just need to decide what you want it to look like," Cami says enthusiastically. "I've seen them pull functions together with literally days' notice. Also, not to share company secrets, but I've known Pete to move bookings to give the right customer the penthouse when it's been booked."

"I can do a mood board for them and create a list of all the things you need. I'll make sure it's perfect. I'm pretty sure there's a gazillion companies that rent beds, screens, etcetera now. It probably won't be that hard even at short notice."

"Do you even have the time for that?" Aurora asks. "Your schedule gives me a headache."

I want to find the time for her. "Sure, I can do most of it while I'm at work. It'll be easy."

"And we definitely can't organize a festival?"

"It's a hard no on the festival," Cami says.

"Okay, I'll call my mom later and tell her to call the hotel. Thank you, guys. So, what do you think about a Reese Witherspoon theme?"

No day starts well with a phone call from my brother.

"Who's dead?" I ask as I answer the phone and put it on speaker. I'm trying to transfer Aurora's birthday cake into a box that will survive my drive to the hotel, while simultaneously trying to finish my book for book club and not fall over Joy, who is currently weaving around my feet.

Only an emergency would make Grayson ring me outside my birthday or a public holiday, and I honestly don't feel mentally able to take on anything else, so it isn't great timing.

"You, potentially. I'm your tsunami siren. Get to higher ground, Hallebear," Grayson says.

"I watched your game last night, so I know you didn't get a head injury. Try explaining, Gray. Just a straightforward explanation, please."

"Mom says you're not going home for Thanksgiving. She called Dad and he said you weren't having it with him. She called me and I said I didn't know what she was talking about. So I suspect any minute she's about to call you."

Managing my mom's emotions is something I don't have time for today. "Thanks for the heads-up. Look, I'm super bus—"

"Are you not going to tell me what's going on?" he says, interrupting me midsentence.

"There's nothing to tell. I'm working." And avoiding Mom. And Will. And everyone else, if I'm being totally honest.

"What about Douche Bag? Is he not upset you're working? You know Mom will recruit him to pressure you into calling out sick or something."

"Douche Bag and I split up months ago, so I don't think he'll care, to be honest." My phone starts beeping to indicate another incoming call. "Mom's calling, Grayson. I gotta get this."

"Wait! This might be the happiest I've ever been. Why did it take you so long? Why didn't I know this? I'm so proud of you."

Grayson has never hidden how much he dislikes Will, so I wasn't expecting him to hide how happy this breakup makes him. I know he'd like Henry, but I won't be telling him, because I know the first thing he'll ask is why I only seem to kiss my friends.

"Because I didn't tell anyone to avoid being burned at the stake. Look, I gotta go. Thanks for the heads-up."

I disconnect from Grayson and accept Mom's call. "Hi, Mom! I'm just getting ready to head out, can I call you back another time?"

Given how Mom totally ignores the fact I'm an adult with commitments and things to do, I'm going to assume the answer to that question is no. In true Mom fashion, she doesn't shoot straight into what, thanks to Grayson, I know she's calling for.

She asks what Maisie should do as her science fair project, then asks me to help her. Then if I think she should dye her hair darker for the winter. How she and my stepdad were called into Gigi's school to talk about her not hanging out with anyone her own age, and that they're worried for her social development. She wants me to talk to her. She asks if I've started planning the itinerary for our vacation at spring break, which I haven't because no one would stick to it anyway.

As she talks, I mentally list all the other things I need to do before I head to the hotel for Aurora's birthday sleepover. I give her the responses she wants when I should be telling her again that I'm too busy to talk, but my conformity eventually leads her to the point I know she's calling me about.

"What are your travel plans for Thanksgiving? I know you and Will usually road-trip with Joy, but I was told he is flying alone."

She practically chokes out the word *alone*. "I was going to call you about it, but I'm working over Thanksgiving, so I won't be coming home. I'm working over Christmas, as well. It's because I'm the newest employee; I have to if I want to keep my job," I lie. "And people have kids, so they already booked their vacation days. I know it's disappointing, but it's only one year."

There's a long stretch of silence. "You can't begin to understand how disappointed this makes me. All of us. Your sisters will be distraught. And what about Will? This is really selfish of you, Halle."

There's a responsibility that comes with being the child that's an extension of the parenting unit: never be the one to rock the boat. You're the anchor that keeps everyone in place. There's an unspoken requirement never to have problems you can't resolve yourself quietly, and it's a condition I've never failed to meet until now.

For as much as not telling my mom about Will was for self-preservation reasons, avoiding hearing everyone else's thoughts and emotions about a situation that only impacts me was a factor, too. Don't get me wrong; if I called my mom heartbroken, she'd be on the first flight out here to comfort me. My family loves me as much as I love them, but my needs have never felt like anyone's top priority, and my breakup would be no exception.

I'd be rocking the boat, and how can everyone else remain steady if I'm not anchoring us down? How can Will and I break up when nobody wants us to?

It's time to put the whole thing behind me, and that's the thing I focus on when I finally summon the courage I've been missing for the past couple of months.

"We broke up, Mom. A mutual agreement that we weren't happy. I'm sure Will won't care what I'm doing."

Silence.

"All couples go through rough patches. Look at me and your father, we took a six-month break when we were in college. It's normal."

I don't need a mirror to tell me what I look like because I can feel the tightness in the muscles of my face. I am the living embodiment of the word *huh* right now. "Mom . . . you and Dad ended up getting divorced."

"After two beautiful children and many happy years together, Halle. One divorce doesn't erase that. I know you have high expectations because of the books you read, but real people have flaws. You included. I'm confident you and Will can work it out, honey. He's your best friend."

"I really need to go. It's my friend's birthday and I'm hosting a sleepover party at the hotel. It's going to be really bad if deliveries arrive before I do," I say, hearing the defeat in my voice.

"Okay, honey. Call me soon, I need you to explain how to do some silly science thing for Maisie's homework."

"Can't you just google it?"

"Probably, but you know I prefer it when you explain things to me. Anyway, get to work and give my love to your friend."

"Bye, Mom."

The call disconnects and I let out a loud, soul-deep groan before carrying on with all the things I need to do.

THE PENTHOUSE SUITE AT THE Huntington is bigger than my house.

It might be bigger than Mrs. Astor's and my houses combined, in fact. Thankfully, Pete, my manager, helped me bring the various decorations up to the hotel while the hotel's event manager coordinated other deliveries.

I'd love to pretend it's because they want to help me, but it's more likely that the event coordinator was given clear instructions from Aurora's mom to do whatever I say, as well as her credit card to pay for all my requests. I think the coordinator was a little put out I was involved, but Aurora is very particular with what she likes, and her mom said I have to approve everything first.

Helping set up is my way of an apology for stepping on her toes.

With the extra hands, everything is set up early, which gives me time to read Gigi's latest English essay, catch up on messages from people wanting to join the Enchanted book club, and rewrite the same two lines of the chapter I wrote last night. I had such big goals when I started that book club, and I feel like I blink once between sessions until it's coming back around. I want to give it more attention, but I don't know how to find the time.

I feel the same about writing, although recent events have caused inspiration to flow out of me. Sure, I rewrite every other word, but at least there are words on the page now. Even if, when I'm being totally honest, until the last week I definitely hadn't been working on it as much as I should.

When the penthouse elevator doors open unexpectedly, someone a lot more interesting than a caterer steps out. "It's very pink," Henry says, looking across the living room of the suite. He's not wrong. Between the balloons, food choices, and inflatable beds set up in front of the movie screen, it feels a little like Barbieland in here. "I feel like I just stepped into the middle of cotton candy."

"That's a funny way to say *wow, Halle, you have such an eye for design,*" I say playfully as he strides confidently across the room toward where I'm working. "Also, aren't you supposed to be at the barber's? Your hair is looking very not-recently-barbered."

When he reaches me, he bends down to kiss my forehead gently while dropping his overnight bag next to the table I'm working at. "You smell good."

I have the overwhelming urge to throw myself at Henry. I don't because I don't know if that's cool, but I really want to. In one way, it feels strange to me that we haven't talked about what, if anything, we are now, but I also kind of like not having another expectation to meet.

He's been busy with an art project and hockey, and I've been organizing this event and getting on top of my other responsibilities, so it feels like we've hardly spent time together, but that was okay. It turns out I needed a little time alone to process my new feelings anyway. It's what I like about Henry; he doesn't expect me to act a certain way.

"Don't distract me. Why aren't you at your appointment?"

He sighs and drops into the chair beside me, quickly leaning forward to peek at my laptop screen. "It's walk-in and I didn't leave home when I was supposed to leave. Then I didn't leave at my backup leave time, and I just kept staring at the time until I got to the point where if I *did* go to the barbershop and wait for the only guy I'll let cut my hair, I'd definitely be late to this."

"How do you ever get anything done?" I ask genuinely. "I would have dropped you off if you needed someone to nudge you."

He runs his hand over his hair, his now-longer curls moving under his palm. "I used to go with a guy on the team named Joe. I put him onto my barber when we met because his hair texture is the same as mine, and he hadn't found a good one yet. It was our thing that we did together. Then we'd watch sports for a couple of hours and hang out. He graduated and moved to Connecticut for law school, so now I have to go by myself."

"You had a date day with your hockey friend? That's so cute!"

I'm *definitely* smiling, but he isn't. He rolls his eyes. "It wasn't a date. It was two guys with the same barber going to get their hair trimmed at the same time. Then hanging out in the same place afterward."

"So you got all your date experience from Joe, and now you're passing it on to me? I love this. How wholesome."

Henry moves forward to take my hands and pull me onto his knee. With our faces level he leans in, his lips practically brushing mine. "There's nothing wholesome about the things I think about when I'm with you. Or when we're apart."

I rub my nose against his slightly and his breathing slows. I lower my voice. "Did you say the same thing to Joe?"

That one makes him laugh. "No, but there's lots of things I say to you that I don't say to anyone else. How long do I have you before everyone arrives?"

Henry's finger travels over my thigh, tracing small circles and swirls while he listens to me talk. It makes it difficult to string a sentence together.

"Less than an hour. Aurora is at dinner with her mom and sister, then I arranged for a car to pick everyone up from her house. The event coordinator was superefficient, so the setup crew and deliveries finished early."

"What do you want to do with time alone in a hotel?" he asks, his voice low as his mouth skims my jaw until his lips find my neck. "After a week without me?"

My skin feels electric. Every cell in my body pays attention when Henry is near me, and the more he touches me the louder they scream for more. More touching, more pressure. Just *more*. It's as exciting as it is totally terrifying.

"I want to go into my bedroom"—he mumbles an *mmm* of approval against my skin—"and take off our clothes." He kisses my neck, and the will to continue dwindles with every microsecond. "And put on our personalized Aurora's-birthday-sleepover pink pajamas."

He stops and slowly leans back so I can see him and his dilated pupils. "We need to work on your delivery, but I'm okay with this plan. And it's been so long since I saw you totally naked . . ." His arm scoops under the back of my knees, and before I can react, he's carrying me across the room toward the bedrooms. "Which one is ours?"

"You broke a rule!" I squeak, flustered by being carried like I weigh nothing. "The same one you always break!"

"Tell it to the board, Captain."

I point toward the door that's slightly ajar. "That's *my* room. You're sleeping out here with the rest of the guys."

Henry uses his back to push the door open properly and walks until he can place me gently on my bed. He crosses his arms and grips the bottom of his T-shirt, slowly pulling it over his head. It lands on the bed next to me. "We both know I'm not."

Desire and anxiety are fighting each other to be my most dominant feeling. Yes, I want to have a repeat of last time, but here? When we'll have to rush and then spend the night hanging out with everyone? I'm not sure I'm there yet. Even the desire to do *anything* with someone is such a strange new thing for me.

"Henry . . ." I say, hating how meek my voice sounds, pushing myself up onto my forearms to look at him properly.

"I know what you want, Halle. Do you trust me?" I nod. "Good. Close your eyes."

I should tell him that I'm unsure, but I'm also curious to see what happens. It's different from how things have been in the past; my anxiety is rooted in being nervous about the unknown. It is, at its core, excitement as much as it's apprehension.

Henry doesn't touch me when my eyes flutter shut. I hear him move around the room and the sound of a zip, followed by more shuffling. My heartbeat doesn't know what it's supposed to be doing and he still hasn't done anything to me.

"Open your eyes, Halle," he says gently.

Taking a deep, and hopefully discreet, breath, I slowly open my eyes.

And immediately burst into laughter.

"I feel like a marshmallow," he says, looking down at the satin pajamas he's now wearing.

The small sense of relief I feel confuses me more than anything. "Baby pink suits you."

Henry pulls the hem of the shirt and shakes his head. I love that his name is embroidered above the chest pocket just like his Titans T-shirts. "Everything suits me. It doesn't mean I should wear it."

"Your modesty is my favorite thing about you," I tease. I sit up fully to get a view of the entire vision, and he really does look cute in pink.

"What's the point of me being modest when I look good in everything I put on?" Taking a step toward me, he grips my knees to pull me to the edge of the bed, stepping between my legs. "I look good in nothing, too. I don't think that's something you want to find out when people will be arriving soon."

It feels like a question and a confirmation that he understands me all in one.

"I would really like for you to prove your claim," I challenge, immediately regretting my confidence when his hands drop to the waistband of his pants. Holding my hands out in front of me in some kind of dramatic protest, I squeak, "Just not today!"

"I know. I'm trying really hard to know, Halle. I'm paying attention to everything so I can get things right with you." Henry takes my outstretched hands and links them at the back of his neck, getting even closer to me. He kisses my forehead, then the tip of my nose, before moving away enough for me to see his face fully. "Just because we did something once doesn't mean we have to do it again or somewhere you're not comfortable."

"I know. Seriously, I do know that, and I understand the whole continuous consent thing. I just"—*don't know how to word this?*—"haven't had the experience of someone making me feel like this. The experience of *wanting* the experience is a new experience for me, y'know? So the nerves of not having experience but wanting it is taking up a lot of head space."

Does he know? Do I even know? I definitely don't know.

"All I got from that is I'm so great at giving you experiences that you're having experiences on experiences on experiences. I want to understand you. Can you explain in a different way? Sometimes it's hard for me to read between the lines. You're better off just telling me directly." I love that he cares so much about understanding me. "Maybe break it down into different points. Start with the first thing you said."

I'm very aware that if I'm grown-up enough to want sex, I should be grown-up enough to talk about it, but boy do I want the ground to swallow me whole.

"I've never actively wanted someone the way I want you. I genuinely thought I was broken in some way for a really long time. I know I'm not, but that's how I was made to feel, and it was hard to unlearn. So that's the first new experience."

"Will didn't make you horny? But I do?" Henry says, a definite hint of smugness to his tone. "Your first new experience is horniness?"

Why did he have to word it like that? "Correct."

"What's next?"

"I'm also experiencing wanting to do something about wanting you. Things were good with me and Will for the first few weeks of our relationship—stop grimacing when I bring him up, please—but I still never had the urge to do anything further than kissing. I do now with you, but I also don't know where the boundaries are. Like, what's out-of-bounds for our friendship? The last time I started kissing my friend he became my boyfriend, and we both know how that turned out. I know you haven't dated anyone, but what if the label is what made it go wrong? I kind of like having no expectations."

"Where do you want our boundaries to be? What label will help you feel comfortable?" he asks so gently that I want to cry. He tries so hard with me when even I don't know how to work out what I want. "I don't not date because I have a problem with it. I've just never cared about labels, Halle. I just know I want you the way you want me. I'm good with doing whatever stops the noise in your head."

"It's cute that you think the noise in my head could ever be stopped," I say playfully, attempting to lighten the very serious mood I've set in my attempt to explain myself. "But this brings me to my next experience, or inexperience, I guess."

I should continue talking, but I don't know how to word it. He nods, encouraging me. "Go on. I'm listening. I'm trying to understand."

"I'm nervous, Henry. I don't know what I'm doing, and what if I'm not good?" I say quietly. "I'm used to being a problem solver, and this is the one thing I don't know how to solve in advance. You have experience and I don't. What if you decide you want to hang out with someone who can have more than one sexual encounter without turning her thought process into a freaking riddle that has to be broken down into sections to be understood? I just said that I like having no expectations, while knowing if you came over one day and said you'd been with someone else it would hurt."

"I'm glad you saved that one until last, because I wouldn't have been able to pay attention to the rest. Why would I hook up with someone else?"

My eyes narrow. "I give you a touching and vulnerable speech and that's all you got from it?"

"It's the only thing you said that doesn't make sense to me, Halle. I don't want someone else. I haven't been with someone in any capacity since I met you. I didn't even realize that it's because I wanted you the whole time until recently."

"Yeah, but that might change. Will got tired of waiting for me to be ready an—"

"And Will is a prick," he interrupts. "But go on."

"And I don't want to lose you as a friend if you want to be with someone less . . . I don't know what I am. Apprehensive?"

Henry cups my face with his hands, his warm palms heating my skin. "I wish you spent as much time imagining things for your book as you do imagining things that aren't going to happen in real life."

"Henry!"

His thumbs glide across my cheeks. "Halle, have you ever considered being chill for five minutes?"

Luckily for him, he kisses me before I can argue, and his joke plus the tender way he touches me does a lot to ease the tension I've developed during this conversation. When his mouth eventually leaves mine, he hugs me tight. Something I didn't even know I wanted until he did it.

Murmuring into my hair, he strokes the back of my head with one of his hands. "I might get to be the guy who gives you all your experience, Halle. That's a big deal to me, too. I don't want someone else with more experience; I want you. And if you decide I don't get to be that guy, I'll still be right here, trying to solve riddles to understand you so I can be your friend."

"How do you manage to take all my bullshit and make it into something really sweet?"

He leans back, his hands reaching to cup my face. "For all you know, I've totally misunderstood everything, and I think we're about to get married. Should we retrace your mental steps to make sure we understand each other?"

I groan. "Do we have to? It's too embarrassing to say out loud again. Maybe I should have just joined a convent right out of high school."

"You're not allowed to be embarrassed; it's one of our rules. What did you call it? Your touching and vulnerable speech. Let me slim it down. Experience one: I make you so horny that it's making you re-assess your whole life." *Give me strength.* "Experience two: you want to do something about those urges with someone, ideally me, for the first time instead of just yourself and your sex app. And experience three, which is actually inexperience three: you're nervous about trying things you haven't done before."

"Bingo." If this was a game show there would be buzzers going off. I nod enthusiastically, because he's said it far better than me even though I think he was trying to make me laugh. "Basically, I'm an inexperienced triple threat and it's pretty busy in my brain currently."

"We can handle it, Cap. We're a team, so you have all the time you need. You already have the advantage that I am so much better for you than Will ever was. And I have a really great idea for get-ting rid of all the thoughts in your head. You just need to lie back and take off your pants. I can definitely get you to be chill for five minutes."

It's the mood lightener I need, and I'm so grateful that we can have these types of conversations in a healthy way. With Will they al-ways turned into arguments. I beam at him. "Your problem-solving skills are unmatched, but I think this time I'll pass, thank you. And no, I've been managing a family since birth. I haven't had a chill day in my life. My natural state is to think of every eventuality."

"Me and another woman can be crossed off your list of even-tualities. Waiting isn't the big deal Will has made it out to be, I promise." The elevator dings loudly outside the room, followed by the sounds of multiple voices, making them very early. "Let me kiss you and show you how much I'm not interested in other people."

He closes the gap between us quickly, kissing me with the determination of a man with something to prove.

And right at that moment is when the bedroom door opens.

Chapter Twenty-One

HENRY

AURORA SLAMS THE DOOR CLOSED, blocking out the sound of gasps, many of which I don't believe are genuine.

"I didn't know you were here!" she yells through the door. "I was giving a tour!"

Halle's hands are pressed against her mouth to cover her shock. I want to kiss her again, but I'm not sure this is the time. I clear my throat. "It's a good thing you didn't take off your pants."

She nods in agreement. "I think you might be right. This is so embarrassing."

I want to tell her being embarrassed is breaking a rule, but people always say some rules are allowed to be broken, so I'm going to give her this one. "They thought we were lying when we said we're just friends and not hooking up anyway. Does that make you feel better?"

Her hands move from her mouth to her forehead as she shakes her head. "No. That doesn't make me feel better at all."

"Is it because you're worrying about what people think of you?" She nods, dropping her hands to my hips and placing her head on my chest. "Okay, well, don't do that."

"Telling me not to worry about something doesn't make me not worry." I silently stroke her hair to comfort her, because I'm out of advice. Eventually she lifts her head to look at me. "I'm being dramatic. It'll be fine, we can just laugh it off, right? We're still just friends, so we haven't been lying to them."

Hmm. Don't like that. Is that what she thought I meant when we talked about no labels? I brush it off. "And I know all their secrets, so if they're annoying, I'll just start dropping them."

"And how do you know all their secrets?" she asks.

I shrug. "People tell me stuff. I think it's because they know I don't care enough to gossip about them."

"Or maybe it's because you're a great friend and a really good listener?"

Once they get their excitement out of the way, I know my friends will be cool with Halle. They all really like her. If they don't chill out about it, I'll cause chaos for everyone. Kris and Bobby, because Bobby hooked up with Kris's sister and he doesn't know; Robbie and Lola, because they argue every week about her moving back to New York when she graduates; Mattie and his toxic ex, who he swore he'd block but is talking to again; and Emilia and Poppy, who break up every time they have a fight, but don't tell anyone because they get back together the next day. I have years' worth of people telling me things I don't want to know.

"It's definitely because they know I don't care enough to gossip about them." She grumbles and throws herself back onto the mattress. I climb onto the bed beside her, nearly sliding off because of the pajama material against the bedding. Lying next to her, I lean in to kiss her cheek, and these damn pajamas tighten against my arms as I move. I'm so hot and I haven't even done anything. "Did Aurora not want to pay for silk or . . . ?"

Halle chuckles. "Some vegetarians don't wear silk, so I didn't want to get it wrong. Look it up; it's a very interesting information hole to be stuck in."

"I know how silk is made. I just forgot she was a vegetarian. You remember everything about everyone; I don't know how you do it. You're a good friend to her, Halle. She'll definitely protect you from the others if they get too excited."

She sighs, rubbing her face against her hands. "Let's just get it over with. It's fine, please don't spill all their secrets."

"You got it, Cap."

IN AN UNUSUAL TURN OF events, nobody said anything when we exited our bedroom.

Not one single thing.

I was instantly suspicious until I saw Russ by the popcorn machine, and he reassured me that after the door slammed closed, Aurora threatened everyone with violence if they made Halle feel the slightest bit uncomfortable or embarrassed.

Halle went for breakfast the morning after we fooled around, and judging by the way Aurora instantly acted protectively toward Halle, I assume she knows. I don't care, Halle can scream it from a rooftop if she wants to. I like the idea that she has girlfriends to talk to. She clearly has a lot going on in her head, and I almost gave myself an aneurysm trying to make sense of it.

I usually shut down when I'm overrun with issues, but Halle's solution seems to be to tie herself in mental and verbal knots. I know she thinks she has to solve all her problems alone, but she doesn't.

I don't know why I'm bothered that she said we were still just friends when that's something I'm used to. I know I sometimes mirror people, but I don't want to start creating problems the way Halle does for herself.

Aurora gives me the same threat of violence when I groan that the first movie we are watching is *Legally Blonde*, so I know firsthand how terrifying she must have been earlier.

Halle and I settle into one of the floor-bed-couch contraptions covering the vast penthouse living room, and I find myself looking at the various artwork on the walls instead of the giant screen that's been constructed to facilitate this extravagant sleepover.

"The interior designer needs to be fired," I whisper to Halle, who is totally engrossed in the movie and her bag of candy.

"Mmm?" she mumbles.

"The artwork doesn't make sense in this room," I say.

"How do you feel when you look at it?" she asks, finally taking her eyes off the screen to look at me. Sporting her own set of pink pajamas, she's braided her hair down each side of her face and taken off all of her makeup. She looks so pretty. And happy. That's my favorite part.

"Inspired," I answer.

"What? I thought you said you don't like it," she whispers after Mattie and Cami turn around from their floor bed in front of us to shush loudly.

"Doesn't matter." I kiss her forehead and her eyes widen, immediately looking around to check that nobody was looking at us. I wish she didn't care so much about what people think.

When she's fully focused on the movie, I dig my cell phone out of my pocket.

JAIDEN

I need advice.

So you came to the expert

Great choice

You're my last resort.

I'm your only hope

Hit me. I'm ready to wow you with my wisdom

How do you know if you're in the friend zone?

Is this about Halle?

Yes.

You're not in the friend zone lmao

How do you know?

People in the friend zone don't get
caught making out in hotel rooms with
the person who is supposed to be friend
zoning them

How the hell do you know about that?

I'm all seeing and all knowing

But yeah, you're good, brother. Firmly
outside of the zone

Why do you ask?

Bobby is a snitch is what you mean.

It was Emilia actually

She now owes me 5 bucks because I
called it weeks ago

She thought I might want to hook up
with other people.

Then she said we're still just friends.

Do you want to hook up with other
people?

No.

Do you want a relationship?

I don't really care what it's called.

It was me not wanting her to date other
people that made me make a move in
the first place.

After a Robbie pep talk when I was
jealous.

That boy really loves a pep talk

Okay, all these things do not put you in
the friend zone

But maybe you guys just need to work
out what you want out of your situation

Like is it just sex? Is it companionship?
Is it both? Is it only when you're both
single?

Has she had a shitty relationship in the past?

Yes. Will Ellington from San Diego.

Yikes. Has anyone told him he's not that great yet?

I plan to.

Maybe she likes no expectations because she's still deciding what her boundaries are

Remember you get to set your boundaries too dude

Give it time. It's new, but if she's as sweet as everyone says she is you should hang on

So I'm overthinking it?

Seems like it. But you know what I always say

Aunts are hotter than moms?

No

Well yes

But no

Communicate is what I always say. Make sure you're on the same page

I've never heard you say that.

I say it all the time

No you don't. You told me to stay toxic.

As a test and you passed by being your nontoxic self

Just talk to her, Hen. You'll work it out.

Okay. Thanks JJ.

You're welcome, brother.

Dare I ask how hockey is going?

Okay so you're gonna leave me on read

I see how it is

It's a good job I love you

Love you, too, J

I feel a lot better when I lock my phone and slip it back into my pocket. Beside me, Halle has fallen asleep, and I let Aurora put on one more movie before I admit defeat and carry Halle to bed. She doesn't even wake up when I lose my grip on her because of these ridiculous satin pajamas we're both wearing and accidentally drop her onto the bed. She's definitely breathing—I've checked twice.

As soon as I climb in beside her, she thankfully shows some sign of life by rolling over to lie on my chest and put her thigh across me like she always does. I brush her hair from her face and she hums happily, her eyes opening slowly. "Why are you so tired?"

"Up late. Busy day. Are we in our room?" she mumbles.

"No. You're trying to straddle me in the lounge in front of everyone."

It's like I've doused her in cold water; her eyes snap open and she pushes herself up with her elbow to look around the room. "You're an asshole," she says, sinking back down to lie on my chest. "That's one way to wake me up."

"Do you want to go back out there? You slept through the end of *Legally Blonde* and *Cruel Intentions*, but I think they're about to put *Just Like Heaven* on. Aurora really likes old Reese Witherspoon movies."

Halle yawns and shakes her head. "I'm happy here with you. On our own. In this huge bed."

"Are you trying to seduce me?" She's staring up at me with anticipation. I drag my thumb across her bottom lip and watch her breathing slow. I lean in and she lifts her head to kiss me gently.

"I wouldn't know how to seduce you," she says. I think about what she said earlier about inexperience.

"When our friends aren't on the other side of the door, I'll let you practice as much as you like."

"My *hero*." She looks up, grinning, but I can tell how tired she is when she immediately lies back down. "Do you think Aurora is enjoying her birthday sleepover?"

"She said it's the best sleepover she's ever been to. What about you? Where does it rank?"

Halle cuddles into me more, moving her head onto my bicep so she can look at me while we talk. "I've never been to a sleepover."

"I am so good at giving you new experiences." I tuck one of my hands behind my head to give her a better place to put her head and let my free hand rest on her thigh. "I wasn't allowed to go to them, either. I didn't care, though. I didn't want to sleep in someone else's house."

"Uh, I think you'll find I planned this, so I gave myself the experience. And it wasn't that I wasn't allowed, I just didn't have any friends growing up other than Will. Grayson went to sleepovers all the time. Gigi does, too, but now that I'm saying it out loud I'm questioning whether she's going where she says she's going after her recent performance."

"Your family makes me happy I'm an only child," I say. "I don't have it in me to look after so many people."

"Surely being the captain of a sports team is like having tons of brothers? And they're not bad. I just only ever complain about them. I should talk about when they're nice to me more."

"It's more like having a farm next to a highway and all the animals keep escaping." I love the feeling of her body on mine when she laughs at something I've said. Even in the dimly lit room, I can tell she's looking at me like I'm the funniest person she's ever met. "Tell me something nice your family has done for you recently."

She thinks for longer than I think she'd be able to justify if I challenged her. I don't challenge her because I don't want her to shut down. I love hearing her talk about anything, and she's one of the only people I can say that about. "Grayson called me this morning to prewarn me about my mom being pissed off I'm not going home for Thanksgiving."

I don't think that meets the criteria of something nice. "Why aren't you home for Thanksgiving?"

"When Will and I broke up, we knew our parents would interfere because they're like that. We agreed that if I didn't go home for the holidays, by the time we're next together they'll be over it. I just didn't get around to telling my mom we broke up until today."

Everything she says generates more questions. "Why are *you* not going home for Thanksgiving? Why not him?"

"I have other options, I guess. I have my dad and stepmom in New York. He doesn't have anywhere else he could go. It was just easier for me to be the one not to go home."

"Easier for him."

"When I saw him, he said we should both go home, but I've already agreed to work. There isn't enough pumpkin pie in the world to make me agree to go home given how unimpressed my mom was. She'll get over it, though. Hopefully by March."

I'm always appreciative of my moms, but I'm extra appreciative when I talk to my friends about their own parents. My moms have never made me feel not good enough, never made me think I wasn't capable of making my own choices, never discouraged me or asked too much of me. It wasn't until I started college and widened my circle that I realized a lot of people aren't as lucky as I am. Sure, they were busy at work, but they always found as much time for me as I needed as well as giving me the best of everything.

"What's happening in March?" She turns away from me to yawn, and I remember that she's supposed to be sleeping right now. "You can go back to sleep if you need to. I'll stop asking you questions."

"That's okay. I like talking to you, and I feel like I should enjoy this bed as much as I can, given I'll never be in this penthouse again. What's happening in March?" she says, repeating my question. "My annual headache. My family and Will's family go on vacation together over spring break. I'm tasked with organizing it every year, and it takes thirty gazillion hours of research and debates, and then when we finally get there, they all ignore my plan and complain the whole time. It's delightful."

Once again immensely grateful for my family. "It sounds the opposite of delightful."

"It is. Every year I debate planning their trip and booking myself to go somewhere else alone. Sadly, I'm pretty sure they wouldn't be able to function without me and they'd end up missing, fighting, or stranded. I mean, they fight when I'm there, too, but at least I know where they all are."

"My parents just use travel agents to book our trips. Have your parents not heard of them?" She laughs again and rolls off me onto her back. I follow her, rolling onto my side and resting my head against my arm. I pull her closer. "You shouldn't go if you don't want to."

"Aurora invited me on a girls' trip during spring break. I've never been on one, or invited to one, and I really want to go. But it's not worth the reaction I'll get. Maybe next year, if she still wants me to go, that is, I can do it."

"I know families are complicated and I've had it easy, but I'm struggling to understand why you don't just say no and do what makes you happy. Why do you have to make sacrifices to please everyone?"

"Yeah, they ask a lot of me sometimes, but at least they always want me around. They say I hold everything together."

"Even if it means sacrificing what you want to hold everything together?"

She's quiet for a moment. "If everything falls apart because I rocked the boat, who's going to notice if I fall overboard? Who's there if I sink?"

I know how deeply Halle loves her family, and from the conversations I overhear they love her, too. I just wish she wasn't weighed down by everyone else's burdens. Conversations like this allow me to learn more about her, which I desperately want, but I can't help but feel unqualified to hand out advice.

"I notice everything you do, Halle. And I bet I could sail a boat if I tried."

She rolls to face me, our stomachs touching we're that close in this gigantic bed. "You do say you're good at everything."

"And Russ is too responsible to let anyone not wear a life jacket. Aurora probably has enough money to buy the Coast Guard," I say. "The guys trained to be lifeguards in high school to meet girls. Robbie would love bossing people around. You're not sinking, Cap. I'm not letting you."

"Despite what you think, you do always say the right thing, Henry."

"Go to sleep; we can talk more about how great I am when you wake up."

Halle leans forward and kisses me slowly. It's soft and sweet, just like her. She rolls over and slides backward until her back is flat to my chest, and that's when we learn there's no hiding an erection in satin pajamas.

Chapter Twenty-Two

HENRY

"We're thinking of starting a podcast."

We're still up north after playing here this weekend, and after our loss earlier—our third in the past two weeks—we decided to brave Faulkner's wrath and use our hour before we head back to Maple Hills to see JJ. I've been trying to drown out the constant noise of my teammates chatting in order to concentrate on an essay that my brain *really* doesn't want to concentrate on, but hearing the word *podcast* come out of Mattie's mouth is enough for me to lower my laptop screen.

"We want to call it *The Frozen Three*," Kris adds.

Bobby nods. "It'll be about hockey."

JJ rubs his fingers against his temple. "Gentlemen, ask yourself this: are three more straight men with microphones what the world needs?"

The noise from the other patrons rumbles around us while Mattie, Kris, and Bobby deliberate over JJ's question. As much as I want to be home in a dark room alone, I'm happy they're all talking about the pros and cons of a podcast instead of my shitty performance.

They keep telling me it isn't my fault, and yet I can't shake the feeling that I'm letting them all down. I don't know how to fix it. Not only that, if I don't finish this essay, then it won't matter how hard I've been trying to be a good captain, because Faulkner will murder me if I get a bad grade.

Halle tried to make me work, but thinking about peeling her clothes off her makes it hard for me to concentrate on some boring essay about a topic I don't care about. I just want to touch her constantly and it's distracting, especially because she wants to be touched constantly.

My free time is filled with a lot of dry humping and jerking off in the shower right now. She hasn't asked for anything more than that, so I figure she's still doing whatever mental gymnastics she was doing last week.

The guys are still talking about a podcast when I get back to my laptop and that little flashing line is taunting me. I can't fail this as well as failing at being captain in the space of a week. I just can't. The more pressure I put on myself, the less I can concentrate on my screen; the guys are getting louder and louder, and it's all getting too much.

By the time we're pulling up in front of our house, I'm mentally done. Coach insisted I sit with him on the bus and talk and talk and talk. Even when Robbie tried to take over, I then had to listen to it. I was looking forward to being alone, but the universe has other plans for me and Halle's car is parked outside of my house.

Companionship is a difficult thing to navigate when I feel overwhelmed. When I know that in all likelihood this person I care about and who cares about me is going to work hard to make me feel better, and with her patience and affection she might help. Of all the people in the world I would want to be waiting for me unexpectedly, she's the one I'd pick.

But in the same reality, the idea of *anyone* being near me, existing in my space and wanting basic human interaction from me, feels like the heaviest weight I can't survive.

Halle approaches me as I climb out of Russ's truck, a glass container clutched tightly in her hands. I meet her halfway down the driveway to get out of Russ's way while he grabs Robbie's wheelchair from the back, and also because I'm not sure I want to invite her in.

"You look really exhausted," she says softly, handing me the container filled with cookies. "I know you're probably holding yourself to an unfairly high standard right now, and I know my opinion on the matter doesn't really count, so I wanted to bring you something nice instead."

I appreciate that she isn't trying to give me a speech on how teams sometimes lose games like everyone else seems to want to. "Thank you."

"I'm going to leave because you look like you need to rest. I'm fighting all my natural urges to try to find the solution to your problem, because I know you don't like to be smothered with attention when you don't feel great," she says, smiling softly. "Call me if you need anything, okay? I'll try not to overwhelm you."

She doesn't hug me or try to kiss me. She just gives me a small wave goodbye, turns around, and climbs into her car. There's a huge part of me that's relieved; I don't want to be touched and asked to talk about my feelings, not even by her, who really, at this point, is the only person I do like touching me. But as I watch her drive away, I start to miss her.

Robbie has lived with me long enough to know he should give me space when I feel like this. Russ has a sixth sense for any kind of negative atmosphere and leaves me alone after making me a cup of tea.

I judged Aurora at first when she said a good cup of tea could solve a multitude of problems, but as much as I hate to admit it, it is comforting. As soon as she bought us a kettle so we'd stop boiling water in the microwave, everything changed for the better.

I still feel like my Word document is laughing at me and my four hundred words as I stare at my laptop screen. Usually an impending deadline would give me the stomach-turning anxiety to produce something quickly, but apparently even knowing Thornton is expecting something from me tomorrow is not enough to get me moving.

I really fucking hate myself for not concentrating when Halle was here to help me earlier in the week. She warned me that I would struggle if I didn't complete it with her because she was adamant I wouldn't be able to do anything while away with the team.

I don't know why I'm like this and it makes me want to tear my hair out.

In my head, I have an ideal scenario of how things will go. Whether that's how I act, how my day goes, what I eat—everything works together in perfect harmony, and I thrive. I don't feel like I'm hyperaware of everyone around me and yet equally completely oblivious. I don't have to concentrate so hard on people's mannerisms and behavior and choices so I can do them, too. I do things in advance, so they aren't something I have to worry about later. I'm a good friend who doesn't struggle to keep up with the people he loves.

In my head, I just exist peacefully and that's enough. I have a routine and it's fucking great.

I tell myself I'm going to work harder to be the version of me in my head, and I'm so frozen by the prospect that I do nothing at all, not even the things I would have done before, and I make everything worse.

Pulling my cell phone from my pocket, I ignore the hundreds of messages in the various group chats that I don't have the energy for and click Halle's number.

"Hey," she says when she picks up a few seconds later.

"I can't write my essay. I'm really struggling to get out of my head."

I expect an *I told you* so or *it's your own fault*; it's what I deserve under the circumstance. Aside from the other stuff keeping me permanently sexually frustrated, I spent our time together last time drawing the painting I was supposed to be writing about on her thigh.

But it's Halle, so what I assume isn't what happens. "What can I do to help you?"

"Are you busy?" I ask, hearing background noise that sounds like she's out somewhere.

"I asked first. What can I do to help you, Henry?"

I can tell she's somewhere doing something, but there's a selfish part of me that desperately wants her to make me feel like this isn't an impossible task. "Can you come over and help? If you're not busy."

"I'll be twenty minutes," she says. "Have you eaten?"

"I've had a cup of that tea Aurora gets from England and a protein shake."

She laughs, and even hearing it over the phone gives me the same serotonin boost I get when I see her do it in person. "That's a no then. Healthy or unhealthy?"

"I want crunchy stuff like cucumber and chips. Nothing sticky."

"Coming right up. I'll be with you soon, so try to relax for now. We'll get it done, Henry. We haven't failed yet, and I'm sorry this one is taking more energy than you have."

"You're the best."

I STARE AT MY CEILING for the thirty-five minutes it takes for Halle to turn up at my house, and as soon as I see her standing on my doorstep everything instantly feels more manageable.

She struggles to hold up the grocery bags since they're so full, but she attempts to show me anyway. "I bought everything that looked crunchy."

I lean forward to take them out of her hands, kissing her cheek gently as I bend down. I want to tell her how much better she makes everything, but Russ and Robbie appear from the den like two dogs responding to a rustling treat bag. Robbie stops next to the kitchen island. "Did you get them?"

I think he's talking to me until Halle responds to tell him yes. Putting the bags on the counter I look between my friends. "What?"

"I need beer if we're going to get through this study session," Robbie says. "But Halle was scared to use her fake ID that isn't fake."

Halle starts unloading the bags, not making eye contact with me until she can't take me staring at her. She clears her throat and steps toward me. She looks up at me with big eyes. "Aurora invited me to go for dinner with her, Poppy, and Emilia earlier. We'd just finished eating when you called me, and I forgot to ask you to check if anyone else needed anything from the store, so she called Russ—"

"And Russ was watching TV with me," Robbie says, interrupting her. "And we decided we should probably be doing something productive instead of watching reruns. So, we're going to all work together and drink beer and eat. And you're not going to struggle in your room alone and blame yourself for shit that isn't your fault when you have people who want to help you."

"I'm not blaming myself for shit that isn't my fault."

Russ takes a bag of chips and opens it loudly, somehow managing to crinkle every inch of the bag. "We win as a team, we lose as a team. No one person is responsible for how we play. It's quite literally a group effort."

"Faulkner wants me to go to his office on Monday. He's not pretending this isn't my fault."

"He wants to check that you're okay, Hen," Robbie says, cracking open a beer and handing it to me. "He might pretend he doesn't give a shit, but he does. He notices the way you retreat into yourself after every loss and he's worried. He might be a hard-ass, but he still has a duty of care. It's why he wouldn't leave you the fuck alone on the bus. Shit's hard, but it's not supposed to ruin your fucking life."

This is the exact reason I stay in my room alone. Halle has what looks like guilt written all over her face. Maybe she didn't know this would be the outcome when I asked her to help me and she involved other people. People who want answers and want to help and want me to act in a certain way.

I want to walk away and lock my bedroom door. That's what my body is telling me to do. Fight or flight, and it's immediately picked flight. It's too hard to say how I feel in a way that will appease everyone's worries when I don't even *know* how I feel to be able to assemble a suitable response.

Overwhelmed doesn't convey how I feel anymore when I know that this anxious weight of impending doom is going to be with me until I graduate or until Faulkner realizes asking me to be captain was a massive mistake and I let everyone down.

Russ is rustling the chip bag again and the TV is playing and Robbie is tapping his fingers against the side of his beer bottle and Halle's finger lightly brushes my knuckles by accident and it's like tiny bugs crawling across my hand and I can't think.

I *can't* think.

"Do you want to go upstairs?" Halle asks, her eyes flicking to where I'm rubbing my knuckles repeatedly trying to stop my hand feeling disconnected from the rest of my body. "Go if you need to."

I nod, and the idea of answering her properly feels entirely impossible as I step around her and head to the stairs. As soon as I enter my bedroom, I throw myself onto my bed facedown, bury my head in my pillow, and let myself pass out.

I DON'T KNOW HOW LONG I'm out for, but when I wake up, there's a lukewarm cup of tea and a selection of snacks next to two Tylenol on my bedside table.

Telling Halle not to be embarrassed about things is second nature to me, and yet I can't shake that same feeling as I take the pills and stand to head downstairs.

Russ is watching TV on his own when I reach the living room, and I can't see or hear Halle or Robbie. He doesn't say anything when I sit at the other end of the couch; he lowers the TV volume. He's watching Halle's baking show with the British people.

"Halle put it on," he says.

"How long ago did she leave?" I ask.

"Couple of hours ago. She took Robbie to Lola's, so it's just us tonight. You hungry?"

As much as I don't blame her for leaving when I wasn't awake to keep her company, I'm now in an even worse situation with Thornton's essay. "We didn't study. I'm going to fail because I have nothing to submit."

Russ doesn't take his eyes off the TV. "Robbie spoke to Coach and told him you aren't feeling yourself. Coach said he'd submit a request to get you a day extension for your essay. Unspecified medical grounds or something. You can hand it in on Tuesday and Halle is going to help you tomorrow. Do you want pizza for dinner?"

"Unspecified medical grounds?"

"Yup. Would it be better for you if I made the decision about dinner? Is there anything you specifically don't want?"

Russ finally looks at me and it's my turn to concentrate on the TV. I nod. "Nothing messy." He immediately grabs his cell phone from the arm of the chair to order something. "Thanks, Russ."

"You got it." He hands me the TV remote, but I have a soft spot for this show. "Is there anything else I could do tonight to help you get to tomorrow?"

It's a weird way to word a question, but one of the things Russ has learned since his dad started working through his addiction is that all you need to do is take one day at a time. He's careful with his word choices, but I like it.

"No. There's nothing you can do."

"Let me know if that changes, okay?"

That's all he says until our food arrives and we sit together eating, watching Halle's baking show, and I don't have to think about anything all evening.

Chapter Twenty-Three

HALLE

In the months Henry and I have been friends, I've never been as nervous to see him as I am today.

Don't get me wrong, I'm excited to see him—I'm *always* excited to see him—but the nerves are an addition today when they've never been there before. I offered to meet him in the library instead of either of our houses. The library feels like neutral territory, and it also reduces the chance of us becoming distracted.

I waited at his house for an hour after he went upstairs yesterday just in case he woke up and wanted me to be there. I could tell from the moment Robbie and Russ greeted us in the kitchen that I'd made a mistake. When Aurora called Russ, it was Robbie who said that Henry needed to know his friends are around him. He's known him so much longer than I have, so I trusted he knew what was right for him—even if my gut was telling me it didn't feel like the right choice for Henry.

It's a lesson learned, I suppose. I was so worried about telling Robbie he was wrong, potentially having him see me as an interference, that I didn't prevent Henry from becoming upset. Even if there weren't tears or shouting, I could tell that things weren't right immediately.

I was fidgeting on the spot, nervous, not knowing how to inter-
ject with a more suitable plan, and I brushed his hand by accident,
and I've never been madder at myself. That was his tipping point, I
think. The step too far for someone exhausted and overstimulated.
I knew it was unlikely we'd get anything done, and that's why I suggested Robbie see if any exceptions could be made. Thornton gave
me an extension last year when I was unwell, so there's no reason
Henry couldn't get one, too, under the circumstances.

I'm thankful we have today to have a do-over. Henry has done so
well this semester, and our system works; we just need to make sure
after I do my bit, he does his bit.

My nerves caused me to leave the house early and I've been
sitting at this table at the far end of the library with two hot choc-
olates from the cafe for twenty minutes. Even with twenty minutes
of waiting, I still don't know how to greet him when he gets here or
if I should bring up last night. My gut is telling me to let him lead
the conversation, that way I'm not going to accidentally cross a line.

Another ten minutes have passed before I see auburn curls poking out of the rim of a Titans beanie.

"Sorry I'm late. Didn't want to come," he says, placing his bag on
the table and getting out his laptop. He pulls out the chair beside me
and kisses the top of my head before taking the seat.

Ouch. "I'm sorry you had to in that case," I say as carefully as I
can, trying not to let that sliver of hurt show in my voice.

He pinches the bridge of his nose between his fingers and sighs.
"I didn't mean that."

Thankfully in my thirty minutes of obsessing over how to act
and waiting, I reread the material we're working with today to jog
my memory so maybe we can get this done quickly. "You did and
that's okay if it's how you feel. You don't have to filter yourself for me.
Should we get this over with then?"

"Halle," he says softly, and the tenderness in his voice makes me dissolve into nothing. I feel how drained he is simply from how my name tumbles out of his mouth. He pulls my seat closer to him and rests his chin on my shoulder. "I said it wrong. I didn't want to have to face you after yesterday. I feel embarrassed about inviting you over then disappearing without saying anything. I've been in the studio and I just procrastinated leaving. I'm sorry I'm late."

"Being embarrassed is breaking a rule, Henry. You're allowed to do what your body tells you to do. Instincts are instincts for a reason. You needed alone time, that's it. No big deal."

He sits back in his seat and my body craves his touch again. "It feels like my brain doesn't work the way it's supposed to sometimes. I try my best to work against it but sometimes it wins."

"Your brain creates the most beautiful artwork and says things to me that make me feel so safe and so cared for. Your brain makes you a friend people like Russ can rely on. Rory told me how responsible you are for bringing him out of his shell. And Nathan trusts you to look out for his girlfriend when he's away, an—"

"And I've hardly talked to her. What kind of friend does that make me?"

"The phone works both ways, Henry," I say, internally gagging when I realize how much I sound like my mom right now. "You're going through a stressful time and she can check in with you, too. You're both equally responsible. But my point is, you and your brain that you say you're fighting are so special. You say it doesn't work properly and I don't know anything about that, but I know that the things you see as differences to everyone else make you who we all care so much about."

"Have you been practicing that speech while you've been waiting for me?"

I smile because there's nothing else I can do when I just carefully navigated trying to tell him how great he is without being too horrendously cringe, and that was his response. "I made it up on the fly. Are you impressed?"

"It's not the best speech I've heard, but I acknowledge your efforts."

I want to kiss him but I'm kind of scared to touch him, so I lean in on the assumption he'll do the rest if he wants to. "I'm sorry I didn't know how to make you feel better yesterday. I'm sorry you're here when you don't want to be."

He leans in, too, his face so close to mine I can smell his cologne. "You're apologizing again."

"And I'm not going to stop until this work is done."

"My body feels really oversensitive today, so I'm not going to kiss you even though I really like it when I do. I also don't want to get kicked out for heavy petting in the library."

I'm about to tell him that nobody says *heavy petting* anymore until he turns and points to a sign on the wall that literally says it. "If we get this finished in the next two hours, I can come to your coach's office with you. I only have class this afternoon."

I fear I might have gone too far, but he smiles and nods. "That'd be nice."

It's NOT UNTIL WE'RE ON our way that I realize I'm so unathletic that I don't even know where the sports building is.

Henry explained it's a little like an evil lair occupied by multiple supervillains and he normally avoids it at all costs. He apparently got locked in there for two hours with his coach after the door jammed when he was a freshman and he's never recovered.

Campus is fairly quiet as we stroll across it toward Henry's meeting, but the calm doesn't stop *me* from worrying that *he's* worrying about his meeting. I decided that distraction might be my best method. "How did you end up being a hockey player? Why not football or baseball or, I don't know, chess?"

"My uncle Miles played hockey until he went to med school. He's technically my biological dad, so I guess I inherited his talent. He's been my mama's best friend since high school, then they all went to the same colleges, so they're all close. My mama grew up playing different sports, so she wanted me to find something I liked as well."

"Did he teach you to play?" I ask.

"Yeah. He's the person who taught me repeatedly that I can be better than anyone in the room if I want to be. He got me my first skates. Took me to my first game. Signed me up for youth league. I became a bit obsessed, the way I do with things I like. My mom was happy that I was working in a team since I also liked creative things but would only do them alone."

A mental image of little Henry playing kids' hockey flashes through my mind. "Does Miles live in Maple Hills? Does he have any kids of his own now?"

Henry takes my hand and pulls me gently to move me out the way of someone texting and walking. His fingers thread through mine and he doesn't let go. "He lived here when I was younger, but he went back to Texas. His mom got sick so now he teaches at a college there. I usually see him a few times a year. I've never known him to even date anyone, so he doesn't have any kids. He's a good guy; I think you'd like him. He reads a lot of books."

"Reading books is definitely the best hobby a person can have." Henry nudges me with his shoulder and rolls his eyes. "I bet he's proud you're where you are now."

"Walking across campus holding hands with a hot girl? Probably."

Now it's my turn to roll my eyes. "Oh, you've got jokes now, huh."

"I wasn't joking."

"I meant the fact you're the captain of your team."

"For now."

"Henryyyy."

"Halleeee," he says, mimicking me.

"I know you'll be with your parents this week for Thanksgiving and I'll be working, but I'm going to come to your game on the weekend. I'll find a way to move my shift around or leave early or something. I want to be there when you get off the ice," I say. "I'm going to wear your jersey and scream your name."

"Can you not make me hard before I go into this meeting, please?" I choke slightly. "Maybe wait to see if Faulkner kicks me off the team before you start moving things around."

"You know that isn't going to happen."

He looks across to me as we stop in front of a building I've never seen before. "Do I?"

Henry holds the door open for me and ushers me to a bench inside the lobby. "Be honest with him, please. Whatever he wants to talk to you about, tell him you're being too hard on yourself."

"I'll be as quick as I can."

MY E-READER HAS HARDLY EVEN warmed up by the time Henry reappears. I look at my phone and he's only been gone ten minutes.

"All good?" I ask cautiously.

"Yes. You can inconvenience your colleagues," he says, like I'm not desperately waiting to find out what this whole thing has been about.

"What did he say? You were really fast."

"He said, 'Are you okay?' and I said, 'Yeah,' so he said, 'You don't seem okay,' and I said, 'I don't like when we lose,' and he said, 'Neither do I, so what're we going to do about it?'"

"Right . . ."

"And I said, 'Win,' really enthusiastically because he likes enthusiasm, and he said, 'Good, was yesterday a onetime blip?' and I said, 'Yes.' And then he said, 'You're allowed to have an off day. You're a human, not a robot.' And I said, 'Good to know.' Then he asked me if I've registered for spring classes yet and I said, 'No,' so he said, 'Go and do it,' so I said, 'Okay.'"

Henry pushes his hands into his pockets and avoids eye contact with me. "So you didn't tell him you're scared to let your friends down and you're struggling to process the tie between the team's losses and your role as captain, and it's making you seriously unhappy?"

"No. It didn't come up," he says casually.

"Henry, for the love of God, please go back upstairs and tell him how you really feel."

"We need to leave or you'll be late for class."

"Henry," I borderline plead. "Please tell him you need more support. What if you lose again this weekend? I despise seeing you be so hard on yourself."

"We won't lose. You'll be there and you're my lucky charm. It's a scientific fact."

"Henry, that isn't how science works. I feel like I don't tell you how annoying you are enough," I grumble, walking under his arm as he holds the door open for me. We're leaving the sports building but it's reluctantly on my part even if it's not on his. "Me being at your games is not a great strategy for success."

"You're the only person who finds me annoying. Everyone else finds me adorable."

Slowly, the Henry I'm used to starts to move to the surface. He still looks worn out but he feels closer than he did before. "You're a menace. I don't know where anyone is getting adorable from."

Hottest guy at this school, yes. Adorable? Not quite.

"To my friends I'm like the younger brother they have to keep alive and out of trouble. You have an audio clip of me making you come on your phone. Very different type of relationship."

I'm surprised I don't fall to the ground. I'm positive my knees wobble a little. "Oh my God, you can't just throw that out there in the middle of a conversation while there are people around us."

He looks around at the one—maybe two—people within listening distance who are clearly not paying attention to us as we all walk in the same direction. "Why not? We haven't talked about it since it happened. I wondered if I'd imagined it because I expected you to bring it up. Have you listened to it?"

"Henry, is this seriously what you want to talk about right now? After how you've been feeling, *this* is what you want to discuss?"

"I'll talk about literally anything if it stops you from talking to me about hockey."

"I'm trying to help you get the support you so desperately need."

"You didn't answer my question. Have you listened to it?" He looks at me and smirks. "Why are you blushing?"

I take another look around us and conclude people definitely aren't listening to us. I lower my voice anyway. "Because you're asking me about masturbating while you walk me to class."

"I didn't. I asked you if you'd listened to it. You're making assumptions about what I think you're doing to yourself while you moan my name on that clip."

"I hate you."

"Do you hate me enough to not want to make more?"

I don't know if this is entirely false bravado considering how bad he's been feeling, and if he's doing that thing he does where he pretends that he's okay. Or if he just really likes getting under my skin and it's genuinely improving his mood.

Of course I've listened to that audio. If this was the olden days, I'd have literally burned out the tape. It's the single most erotic experience of my life and I have it recorded. I don't know what's so hot about it other than the fact it's Henry. I've been using audio apps for a while and there's nothing on there that even comes close to how good this is.

Nothing else has happened between us since then other than, as the library sign would say, heavy petting, and lots of cold showers.

And listening to the audio clip with my vibrator, obviously.

Maybe it's because it makes me feel powerful in an area of my life that I haven't felt powerful in before. Maybe it made me feel desired and satisfied and happy.

Maybe, just maybe, it's Henry Turner.

"I've listened to the clip, Henry. In bed. In the bath. When I'm supposed to be studying."

We reach my building and he holds open the door for me. "And what's your professional review?"

"Professional review? Eleven out of ten. EGOT status pending for an excellent performance."

"Thank you to the Academy in that case," he says.

It's a lot busier here than it was outside, which massively reduces my willingness to discuss what I'm doing when I'm home alone. I don't know if I just watched too many college shows when I was growing up, but it really does feel like everyone notices Henry as we walk by. His posture stiffens, face hardens. It tells me it's not just in my head, and perhaps the idea of being perceived isn't what he wants right now.

"Hey, my room is right round this corner. Why don't you head out? It's super busy here today."

"Okay," he says. "Thanks. I'm pretty tired, so I might not be around later, but I'll speak to you tomorrow?"

"Thank you for telling me that. Yeah, I'll speak to you tomorrow."

He doesn't hesitate to get himself away from this hallway and I can't blame him, because people definitely seem to watch him leave the way they watched him arrive. Nobody pays attention to me as soon as he's gone, and when I sit down in class, thinking far too much about the audio on my phone, Aurora drops herself into the seat beside me. "I hope you're in the mood to hear me complain about Chaucer."

Consider my mood officially killed.

Chapter Twenty-Four

HALLE

I HAD EXPECTATIONS OF WHAT my adult life might look like.

It was going to be sophisticated and full of adventure. I'd meet interesting people and do interesting things, and I'd be hot and happy.

It certainly did not involve me lying on my living room floor on a Tuesday evening with a slightly stale bag of chips and a pile of tissues because listening to "Marjorie" makes me miss my Nana and I can't stop crying. But I also can't stop listening to it.

I lifted my legs to rest them on the couch twenty minutes ago while balancing my laptop on my stomach, and I'm comfortable enough to stay here forever. Joy likes our floor life, too, and has taken to pawing her way across my hair in an attempt to make herself some kind of bed.

I'm supposed to be studying for my finals. I'm supposed to be hanging out with Henry. I'm supposed to be helping Gigi. I'm supposed to be baking for book club and finalizing the questions because I promised to still hold the session for people in town for the holidays. I'm supposed to be cleaning. I'm supposed to give Mrs. Astor a ride to the grocery store. I'm supposed to check in with Cami when we're not at work. I'm supposed to look up Maisie's science project. I'm supposed to plan the vacation. I'm supposed to find Mom's Christmas gift from all of us right now even though I have a month because my siblings are useless and impatient. I'm supposed to be writing.

God, I'm supposed to be writing so much, and like everything else it's a complete lost cause.

After declaring, with all the determination of a woman with actual life goals she intends to see through, that I was going to put myself first, it appears that I have failed miserably. So, so miserably, and when I realized that I've been reading the wrong book for book club, because I forgot I said it would still happen and then confused my months, and that I couldn't read it *and* do all the other things, I had to lie on the floor.

It's hardly the life I imagined for myself, but in a kind of near-delusional state, I've accepted it pretty quickly. My floor angle gives me the perfect view of the front door, so it's easy to see Henry walk in and take one very long, very confused look at me before walking over and lying down beside me.

I'm sure this isn't what he was expecting when he finished practice and asked if I wanted to hang out.

Joy quickly abandons her hair bed and climbs onto the center of Henry's chest, purring happily as he strokes her. He turns his head to look at me. "Did you fall over?"

"Yes." I reach for my phone and turn down my sad Taylor music playlist because Henry's just gotten through his funk, and he doesn't need to see me bawl my eyes out if "this is me trying" comes on.

"Why are you sad, Cap?" he asks.

"I'm not sad," I lie. "I'm a ray of sunshine like I normally am."

"You're not a ray of sunshine," he says casually, lifting his legs to rest on the couch to mirror me. "You're the period of calm after a storm or, like, I don't know, a well-fed panda."

I snort, and I've given up pretending that snorting isn't a thing

I do, because it apparently is in Henry's company. "How poetic of you. I'll put it in my bio. Halle Jacobs: Aspiring author. Professional people pleaser. Calm like a well-fed panda."

"Halle Jacobs: Actual author. Excellent baker. Calm like a well-fed panda. Best ass in LA."

I hate that he's making me laugh when I really, *really* just want to have a totally overdramatic and chaotic meltdown. "Okay, now I know you're making fun of me."

"I've seen a lot of asses. I can confirm yours is my favorite." I scowl at him while he lifts himself to stand. Henry is clearly a man with a plan and I watch his every move as he takes my laptop from my stomach and puts it on the couch. My phone goes next, then my e-reader, and when the nest I'd built around myself is clear, he picks me up from the floor and drops me onto the couch. Sitting beside me, he drags me toward him with ease, and pulls my leg across his hips to maneuver me on top of him. It takes a little effort, since I'm being uncooperative, but he manages it, and I have no choice but to rest my chin against his chest as I straddle his lap.

He tucks my hair behind my ears and sighs. "Why are you so unhappy?"

"Because you haven't given me enough bamboo, clearly," I mumble, refusing to look up.

He tucks his finger under my chin, tilting my head back so he can look at my face. "What's wrong, Cap?"

Out of all the things I could possibly start with, I start in the most unreasonable place first. "Do you call me Captain because I'm in charge? Because I don't want to be in charge of everything. I'm tired of being in charge of everything, and everyone, and having to be the leader. I don't want to be the captain or the family manager. I'm so tired and it's all falling apart."

"So when I don't want to be captain everyone has a problem, but when you don't it's fine?" I think he's using humor to lighten the situation, but I'm too miserable to laugh. Henry lowers his finger from my face and wraps his arms around me to pull me tight to his chest. He strokes my hair, and after having Joy prance through it, it feels nice. "Maybe at first, but now it's because we're our own team and we're equals. Being captain feels better if I think I'm doing it with you. I'm sorry that you've been doing the bulk of the leading; I'll try harder for you."

I feel like my insides crack. "That's actually really sweet."

"If you don't want me to call you Cap anymore, I'll stop. There's no shortage of nicknames I could give you. Panda rolls right off the tongue."

"I don't want you to stop," I admit. "I want to be in a team with you."

"Now that you've hit me with your most *pressing* issue, what else made you cry on the floor?"

I, in the calmest and most well-structured-and-not-at-all-tearful way, explain that everything has snuck up on me and collapsed, and now I feel like I'm buried beneath the weight of everything and everyone.

All the plates I keep spinning all year to make sure everyone else is okay are starting to drop to the ground and smash. And it's when I realize how much of other people's lives I take on that it suddenly makes sense why I miss Nana, the one person who never made me feel burdened. I leave out the part about my book, or lack of book more appropriately, because I know that he'll put it down to experiences, which isn't the problem.

I'm the problem. My lack of commitment to something very important to me is the problem. Henry not taking me on dates because we spend our time doing other stuff isn't the reason I'm in this mess. Him asking me how it's going and me saying great when things aren't great is a problem I've created for myself.

If I tell him the truth, he will think he's letting me down, something he already battles with because of hockey pressure, and I can't face seeing him beat himself up over another thing that isn't his responsibility.

"Okay. To start, I think you should stop listening to that song about the grandmother," Henry says firmly. "And you need to start saying no to people. Me included."

"You make it sound easy. It isn't easy, Henry," I mumble, head still firmly buried in the warmth of his chest.

"It is. I say no all the time. Ask me to leave."

"No, I don't want you to leave," I say, sitting back to look at him in what feels a lot like terror.

"See? Look how easy saying no is. You just did it. You're so smart." He uses both of his thumbs to wipe under my eyes and cups my face. "Crying people make me feel stressed, so you have two more minutes to get it out of your system and then we're going to fix everything, okay? You're allowed to have an off day, Halle. You're a human being, not a robot."

I shake my head. "No, I need at least five."

"See? You said no again. Keep it up, champ."

Instead of crying, I spend my five minutes clinging to Henry and letting him stroke my hair. His steady heartbeat is soothing, and he's quick to reach for my phone to skip when the familiar notes of "Marjorie" start to play again. When my five minutes are up, he forces me to stand. I can't lie; the desire to lie on the floor again is still there.

Henry stands, too, positioning himself in front of me in a way that would realistically stop me from dropping to the floor. "Get changed into something comfortable. Wait, shower first and wash your face, because you have black eyes from your makeup. Then come back down."

I head toward the hallway to immediately do as I'm told, and jump when he slaps my ass. When I look back at him over my shoulder, he's smiling. "I told you. Best ass in LA."

I turn to head toward him, and his hands scoop under the backs of my thighs to lift me as I wrap my arms around his neck and my legs around his hips. "I like you."

He kisses me gently. "I like you, too."

I unwrap myself and head upstairs, and when I finally come back down looking and feeling significantly better, Henry is on the phone with someone in the kitchen.

"Can you do it or not? Yes, I understand. No, I don't care. Yes, I'm sure she thinks it's sexy. Yes, I'm contributing. Just email it to her when you're done. Do you have her number for the voice note? No, she doesn't want pictures of you reading it. Okay, thanks. Bye."

My eyes scan across the work surface in front of him where there's ingredients everywhere and my oven is on. "What's happening?"

Henry grabs an apron from the hook on the wall and pulls it over his head. "I'm baking your cookies for book club tomorrow. I've watched you do it a million times, so it'll be easy. I have your nana's recipe and a strong desire to not be haunted by her if I fuck it up."

"Oh," is all I manage to say as he rounds the breakfast bar and pulls out a stool for me, nodding toward it for me to sit.

"I talked to Mrs. Astor while you were in the shower, and she gave me her grocery list. Russ is going to the store now to pick it up for her, while Aurora creates a short list for your mom's Christmas present. She said to text her your budget. Cami is fine; I called her but she was in the middle of a Pilates class and only answered because she assumed it was an emergency. You might want to follow up."

I will not cry. I will *not* cry. "I will."

"Jaiden claims he won every science fair at his school. I don't believe him, but he does have a degree in chemistry, and your sister is eight, so I can't foresee a problem. He's going to send over some ideas and research direction when he gets home.

"Bobby claims he already read your *actual* book club pick but he's going to skim it to remind himself, then send you a detailed voice note about everything that happens. As well as some questions you can ask. He did offer to run the session for you, but I assumed you wouldn't want that. I recommend that you don't want that."

"But isn't everyone busy going home for Thanksgiving? Or studying? I don't want people to get behind when finals are coming up."

"People want to help you, Halle. And I think you're the only person I know who's already started studying."

I'm staring at him in awe, and in return he looks at me like I have two heads. "Thank you."

"Why are you looking at me weird?"

"Because you stopped the boat from rocking," I say, feeling the relief and appreciation meld.

"I don't know what that means," he says, turning my electronic scale on. "I made the executive decision to say fuck off to planning the vacation. So all that's left is that you need to talk to Gigi, and then study if that's something you feel like you should be doing."

"Will you kiss me?" I ask. "I promise I'm done crying."

"No," he says, and honestly, it catches me off guard. "Because if I kiss you, I'll want to do more, and I have already washed my hands. Ask me again when I'm done."

"Yes, Captain."

GIGI SPENDS OUR ENTIRE VIDEO call asking me repeatedly who she can hear in my kitchen.

I'm thankful that Henry told me to put my headphones on, saying if he wanted to listen to children complain about homework, he'd spend time with his teammates. I pointed out he's complained for the past three months, and he told me it didn't count because I think he's hot.

I'm still not sure how the two things are linked, but I do think he's hot.

After watching him concentrate on the recipe book over the top of my laptop, I'm inclined to agree with him that's he's good at everything. It takes longer than normal to get Gigi off the call, not because she suddenly developed an interest in me but because she's nosy.

Shutting my laptop, I watch Henry watching the cookies through the oven door as I stand and stretch. He assembled the ingredients more slowly than I do because he's so determined to get them right the first time. "They bake slower if you watch them."

He turns his head to look at me, eyebrows pinched enough for a tiny line to appear between them. "That sounds like a lie."

"It's true," I say as confidentially as I can without laughing. He stands straight and walks around the counter to my side, leaning in to kiss my temple. "Every baker knows."

"How do you feel now?" he asks, tucking my hair behind my ear and rubbing his thumb along my jaw affectionately.

"Better. So, so much better, but equally like I need a full-body massage to get rid of all the tension."

His hand travels from my jaw down my neck, and along my collarbone gently. "There's something I can do that will definitely get rid of all the tension in your body, and I bet I can do it before the oven timer goes off."

"I'll take those odds."

Kissing me gently first, Henry drops to his knees, and it's possibly the most devastating sight I've ever seen. I've never been so grateful to be wearing a dress. His hands run up the outside of my thighs, gliding past the hem, settling on the band of my underwear. "Have you done this before?"

He watches me, his tongue tracing his bottom lip as he waits for an answer. "No, but I want to know what it's like."

"Good. So do I. Lean back against the counter."

He pulls my underwear down my legs, lifting each foot by the ankle so I can step out. Kissing up the inside of my thigh, he hooks one of my legs over his shoulder, and his head disappears beneath the skirt.

It's hard not to wonder at what point my legs will just give out. Or my heart. Not sure which one will go first.

He spends time kissing and touching my inner thighs and ass, keeping me in place while I try not to wiggle away from him as the sensation of his evening stubble against sensitive skin makes me squirm.

His tongue parts me and my breath hitches, my head falling back as he licks and sucks. My skin feels like it's fizzling and my hands grip the countertop behind me to keep me upright. Whimpering his name earns me a slap to my ass, and when I moan again, he slowly slips a finger inside, working me until he can add another.

Everything that follows seems to happen in a blink. Pleasure rolls through every bit of me, building and building while I get used to feeling so full. He moans as I squeeze around him, flicking his tongue against me at the perfect speed and pressure.

"Henry," I moan. His free hand leaves its hold on my thigh, finding mine and letting me cling to him tightly.

My legs almost buckle as stars shoot behind my eyes; he's careful as he lets me go, sensitive and swollen, pulling up my panties and standing up to face me.

I should say something, anything, maybe write him a thank-you letter or erect a monument in his honor. But I don't need to, because the oven timer goes off, and the smug look on his face is all the appreciation he seems to need.

Chapter Twenty-Five

HALLE

THE NOISE FROM THE ARENA lobby is yet to die down even long after the game ended and people started to leave.

I managed to secure myself one of the tall tables and seats that border the room to attempt to draft a chapter. Henry tasked me with saying no more, which I'm putting into practice by telling *myself* no when I try to do anything that isn't working on my WIP now that Thanksgiving is done.

The manuscript was a good distraction from how sad I felt on Thursday after I got home from work to an empty house and Gigi and Maisie were too sleepy to talk. Mrs. Astor hosted her family and was sweet enough to leave me a plate in the fridge. She also stole my cat, but she did have the courtesy to forewarn me. One of her granddaughters is autistic and Joy helps her regulate at busy family events, so I don't mind sharing her.

A work in progress at least needs to be in progress, and now the load feels lighter, even if it's only temporarily. I need to stop feeling sorry for myself for being behind and actually do something about it.

I've been surprisingly—or unsurprisingly, depending on how you look at it—productive after my total meltdown. I realized I wasn't uninspired, something I previously struggled with; I've been distracted.

Sure, I doubt anyone would judge me for spending so much of my time under a sweet, hot hockey player, but still, I'm a woman with goals. I can have it all and I will, I just need to actually try. I can't continue to be distracted by a pretty face and a stellar personality. Even if it is *the* prettiest face and the *most* stellar personality.

Speaking of *the* prettiest face. Henry exits the door that now has two No Entry signs much to the happiness of the people still hanging around. There's cheers all around when they spot him, and as happy as it makes me to see him be celebrated, I cringe for his sensitivity to loud noises.

I attempt to focus on planning how I'm going to make my make-believe people kiss and fight, instead of trying not to laugh at how unimpressed Henry looks as people stop to talk to him. When two women approach him, his name on the back of their jerseys, the ability to pay attention to my laptop gets that little bit harder.

I can hear one of them laughing loudly from across the room, and the other puts her hand on his arm. I don't hear what Henry says, and I'm still pretending to be working when I spot him walking toward me in my peripheral vision. He stops next to me, the chair I'm sitting on putting us at similar heights so I can see how big his smile is when I turn to face him. "Hello. You won," I say simply. "Two days in a row and I saw them both. Does that make me your biggest fan?"

"Of course I won." He kisses me hard, dropping his bag on the floor to tangle his hands in the hair at the nape of my neck. He only breaks us apart when the passing hockey fans start whooping. He rests his forehead against mine. "You're my lucky charm. I told you: science."

Kissing in front of people is not something we do, even after the incident at the hotel, but as the two women in the Turner jerseys storm off, I suspect maybe the kiss wasn't for my benefit. "You can just reject people, y'know. You don't need to put on a show for them."

He leans back to look at me, his hands still resting on my neck. "What are you talking about?"

"Kissing me. The girls in the jerseys. Just tell them no."

"I did. Then I came over here to celebrate our win."

"Hmm," I grumble. I still feel like he was using me to send a message to people he's too tired to deal with. "If you say so."

"Are you being unreasonable to start a fight?" he asks. "It's fine if you are, but can you save your rage until we get home? If we're going to fight about this, we should fight about it somewhere we can make up."

I stare at his chest and shrug. "We're not fighting, and I'm not being unreasonable."

"My bad. I meant dramatic." I mumble that I'm not and he tugs a little on my ponytail to force me to look up at him. "And you are." He pecks my lips and I melt like the weak woman I am. "But I don't mind. We haven't had a fight yet. It's a good experience for you."

"If you tell me I'm dramatic one more time we *are* going to be fighting," I drawl.

He grins, and after a losing streak, seeing him genuinely happy after a game is a dream. "You're not doing a lot for your 'I'm not dramatic' case."

"We're officially fighting," I declare. In my head I sound serious and intimidating, but he gives me that damn smirk and kisses the tip of my nose, and it's clear he does not care one bit.

"Two wins and a fight with you? I'm so lucky. I have to get back, but you're going to wait here, right?" He peeks at my laptop screen where my Word document is open. "What are your imaginary friends doing today?"

It sounds patronizing, and it is in reality, but Henry started calling my characters my imaginary friends when I said it felt weird calling them their names, and I like when he shows an interest now that I have something to actually tell him. "They're not communicating and instead are dancing around what they want from each other."

He scoffs. "Sounds like us."

"We communicate," I argue. "We just communicated that we're in a fight because you kissed me to get rid of some women you're too tired to entertain."

"Halle," he says softly. "The only person I want to entertain is you. You and your dramatics keep me totally occupied. I kissed you because I'm a really big fan of kissing you. Some might say obsessed. It's the first thing I thought about doing when I got off the ice. Being here listening to you create imaginary conflict is going to get me into an *actual* conflict with Faulkner, but it's worth it."

"An obsession sounds pretty dramatic if you ask me," I mutter, burying my head in his chest to hide my face from him. "You should go do your leadery duties and leave me to my imaginary friends, I guess."

"I'm excited to fight with you when I'm done," he says, kissing my forehead.

"Can we save the fight until a later date? I'm kinda a big fan of not fighting with you ever," I say teasingly.

He nods as he laughs, walking away. It's not until he's going back through the no-access door that I realize quite how many people are watching me. I dig my headphones out of my purse and concentrate on my characters dancing around what they want from each other, and *definitely* not on Henry saying that sounds like us.

THERE IS NO FEELING MORE unnatural than silence in Henry's house.

While everyone piled in here earlier to celebrate their much-wanted wins, when they all headed out Henry told them he was staying in tonight with me. I'm pretty sure he said "with Halle" so they couldn't argue with him, and I don't mind being his get-out-of-jail-free card if he's tired from the adrenaline.

As soon as I made myself comfortable on his bed with my laptop he disappeared into another room, and when he came back, he was wearing his painting clothes and had a fresh canvas under his arm. He did not entertain my excitement that I was going to see him do something more than sketch. Instead, he sat on the floor and opened a small palette of paints, and that's where he's been since.

I don't know what he's painting, but given he's never let me see his work properly before, I'm too scared to ask in case it causes him and his canvas to scurry off somewhere else in the house.

"I can feel you watching me," he says as he swishes his paintbrush against the material.

"Watching sounds creepy. I'm admiring. I love your artwork—the little you show me, anyway."

I only get to see the things he does for me, not for himself. The drawings of Joy, the flowers he draws because I prefer them to real ones now, the portrait of Quack Efron being a distinguished gentleman wearing a suit, and not forgetting the things he draws *on* me.

Henry places the paintbrush between his teeth and stands from the floor with his palette and the towel it was sitting on. He throws the towel onto the bed beside me and puts the paint down. With one hand he closes my laptop and puts it on his bedside table, takes the paintbrush out of his mouth with the other, and sets it next to the palette.

"What're you doing?"

He climbs on top of me, straddling my hips so I can't move. "I'm painting. Can I lift your shirt up?"

"You're going to paint on my stomach?" I ask, already knowing the answer before he nods. "It's not flat."

"I have seen your stomach before," he says, like I'm ridiculous for even pointing it out. "Why does that matter?"

"It's just not toned, and I have some marks," *and I'm pretty sure there's a few black hairs beneath my belly button that I haven't tweezed.*

"It isn't weird to me that you have stretch marks." He pulls the arm of his T-shirt up and flexes, twisting until I spot the faint faded lines on his biceps. "I have them. You don't need to feel insecure."

I wouldn't say I immediately feel super defensive, but there is an aspect of how I want to react that is to defend myself. I know my body isn't what society would define as perfect, but I've worked hard to love myself through the years when it's felt like everything is designed to convince me not to. "I'm not insecure. I like my body," I say. "Other people seeing it isn't something I'm used to, that's all. I was just worried it wouldn't be a good canvas."

"You're my perfect canvas, Halle. Every part of you. But good to both of those things. I like your body, too, and I like being the only one to see it."

Perfect canvas. "What are you going to paint?"

"You'll have to wait and see."

I lift my T-shirt and tuck it under my bra to keep it out of his way. He doesn't talk while he gets to work. Starting with large strokes across my ribs and below my belly button, followed by hundreds, if not thousands, of smaller dabs and flicks. He hums to himself, occasionally pausing to sit back to assess his work.

Every brush stroke feels like a kiss against my skin, and when he checks if I'm okay, I can only nod, because the tenderness of it all is too much. It feels so personal and so special, and he wants to do it with me.

He climbs off me and works from my side, lying on his stomach. Then my other side, then between my legs. Every so often he asks me if I need anything, but I say no because I don't want this to end.

It does end and he makes me lie on the bed until it dries so I don't ruin his *masterpiece.*

"Do I get to paint on you next?" I ask, moving very slowly as he helps me get off his bed and walk toward his full-length mirror.

"No. I've seen your doodles. You're really bad at art."

"You're so rude sometimes, do you know that?" I grumble, scowling at him over my shoulder as we walk across the room.

He covers my eyes as we take the final few steps. "Everyone tells me not to filter what I say until it's time to tell them they're bad at art. Are you ready?"

"Show me."

Henry takes away his hands but stays close behind me; his face presses into my neck, kissing over where my pulse is hammering. Lilac and lavender swirls intersect with pearlescent white clouds across my rib cage; soft hues of pinks and blues and greens decorate my skin in the most delicate way. White and yellow blend seamlessly into it all. It takes me a second to realize what it is. "You like meadows. It's the first thing you ever drew on me."

"I spend a lot of time daydreaming about lying in them. Feels like it would be peaceful. I've developed a fondness for daisies, too."

There's an *H* on the lower left corner of my stomach in thick, black cursive. It's the only bold color on my stomach. "You signed me."

His fingers dance across the skin beneath his initial. "How does it make you feel when you look at it?"

"Pretty," I respond, answering honestly and feeling more vulnerable than I have before. "You always make me feel pretty."

"You feel like that because you *are* pretty, Halle."

"Promise me you'll let me experience going to a meadow with you."

"I promise."

Chapter Twenty-Six

HENRY

Finals is the only time of the year when I feel like I have the upper hand academically over all my friends.

I always do well in my exams because I've found a system that works to get the best out of me. Practical work has never been a stress for me because I enjoy it so much, and written work falls into my system. It's simple: I let the impending dread build and build until I start to convince myself that if I don't start doing *something* there's no way I'll pass, and then I start studying.

Is it the perfect strategy? No. Is it perfect for me? Yes, and it's never done me wrong.

Poppy stared at me with her mouth slightly ajar while I explained it to her and Halle. I told her I wanted to react in the same way when I found out she wants to be a kindergarten teacher.

Sure, my method isn't as tidy as Halle's highlighted timetable or Anastasia's not one, but two planners . . . But I'm the only person not freaking out yet about our imminent end of term exams, and holy shit does it feel good.

My and Professor Thornton's professional partnership is about to come to a grinding halt, and I've never felt better about never having to talk to someone ever again. I survived, largely because of Halle's kindness and determination, but I survived.

Now I just need to continue to survive hockey and I might not entirely fuck up my college career. Halle looked at me with pure panic when I told her I'd be putting in extra time at the gym instead of following her meticulously planned lead. It's safe to say she doesn't believe me when I say I thrive under pressure.

She pointed out that her concern isn't lack of belief in me, it's because every time I've been under hockey pressure, like losing, I've had what she calls a "meltdown."

I can't see her point.

WHEN EVERYONE COLLECTIVELY AGREES TO concentrate on textbooks instead of beer pong tonight, I try my hardest to look disappointed.

Halle and Aurora are giggling across from me, whispering to each other like a couple of kids. "What?"

"Nothing," Halle says quickly, eyes flicking back down to her paper.

I look to Aurora, saying nothing because I know I don't need to. She'll tell me if I stare at her long enough. It's around twelve seconds. "You're just a terrible actor, Hen. I've never seen anyone look so relieved not to get to go on a night out."

"I'm devastated, Aurora. I'm surprised you can't tell."

To me it sounds convincing, but for whatever reason they start giggling again. I don't know whose idea it was to have a late-night group study session, but if it means I don't have to go to a sweaty frat party, I'm all for it.

The front door opens, and Russ and Robbie appear holding bags of food. Russ looks at me and nods toward the den. "Can I talk to you?"

"Sure." I follow him and sit at the table, and hold my hand out for Russ to give me the burrito he just got.

Russ immediately places a laptop in front of me. When he lifts the screen, I realize what this is about. The student portal is staring back at me like something from my nightmares. "Do it, Henry. Or I'm not giving you your food. You can't run off to Halle's place and avoid me now. We're all here and you're doing this. I promised you I'd make you."

He takes my food out of the bag, holding the foil wrapper out of my reach. We both know I'm faster than he is. If I went for it, I could probably get it before he has a chance to fight me off. "You're being ridiculous."

"Press the buttons, Hen. Do it or I'm putting your dinner in the trash."

"Did you offer me a burrito with this in mind?" I ask, swishing my finger across the mouse pad but not clicking on anything.

"Yes."

"I'm not a dog," I grumble.

"Did he do it yet?" Robbie yells from the kitchen. He rolls himself into the den where we're sitting around the table, apparently where I'm signing up for classes, not where I'm eating a burrito.

Robbie hands me a plate for the food I don't have and takes his spot at the table beside Russ. "What do *I* need to do to get *you* to do what you need to do for next semester?"

"Does that even make sense?" I ask, making him roll his eyes at me.

"You promised me a month ago you were going to sign up for your classes on time. It's important that you don't have this weighing on you. It's important that I don't get fucking fired by Coach if we have a repeat of September. I'll give you anything, Hen. Name your price and just sort this out."

I must have forgotten to tell them that Halle made me do this two weeks ago, but I'll always seize an opportunity to get something from Robbie.

"Just log in and tell me what classes you want to take, and I'll do it for you," Russ says. "Then you can forget about it until after the New Year."

"I haven't decided what I want to do yet," I say, enjoying how both of their eyes widen. "I might take Thornton's other class."

"What do you mean, what you want to do? You've been complaining about him for literally months," Robbie snaps.

Russ unwraps his burrito slowly and I stare at mine longingly. "Is that the one Aurora and Halle are doing? The sex one?"

Robbie stops eating his own food and glares at me. "*Please* tell me you aren't considering putting yourself through more misery just to study sex with Halle. Do it in your bedroom like a normal couple. Don't get fucking graded on it."

I ignore when he and Russ both mutter *we're not a couple* under their breath before I can.

I shrug nonchalantly. "It sounds interesting. I like eighteenth-century art."

"You need to get laid," Robbie says, like I'm not incredibly aware of that fact. "You've lost your mind. Henry, promise me you're not going to do it. You can spend every spare second with her if you want to; you don't need to be with her during college hours, too. You don't like him, remember? Just because Halle is fucking brilliant and made it easy for you doesn't mean you should go through it *again*."

"It wasn't that bad," I say, and his face starts to redden.

"I think you're looking at it with rose-tinted glasses," Russ says carefully. "I know Halle made it manageable for you, but when she wasn't here you complained about Thornton a hell of a lot."

"I don't remember that," I say. Robbie is now very red. There's a vein in his forehead I only usually see when we're losing.

"Well I do," Robbie snaps. "You complained a fuck ton. So much that I felt like I was taking the class with you."

This is more fun than seems fair. "If JJ were here, he'd tell me to do it. And he'd let me eat my burrito."

Robbie snorts. "JJ told you to get your dick pierced and you told him that you'd rather swim with hungry sharks than ever take his advice. But sure, you'd listen to him about this. It's funny how you say 'ask JJ' and not Nate, who absolutely would not allow you to take a sex class."

To Robbie's credit, that's exactly what I said. However, I've taken JJ's advice more recently and it hasn't all gone horribly wrong yet.

"Did you start doing brain training or something? Why do you suddenly have the memory of an elephant?" I ask Robbie. "And you know it's not a sex class, right? It is definitely about art and literature."

Robbie looks at his watch, then back at me. "It's been five minutes of nonsense and not five minutes of you prioritizing your education. I'm being serious, Hen. Name your price."

"My price is my burrito. Give," I say to Russ, pulling the laptop toward me at an angle where they can't see the screen. Russ hands it over and they both sit, breathing loud sighs of relief, and unknowingly watch me type Halle an email about my burrito.

AFTER A COUPLE OF HOURS of everyone pretending they're studying, Halle and Aurora leave with the other guys to their respective houses. I want Halle to stay, but I also want to work on her Christmas present, which I only decided to make a couple of weeks ago. She was cool with it and said she'd use her free time to study without me trying to distract her.

I've noticed she says I distract her a lot, and I've been spending a lot of time trying to decide if she's hinting that I should stop. If it was anyone else, I'd ask them outright, but with Halle, I know that she'd tell me whatever she thinks I want to hear.

When I ask her if she's regretting not going home for the holidays, she tells me no, but I think I can tell that it's not the truth. She looks down before she smiles, and she lifts her shoulders up high, tilting her head to the side before saying, "It is what it is."

Cami and Aurora said Halle says the same thing to them, which makes me want to do something extra special for her. And the good thing about Aurora is that she loves interfering in making plans.

I'm about to find my tablet to continue with Halle's gift when I hear my name being yelled from downstairs.

"What?" I shout down in response.

"Halle is calling you. Take your phone off do not disturb!" Russ calls back.

Oh shit. Six missed calls.

"Sorry! Ringer is off," I say when Halle answers my call. "What's up?"

"Is my laptop charger at your house?" she says frantically.

Looking around my room, I spot it on the floor beside the slippers she left here. "Yeah."

"I'm on such a roll with this chapter and my laptop is going to die. I'm going to forget everything I want to write. Oh my God, I can't believe I left without it! What was I thinking?" she says. I can hear her rummaging around on the other end of the line. "Can you bring it over, please? I'd come get it, but I need to get this out of my head."

"I'm on my way," I say, silently proud of her for asking. "I'll be quick. Don't forget anything."

"Hurry!" she yells as I grab a sweatshirt and put the charger in the pocket.

Russ lets me borrow his truck so I don't have to jog over there, and it's another reminder that I really need to get my own car at some point. Looking at cars is boring, and every time I try to pick one I end up distracted.

It only takes ten minutes from leaving the house to pulling into Halle's driveway, and when I walk through the door she constantly leaves unlocked when she shouldn't, she's lying on her living room floor surrounded by sheets of lined paper covered in a more frantic version of her neat handwriting.

"Laptop died!" she says, tearing the paper from the pad and tossing it onto the growing pile. "Can't talk."

I don't say a word as I plug the charger into the socket and connect it to her laptop. Picking up Joy, who's wandering dangerously close to Halle's pile of papers, I tuck her under my arm as I walk around the kitchen, putting snacks onto a plate and grabbing a bottle of water from the refrigerator.

I put them on the floor beside where Halle is lying and drop myself into the chair with Joy.

It's fascinating watching her process be so raw. Normally when she writes it consists of her groaning at her laptop or being so into it she zones out and doesn't hear me talking to her. When I remember to ask her how the book is going, she changes the subject quickly or ignores it if what she's done is good.

Joy is purring on the center of my chest while I watch Halle throw her pen down and lie against her forearms. "Hi."

"Hello. I plugged in your laptop."

Lifting her head, she looks at all the pieces of paper scattered around her. "I was scared I'd lose the scene."

Moving Joy to my side, I hold open my arm. "Come tell me about it."

Halle climbs from the floor and shuffles over to my lap, maneuvering her legs over the arm of the chair. "I don't really know what to tell you. It probably won't make any sense when I read it back."

"Tell me anything. I like listening to you talk."

I run my hand up and down Halle's shin as she tries to work out where to start. "I'm trying to finish the second act, but because my twist is that she's marrying someone else, I've been writing their relationship basically not knowing who she's going to marry instead."

"Still rooting for my guy, but go on."

"And then I was like, he's standing at the front of the church, and why would your ex be at your wedding for starters—great plot hole, Halle—but *why* would he be at the front? Then I realized what if she was marrying someone he knows, like his best friend?"

I don't like where this is going, but she's so excited I don't want to stop her. "And it got me thinking about how when Will and I broke up he kept all the friends, but what if they broke up but she kept the friend? His best friend. Or they grew closer because they both wanted something more from this same person, and the thing that was missing brought *them* peace with each other as they both grieved what could have been romantically and platonically?"

"So that's what you've been writing? Her and his friend?"

"Kinda. Starting to set it up anyway. The thing I keep thinking is, what is the price of love? And how much is too much? At what point do you look at the choices you're making and decide the price is too high? How much should we sacrifice for someone we care about?" She's glowing, and I can't stop watching her. "I'm approaching this last act, and I honestly have no idea what's going to happen, so I just wanted to get all my thoughts down while I could before writer's block could hit me." She cups my face with her palm and kisses me gently. "Thank you for coming over so quickly."

"When did you know you wanted to be an author?" I ask. I can't believe I've never asked her before.

"When I was about six or seven. My mom took me to a kids' event at the library where the author was doing a reading, and I just thought it was so exciting and special. I can't even remember who the author was, but everyone was hanging on her every word, and I decided I wanted to do that."

"I want to see people hanging on your every word in a library," I say softly, resting my hand on her thigh.

She picks it up, kissing my knuckles gently. "Hopefully."

Chapter Twenty-Seven

HALLE

THERE'S SOMETHING ABOUT WALKING OUT into the fresh December air knowing I don't have to think about college again until the first week of January that makes everything in my life so much better.

Henry is engrossed in his cell phone on a bench when I walk out of the English building with Rory. He's completely oblivious to the group of women talking about him to his left when we walk toward him. He looks up as I reach him, smiling at me in a way that makes my heart pound.

"Is the oxygen oxygening more today?" I ask when he stands, pushing his phone into his pocket and kissing my cheek. "Or is it me?"

"Halle's being weird today," Aurora says. "Like, really super weird and unnaturally joyous."

His eyebrows crease, nose scrunching in the way it does. "It's you. Air is air."

"I have so many things I'm going to achieve over winter break and I'm excited to not feel like a failure anymore," I say. "I'm going to get ahead in everything and get my life in order."

"Sounds boring. How much more in order can your life get?"

Henry says, pulling my book bag from my shoulder and slinging it over his.

I don't bother answering him because he has no idea how many half-written and half-thought-out chapters I have collecting virtual dust on my laptop right now. I also need to type up the chapter I for whatever reason decided to write by hand. My first draft was supposed to be done so I could spend the next couple of months editing before I need to submit in March. I still haven't finished the second act, and God knows what will happen when I get to the third.

I'm so behind, but I've decided to see spending Christmas working as a blessing and not a disappointment, and that when class starts again, I'll be back to my usual undistracted and organized self.

"Yeah, I'm with him. You're one of the most put-together people I know," Aurora says, turning to face Henry. "But speaking of people who don't have their lives together . . . How's the soul-crushing panic treating you? When's your last exam?"

"You're being very judgmental about my choices for a person deeply in need of therapy," Henry says, and while my instinct is to gasp, Aurora laughs. "It's this afternoon and I'm genuinely not worried."

"I also think lying is fun." She looks down at her cell phone and smiles. "Russ just texted to say he's finished. We're going Christmas shopping; do you need me to pick anything up for you?"

I think she's talking to Henry at first, but then I realize she's looking at me. "Sorry, what?"

"Have you finished your Christmas shopping, or do you need some help? We're going to the mall, but if there's something specific you need, I can use the personal shopper service my mom has. They'll gift wrap and arrange for it to be mailed to Phoenix for you, too."

I know it's not a huge deal, but Aurora's offer catches me off guard. She already did me a huge favor by helping me organize the gift from my siblings when they were hounding me; I'd never expect her to help with anyone else.

I also can't think of a time when anyone has offered to help me at Christmas. I'm always in charge of making sure everyone has the right gift for everyone else, and people think nothing of it.

"I've finished already, but thank you for offering."

"No problem! Text me if you think of anything. Bye, lovebirds."

Aurora lifts her phone to her ear as she walks away, and when she's out of earshot, Henry finally talks. "I have two hours to kill. Do you want to break the 'No heavy petting in the library' rule with me?"

An unexpected laugh bursts out of me and he pulls me closer, laughing too. His hands settle on my neck, tilting my head back gently to look up at him. "As festive and not at all voyeuristic as that sounds, I promised I'd work at Enchanted for a couple of hours to help with the last-minute gift-buying as people start to leave town for Christmas."

He pouts. Like actually. "Are you saying no to me?"

"You do keep telling me that I should say no to people."

His thumb rubs along my jawline. "I mean everyone else, not me."

"Ah, well, the instructions were unclear, so I'll be saying no to everything you ask me from now on."

"That's not going to happen, though, is it? I'm taking you out later to celebrate surviving Thornton."

I feel like everyone is looking at us, but I'm trying to tell myself it's in my head. We're standing so close together, talking in hushed voices, while Henry touches my face gently. I don't know how we ended up here, but I don't want it to stop.

"I just told you I'm saying no to everything you ask me," I tease.

"And I didn't ask you." My mouth opens to object, then closes, then opens again, but I don't have anything to fight back with because he's got me there. "Are you being a goldfish? What's happening?"

"You, Henry Turner. You're happening. You are constantly happening to me."

He leans in slowly, grinning before kissing me in a way that makes my entire body tingle. "Is that a good thing?"

"Yes."

"I told you saying no to me wasn't going to happen."

"What should I wear later?" I ask, apparently accepting his non-invitation with no objections. "For our plans."

He tucks my hair behind my ear. "Something you like."

"You are so, so helpful."

"I know. It's one of my many talents."

THE DAY HAS FLOWN BY and I'm grateful that I don't work in retail full time.

In a bid to decompress from the chaos that was working in Enchanted, I attempted to work on my book, and as a result have left myself with not enough time to find matching shoes. By the time Henry lets himself into my house, I only have one. It takes all my powers not to drool when I look up from where I'm kneeling on the floor of my closet and spot Henry standing there in a suit and white shirt.

"Why are you eye-fucking me?" he asks, leaning against the doorframe calmly.

"I'm not!" I argue, although I definitely might be. "Okay, it's the suit."

"You see me in a suit every week."

"*That* suit is different." I don't know anything about men's fashion, but this one looks like it was made to mold to every muscle in his body. Not too tight, just enough to accentuate his physique. "You look *really* good."

He just smiles, which I'm going to accept as agreement. Henry reaches into his inner suit pocket, pulling out a folded piece of paper. "I was going to do flowers, but I thought you might be bored of them."

"I could never get bored of anything you create." I open the piece of paper he hands me and find a drawing of me staring back. I'm in my living room reading a book with Joy in my lap. It looks like a photograph. "Did you do this from memory?"

"Yeah. I started it a couple of weeks ago, but I finished it last night."

"I thought you said you were studying last night!" I say, my voice creeping higher than it should.

"No, I said I was busy working. I never said I was studying." My jaw drops. "Halle, if you're going to stay kneeling on the floor in front of me with your mouth wide open, we might end up having a very different evening than the one I've planned. Just say thank you and hurry up."

Every inch of my body gets hotter. "Thank you."

"You're welcome, and you look really good, too."

Henry watches me until I finally find my other shoe, and holds out his hand to help me from the floor. "I have two shoes. I'm ready. Do I get to know where we're going yet?"

"No," he says, smiling. "It's a surprise."

We put the makeshift cardboard wall around my Christmas tree to prevent Joy from trying to climb it and leave her with Destiny's Child's Christmas album playing for company. I truly believe that Henry would bring her everywhere we go in one of those cat backpacks if I let him.

We sit in a comfortable quiet, letting the radio fill the silence between us as we idle in traffic. His hand is holding the inside of my thigh, and I'm trying to hold myself together.

He turns the radio down, twisting in his seat to face me as we slowly creep down the highway. "Have you written anything today?"

"Maybe like a thousand words before I started getting ready. I was pretty tired after helping at the bookstore."

"And what were your imaginary friends doing for those thousand words?" he asks, eyes darting between the road and me. "Is she dating his friend yet?"

"No, the book moves around in time so you see the key things in their story. I'm writing the past when she's worried she likes him more than he could ever like her, because he isn't a relationship guy. She's scared to get hurt and she's keeping bits of herself back, which he hates. She wants him to prove that he deserves those bits before she hands them over, and he wants her to just trust that he can be the person she needs because what they have is special enough for the risk."

"And can he? Change for her?"

"No."

He keeps checking between me and the road, which is how I catch his furrowed brow. "Why not?"

"You're asking me to spoil the book for you?" He nods. "I don't know yet. I'm working it out as I go. Mainly because I question if one person *should* change to be in love with another person. At what point do you eventually revert back to the person you were? And is the love even genuine if you had to become someone else to achieve it?"

"I disagree," he says. "I think the right person makes you the person you were supposed to be in the first place. I don't agree that you become a different person. That suggests people can't change through all the other factors that make people evolve that aren't romantic."

"What makes you say that?"

"I've seen my friends change for the better because they fell in love with the right person. If people only fell in love when the other person became their perfect match, messy relationships wouldn't exist. People can't control when they fall in love. You wanted to love Will, but you couldn't."

I take in what he's saying, and it seems so different from our first date when we talked about my idea. "What happened to not valuing romantic love above the other types?"

"What happened to complicated is exciting?" He squeezes my leg playfully. "Does she really have to marry someone else?"

"I haven't written it yet, but yeah. That's the plan."

"I'm going to keep asking." He tsks. "I still have faith in my imaginary man. He's going to pull it out of the bag and win her."

The traffic picks up and we revert back to our normal comfortable silence. I realize where we're going when Henry takes a familiar exit, and I'm immediately glad I found my other flat shoe. I've always intended to visit the Byrd & Bolton art gallery, but I haven't had anyone to go with.

Henry climbs out of the car, immediately walking to my side and opening the door for me. He holds out his hand. "You've really got this gentleman thing down," I tease.

"It's the suit." He threads his fingers through mine like he did earlier. "Makes me act up."

He produces two tickets when we reach the entrance and scans us through the barrier. "I've always wanted to come here," I admit. "Thank you for bringing me."

"I've been wanting to bring you for a while. I was just hoping I'd have something special to show you here."

I let him guide me through the first floor; his hand grips my waist to gently tug me out of the path of someone staring at a pamphlet as they walk toward us. His finger runs down the length of my forearm. "You have goose bumps. Are you cold?"

"The AC is a little high," I flat-out lie. Lying might be bad, but so is admitting that my body does weird, uncontrollable things in his presence. "It's my fault for wearing this dress."

"The dress is perfect, and you look perfect in it," he says, shrugging off his suit jacket. Before I have time to object, he places it over my shoulders. "I don't want you to be cold."

"Thank you," I say, but it comes out as more of a whisper.

"Why are you whispering?"

"I don't know."

Henry gives me a funny look and retakes my hand. "It's supposed to be around this corner."

We pass signs for a local up-and-comers exhibition on display through December. He stops in front of a large painting.

It could be a photograph, it's so intricately detailed. The women are sitting together at a table outside; light blue sea and small white buildings are their backdrop. Their intertwined hands rest on the table between wineglasses, and their faces are turned toward each other. The woman on the left has pale white skin and dark blond hair, cut to a length that just skims her collarbone. Her blue-and-white collared shirt is unbuttoned at the top, and I can just about make out the *Y* and *H* initials hanging from a delicate chain around her neck.

I'm captivated by how the artist has shown her laughing; I feel like I'm intruding on a private moment.

The other woman has rich brown skin and long reddish-brown hair braided down to her chest, where it turns into perfectly identical curls. Her bone structure feels familiar, like I've met her before. The part of her outfit I can see is the softest shade of buttercup yellow, but the thing I can't take my eyes off of is her smile.

It's mesmerizing, and even as someone with no knowledge of art, I can tell the time and care that's gone into this piece. Someone who loves these women painted this; I'm sure of it.

Beneath the name of the painting is a much smaller rectangular plaque with black letters sitting on a white background.

TWO WOMEN IN LOVE
HENRY TURNER

"You painted this?" I'm trying not to let the shock show on my face, since it feels like I spend a lot of time with my mouth hanging open around this man. "Henry, it's stunning. Are they your moms?"

He nods. "I'm glad you like it. Okay, we can go now," he says, placing his hand on my waist.

"Wait!" I whisper, twisting to face him. "You're showing me your art, Henry."

"Why are you telling me like I didn't organize this?"

"Because this is monumental for me. You don't like people looking at your work and you're voluntarily showing me work that isn't of me or on me. Can you understand how special that makes me feel?"

"You are special, Halle," he says, leaning forward to kiss my forehead.

"Please tell me about the painting, Henry. When did you do it? It must have taken hours. Where is it?"

"I did it during summer break. Russ was working at a summer camp; Nate, JJ, and Joe all moved away; Robbie was with Lola and visiting his parents. I had a lot of free time. It was on their anniversary vacation to Greece last year. They borrowed my camera for the trip, and I found it when I was looking for something else. They look so happy in the photo. I decided I wanted to paint it."

"What do they think of it?"

"Wow, you're asking a lot of questions tonight. They haven't seen it yet. I forgot to tell them I'd submitted it. They both have some vacation time for Christmas, so I'll ask if they want to see it one of those days I'm home."

"They're going to want to see it, Henry. They're definitely going to want to. I'm so proud of you, and I'm so honored that you've shared it with me. Do you want me to take your picture with it or something? This is so special. I feel like we need to commemorate it somehow."

Henry looks down at me like I have three heads. "I'm good."

"Don't you want a picture to show people? Or to remember it?"

Short of picking him up and putting him next to the painting, I *will* convince him.

"If people want to see it, they can come here. It's an art gallery," he says calmly. People pass by us, not stopping to pay attention to the two people standing face to face, debating with each other. "I don't care about these hypothetical people. I wanted to show you and I have."

"But I want the experience of taking your picture next to your beautiful artwork," I say, definitely pouting. Childish, but hopefully effective.

He shakes his head, the corner of his mouth tugging up into a smirk. "I'm too busy to take a picture." He lifts both of his shoulders and tilts his head, giving me a look that says "Waddaya gonna do?"

"You're too busy?" I repeat.

"Number one in the Henry and Halle code of conduct rule book: we have to be honest about how busy we are."

"You're—" God, he's smiling really big now. "Insufferable."

"How about we compromise?" Both of his hands find my waist and my pulse ping-pongs around my body as he walks me backward slowly. There's no sound except my feet hitting the floor and our breathing. When I sense the wall behind me he stops moving, letting go of me to take a few steps back himself. He pulls his cell phone from his pocket and holds it up. "I'll take your picture with it."

"You're joking."

"If you want this picture to turn out nice, I recommend you stop talking and start smiling, because you look possessed in that last one."

"You're rid—"

"Oops, there's another one."

"Fine!" I snap, smiling next to his painting.

After ten seconds he finally lowers his phone. "Beautiful."

"Do I get to see?" He nods and walks over, handing me his phone. "I'm deleting the bad ones."

"But they're my favorite," he groans as I pull up his camera roll.

He wasn't joking—I really do look possessed. I spend more time deleting awful pictures than I do looking at nice ones, but at least I know I'm not going to come here one day and see it hanging on the wall.

"Are you done being a photography critic? We have a dinner reservation and I'm so hungry."

"I'm not done looking at your work," I say. We stand side by side in silence, elbows touching, looking at the two people who made Henry Turner the man he is. "How do you feel when you look at it?"

He mulls over my question for a little while, but I don't mind waiting. "Lucky. What about you?"

"Grateful."

Chapter Twenty-Eight

HENRY

Normally I don't love our Christmas party, but this year it feels different.

Robbie has relaxed a little with his party antics since starting grad school. I know he has a lot of work on his plate as well as trying to prove to Faulkner and the college board that he's responsible enough for a permanent job at the end of the year. We're still having our normal fancy dress party, but he hasn't gone over-the-top the way he has in previous years.

He says it shows maturity and didn't like when I said it seemed like poor time management, since he forgot to order the decorations by the cutoff.

That said, our house still looks like Michael Bublé himself threw up on it. Michael—and I've been forced to listen to him enough that I feel like I can call him by his first name—has been playing for the past week. In between exams, we slowly decorated the house to meet Robbie's standards. Lola tried to help, but she's easily distracted and not great at taking directions. Ironic for someone who wants a career on stage. I immediately banished Aurora and Poppy for similar traits, but Halle, Cami, and Emilia were very helpful.

I'm already drunk when guests start showing up, which makes everyone patting me on the back for our recently improved game performance more tolerable. People keep stopping to say hi to me and chat while I'm trying to mix a punch bowl for Halle. Multiple women I've hooked up with keep trying to talk to me. I have been politely telling them I'm not available, which results in their faces dropping before walking off.

Sure, I might not technically have a girlfriend, but I'm definitely not available, and the person I'm not available with really likes this punch I'm trying to concentrate on.

After people we know had their drinks spiked a couple of months ago, we stopped making random shared drinks, but tonight is the exception because I'm going to guard it with my life.

Cami is coming and it's her first party since October, so we have a system to keep drinks separate from the rest of the party to help her feel comfortable. Poppy has stopped drinking alcohol altogether after she said she found herself panicking as soon as it started to have an effect on her.

Russ leans against the counter beside me. "Breaking hearts isn't very Christmasy."

The only thing I've broken today is the mistletoe above the front door. That went straight into the trash. There's no way I was giving one of the guys the opportunity to kiss Halle when she gets here. "What are you talking about?"

"There's, like, three women outside comparing conspiracy theories about why you're not paying attention to them." He sips his beer to stop himself from laughing. "They might need a support group once they see that post."

"Why is everyone around me so annoying?"

I woke up this morning to a million messages in our group chat because the insidious UCMH gossip page posted me kissing Halle after her exam yesterday. I didn't look at it properly because I don't care, but Halle was very embarrassed until I reminded her that she isn't allowed to be embarrassed with me.

I add the final pour of vodka and grab us a cup to test it. When Russ takes a sip and his eye twitches and face tightens, I realize I forgot to add in the orange and pineapple juice, and I've basically given him lemon-flavored liquor. "My bad, buddy."

"I feel like my tongue is sweating. Is that possible?"

"It's the lemon . . . Or maybe the tequila and vodka, I can't be sure," I say, laughing at the way his face is twisting.

"Not to make this weird, but I'm glad you have your spark back after that bad time," Russ says, and that's when I realize he's a little buzzed, too. "You're a great friend and a great captain."

"Why are you making things weird?" I ask.

He rubs the back of his neck with the palm of his hand, then pretends to fix his Santa hat. "I've said it now so there's no going back. I'm just gonna go wait for Rory to show up and for Robbie to announce the game."

If Halle blushes occasionally, then Russ blushes often. All the way to the tips of his ears. I'm not a huge fan of heart-to-hearts—they always feel awkward and unnecessary—but I believe it takes a lot to start one. "Thanks for saying it. I appreciate it."

Thankfully, it doesn't take long for the girls to show up. Halle told me her favorite part of doing anything now is getting ready; she always wanted a big group of girlfriends she could do things with and now she has one.

I can see the white halo on her head bobbing through the crowd as she makes her way toward me in the kitchen. Her white dress stops halfway down her thighs, and she has white feathered wings poking out on her back.

"Are you a Quack Efron?" I ask, looking her up and down.

She throws her arms around my neck and kisses me, which catches me off guard more than anything. When she leans back and looks up at me, I realize that she's buzzed. She told me earlier that it's my job not to let her get drunk so she doesn't turn into a hungover nightmare. It's a plan I can get on board with. "A duck? I'm an angel!"

Aurora appears behind her dressed in green. "And what are you?" I ask her.

"I'm a Christmas tree, duh." She motions to her green dress like I was somehow supposed to get that from just looking at her.

"You both look great for a chicken and a plant." Emilia and Poppy appear behind them with Cami and I try to guess what their outfits are supposed to be before I have to go through this again. "Are you two supposed to be dominoes?"

Emilia snorts, but Poppy, who I assume oversaw costumes judging by her reaction, looks offended. "We're snow women!"

I finally look at Cami and I want to give up immediately. "Did you get into patchwork quilting during your partying hiatus?"

"I'm clearly Sally from *Nightmare Before Christmas*." She folds her arms across her chest. "What are you supposed to be?"

"First of all, that's a Halloween movie." I point to the same hat I've been wearing for three Christmases. "And I'm obviously Santa."

The five of them stare at me with the same expression, but I can't place what it is. Respect, maybe? Awe and wonder? Halle's arms leave my neck and travel down my body until she reaches the hem of my shirt and pulls it out. "You're not even wearing a costume."

I shrug. "I'm an undercover Santa. I'm checking if the information I have on my list is correct—or something."

"You're Santa's auditor." Aurora's head shakes slowly. "Unbelievable and yet so on brand. Props to you for your consistent dedication to the bare minimum."

"I go above and beyond where it matters."

"So I've heard, lover boy," she says, and Halle slowly turns to look at her.

I look across the five of them. "Did nobody think to be the Spice Girls? Well, Christmas Spice Girls?"

"How on *earth* do you know who the Spice Girls are?" Aurora says, shaking her head.

I think she's irritated I saw the resemblance when she didn't. I don't know how they missed it, considering they all fit the bill perfectly. "I played with JJ for two years. You don't make it out of that experience without knowing who the Spice Girls are."

"Why didn't you tell me? That would've been such a good outfit."

"I can't do everything for you, Aurora. I was busy coming up with my own outfit. At least you have something for Halloween now. Which is lucky, since Cami is already wearing her Halloween outfit."

"You're not even wearing a costu— No. Never mind," Aurora says, interrupting herself. "Y'know what, it's Christmas. I'm not letting you get a rise out of me for your own amusement. I'm going to find my boyfriend because I bet he can tell I'm a tree."

"He's in the den," I say, nodding toward the adjoining room. "He's also an undercover Santa."

"Uh, not if I have anything to do with it," she says as she walks off.

I explain the drinks situation and try to reassure the rest of them that they'll have a good, safe time. Emilia, Poppy, and Cami thank me and follow Aurora to the den, leaving me alone with Halle.

"You look beautiful," I tell her. "The most beautiful swan I've ever seen."

She pins me with a look as she shuffles her wings. "Oh, so I'm a swan now? I wanted to be a donkey, but I wasn't allowed. *Apparently*, a donkey wouldn't make you fall to your knees and be overcome with desire. Because that's something that's important."

"Aurora says weird stuff sometimes."

"Oh, it wasn't Aurora. It was Jaiden. He called Emilia while I was there and wanted to know what my outfit was."

Her eyes flutter closed as I run my finger beneath where her cheekbones are shimmering under the lights and tuck her hair behind her ear. Something I do because I like to hear the way she tries to steady her breathing when I touch her unexpectedly. "We should really have a rule about listening to JJ about anything."

She looks down at her dress then back up at me innocently. "I guess you're right. It definitely didn't make you fall to your knees."

"I've wanted to get on my knees for you from the second you walked in, but it wasn't because of your dress. It's because of how much I like making you come."

Her cheeks turn red immediately, and I feel a kind of smug satisfaction from getting a reaction out of her. "It amazes me how you can go from sweetly reassuring our friends that their drinks will stay safe to this in under five minutes."

I pick up the punch bowl and ladle from the counter and start walking toward the den with her. "You'd be amazed what I can achieve in under five minutes."

THE HOUSE PARTY HAS OVERSPILLED into the garden, and it feels like every person at UCMH is in our house right now.

I took a seat on the couch in the den and put the punch bowl on the table beside me earlier, and it's where I've stayed. I've noticed that now Halle is with me, people don't talk to me as much because they all want to talk to her.

I *love* it.

If anyone tries to include me by asking me a question, I defer to my little social butterfly and I'm back in the safety zone again. The only bad part is when she gets up to use the bathroom and I have an unestablished amount of time to fend for myself. She goes with her friends, and they take a fucking lifetime.

Mattie drops into the seat beside me. "Did you know about this?"

"Define *this*."

Mattie gestures to Robbie on the other side of the room talking to a more animated than normal Bobby. "There's no game!"

"So?"

Robbie follows Bobby across to where we're sitting, rolling his eyes dramatically. "He's not joking," Bobby says as he throws himself onto the couch, making it shake.

"I feel like I'm missing an important part of what's happening," I say, looking between my feuding friends.

"There's no game," Robbie and Bobby say at the same time.

I try hard to understand what's happening with the various grievances I'm made aware of on a day-to-day basis. Nate played mediator and now it falls to me, but this one has me totally lost. "So?"

"If there's no game, what's the point? Why are we all even here?" Mattie groans.

The circle grows as Russ and Aurora appear and Halle returns from the bathroom with Cami. "What's happening?"

"It's my new low-key vibe," Robbie explains, without really explaining. "The days of drunk Jenga are behind me. Plus, we all know how that ended last time."

"Uh, how did it end last time?" Cami asks, filling her cup from the punch bowl beside me.

"Russ and Aurora fucked, and Henry ran down Maple Avenue naked," Mattie says. "Two beautiful things that wouldn't have happened if you didn't stay true to yourself, Rob. Nate and Stassie, you and Lols . . . it happened at *your* parties. Where there were games! Hen and Halle, too! *You're* the invisible string, brother. Why are you holding out on the rest of us?"

"Does he always talk like this?" Cami asks, looking at Mattie with a disgusted, but kind of amused, expression. "Like if he just keeps going people will believe what he says? Because I'm almost one hundred percent confident that's not what invisible string theory is about. Me and Halle listen to the song about it every single work shift."

"Yes," multiple people say at once.

"When he's really drunk he likes to reimagine things to suit whatever he's trying to do," Robbie adds. "You don't need a drinking game to have a good time, Mattie."

"Wait, we didn't meet at a party," I argue, glancing at Halle, who looks like she's questioning why she ever wanted friends. "We met in a bookstore."

"That you were at with Aurora, who you wouldn't know if Muffin hadn't slutted himself out after—drumroll please—a game at Robbie's farewell and fuck-off party," Bobby says. "I'm seeing the vision. Robbie, you need to come up with something quickly. The expansion of our friend group relies upon it."

"I'm good with not expanding," I say. "If anything, I think we're good to lose some people."

"You'll miss us when we graduate," Kris says, appearing behind Robbie.

"Where did you go? You missed Mattie being really weird," Russ says.

Kris holds up a red package. "I ran home to get UNO, Muffin. Because I'm not witnessing the downfall of Robert Hamlet in my lifetime."

"And what are we going to do with UNO?" Robbie drawls, twisting in his wheelchair to look at Kris behind him.

Kris shrugs, and it's clear he hasn't thought that far ahead. "Anything can be made into a drinking game; you taught me that."

Robbie turns back to face me and pinches the bridge of his nose. "I have to fly home in the morning. If I miss my flight, one of you is driving me to Colorado."

"That's the spirit!" Mattie says. "I'll find the shot glasses."

I stay in my seat beside the punch bowl and watch all my friends head toward the dining table. I think half of them are following out of curiosity to see what Kris manages to come up with, and the others somehow believe Robbie is the key to them getting laid.

Halle sits beside me and watches in silence. I put my arm across her shoulders and she cuddles into me, smiling up when I kiss her temple. "You don't want to play?"

She shakes her head and rests it against my shoulder. "I'm good here with you."

"You don't want to test if Robbie's party game is the center of a happy relationship?"

"Nope. Like I said, I'm good here with you."

"Halle?"

"Yeah?"

"Where did your eagle wings go?"

Chapter Twenty-Nine

HALLE

IF I EVER UNEXPECTEDLY FIND myself in a position of any sort of power, there are a few rules I'll immediately put into place:

1. You cannot answer the question, "What do you want for Christmas?" with, "Nothing. I don't need anything."

2. When someone says that they're taking you away for the night and you ask, "What do I need to pack?" they cannot answer with, "Whatever you feel comfortable in."

3. Christmas traffic is illegal.

When Henry told me that he wanted to take me away for the night because I'm now working double shifts from Christmas Eve until the day before New Year's Eve, I didn't expect it to result in this level of stress. I don't even want to do double shifts, but when my manager asked me to because someone quit unexpectedly, I didn't want to let him down when he said everyone else had said no.

As grateful as I am for the extra money, especially because nobody told me how expensive having a social life is, it's really thrown a grenade at all the things I hoped to catch up on during winter break. I'd fully intended to get ahead, and now I guess I'll have to work harder and stay up later to do it.

Something I wish I'd worked a little harder on is packing a bag for this trip. Joy is on vacation at Mrs. Astor's house, living her best life getting all the attention from the visiting grandchildren. And here I am, on my bedroom floor surrounded by clothes.

After I spend five minutes staring at them, hoping they'll compile themselves into some kind of outfit, Henry walks into my bedroom. "Wow, you're messy," he says, sitting on my bed behind me.

"I love it when you compliment me," I drawl, rummaging through my clothes. *Why is everything the same color?*

"Your tits look great today, and I like your hair like that."

It's enough to get me to break the staring contest with my floor-drobe and look at him. "Huh?"

"You said you love it when I compliment you. I can keep going; I have a long list of things about you that I like."

"That's not . . . That's . . . Thank you?" I say, unsure what there is *to* say.

He leans toward me from the bed, and I think he's trying to kiss me until he starts to squint. "Why do you only have stuff on one eyelid?"

"That's a really great question." I cross my legs and try to sit back to look at him comfortably, but I can't find a place to put my hands because of all the clothes, so I opt to climb onto the bed beside him instead. "Because my mom called when I was putting makeup on to beg me to book a flight home and call out sick. I couldn't get her off the phone, and then I realized you were on your way and I hadn't packed anything."

Not that I'd admit it to Henry, but there was more than one time where I *almost* agreed to let my mom book me on a flight. She's upset I'm not there, and as much as I've tried to make my peace with it, I'm upset I'm not there, too. "Was your mom okay? Are you okay?"

I nod, although it lacks conviction. "I knew she was *really* sad when she gave up on trying to make me come to Phoenix and started trying to convince me to go to my dad's. She just doesn't want me to be so far from people who love me on Christmas. I said no and stuck to my guns."

Henry holds out his arm and I slide under it, breathing him in deeply when he kisses the crown of my head. "You won't be. Do you think if you weren't people-pleasing your manager you would have given in to people-pleasing your mom?"

"Can you let me have this moment? Tell me you're proud of me for not being a people pleaser to the person who made me a people pleaser!"

"I'm proud of you. I'll be so proud when you finish getting ready so we're not late. That will really *please* me."

"You're annoying," I grumble, turning to my messy floor.

He laughs. "That's not very festive."

WHEN THE HIGHWAY SIGNS SAY Malibu, I realize I have no idea what he has in store for us.

Henry ignores all my questions as we pull up to the valet at a fancy hotel. He walks around the car to open my door, helping me as our overnight bags are collected from the trunk.

"This is a really nice place," I whisper to him as we climb the carpeted staircase to the lobby entrance. With only a couple of days until Christmas, there's an expensive-looking red bow and various festive ornaments decorating the entrance. "I don't think I've ever been anywhere this fancy before."

Thankfully, when Henry arrived at my house wearing dress pants and a shirt, I realized I needed to wear and pack something besides sweatpants.

"You work at The Huntington," he says, like I'm ridiculous.

"That isn't the same thing! I think I'm underdressed."

"I don't gamble, but if I did, I would bet you that Aurora calls you a goddess or tells you she wants to bow at your feet in the first ninety seconds. You look incredible, Halle. Like you always do."

"Thank you, I'm ju— Wait! Is Aurora here?"

Henry groans, stopping on the last step before the doors. "Oh fuck. I wasn't supposed to tell you that. I mean, she's never on time, so if I tell you she isn't here, I'm unlikely to be lying. C'mon."

He takes my hand and leads me into the hotel lobby, where to my surprise and confusion, Aurora and Russ are standing. "Oh my God."

"Merry Friendsmas! Or Christmas Eve eve!" Aurora says as she approaches me, immediately pulling me into a hug. "I love that color on you. You look incredible! I sort of want to bow at your feet. Why do you look so powerful and goddessy?"

"Told you. Why do you ever doubt me?" Henry mutters beside me. I nudge him with my shoulder playfully, and he keeps me close by wrapping his arm around my waist. He looks at our friends. "I didn't think you'd be on time."

"You're one to talk," Aurora says. "You're constantly showing up late!"

"I'm late because I don't want to go, not because I can't be ready on time. It's different, Aurora," Henry counters. Which, to be fair to him, *is* true.

"We're early because Ror wanted to get away from the sibling rivalry," Russ explains, trying his hardest not to laugh.

Aurora rolls her eyes, and I can't help but ask because Aurora's family life is already a little strained. "Elsa?"

"God, no. My sister doesn't do family; she's in the Maldives. It's that goddamn cat my mom stole." Aurora holds up her arm to show us multiple angry-looking scratches covering the area between her wrist and elbow. "There isn't even any rivalry; he's already won, and he knows it. He left a dead mouse in one of my shoes last night. Mom keeps trying to tell me it's good luck and to stop being so negative all the time."

"Have you considered that you've done something to offend the cat?" Henry asks her, looking at her phone screen as she holds up— yep, that's a dead mouse in a shoe.

"Why are you victim blaming me? On Friendsmas?" Aurora says.

"Okay, I sense a debate brewing, and I would like to eat before the year ends, so maybe we should let them know we're here," Russ says, quickly interjecting between his girlfriend and best friend.

It's funny, because Henry and Aurora seem to really like arguing with each other. I've watched them turn the smallest of things into a debate where their sole aim was to annoy each other as much as possible. As the peacekeeper in my family, I can confirm with absolute certainty that they act like siblings. Henry always says he's glad he's an only child without realizing he has a younger sister in Aurora and an older sister in Anastasia.

The amount of food we order is excessive, but somehow, we manage to eat it all. Henry has booked us a night at the hotel, so knowing my bags are upstairs makes Aurora try to convince me to get changed into pajamas with her to accommodate her food baby. It takes longer than it should to make her accept that the restaurant wouldn't like that. By the time Henry and I are heading upstairs to our room, any of the negative feelings about not spending this time with my family are long gone.

Our bags are sitting by the door, and when we enter our room, I see several identically wrapped presents under a beautifully decorated Christmas tree in the corner.

"It feels illegal to be thinking about opening presents before Christmas," I say, watching Henry pick them up from the floor and put them on the bed. "What are you doing?"

"Breaking the law. Come sit." He pats the bed beside the pile and it's a conscious effort not to moan when my butt sinks into the mattress. Gently taking my ankle, Henry unstraps my shoe and drops it onto the floor behind him, repeating with my other foot.

I watch him shrug off his blazer and kick off his own shoes, followed by undoing another button of his shirt and rolling up the sleeves. He climbs onto the bed beside me, looking more like he's going to be modeling for a magazine than hanging out with me. "It might be the wine talking, but you are *so* beautiful," I say. "Like you should be on magazine covers."

He smiles as he reaches for one of the presents. "It isn't the wine talking. Here, I want to watch you open this one first."

I recognize the brown paper wrapping immediately. Henry turned up at my house asking to steal my paper because he hadn't bought any and didn't want to fight for parking at the mall with the people he said "were too unorganized for Christmas." I pointed out that *he* is too unorganized for Christmas, but I can't remember what was said after that because he kissed me.

To his credit, there are tiny pencil drawings of various Christmas-themed items all over the top, so he did try to customize it as well as adding a beautiful bow that also looks very familiar.

Henry promised me he wouldn't buy me more than one present, but there are three in front of me. I count from one to three out loud, tapping my finger on each ribbon. "One. Two," he says, tapping on his own gifts because I also ignored the promise.

"Okay, I broke it, but you broke it more."

"We said buy and I didn't buy one of them. We're even."

"If I knew stealing was allowed, I'd have gone all out."

He laughs, leaning toward me to kiss me slowly. His hand holds my neck, keeping me in place, but there's nowhere I'd rather be anyway. He eventually stops and rests his forehead on mine. "Start with the slim one."

It always amazes me how Henry just functions like a normal person when I need five to ten minutes to recover after every kiss. He sends my entire body into chaos every time he touches me, and I'm unsure I'll ever get used to it.

The "slim one" is more envelope than box, but he managed to wrap it anyway. There are small doodles of animals in Santa hats, and when I spend time admiring each individual drawing, he grows impatient and pokes me in the waist playfully, making me squirm.

"I'm doing it!" Carefully pulling apart the paper, I find it is in fact a wrapped envelope. Unsealing it, I skim the contents then read out loud. "'Ms. Jacobs, thank you for supporting our conservation efforts, and those of our partners at our research and breeding facilities in Sichuan, China. Please find enclosed your welcome pack, including recent pictures of the adventures of Bao. Bao is a five-year-old giant pan—' You got me a panda!"

"I don't think you *get* the panda, but you get updates on the panda, yes. They're sending a stuffed toy, which is great, because I don't think the ten I already won you are enough."

"The adventures of Bao sounds like a children's book I'd want to read. You could illustrate it. This is so great, thank you so much."

"Open the next one."

It's super light when I pick it up, almost like there's nothing in it. There are Christmas cookies drawn all over this one. I'm confused when I carefully remove the wrapping and it's a shoebox, given there are clearly no shoes in it. When I finally lift the lid I'm even more confused to find a QR code printed on a piece of paper in the center of the box. "I don't know where my cell phone is," I say, patting the bed around me for it.

"Use mine." Henry hands me his phone, and the first thing I spot is me. Literally. The picture of me at the gallery is his lock screen. When I type four zeros, the easiest password in existence, a different picture of me, one where I'm asleep with Joy, is peeking through his collection of apps.

Pulling up the camera, I finally scan the code, and my nana's handwriting fills the screen.

"What is this?"

He leans over, pinching the screen to zoom out, and it immediately becomes clear. It looks exactly like the recipe book that lives in my kitchen, but the digitalization has made it darker and more visible. The cursive is perfect. I've looked at these pages more times than I can count, and it's identical. The only difference is, where there was previously a picture of the dish cut out from a magazine, there's now a drawing.

Henry swipes his finger across to go to the next page, and the next, and the next.

"The drawings are placeholders. I photographed each page with my camera, but because the magazine cutouts are so old, they need to be scanned in. They were losing too much quality, but I couldn't take the book to scan it without you noticing."

I'm speechless, but I manage to force out a word. "How?"

"Mrs. Astor helped me break in while you were distracted by Cami."

"I love the drawings. I love everything," I say, suppressing the urge to sob. "This is the most thoughtful thing anyone has ever done for me."

"I have nightmares that I'm going to accidentally ruin those recipes. Burn down your house, spill my drink, put it in the oven by mistake. I know how important they are to you, which has made my imagination go wild. I'm going to continue not to ruin your prized possession, but I figured if I was anxious about losing them you would be, too. Now you have a backup."

"I'm struggling to find the words to explain how much this means to me."

"Please don't cry. Anastasia said you would cry; I hate it when she's right."

"My presents for you *aren't* thoughtful," I say, stressing *aren't* like my life depends on it. "I didn't realize you were coming here with a game plan to win best Christmas present."

I sniff, and the fear in his eyes is evident. "I always come to win. Last one, open."

Handing him back his cell phone, I reach for my final gift. This one, although small, definitely has something in it. The wrapping paper is decorated in candy canes, so I assume it's food related again.

The small green box doesn't have a brand name that I recognize, so when I open the lid I'm not expecting to find a necklace. The letter *H* is small and delicate, hanging from the chain in the middle of the box. Definitely not food related. "I love it. Wait, that's your monogram. Henry, this is your handwriting!"

"It is. I had it made for you."

"Is the *H* for Halle?" I ask carefully. "Or Henry?"

"You get to decide," he says. "What do you want it to be for?"

My finger brushes against the felt cushion. "Henry."

"That's what I hoped you'd say. Want me to put it on you?"

I nod and we both climb off the bed. He takes the box from my hand and stands close to my back. As I pick up my hair, his arms thread through mine to put the necklace around me, his fingers skimming the nape of my neck lightly, making me shiver.

When he's done, he takes my wrists to move my hands away, letting my hair drop. Using his finger to move some of my hair away, he presses his lips against my shoulder, moving slowly until they reach my neck.

I can feel him everywhere, though only his mouth is touching me. My skin vibrates when he talks. "Merry Christmas, Halle."

Chapter Thirty

HALLE

Henry Turner kicks my ass at gift giving.

Spinning to face him, I lift onto my toes to wrap my arms around his neck, burying my head in the curve of his shoulder. His arms circle my waist, hands linking at my lower back, holding me as tight as I'm holding him. "Are you stalling because you think your presents aren't going to be as good as mine? . . . Ow. Don't poke me."

Leaning back, my hands cup the back of his neck. His hands travel farther down my body before stopping on my ass. "They're not. I can tell you that right now. Lower your expectations significantly."

Henry grabs my upper thighs and lifts me high enough that he can throw me onto the bed. "It isn't your fault I'm more thoughtful than you. Don't worry about it."

"Just open the damn presents before I cancel Christmas altogether."

"Okay, Grinch." He holds up his hands defensively, grinning. Henry reaches for one of the boxes and I sit up from the spot he threw me onto, crossing my legs to watch patiently. "Didn't bother to draw on the wrapping paper? Okay, lazy."

I throw one of the pillows from the bed at him but he dodges it with ease. He rips the brown paper off, and I swear he goes slowly to get a reaction out of me. Finally, the brand comes into view, followed by the picture of the headphones I chose for him. "They're noise canceling," I explain. "I know you have some headphones already, but when I borrowed them that time to listen to an audiobook, I realized how much noise they let in. These ones will shut everyone out if you need them to."

"What do you mean, lower my expectations? This is amazing, Cap. I love not having to listen to people talk." He looks genuinely thrilled as he examines the box. Then he finds the extra bit. "There's a code stuck to it; do I need that?"

"Yeah, if you want to listen to the audio I made for you."

His head shoots up, looking right at me. "Audio?"

It felt a little unfair to me that I have something intimate between us and he doesn't. But I'm also glad Henry said the only person who should have the one we made is me. I've listened to it *a lot*, and it's really clear that it's us from the talking. While I believe that Henry would never, ever share it with anyone, I still know that the smart thing to do is to protect myself first. Even though I trust him not to betray me, there are so many other external factors that could go wrong.

This audio could be anyone, because the only name on it is his. "For when you miss me," I say. "Open your other present."

"Why? Are we not having a listening party?" I roll my eyes as I climb off the bed. I start to collect the stray pieces of wrapping paper, putting them in the trash can beneath the desk.

"No, you can listen to it alone on your new headphones."

I take my gifts and the headphone box—although he resists—and put them on the table, leaving the bed clear of everything but him and his final gift.

He shakes it, and the nerves I've been suppressing all day erupt in me like a volcano. "It's very light. Did you make me a recipe book, too?"

"I didn't. I thought about it, but then I realized finding out you're a naturally gifted chef would be annoying for me as a habitual food burner."

He tears the first strip of paper and I reach behind me to pull down the zipper on my dress. My hands are shaking, but it's from excitement as much as anything else. He slides the box out, the brand name in bold red letters on the lid. Looking up at me with understanding, his eyes immediately follow my hands as I push each sleeve over my shoulders. "The lingerie isn't in the box, is it?"

I shake my head as I push the dress down my stomach, revealing the delicate floral and nude lace bra. It goes over the matching garter belt next, then over my hips so he can see the matching thong until the dress slides down my thighs, revealing the straps to the stockings, and pools on the floor. It's exhilarating and nerve-racking, but I feel so pretty in it. Vulnerable, but pretty. "The lingerie isn't in the box," I say, my voice thankfully staying steady.

Henry climbs off the side of the bed, walking around slowly until he's standing right in front of me. He pushes my hair behind my shoulders gently, tucking any strays on my face behind my ears, then he takes the *H* and repositions it so it's sitting perfectly on my chest. With his finger, he nudges my chin up to look at his face. "You are the most beautiful thing I've ever seen in my life."

"I think that about you every day."

Henry leans in slowly, his hands entwined with my hair as he kisses me gently, giving me the most ridiculous urge to pop my foot up like a cartoon character. Maybe it's because when he touches me life feels too good to be real.

I unbutton his shirt until I reach the last one, and he only lets me go to shrug it off before holding my face tenderly. His tongue moving against mine makes it harder to concentrate on undoing his belt, but I manage. My hand brushes against him as I pull his zipper down and he groans into my mouth.

The pants fall to the ground and he steps out of them, walking me backward until the backs of my thighs hit the edge of the bed. "I'm ready. I have some things in my bag that might help make it easier."

"Ready?" he asks, tracing my jaw with the backs of his fingers. "Ready for what?"

"To have sex? The lingerie . . . I thought I was being obvious. I'm sorry . . ."

His eyes widen slightly, and he kisses me before saying anything at all. "Don't apologize, Halle. It's just good to say it so I don't assume the wrong thing. Lie down and I'll get the bag. You've clearly thought a lot about it to be so prepared. That makes me feel good. I've been scared of making you feel rushed."

I've thought a lot about it, but I also confided in Cami that I was ready when she helped me after I decided I wanted to start taking birth control. She gave me a list of things to bring like my vibrator, lube, a towel in case I bleed, and condoms. It was her idea to wear the lingerie and give him the box.

I tuck myself under the covers and watch Henry grab the other things from my overnight bag. He places them on the bedside table and climbs in beside me. "You haven't made me feel rushed. You're so patient. I'm so grateful."

Patient feels like an understatement. There was part of me that thought maybe he wasn't interested because I'm not used to not being hounded about it. Then I realized no, this is just what it's supposed to be like.

"I'm glad, but don't be grateful for the bare minimum you deserve." We lie on our sides facing each other, and Henry pulls me closer until our stomachs are touching. His forehead presses against mine. "We can stop if you change your mind, okay?"

"Henry," I whisper.

"Yeah?"

"You're my best friend."

His lips brush mine gently, sending sparks of electricity across my skin. "You're my best friend, too."

"Please be gentle." It comes out so quietly I almost imagine I've said it until he answers me.

"I promise I will be."

Henry grips my leg and pulls it over his hip. Rolling onto his back, he guides my body on top of him. With one hand on my ass and the other in my hair, he brings my mouth to his. It's different. It feels hotter and dirtier, his normal careful restraint gone, and he grinds himself into me. With my legs spread across him, I can feel how hard he is. My hips roll and he moans in a way that makes me throb. The friction is incredible even while we're still wearing underwear.

Reaching to the bedside table, he grabs my vibrator and hands it to me. I sit up straight and he grips my hips. "Show me how you use it on yourself."

I know my cheeks are heating up, but now isn't the time to feel shy. "I normally lie on my back," I say as I climb off him and lie beside him. Unclipping the stockings, I start to take off the thong. Henry moves in front of me, helping pull it down my legs until it's removed completely. My heart is pounding as his hands rub up my shins to my knees. He pauses, watching my face carefully before slowly guiding my legs open. It's as exhilarating as it is vulnerable. Putting the vibrator on the lowest setting, I lose myself to it while Henry kisses my neck, chest, jaw. My hard nipples are poking against the lace, but he ignores them, focusing on all the other bits of me he has access to.

His fingers touch below the vibrator and my pulse soars. I nod at him desperately, eyes shutting tight when he slides a finger into me, then another.

"Touch me," he says. His voice is gravelly in a way I haven't heard before. I reach my free hand toward him, and he helps by moving his body into the right position for my hand to slip beneath the elasticated band of his boxers and close around him. "Oh fuck. That's it, Halle. Grip it tight," he groans.

Hearing him talk like that makes me shatter into a thousand tiny pieces so quickly that it surprises the both of us. I turn off the vibrator as he removes his fingers, my own hand still wrapped around him, he looks at me with the biggest grin. "You like being told what to do in bed."

I think about it before realizing he's totally right. "I think it's because I like not having to be in control of everything. I like not having to make the choices."

"My sweet girl," he says carefully. "I want to know everything about you."

It's wild for me to realize that whenever I think of the first time I ever had sex, I won't have to remember a time when I wasn't ready with someone I didn't truly want to be with. I'll get to think of this moment, here with Henry, where he makes me feel as special as the whole night sky.

He holds my wrist at first, guiding me up and down, focusing on the tip until I get it right and he lets go. He explores my body with his hands, brushing and touching, until he gets too close and tells me to stop what I'm doing.

When he reaches for the condoms, he also grabs the lube and towel. "I read online the first time is easier from behind," I say when he gets onto his knees to spread the towel across where our hips will be. "I don't know, though . . . obviously."

"Next time, let's keep these on." He directs me over the towel and starts rolling each stocking down my leg. The garter belt goes next, followed by my bra, until I'm totally naked with my legs spread open for him. I've wondered if I'd regret it when I got to this point, but as his eyes rake over me, dark and heavy, I realize there's no chance. "You're so perfect, Halle. I've dreamed about having you like this."

"Henry . . ." It's a moan and a plea, I don't even know. I just want him.

"We can do whatever makes you feel the most comfortable. But do you want to look at the pillow or the headboard? Or would you rather be looking up at my face the first time I slide inside of you?"

I swallow so hard I swear it's audible. My skin prickles. "I want to be looking up at your face."

"Good. Because I want to see yours, too. Stay on your back to start, and we can try the other way if it's not good. I'm going to make it good for you."

"I had a sex dream about you once. Weeks ago, and I couldn't look at you," I admit, sort of frantically, while I watch him push down his boxers and roll on the condom. It's so thick and heavy. I know biology is on my side and I'm designed to take it, but holy shit. "My subconscious hasn't done you justice."

"We're going to revisit this conversation." He looks so smug, and it truly makes me relieved I didn't tell him at the time. "For now I'll have to give your imagination a lot of material to work off then."

I love that we're not rushing. At no point do I feel like I've been groped or pushed. But I really, desperately, borderline obsessively want him to put it in.

"Henry, please. I'm aching and my body feels a little like it's going to burst into flames."

"And I'm supposed to be the impatient one." He positions himself over me, lips pressed against mine as I feel him nudge into me. It's unlike any sensation I've had before. "Oh shit, Halle. Fuck, you feel so good." He kisses the corner of my mouth. "Are you okay?"

I nod, clinging to him desperately. "You're bigger than your fingers."

"I know, I know." It almost sounds like an apology. "You're so wet, though, it'll get easier. Pass me your vibrator and take a deep breath to relax."

Turning it back on to its lowest setting, he wedges it between us against my clit and my whole body shakes. He isn't hurting me; it's just a strange sensation to finally feel the throb ease while also feeling like I'm being stretched, and everything's more heightened.

I take hold of the vibrator so he can put his hands in my hair again the way I like, and wrap my legs around him, crossing them at the bottom of his back. The angle does something, because I watch his eyes roll back while he sinks in deeper. His stomach flexes, and when he focuses back on me, there's something I can't read, but I know I feel it, too, whatever it is.

We get into a rhythm, a perfect one. Both of our bodies are glistening with sweat. Henry's mouth closes around my nipple, then the other one, sucking and teasing as his hips roll backward and forward against me. It's too much. Too good.

My fingers sink into the hard muscles of his back, clinging to him like he's the only thing keeping me on earth. He goes a bit harder, a bit deeper, the sound of our skin meeting while he moans my name. It all makes me unravel. My legs tighten around his hips, pushing him deeper with my feet. His head buries into my neck, kissing and sucking the sensitive skin. My back arches, pushing me into him as if I could get any closer.

His hips jerk and I feel him swell and twitch, sealing this whole thing.

I don't want to let him go as he lies on top of me, the pair of us panting. There's an almost emotional reaction bubbling to the surface, but this couldn't have been more perfect.

"Are you okay?" he asks carefully, kissing my eyelids, then my nose, then my lips.

"I'm starting to get a little bit sore," I admit, wincing when he pulls out even though he's gentle.

"I'm going to run you a bath, okay?" he says.

I nod. "That would be nice." I hate it when he climbs off me, but I rationalize that at some point he does need to clean up and dispose of the condom. "Henry," I yell as he rounds the corner toward the bathroom.

"Yes, Cap?"

"I wouldn't have wanted it to be anyone other than you."

There's an almost bashful smile I haven't seen before as he nods. "I feel the same."

Chapter Thirty-One

HENRY

I DON'T KNOW WHY IT'S when I'm trying really hard not to be a distraction that I suddenly think of every single thing I've ever wanted to say to Halle.

She's typing away on her laptop, ideas for her imaginary friends coming thick and fast, and I don't want to stop her when she's on a roll. But at the same time, I really want her attention. And she'll give it to me if I ask, which is why I'm trying hard not to.

It started when I arrived and she said happy New Year's Eve, which I argued wasn't a thing that people say, and she argued that it was. So I looked it up, and ended up reading up on the origins of the New Year's celebrations and I want to tell her, so she knows I'm right.

After Halle worked double shifts for the past week, you'd think she'd give herself a break from working on her book, but she seems to have found her stride. I wasn't supposed to see her all week because I was home for the holidays and she was swamped with work, but I somehow managed to sleep here every night, then go back home.

My mom asked if I'd taken up stripping because I disappeared in the evening and came back in the morning.

I can see her cheeks above the rim of her laptop, which is how I spot them turning a deep red color. She looks paler than normal, but she says she isn't sick. Her eyes flick up to me like she knows I'm watching, then shoot back to her screen. "Stop surveilling me," she whines. "It's creepy."

"I'm not surveilling you. I'm admiring you. Why are you so flushed?"

She moves in her seat, tucking her feet under her butt. "No reason."

Her voice comes out higher than normal, a sign I've learned means she's lying. "What are your imaginary friends doing that's making you so pink?"

"Nothing!" Another lie.

"Halle Jacobs, are you writing about sex?"

"No!" Another lie.

"I'm trying not to distract you but you're making it very hard." I watch as she snaps her laptop shut and walks across to where I'm sprawled on the couch. She climbs on top of me, slotting perfectly into the gap between my body and the couch. Her leg is draped over me; it's natural to us now. We work so well like this. "Okay, now you're just distracting yourself."

"I deserve a little break." She reaches up to kiss the underside of my jaw. "And I was writing about after the first time they have sex. When they're in bed talking."

"What are they talking about?"

Weirdly, she shrugs. Difficult to do while she lies on me and not the kind of unsure action I've watched her do before. "What it means now that they've done it. If it changes anything between them. What their future might look like."

"Is that what you wished we'd done when we had sex?" I ask. Maybe I should have thought about this, but really, I didn't know I had to. I'm always concerned with making sure she's okay, she liked it, I wasn't too rough or too soft or any of the other combinations of mistakes that I might have made. "Should I have brought it up?"

"Which time? I don't think we leave much time for conversation." She laughs, but she hasn't said no. "I could have brought it up. Any of the times. I guess for me I kind of don't know where we're at. You passed Thornton's class; you don't need me anymore. My book is about three quarters of the way to being done, and you've given me more experience than I ever could have asked for."

"I do need you, Halle. I want you. I'll give you whatever you want, but I want to be where you're at," I tell her honestly. Yes, surviving Thornton was the original objective, but I have a much bigger purpose now. "What do you think?"

"You're not going to like it when I talk about him."

I groan and she pokes me in the cheek. "Go on. I'll cope."

"Calling Will my boyfriend destroyed our friendship. I'm scared that if we try to put a label on what we have it'll change things. I don't want things to change between us. I like them exactly as they are. We tell each other what we need, we see each other as much as we can, the sex . . . the sex is incredible. You make me laugh, you make me feel so cherished, Henry. What if I'm just not supposed to be someone's girlfriend? I don't want to risk it all going wrong. I just want to be exclusive. Am I asking for too much?"

It's funny, because I've never really thought about being someone's boyfriend until her. "No, you're not asking for too much. I'm not sharing you and I've never understood labels. I don't care what we're called. Nothing needs to change. Other than maybe I'll be the one helping you out with your sex class with Thornton."

She giggles, her body vibrating against mine. "Please don't call it a sex class with Professor Thornton. It might make me throw up." I *love* listening to her laugh. "Can we promise that if either of us suddenly feels attached to a label that we'll ask the other? And maybe we can see how we feel again and talk about it later. Am I making this too clinical?"

"No. You're being honest and I like honest. We tell each other what we want, and we respect each other's needs. It's what we do now, Halle. I don't see how it can go wrong." I slap my hand down against her ass. "Go write. I have a really interesting story to tell you about the origins of New Year's when you're done."

"Don't threaten me with a good time."

AFTER THE QUIET OF HALLE'S house, returning to my house always feels like walking into a zoo.

She's close behind me, her fingers threaded through mine as we walk into the mess of all the people who do not live here.

After she finished her chapter earlier, she climbed back on top of me, and what I thought was going to be a celebration of its own turned into her falling asleep on me with Joy. She says she's not sick, but I definitely think she's getting sick. Her eyes are redder than normal, and her skin is pale and clammy. When Russ texted me to say that people were going to order food and hang out at the house tonight instead of finding a party or going to a club, we decided to join them.

I set the cat carrier at my feet as Halle nudges me. "Gigi is calling. I'm going to take it in your room. Make sure she doesn't pee anywhere."

"Oh my God," Aurora squeaks, immediately jumping up from the couch and dropping to her knees in front of the carrier. "I didn't know you were going to be coming, too!"

"She can't answer you, Aurora," I say. "She's a cat. Also, cats don't seem to like you, so maybe don't get too close to the door."

Robbie is spending New Year's in New York with Lola's family, and Russ has promised to help me scrub this place of every single cat hair tomorrow before he gets home the day after.

"Why is she here?" Aurora says, unlatching the door and reaching in.

"I don't want her to be afraid of the fireworks if she's alone." Halle told me that Joy has slept through every New Year's Eve since she was born, but I'm not convinced. "And she's cute."

"She is cute," Aurora says, talking to her like she's a baby. Which I definitely don't do. "Hi, pretty girl, you are so lovely."

My phone vibrates in my pocket, which is the only thing that can drag my attention away from Aurora potentially stealing Joy's affection from me.

HALLE

UPSTAIRS!
NOW!

"Don't lose her," I say to Aurora as I head toward the stairs.

When I push the code into my bedroom and see her standing in the middle of the room with her hands on her hips, I think maybe I've misread the signs. "Am I taking my pants off or what? Because you sounded horny, but you look mad, so I'm confused."

"Look at my neck!" she yells, pulling the collar of her sweatshirt to the side. There's a reddish-purple mark on her neck that I don't remember seeing before. "You gave me a hickey!"

I shake my head. "That doesn't sound like something I'd do."

She pulls the sweatshirt down farther so I can see the same marks on the top of her breasts. "I haven't been letting anyone else put their mouth near my chest, so I'm pretty confident when I blame you. Gigi just spotted the one on my neck and now I'm never going to hear the end of it."

"That doesn't quite sound like proof, though, does it," I say, trying not to show the weird kind of pride I'm feeling. I like knowing her enough to know how to joke with her. "Do you have your makeup bag with you?"

"I tried concealer, and it didn't work," she says with a huff.

I kind of like it when she's feisty, too.

"That's because you need to color correct it first. Do you have any stuff for that? I don't really want to have to find the Halloween face paint." She nods, her pout still making me want to kiss her. After searching her bag, she produces a color corrector palette and a sponge. I pull her collar away and brush her hair back with my hand. "It's just color theory, Cap."

"Do not be sexy about art right now. I'm mad at you."

"Do you want to give me one so we're even? I don't mind. You can leave them all over me." She's trying not to laugh. "You're cute when you're pouty."

"Just hurry up before one of the guys launches Joy's online cat career."

I dab quicker, the colors immediately changing like I knew they would. "So to be clear, I'm not taking off my pants?"

AS FAR AS NEW YEAR'S Eves go, I think this has been one of my favorites.

It's taking a lot to control my jealousy as Joy trots between each person, looking for attention. Halle has kissed my cheek occasionally, promising me that she can tell she still likes me best. When Joy eventually grows tired of Mattie and Bobby trying to take her photograph with her paw on a puck, Halle picks her up off the floor and she settles on our overlapped knees.

With only five minutes until midnight, it's nice to know whom I'll be kissing, even if that person has fallen asleep on my shoulder. I'm still really worried she's sick and she's going to be too stubborn to admit it.

Everyone is talking about the point of New Year's resolutions. Poppy goes first. "I want to start journaling. I feel like I learn so much and I can never remember it."

"I want to start Pilates," Emilia says.

Russ takes a swig of his beer, a defeated air to him when he speaks. "I want to fix my relationship with Ethan."

"I want to make my relationship with my dad worse," Aurora says, lightening the mood. "And read the books on my TBR."

Mattie clears his throat and looks only at Aurora when he speaks. "My resolution is to get VIP passes and access to the Fenrir paddock at the Nashville Grand Prix."

Bobby nods. "That's also my resolution."

Kris joins them. "Mine, too."

Cami goes next. "Mine is to be more toxic and make more men unhappy."

Kris shakes his head as he sighs. "We'd be so good together if you only gave me a chance."

She tilts her beer toward him and winks. "Keep dreaming."

"Go on, Hen. What's yours?" Russ asks. Halle lifts her head from my shoulder, apparently awake now.

Even though I knew they'd ask me eventually, I still didn't know what I'd say. I've never set New Year's resolutions because I never stick to anything. I can't even stick to a routine of things I *have* to do.

I want to enjoy hockey again without all the anxieties that being captain has brought. I want to be a good friend to everyone, not constantly worrying that I'm on the brink of letting everyone down. I want to make Halle happy. I want to remember to check in on Anastasia more. To text people back. To not spiral when things get too bad. There are so many things I could say, but I don't know how.

"I want to prove that Robbie is lying about his cat allergy." The room laughs, the dopamine hits me the way it always does when I say the right thing. "Go on, Halle. Last one."

"The TBR was a good one; I can't remember the last time I read a book that wasn't for book club or college. Be distracted less, maybe? Yeah. Be less distracted from my goals."

Russ unmutes the rerun on the TV and the people in Times Square let us know it's only one minute until midnight.

The countdown begins from ten and there's one more thing I need to say. Lowering my mouth to Halle's ear, I whisper low enough so only she can hear me. "You're the best thing to happen to me this year."

"That's how I feel about you."

She smiles, and the rush is better than everyone laughing at my joke, no question. And when the countdown gets to zero, I kiss her for the first time this year.

Chapter Thirty-Two

HENRY

"Stop staring at me."

Halle doesn't sound like my Halle when she snaps at me for the tenth time today. Her voice is rough, nasally, too, congestion making her sound like she's trying to talk with a marshmallow up her nose.

When her head tilts up from its normal position of facedown in the pillow, the tip of her nose is pink, eyes watery with dark marks under them.

"You need to go to the doctor," I tell her for the tenth time. One each for every time she's told me to stop staring at her. "Why are you being so stubborn?"

She sniffs loudly. "Because you told me I had to start saying no to people. So, no."

"I also said I didn't mean say no to me."

"I have a little bit of a cold or something. Whatever wiped everyone out two weeks ago has clearly finally reached me. I'm fine, Henry. It'll pass, I promise."

"Did all your sneezing give you a concussion? You started the epidemic that wiped everyone out. You've been sick all month; it isn't normal. You need to go to the doctor."

After telling me I was wrong all day on New Year's Eve, Halle started complaining about feeling unwell on New Year's Day. She said it was because she'd worked so many hours then stayed up late with me. She said it'd be worth it when she gets paid and can buy new clothes for her vacation. An unfortunate reminder for me that the vacation is still happening.

College restarting brought hockey with it, and despite my insisting she stay home to rest, Halle dragged herself to our Saturday game after we lost our first game of the year the day before. I'm pretty sure she slept on Poppy's shoulder the entire time and didn't see one second of play.

Calling her my lucky charm has made her superstitious, which, as our luck in her presence continues, the team is kind of feeding in to as well. We've played away for the past two weeks, and instead of using her time without me to sleep, she helped answer a cry for help from Enchanted when their weekend guy called in sick.

I pointed out that *she* probably gave it to him, which was not gratefully received.

"The doctor will tell me to rest," she mumbles into the crook of her arm, not bothering to look at me. "I'm not vomiting anymore. And I'm not pregnant, if that's what you're worried about. I think my body is just rejecting me having such a stellar work ethic."

I slow-blink at her even though she can't see me. "I hadn't even thought about that. I don't think a symptom of pregnancy is looking like you're on the brink of death."

"You clearly haven't seen *Breaking Dawn*."

"You think I lived with Anastasia and Lola and didn't have to watch *Breaking Dawn*? Be serious. I'm worried about you. I fell into an information wormhole on WebMD and I'm struggling to be cool with you not being looked at."

She pushes herself up from my bed and sits on her heels facing me. She's so beautiful, even when she's snotty and gross. "I'm a vision of health and wellness."

"Let me take you out then if you're so healthy and full of energy."

The way she looks at me is the most alert she's looked in weeks. "Huh?"

"I want to give you a new experience. Let's get ready and go, Cap!"

"Henry, we don't need to do that anymore. You've escaped Thornton and I haven't written a word in weeks. Forget about it."

"No, I want to give you an experience. Let's go."

Reading body language is not always my strong suit, but Halle's practically writing this one on the wall for me to read. She's tired. She's achy. She low-key hates me for putting her in a situation where she has to admit defeat or do something she doesn't want to do. Breathing out a heavy sigh, she surrenders. "Fine. Let me get ready."

EVEN IF HALLE DIDN'T LOOK like she should be painted into *The Triumph of Death*, I'd be able to tell she isn't healthy based on one thing alone: she isn't asking me where we're going.

By the time we're pulling up in front of my parents' house, she's asleep. Which is telling, considering it's not that far from her house. I don't like waking her up when she's sick, but I've overthought every single possibility for the past three weeks. I've ended up fixated on every sniff and cough, trying to determine exactly the tone of the cough so I could match it to the chart I found online.

Watching her try to act like she was totally fine while she had some kind of stomach virus and threw up repeatedly was the weirdest experience of my life. I don't understand why she won't take care of herself properly. Nobody was going to die if she didn't do the thing she'd said she'd do for them. Everyone would have understood, but it's the most impossible task to her just to admit that she needs a break.

When I went to Halle's work to deliver her more medicine, Cami said Halle's scared if she stops doing all the things she normally does it'll make her mom fly out to try to look after her. Given her mom is still holding out for Halle Ellington, and I exist, more mom time isn't something she wants right now.

"We're here, sleepy girl," I say, nudging her gently.

She frowns, looking around to work out where we are. Rubbing her eyes with the back of her hands, she leans to look out of the window properly. "Are you making me join a sorority? I thought about it freshman year and decided it isn't an experience I want. So can we go home now?"

"This isn't a sorority house. Come on, let's go inside."

I don't give her a chance to argue with me when I climb out of the car and head up the driveway. I hear the car door shut and her feet hitting the concrete. "Henry, wait up! Where are we?"

Using my keys, I open the door and usher her in. "My house."

As soon as I step through the threshold, I can smell soup on the stove. I called my mama while Halle was getting ready and asked if she would just take a look at her to make me feel better. We argued about whether this constituted as bringing a girl home, and eventually settled that it doesn't, because I'd never bring a girl home while Mom was at work.

Halle grabs my hand, stopping me from progressing farther into the house. "You brought me to meet your *moms*! I haven't even brushed my hair today!"

"That's not my fault; I did tell you to get ready. I thought it was supposed to look like a nest. It's that thing. A messy doughnut." The color is returning to her cheeks, even if it's from anger. "And it's only one mom. The other one is at work."

"You're seriously doing this to me? *Seriously*?"

I'm beginning to think I might have fucked up. "I just want her to take a look at you and promise me you're not dying. Because even though logically I know you're not, there's a tiny little voice in my head that tells me that you might be. But you"—I lower my voice so it doesn't echo through the house—"won't. Get. Help."

"This just gets worse. Okay, okay. I'll do it for you. I'm sorry that you've been worrying about me."

"Don't do it for me, do it for you. Care about the fact you're sick. That's all I want." Wrapping her hands around my waist, she buries her head in my chest. I hope her nose isn't running. I kiss the crown of her head, and the nest tickles my nose. "I like this, but every day we get closer to your germy ass making me sick."

"Are y'all coming to say hi or are you going to make a run for it?" Mama shouts from the kitchen.

"Your mom has a southern accent," Halle says, looking up at me with big eyes.

"Do you not listen to me? I told you she's from Texas."

She laughs, closing her eyes as she shakes her head. "I know, but for some reason, I just expected her to sound like you, but, I don't know, more feminine. It's silly, I know."

"My mom has a Boston accent because she's from Boston. Just to clear up any confusion when you meet her."

"Got it, smarty-pants. Okay, if she hates me, you have to convince her to give me a second chance because I'm not at my best," Halle says, buttoning up her cardigan and straightening her dress. She unbuttons her cardigan again. "I don't know what I'm doing; I'm too hot and flustered."

"Come on. She's going to love you," I say, taking her hand.

Thankfully, Halle doesn't make me drag her into the kitchen with me, but there's definitely a hint of reluctance in her walk. I keep hold of her hand so she can't run away, and as suspected, Mama is adding herbs to a soup pot next to her work laptop and a glass of wine.

"Hi, baby. Soup is almost done." She looks up from the pot and straight past me to Halle. "Halle, it's so nice to meet you, honey. I'm Maria." She twists one of the knobs on the stove and takes off her apron, rounding the kitchen island quickly with her arms open. "Please don't look so scared. Henry said you haven't been feelin' so good. Poor girl."

Mama embraces Halle, but Halle doesn't let go of the tight grip she has on my hand. Instead, uses her other hand to receive the hug, and seeing Halle so nervous makes me think maybe I should have just taken her to her doctor's office instead. When Mama finally lets Halle go she takes my face between her hands and kisses me on the cheek. "Did you get taller?"

"Why are you acting like you didn't see me last week?" I guide Halle to a seat at the island in front of the pot.

"And why are you acting like you aren't still growing?" she counters, returning to the stove.

"I didn't get taller in the last week."

"Halle, darlin'. Do you want your noodles in your soup or on the side?" Halle looks to me for guidance like it's some kind of test. "When Henry was a toddler, every few months he'd get strep throat and all he'd eat was chicken noodle soup. But he would not eat it if there were noodles touching his carrots. He wouldn't tell us that, though; we had to figure out why he was crying through a process of elimination."

"And I've heard about it ever since," I mutter.

"Talk loud enough to be heard or be quiet, baby," Mama says, not missing a beat. "I think I cooked more soup than every family on the West Coast that year. So now it's a family tradition to serve your noodles on the side, but I'll put yours in the bowl for you if you like."

"On the side sounds good, thank you," Halle says, sounding more polite than she's ever been to me.

Mama and Halle talk. Well, Mama asks Halle questions about where she's from, what she's studying, what her hobbies are. And Halle answers in the same polite tone instead of saying, "Leave me alone, I'm sick." My fingers tap against the marble counter and my foot bobs up and down as I listen to them go on, and on, and on.

"What's got your feathers ruffled?" Mama says to me with a pointed look.

"Are you going to examine her? She's really sick." I have too much energy in my body, and I can't sit still. I just need to stop obsessing over it, but I can't. Her expression softens.

"I thought it would be polite to let the poor girl eat a hot meal before I start poking at her, Henry. I hear you're stubborn, Halle." Halle's mouth opens, but no sound comes out. "Which suits my son, who is stubborn as a mule when he wants to be. Isn't that right, baby?"

Now it's my turn not to have anything to say, because how am I catching strays when Halle is the one in the wrong?

Mama laughs to herself. "Lookin' like a couple of goldfish. Let me find a thermometer."

When she disappears, Halle turns to me. "I can't believe you told your mom I'm stubborn! She's going to think I'm difficult and unappreciative now. That's going to be her first impression of me. I'm not even stubborn; I literally agree to do everything for everyone all the time and that's why I'm sick."

If she's annoyed, then I'm more annoyed. "Exactly. You do everything for everyone all the time and you get sick and you don't ever put yourself first."

"It's never a problem when I'm doing things for you!" she says, and I want to argue back, but she's right. I treat it differently when it benefits me. "I didn't mean that, Henry. I'm sorry. I'm just grouchy because I'm tired of being sick. You're right; I should have gone to the doctor last week. I was just . . . I don't have an excuse. I'm sorry I made you so worried."

"I don't want to be top of your priority list. I mean, I want to be second, but I want to be after you. I want *you* to start prioritizing yourself over everyone else."

"I hear you," she says. Quickly looking around the room and confirming we're alone, she leans in to kiss my cheek. "I don't want to give you my germs."

"That's okay. We'll make up for lost time when you're better."

———

MAMA SAID HALLE HAS A straightforward—not fatal—illness, and with a few days of real rest, hydration, and medicine she would recover.

On the drive home Halle called her boss and told him she wouldn't be in this week, and also called Inayah to cancel book club. Then she called Mrs. Astor and asked if she'd mind looking after Joy for a few days while she stayed with a friend. For some reason, the way she said friend made me feel unhappy. Maybe it was because I wanted to bring Joy with us, but apparently testing if Robbie is lying about his cat allergy is mean and probably illegal.

"Mrs. Astor tells me I look like her husband every time I talk to her. I asked to see a picture and he's an old white guy with no hair," I say to Halle when I get back from taking Joy next door.

Halle looks up from packing her bag and laughs; it's the brightest I've heard her sound in weeks. "She means future husband. It's a joke she and my nana used to share. A bit like a, *Oh, you feel like boyfriend material* type thing. Like, *Oh, you look like my husband. Which one? My next one.* She's hitting on you, Hen."

"Are you going to go fight for me?" I ask, watching her immediately roll her eyes.

"Absolutely not."

"You answered that quick. Why not?"

"Because I've known that lady since I was a baby," Halle says. "And mainly because I know she did martial arts in the seventies."

"I'd fight for you if Mrs. Astor was a Mr. Astor, may he rest in peace."

She adds what I hope is the final thing to her bag, then starts to zip it up. "I'd never want you to fight for me with anyone over anything. Fighting is for fools, and you are not a fool."

My eyebrow creeps up a little. "Fighting is for fools?"

She laughs, rubbing her fingers against her temple, which tells me she's due more medicine soon. "Grayson used to get into fights *all* the time when we were younger, and it's something my mom said to him. She had it made into one of those motivational cross-stitch quote frame things. Like the ones you get about Jesus. I think he still has it; I'll get him to send a picture if he has."

"Fights about what?"

She sighs. "I don't even know. Mom used to say it was just boys being boys, which is a bullshit excuse in my opinion. Grayson wanted to live with Dad when our parents split up, but Dad didn't fight for custody of us. Then we moved to Arizona, which Grayson hated. He was horribly bullied for sounding different, and he was small but really broad when everyone else was having a growth spurt and thinning out. I think it all just made him a super angry kid."

"Is he still like that now?"

"Angry? No, he's actually pretty chill now, just quiet. It was really hard on Mom because she was pregnant with Maisie. She had Gianna half the time, and Gi just didn't understand why she suddenly had this woman acting like her mom, so she was a terror. And then every other day, Grayson's school was on the phone saying he was going to get kicked out if he didn't fix his behavior."

"How did you feel about it?"

"I hated Grayson coming home bruised; it used to really stress me out because it made me think maybe I'd get bullied when I went to high school. I was taller than the other girls in my class and puberty slammed into me like *I* was the running back. I've always had bigger boobs, wider hips, thicker thighs, etcetera than everyone else, but I didn't get bullied. No one paid attention to me really, but I still hate fighting because of how miserable everyone was while Grayson was acting up. Nobody knew about the bullying thing until later."

Every time Halle tells me something about her life, I'm mad at myself for not asking earlier. I want to sit her down and learn everything there is to know about her. "What made him stop fighting? Was it the cross-stitch?"

"It was not the cross-stitch, I'm afraid." Halle chuckles, but then it turns into a coughing fit, which reminds me to come back to this later. "So this sounds like it's been lifted straight out of *Forrest Gump*, but I swear it's true! He'd pissed off some guy in his class over something and they were going to fight after school.

"When Gray turned up there was this gang of kids there, so he ran. Our high school football coach saw how fast he was. Found out who he was, which meant finding out that he was an angry little nightmare on the brink of expulsion. He hauled him in, sat him down, and said if he stopped fighting and giving shit to all his teachers, he'd let him train with the players. If he stuck to it for the rest of the year, no incidents, he'd put him on the team."

"I take it there were no more incidents?"

Halle chokes out a laugh again even though this story isn't very funny. "No, there were incidents. And every time there was one, Coach reset the clock to zero. But that stubborn old man never gave up on him, and eventually Grayson made the team. Bullying stopped as soon as he was appreciated for being small and wide. His grades improved, he got into college, and the rest is history."

"And what was happening to you? Grayson was fighting, Maisie was a baby, Gigi was confused. What were you doing?"

There's a sad smile that she wears sometimes. One that doesn't meet her eyes like when she truly smiles at me. "Well, we became a football family, so I spent a lot of time sitting on bleachers reading while we supported Grayson. I helped with Maisie's diaper changes and keeping her entertained so Mom could have a break. Then Gigi moved in full-time, so that was another adjustment for everyone. I spent a lot of time hiding out at Will's house that summer."

"Is that how you became friends? Hiding from your family?"

"I wasn't hiding from them. Mom and Paul, Mom especially, just had so much going on that I didn't want to ever add to the stress. It's hard to get yourself into trouble when all you do is read books. Will was very confident and he just welcomed me with little effort on my part." Why did I ask about Will? Why do I like annoying myself?

"I guess that makes sense."

"I just didn't have any responsibilities at Will's house. Nobody asked me to do anything, I never ended up covered in baby spit-up, and Will was just so laid back about everything that it was a respite from always trying to keep the peace in my own house. I know I don't talk about him positively now, but I needed him then. He made me feel less lonely."

She rubs her temple again, and it's a swift reminder that she needs to rest. And I don't want to hear Will's redeeming qualities when he treated her so badly and she doesn't really see it. "I'd like to see the cross-stitch if your brother has it," I say, changing the topic. "Are you ready be taken care of?"

She nods, looking around the room for any last-minute things, and she clearly spots one because she makes a little squeaking noise. "How do you feel about me bringing Quack Efron?"

Chapter Thirty-Three

HALLE

THE FUN PART ABOUT SPENDING so much time with someone who always says what they're thinking is that when they're trying *not* to say what they're thinking, it's painfully obvious.

There's been a nervous energy in the air all week, and I put it down to Henry desperately wanting to make me feel better. I feel bad about making him worry, and if I'd known it was so serious that he was willing to introduce me to his mother, I'd have maybe listened to him a little sooner.

It's hard being the person who needs to slow down when you're the one who is always picking up the pieces for everyone else. Henry was right, though, and my pieces were flying all over the place.

Now that I'm finally feeling more like myself, it's my turn to convince Henry to prioritize his health. He's been going all out in the gym and doing extra hockey sessions with his teammates for weeks. He claims it's because the best leader is one strong enough to lead his team—which I'm pretty sure is a quote he found online—and that it isn't anything to do with the fact he's playing against Will on Friday.

I guess it feels like a long time coming for him and probably like he's got something to prove. He's dancing around the truth, and I'm letting him, because I know all he's heard from the guys is about how they won't be able to face me if they get beat. I've tried to say I don't care, but nobody seems to be listening to me.

The only plus side to Henry's overthinking is his bid to distract himself, which so far has involved: bending me over, climbing on top of me, pulling me on top of him on every surface of his house, my house, and—as much as I'm horrified to admit it—my car.

My legs wobble when I try to use them, and instead of giving me the sympathy I so clearly deserve, he gave me a detailed breakdown of how lifting weights could help stop it. Then he makes my legs shake all over again.

I've read enough romance books to wonder how the leads get anything done when they're constantly pawing at each other, but I honestly get it now. I have little to no interest in ever getting dressed and leaving the house. Which means every time I think I should really just ask him outright what's bothering him, so I can reassure him again that I don't care about Will, I instead immediately allow him to distract me.

The movie we put on has only been on for five minutes, but already he's trying to get access to kiss my neck and his hand is traveling across my stomach. "Are you not tired?" I say, my eyes shutting tight when he begins to kiss down the column of my neck.

"Of you? Impossible," he murmurs.

My body reacts to him like it hasn't been touched in years, not hours, but I need to exercise some self-control like the adult woman I am. I think? A voice somewhere is telling me that's right, but a much louder, much more turned-on voice is telling me to take off my clothes. "Should we talk about the elephant in the room?" I ask, silently congratulating myself for verbalizing my thoughts and not just giving in.

His breath is hot on my throat when he speaks. "I didn't win you an elephant, but we can go to Santa Monica right now if that's what you want."

"You're ridiculous. I mean the reason you're taking all your nervous energy out on my body instead of talking about it."

He nudges one of my knees with his and climbs between my legs, pressing himself into me so I can feel how hard he is. "I'm not nervous about the game. I doubt I'll even see your parents."

"So you *do* know what I'm talking about! Henry, get off me! Let's talk about it."

He groans as he dramatically climbs from between my legs and throws himself onto the mattress. "There's nothing to talk about. I'm not nervous."

It's no accident that my parents booked their annual January trip on the weekend when Will is playing at Maple Hills. I blame me not realizing the dates overlapped on the fact I was so sick when they called to remind me a few weeks ago. I've already made my peace with this weekend being hell, but I hate that it's been weighing on Henry's mind all week.

"You know it doesn't matter to me if you win or lose, right? And if you don't want to see my mom and stepdad that's totally fine with me. I hadn't even considered you would want to since you'll be so busy with the team, and you also call them annoying every time I speak to them on the phone."

"I want to beat him for you," he says. "I want to embarrass him the same way he made you feel embarrassed and belittled. I want him to be miserable every second he's on the ice."

"That's all very admirable of you, but I need you to know that I don't care. I'm going to be there for you and you only—well, the guys, too, but mainly you. If you win, you win. If you don't, no big deal."

"Is this the bit where you copy what they say in the movies like, *You'll always be a winner in my eyes*, or something cheesy?"

"Is that what you want me to say to you, my little winner?" Henry rolls his eyes at me but slides closer, cupping my cheek with his hand. "You'll always get reassurance from me. We're a team, remember?"

"Do you think your parents will always dislike me because I'm not Will?" Henry isn't someone I'm used to sounding uncertain, so the sliver of vulnerability in his voice as he moves his hand from my face to twirl a strand of my hair between his fingers crushes me.

"They won't dislike you, Henry. They don't even know you. If they knew you, they'd love you. You are a person who makes their daughter infinitely happy, and in the grand scheme of things, that matters more than someone in my past."

"You sound like you think you're right, but I also don't believe you."

"I think you need to do something productive to keep your brain busy." I push off the hand that immediately grips my thigh, adding, "That doesn't involve pawing at me. Why don't you paint? Or draw? Or, I don't know, get your tablet and give me a structural breakdown of every single piece you've ever created including pictures?"

I expect an argument, but I don't get one. "Okay," he says. "Wait here."

Henry disappears from his room, and I'm left on his bed, confused and very skeptical. When he comes back into the room, he holds out his hand, gesturing toward his door with his head.

"No," I say, my eyes narrowing in suspicion. "I feel like you're up to no good."

He gives me the mischievous smile that makes me melt. "I'm doing what you said. I'm keeping my brain busy and no one else is home, so come on."

Taking his hand, I maintain my skepticism as he leads me out of the room and into the one next door. I don't think I've ever been in this room. There's a bed pushed up against the wall with no bedding on it, and unused canvases leaning against the closet. "Is this your secret lair?"

I sit on the bed as he walks around the empty floor. "It's JJ's old room. We were supposed to have another guy move in, but it didn't happen, so it only gets used if the guys stay too late. There's more floor space after I pushed the bed against the wall. I work in here sometimes."

"Very convenient . . ." *I'm still suspicious.*

"Do you want to paint something with me?" he asks, spreading a protective sheet across the hardwood floor. "I have a very specific idea."

It takes me ten times longer than normal to blink because of the shock. "You're joking. You're going to let me be involved?"

"I'm not joking." Pushing the canvases out of the way, he opens the closet door and reaches in, pulling out what looks like a rolled-up cotton canvas and a sealed pack of different-colored paints. "But it'll be messy. This is body paint."

Putting the paints on the floor beside his feet, he gets on his knees and unrolls the canvas in the center of the protective sheet. One hand reaches behind his head, tugging his T-shirt over his head and throwing it behind him.

"What do you want to do?" I ask, taking off his sweatshirt that I stole. Henry stands from the floor, pushing his sweatpants down until he's only in his boxers.

"I want to take off all your clothes, cover you in paint, and fuck you right here on the floor," he says, pointing to the center of the canvas. "Respectfully, of course."

I have been saying I wish I knew more about Henry's creative process . . . "I love art."

He walks over to me as I stand, his hands tug at the bow keeping my sweatpants tight, and his mouth captures mine delicately. "I love art, too."

He's careful as he walks me backward, pulling my T-shirt over my head and letting my pants drop. His hands link at the back of my neck and I realize he's taking off my necklace. "No," I say, my hand clamping over the *H* protectively. "It's bad luck if I take it off."

"Do you want it to get ruined by body paint?" I shake my head. "Nothing bad is going to happen because you took it off."

Weirdly, it's taking off the necklace that makes me feel the most exposed, and not the fact he's stripped me down to my underwear. He disappears into the bathroom and reappears with a foil packet and throws it beside the canvas. Picking up the paint bottles from the floor, he breaks the plastic seal binding them and asks me to pick a color. "Purple."

Henry puts the others on the floor and has me take a few steps backward so we're both standing on the protective sheet. "I'm going to take my underwear off and then yours. Are you good with that?"

I nod, my body feeling extra jittery. I feel like I'm watching his every move with the most intense interest. He's already getting hard when he drops his boxers, then my panties, and when he undoes the clasp of my bra and slides the straps over my shoulders, my nipples stiffen.

"It might be a little cold," he says, opening the lid of the paint bottle. He gives me one last fleeting kiss before squeezing the bottle onto my chest. I flinch a little and goose bumps spread across my skin. The paint begins to run; he catches one droplet with his thumb and presses it between my collarbones. "No bad luck," he says as he signs my skin with the same *H*.

I pick up a bottle from the floor, not even looking at the color as I open the cap and squirt it against his chest. Henry takes it from my hand and squirts it across my legs.

The pattern continues. Laughing, grabbing, painting, kissing. He maneuvers us down to the floor, the paint he squirted against my ass sliding against the fabric. His hands cup my breasts, leaving large blue handprints. The blue swirls into the pink as his thumb grazes my nipple.

We compare who has the cleanest hands, and when I win, I rip the foil and roll the condom onto him. Even with all the practice, there's still a split second where I think I'm not going to be able to remember how to do it.

He lines himself up, and my body melts when he pushes in gently. "You feel so good," he whispers, his hands planted firmly beside my head as his hips move against mine.

Everything about him feels perfect.

I whimper in protest when he pulls out, sitting on his heels as he reaches for more paint. Holding my leg up by my foot, he takes off the lid entirely and pours the blue paint from my ankle to my knee. He repeats on the other side with red. "What are you doing?" I ask, sitting up on my elbows to watch him hard at work.

"Blue and red make purple. Get onto your knees."

"Yes, Captain." The way he glares at me is worth it when I move onto my hands and knees and he pours more paint across my ass and slaps it. I follow his lead when his hands push my shoulders down until my chest is touching the canvas.

Henry takes hold of my hips, moaning loudly when he sinks into me again.

The sound of paint splashing as his skin slaps against mine is pushing me toward the edge. Putting my cheek flat on the ground, I reach back for his hand. He's holding it tightly when we both come, collapsing onto the material.

There's a period of silence, as there always is with us while we try to return to earth from the stars. I didn't realize I could feel like this.

"Halle," he says gently.

"Yeah?" I respond, my heart hammering in my chest.

"You have paint on your cheek."

The hammering slows down. "Thanks for letting me know."

THE SHOWER TAKES TWICE AS long as the art because we're so dedicated to making sure no paint is missed.

I'm pretty sure I'm going to be finding specks of purple for a long time. "I need to go home and clean up for my parents arriving tomorrow," I yell from his bathroom as I pull on one of the Titan T-shirts with his name on it.

Henry appears in the doorway, his pants low on his hips while he rubs body butter across his chest and biceps. "You can't go outside with wet hair. You'll get sick again. I only just made you better."

"That's a myth. I'll be fine. And if I'm not, I'm kind of a big fan of you looking after me."

He frowns. "At least put it in a nest or something."

"It's a real good job you're so pretty because you sure can be bossy." Reaching beneath the bathroom counter, I find his box of stuff. There's a tiny label on the front of it that didn't used to be there: Halle's. "I missed a chapter."

"What? Of your book? It's probably because you get distracted so easily."

"No, not my book, and don't even get me started on who gets distracted easily. I missed a chapter where you put my name on this stuff."

"Oh," he says like this isn't a huge deal. "I got Anastasia a label maker for Christmas, and I was teaching her how to use it. It's your stuff so it needed a label."

My heart feels like it's lodged in my throat. It's the smallest gesture, and yet it's so huge to me. But he will actually throw me out if I start crying over a label, so I need to pull myself together. "You make me feel so special, Henry."

"Good," he says. "You are special."

"I should go. I really do have a lot to do." *Like cry in privacy.*

"Do you need help?" he asks.

"Thank you, but you're more of a distraction than you are help."

"I wasn't offering—I was going to tell you to speak to Russ. He's great at cleaning."

I roll my eyes as hard as I can as I shuffle past him. He blocks me with his arm, kissing my neck and poking me in the side. "Goodbye, Henry."

"Bye, Cap." He catches me before I can fully turn, kissing me in a way that has my already unreliable legs on the brink of collapse. "Halle, wait!"

He jogs out of the room, leaving me very confused. When he returns, he holds up my necklace. "No bad luck."

I know I have a goofy grin on my face the entire ride home. I catch it in my mirrors every so often, but I couldn't get rid of it if I tried.

Well, until I pull into my driveway and find a car I don't recognize and my lights on. A normal person would think they're being burgled. A normal person would panic and call 911; they wouldn't let themselves into the house with their potential robbers. But I'm not a normal person, and I know this is so much worse than being robbed, because when I walk into my living room, my mom and stepdad are drinking a bottle of wine with Will and his parents.

"Surprise, Hallebear!" Mom shouts, jumping up from her seat to hug me tight. "Why do you have paint in your hair?"

Chapter Thirty-Four

HALLE

IF THERE'S A HIGHER POWER, it fucking hates me.

There's no other explanation for why my worst nightmare has dropped on my doorstep a day earlier than planned. Not even my doorstep—they're in my house. Because apparently my parents think it's totally normal to let themselves into a house they don't live in. Okay, maybe Mom owns the house, but still. I could have been here walking around naked. Henry could have been here walking around naked.

My mom takes great joy in explaining that Will's coach let him travel early since his parents were flying in for the game. She says it like it's a wonderful thing, and I can't process the words to express how it does not feel like that. I want to ask why they didn't just fly to Will's house and travel with him tomorrow, but it feels like a hallucination and I'm not quite sure how to deal with it.

I wait until they're all talking about how excited they are to go to the game before pulling my cell phone out of my pocket. I bring up my chat with my friends.

SPICE GIRLS

HALLE JACOBS
What's the code for when you get home

and your ex, his family, and your parents
        have let themselves into your house?

POPPY GRANT
Is there a color more urgent than red?
Like code super red?

CAMI WALKER
fuck the code babe, RUN

EMILIA BENNETT
Do you want us to come and save you? I
can call in a gas leak and get your street
evacuated

AURORA ROBERTS
leave them in your house and we can
have another sleepover at the hotel!!!
don't forget Joy though

                                HALLE JACOBS
        I'm wearing Henry's Titans T-shirt and
                        Will is just STARING at me

                                HALLE JACOBS
        It literally says HENRY right on my breast

POPPY GRANT
Bark at him

AURORA ROBERTS
bark at him

EMILIA BENNETT
Bark at him!

                                HALLE JACOBS
                He's asking what I'm laughing at

CAMI WALKER
woof woof woof woof woof

POPPY GRANT
Tell him you're laughing at his absolute
audacity to turn up at your house

EMILIA BENNETT
Have you told Henry?

                                HALLE JACOBS
                No. I literally just took my phone out to
                                        text you guys

AURORA ROBERTS
yeahhhhhh. maybe like, don't? unless
you want him to turn up

CAMI WALKER
agreed. i mean as a spectator, i would
like to see it . . .

CAMI WALKER
but as your friend, i would not

> **HALLE JACOBS**
> I have paint in my hair and my mom
> wants to know what it's from

> **HALLE JACOBS**
> She does not want to know what it's
> from

AURORA ROBERTS
tell her you're letting an arty guy rail you
and see what she says

> **HALLE JACOBS**
> Would rather die

> **HALLE JACOBS**
> Putting my phone down

> **HALLE JACOBS**
> Pray for me

CAMI WALKER
i'll ask my granny to light a candle for you

CAMI WALKER
it's the middle of the night in ireland
though so you'll have to wait

POPPY GRANT
I have a Dolly Parton candle will that work

> **HALLE JACOBS**
> I think so because this can't get worse

Tucking my phone away, I start trying to mentally run through all the things in the house I would have hidden if I hadn't been blind-sided. Laundry on the guest room bed, litter tray that needs to be cleaned, various books decorating every surface. Oh God. There are condoms in the bathroom. Apparently it can get worse.

It's like someone lit a fire under me as I spring from my seat.

"Honey, where are you going in such a rush?" Mom asks, freezing me on the spot.

"I need the bathroom, sorry. Be right back."

I'm practically an Olympian the way I sprint up the stairs. Maybe I was wrong, maybe Grayson didn't get all the sporty genes. When I throw myself through the bathroom door, the offending black box is staring back at me. I think if it could talk it would tell me to grow up, but it doesn't stop me grabbing it to hide from my parents.

What I don't expect to find is that the box is empty.

HENRY TURNER

> Did we use all the condoms in my bathroom?

Are you hitting on me?

> 🙁 I'm being serious.

No, made a pretty big dent though.
We can try harder next time.

> The box is empty.

Weird. Maybe Mrs. Astor doesn't want me to hook up with you.

I have some. Come over and I'll show you.

> I believe you. I have the paint in my hair to prove it
>
> & I left like fifteen minutes ago!

Why leave at all? That's what I want to know.

Come back. I miss you. Bring Joy.

Robbie probably won't die.

> I can't 🙁 My mom and stepdad surprised me by coming early

It wasn't them though don't even say it.

> Don't even think it.

😬

After my Christmas present, I now know that Mrs. Astor uses her emergency key liberally, but I can't imagine she'd steal condoms

before the mixing bowl she's been eyeing since Nana got it in the
nineties.

As I exit the bathroom, box in hand ready to go into my bedroom
trash, I decide that I have a ghost. Which is what causes me to jump
out of my skin when I venture into the hallway and Will appears
from the darkness like a freaking ghoul. "Oh my God, you made me
jump."

He laughs and holds up his hands defensively while I hide the
box in my hands behind my back. "Sorry, I didn't mean to scare you.
I wanted to use the bathroom."

"Did you not want to use one of the other ones?"

Will shrugs, looking toward the staircase then back at me. "Let's
talk in your bedroom, Hals."

"Let's talk right here. Or you can just meet me downstairs after
you've used your bathroom of choice."

"I didn't know you didn't know we were coming. Nobody told
me it was a surprise for you. I would have given you a heads-up if I'd
known. I wasn't trying to catch you off guard."

The tenseness in my body relaxes a little. My shoulders drop an
inch. "Oh. Don't worry about it. Their intentions were good and it's
nice to see everyone."

He nods. "Yeah, we missed you a lot at Christmas. Dinner was a
disaster without you making everyone stick to the schedule; we ate
two hours late. I texted you. Didn't get a response, though."

I wish I'd barked at him when I first stepped out of the bathroom.
"Yeah, Gigi told me it was pretty stressful. And sorry, worked double
shifts. I must have read it by accident."

"No worries, no worries. How long have you been with your new
boyfriend?"

It's a funny thing when your gut picks up on something before
the rest of you does. This is why I feel so unsettled around him. "I
don't have a boyfriend, Will."

"Don't treat me like I was born yesterday, Hals. The condoms and the guys' name on your tits suggest otherwise."

"Okay, this conversation is over."

I step around him to head into my bedroom; he thankfully doesn't follow me in. After disposing of the box, I quietly realize as it stares back at me from the wastebasket that I don't have a ghost, I have an ex.

I leave to get downstairs quickly in case he actually did need the bathroom, but he's still in the hallway waiting for me. He is leaning against the wall with his arms folded, only standing up straight again when he spots me. I'm fully intending to ignore him and go downstairs, until he speaks.

"I feel like every time I see you, you're different."

The question stops me in my tracks. "Excuse me?"

"You cut your long hair. You changed your makeup. You started wearing jewelry. You're obviously having sex now. You even smell different. Did you change your perfume for him, Hals?"

My hand closes around the *H* hanging from my neck. "I wanted to do those things for me. Nobody asked me to. Nobody made me."

"I see your stories, and you're out all the time. Even when I don't look, I fucking hear about it thirdhand from my mom. *Halle's new friends got her VIP tickets to a concert; Halle's new friends invited her to Europe to go to a Formula 1 race in the summer; Halle's new friends took her to a fancy restaurant in LA; Halle's new friends took her to an NHL game.* Do they even know the real you? Shit, do you even know the real you at this point?"

"You don't know what you're talking about, Will. Let's go downstairs."

I wish I'd stayed at Henry's house. At least if I had I could have avoided this conversation. "Why am I the only person you wouldn't put first?"

It's the softest he's sounded, and yet it makes my blood boil beneath my skin. "What are you even talking about? I put you first with *everything*! I didn't cut my hair when *I* wanted to. I planned my schedule around you and hockey. I spent *hours* in the car driving to see you. I worked my ass off trying to be nice to your friends so they'd like me! If I didn't put you first in everything then we wouldn't even be friends in the first place!"

"Whoa, that's not true or fair! I was your friend when you had zero. Maybe you don't remember that now that you have the Maple Hills friends you always wanted."

There's a sliver of hurt in his voice, and that's what tells me something deep down I've always known: he has no idea the type of friend he is. "Will, if we weren't neighbors or our parents weren't best friends, and I didn't overcommit myself for other people's benefit, we would have stopped being friends when we were, like, I don't know, twelve? Thirteen?"

"That's not true, Hals."

"If I didn't practically do your homework for you for eight years, let you copy my test answers, be your designated driver, or give you an alibi because your parents thought if you were with me then you definitely wouldn't be getting into trouble . . . we would not be friends."

"Halle . . ."

"If I didn't help you with every single college application, we would not be friends. If I didn't babysit your siblings with mine so you could go out, you and I would not be friends."

"Halle, stop."

"I can keep going. I have a long list of things that I've done for you over the past decade because I didn't know how to say no. If you were my friend, you would have stopped me. You'd have shaken me and told me that I didn't need to do things for you to keep you. You'd have told me to stop letting everyone use me like a doormat.

"If you were my real friend, Will, you would have told me to make myself my number-one priority. You'd have told me to say no to people. You think you *know* me because you've known me the longest, when really all you've known is the person I've conformed to to make everyone else's life easier."

"You don't know what you're talking about, Halle."

"Tell me something you like about me then! Tell me something that isn't directly related to me doing something for you, or someone else, and maybe I'll believe that I'm wrong."

He doesn't have anything, and the irritation is written all over his face. "I don't know what you've been dreaming up, but these new friends of yours, they're going to drop you as soon as Henry Turner gets bored of you."

The problem with knowing someone so long is that they know exactly what to say to get beneath your skin. "I'm not listening to this. Go to your hotel and avoid me until you fuck off back to San Diego. We are not friends. We're not going to be friends again."

"You might want to rethink that, because they're not your friends, Hals, and I've heard he has a reputation with women for a reason. Why would he want to keep you when he's got what he wants from you already? I mean, props to him for getting you to fuck him when I tried for a year and couldn't get you to do it."

"I fucking hate you."

"You don't. You're too nice for hatred. I'll let you be mad at me for a bit because the truth does hurt, but when you realize I'm right, I'll forgive you, because that's what real friends do. And during spring break, I'm going to show you that I am your real friend and things can go back to normal."

"Leave, Will. Now."

This time, he does what I ask and heads down the stairs. I stand frozen in the same spot, rigid as I try to listen to his voice downstairs. When I hear the front door open and close I head into my bedroom. I want to cry, but nothing will come out. Shock, maybe? That certainly wasn't a conversation I expected to have today.

My first instinct is to call Henry, but I know he should be getting into the right headspace for the game tomorrow. I pull my phone out of my pocket and pull up my chat with the girls, but the idea of telling them what he just said makes me feel nauseous. Not because I think they'll judge me for being friends with Will for as long as I was, but because what if he's right?

If I tell them what he said, and they call him a liar, if they drop me, does that mean it'll hurt twice as much? Is it easier to live in ignorance and hope you know the people you call friends?

When I feel ready to fake my way through the rest of the evening, I head back downstairs to the living room. To my utter dismay, Will's parents are still here with mine. Now that the initial shock of them visiting has worn off, it makes me realize that only my mom and stepdad are here.

"You okay, honey?" Mom asks as I reenter the room. "You've been gone a long time."

"Sorry, I've been sick all month. I just needed a little break. Hey, Mom. Where's Maisie and Gianna?"

"Oh, they're at Sylvia's," she says, referencing Paul's mother. "We decided to have a mini break and do some sightseeing, and we couldn't take them out of school."

"Oh, I was looking forward to seeing them."

"Well maybe you could try coming home and you would get to see them," she says, smiling over her wineglass. "You'll see them in a couple of weeks, Hals."

"Wait, so you're having a long weekend. Where are you staying?"

She looks at me like I just asked her for the nuclear codes as I take a seat in the chair opposite her. "Here, obviously."

"You didn't think to check that's okay? I have plans with my friend. She's coming over so I can help her with a group project for a class we have together. Her group is really unhelpful and she doesn't want to fail and—"

"And you can do all those things while we're here, Halle. We will stay out of your way," Mom says, interrupting me.

I know that she isn't wrong, but it still rubs me the wrong way that she didn't think to ask. She assumed I'd be okay with it, but

I guess she wouldn't think otherwise when I'm always okay with everything. I know it's my argument with Will that's making me irritable, but I know she'd never assume Grayson could house them for a couple more days. She'd always check first. "Sure."

There's a weird tension in the air, but I don't know how to break it. Will's mom steps up, clearing her throat. She holds up Henry's sketchbook, something I definitely would have hidden away if I hadn't been ambushed. "Did you take up drawing, Halle? They're very good."

"They are, but it's not mine. It's a friend's sketchbook. They must have left it here by mistake."

"Let me see," Mom says, switching her wineglass to her other hand to reach across and take it. A piece of paper falls out of the side and onto the floor. If I wasn't so anxious I'd laugh at the prospect of having to explain the lore of Quack Efron and his suit to the room. "They're all of you."

"They're not all of me," I say, pulling my knees up to my chest and clinging to the *H* on my necklace, hoping she doesn't notice it exactly matches the *H* Henry signs his work with. "A lot of them are of Joy, and flowers."

Will's dad clears his throat, clearly uncomfortable. "I think we should probably head to our hotel and leave you three to catch up."

It's impressive, the speed at which they manage to leave; if only they were taking my parents with them. Mom is still flicking carefully through each page and I have no idea what's going through her head. Eventually, she puts the sketchbook on the coffee table beside her and looks to my stepdad. "I think we should head to bed, too, Paul."

Mom stops in front of me on her way out of the room, bending to kiss the top of my head. "Night, honey."

Paul is close behind her, and he ruffles the spot my mom just kissed like he's done ever since he inherited me as his kid. "Love you, Hallebear."

Hearing them leave the room, Joy wakes up from her nap. I wish she could talk, because she'd tell them how much better Henry is than Will.

Chapter Thirty-Five

HENRY

It's hard to believe all the people telling me today isn't a big deal, when every single person who knows me and Halle has checked in.

Last night after Halle went home, as a team, we decided what our perfect routine would look like. My history would suggest it was a pointless activity, but throughout today I've done every single thing we said we were going to. And so did the rest of the guys. Weirdly, it's proven my own point that I feel better with a routine. Maybe this is the start of me being able to stick to it.

I haven't skipped one stretch, one ounce of protein, or zoned out of one motivational talk. In a way, it's reminded me how much I loved just being a player on the team, without this constant nagging in my head that I need to be doing something more, being better, being the leader. Today we're on the same page: we all want to see Will cry at the end of the night.

Everyone is as invested in this as me, except Halle. Every silly superstition my friends have has been stuck to. Even as far as JJ wearing his lucky pants up in San Jose, Nate only listening to rock music, Joe always putting his right shoe on first and getting his grandma to do her special prayer she used to do on game days.

It sounds extreme—paranoid, definitely—but everyone knows how much Halle means to me. Will is arrogant on the ice, and I know from Halle he's had his ass kissed his whole life. There's nothing I can say to him that'll hurt him more than beating him this weekend.

I'm the last off the ice when our warmup is done. I've been getting my head in the zone all day. I feel good, the team feels good—all that's left for me to do is survive Faulkner's motivational speech.

I'm about to pass no-man's-land—a small stretch created by a planning error that connects our hallway to the visitors' hallway—when I hear my name being called. I know immediately I should ignore Will, but when I hear him call me a fucking coward I can't help but stop. The guys in front of me making their way into the locker room do the same, turning around to see what's happening.

"Looking slow out there," he says, in the most pathetic attempt to goad me. I'm in the best shape I've been in. It's the most effort I've put in.

Pulling off my helmet and tucking it under my arm, I ruffle my hair to unflatten it and scoff. "Thanks for the feedback. Show me where I asked."

I don't understand what Will is hoping to achieve. Everyone who has ever played here knows this area is out of bounds. We don't mess with each other off the ice. It dates back to when the Titans were known for pranks and people would use this spot to get into the other locker room. There isn't anything he can say to shake me.

I think he can tell he isn't going to psych me out because he starts smiling. "How're you liking my leftovers?"

"If you don't think you can beat me out there just say that." I turn to head back to the locker room with my teammates, who are still standing by, but he just doesn't know when to stop.

"Have you seen all Halle's scars yet? She has a few. Always saving Maisie from falling over and hurting herself instead. Or the birthmark on the inside of her thigh? I liked discovering that one."

"Fuck off, Ellington," I call over my shoulder.

"Don't walk away from me," he yells. I turn to face him again, taking a few steps toward him. I'm bigger than he is, and the difference is, I don't need to fight him. I don't want to fight him. Halle laughing her way through saying, *Fighting is for fools, and you're not a fool,* plays in my head like a song. She hates fighting and she'd hate me fighting. And I have her, and he doesn't. "See? We can talk like adults. We should be best friends actually; we have a lot in common. I should be thanking you for keeping my side of the bed warm."

"I already have a best friend, thanks. Her name is Halle. That isn't something you can say anymore though, is it?"

I know I've hit a nerve. Bulldozed the nerve, in fact. "Do you like the things I taught her? I don't feel like you're very grateful for me making her less of a frigid bitch."

The guy behind me lunges forward but I block him from reaching Will. It's Bobby I realize afterward. "Shut your fucking mouth, you prick," he snarls.

Will holds up his hands defensively. "I'm just trying to say thank you for breaking her in for me. You saved me a job when we go on vacation together."

My blood feels like it's boiling. I don't need to react to him. I don't want to. Halle wouldn't want me to. I want her parents to like me, and they won't if I beat the crap out of Will. I can't let the team down. I can't let myself down.

"She'd never touch you," I say. "Fuck off back to your own locker room. And don't talk to me again. Don't talk to Halle again."

Bobby is still close behind me. I hear what sounds like Kris's voice with him but I don't check. Will seems like a punch-to-the-back-of-the-head kind of guy. I doubt he'd ever be able to win anything fairly.

He laughs, but even I can tell it's forced. "I'm excited to see if she likes it rough. I bet she does, right? She's such a fucking people pleaser I bet she'd do anything I asked. I'll try to send her back to you in one piece, Turner."

I feel sick. I don't know how I ended up being the one holding the others back. They're yelling at him right down my ear and I just want to be in my own locker room. There can't be a fight on my watch. "I get it now," I say to him calmly over the yelling.

"You get what?" he sneers.

"Why she could never love you."

Will snaps, lunging forward for me, but I'm quicker than he is. The guys behind me rush forward, and somewhere in the chaos an elbow hits beneath my eye. It's all over quickly as someone drags me back and someone else pulls Bobby off Will. I see Kris go for him and get yanked back. It's all a blur. The shouting alerted Will's team and they drag him back; looking at his split lip, I see Bobby definitely got the best of him.

The minutes that pass become an adrenaline-filled maze of people and doors. My ass hits the bench and it's one second before my name is being screamed. Months and months of this same room and that voice shouting my name fills me with the same sickening dread.

The locker room is in chaos, but I ignore it as I walk into Faulkner's office and shut the door behind me.

"What in the fuck just happened out there?" Faulkner yells louder than I've ever heard him. My ears sting and my skin feels like it tightens across my whole body. Like it's suddenly not enough to fit me.

"A fight, Coach."

"A fight about what?" he yells. I really wish I could ask him to stop yelling or that I had those earbuds Halle bought for me.

"I can't tell you, Coach." He brushes his hand over the top of his head, and I still haven't had my answer about what he thinks he's brushing. Now isn't the time to ask. It's never the time.

"You can't tell me?" He spits out the words like they're unrecognizable to him. "If you don't tell me what on God's green earth made the captain of *my* team get into a fight before the start of a game, then you're not going on the fucking ice. Start explaining, Turner. Now."

Will just said the most disgusting things about Halle and she's going to be so embarrassed. Even though I'll tell her she's breaking a rule, and that she doesn't need to be embarrassed about it, she's going to be. Will might tell his team what he said, they might laugh about it. The thought makes me want to throw up.

I know Bobby won't tell anyone, and neither will Kris. I don't know who else on the team might have heard, but I trust my friends enough to know that they're about to be told they didn't hear shit. That there will be a problem if they utter even a syllable that sounds like what Will said. My friends are good like that; Halle's friends are good to her.

"I can't, Coach. I'm sorry."

There's only one thing I hate more than Coach Faulkner screaming at me: his silence.

I count his breaths, in and out. In and out. In and out, until he finally speaks. "There's only one thing that'd make someone on this team act this damn foolish. Who is it?"

I clear my throat. Pointless. My mouth is dry. "It doesn't matter who she is."

"I'm not playing around with you here, Turner. This isn't a fucking negotiation. I get to know what happens in my rink. You tell me. That's the deal we agreed upon when you joined this team. You're the captain, for Christ's sake. I need better from you."

It stings when all I've done all year is try to do my best. "You have two daughters, Coach?"

His eyes narrow at me. "You are on thin fucking ice, Turner. Think *very* hard about what you're about to say next."

"Would you do something you know would hurt and embarrass them . . . for hockey?"

"I'm not running hypothetical situations with you. You fucked up." He cradles his head in his hands and shakes his head so violently the desk moves. "We have a team out there that needs to go and win this game. Are you going to be honest with me or not?"

"I shouldn't have to hurt someone I care about to prove to you I'm good enough to play on this team. It's not what being a good leader is, Coach. If you're going to sit me out because I was in the wrong place at the wrong time with someone looking for a fight, then fine."

Faulkner stands from his desk, and I swear the whole room shakes. "If you're not prepared to do things you don't want to do, maybe we need to talk about whether you have the right attitude to be captain. Wait here. Hopefully when I come back, you'll have come to your senses."

The door slams behind me, the brief moment it opened telling me the locker room is dead silent. Something I'd have previously called impossible if I didn't know they'd all be trying to listen to what's going on in here.

I hear Faulkner scream that he doesn't want to fucking hear it, and for everyone to get their head out of their asses and into the game. I rest my head against the desk and breathe out a sigh.

The idea of having my title taken away feels a lot like relief.

And I honestly don't know how to process that. Sometimes it feels like I have too many emotions, and other times it feels like I have none. Sometimes I feel like I understand everything going on around me, and other times I feel like I'm surrounded by people who speak a language that I don't speak.

Hockey and art have always been great equalizers for me. When it didn't matter so much about what I said, and there was a guideline for how I acted. Rules I could follow, mistakes that could be easily identified and fixed. It's almost the opposite of the fluidity of art, where there isn't a way for me to get wrong what I'm trying to create.

It has the structure I crave coupled with the this-could-go-anywhere I love when I create something new.

I love being on the team, and when I'm honest with myself, I don't love having the team look up to me. Becoming captain took away my great equalizer and overcomplicated my emotions that had previously been sound.

How can I be honest about how I'm feeling when I know it'll let my friends down?

How do I let go of the thing I've clung to so tightly all year? Something that has always felt like I'm seconds away from being stung by wasps?

What if Faulkner tells me I haven't been doing a good job, and it's all been for nothing?

I hear the familiar sound of the guys cheering, hyped up to get out there and win.

Faulkner wants me to wait here, but I can't. I can't tell him to his face that I'm as relieved as I am. I wait until I know they're gone, then I leave Coach's office.

I get changed as quickly as I can, shoving my things into my bag and getting out of the locker room. As I approach the door out into the foyer I can hear people screaming at each other. Leaning against the wall beside the door, I open it the slightest amount to listen, and that's when I realize one of the voices is Halle's.

Chapter Thirty-Six

HALLE

THE WHOLE ARENA IS BUZZING and I can't get myself to feel anything beyond pure nausea.

Cami hands me a giant soda cup that she previously suggested I use as a weapon against Will's parents if I need to. She also offered to add a splash of vodka for courage—courage I desperately need with my mom sitting on my right wearing Will's name on the back of her jersey—but I politely declined.

There's only one thing that's going to make me an anxious wreck this weekend: he has blond hair and a bad attitude and will be getting on the ice at any moment.

I've always desperately wanted close friends, but I never truly understood what it meant to have them until the moment Aurora bribed the students beside us to switch seats. All so I didn't have to sit with my family on my own. She said it would be her worst nightmare, and she couldn't live with herself if she let me go through it alone.

As soon as the first player steps onto the ice, I take a deep breath and shrug off my jacket, the UCMH logo bright and bold in the middle of my chest with TURNER running across my shoulders.

"Halle," Mom groans as soon as she sees the orange. "I thought you'd wear Will's jersey. This isn't very supportive of you."

I take a big sip. "I'm making a point to support my school and my friends."

"You're making a very insensitive point. It's not fair to rub Will's nose in it, knowing you have a new *friend*. I think you should wear Will's jersey tomorrow."

I feel like I'm going to be sick and nothing's even happened yet. One by one, the team steps onto the ice. I count them. There's something wrong. I turn to Aurora in the seat beside me. "Where's Henry? And Will?"

I watch as every other player arrives, except for the two of them. I can hear Will's parents start to mutter, then my stepdad's voice. I wait, counting to sixty in my head like maybe there's just a little delay and they'll be out any second. They're not coming. Something's wrong.

Standing, I'm immediately stopped by a hand on my wrist. "Where are you going?"

"I'll be right back," I say to Mom, handing my drink to Aurora.

"Do you want me to come with you?" Emilia asks as I pass her.

"No, I'll be right back."

I fight through the lines on the stairs as people try to get to their seats to watch the game begin. It's like trying to run through sand, and every person stepping into my way is just frustrating me more and more. My mind is jumping through every possibility and none of them are nice.

Adrenaline is fueling me as I stride toward the no-access door, praying I find Henry somewhere on the other side of it.

"Halle!" my mom shouts behind me. "For God's sake, slow down!"

"Mom, it's fine, go back to Paul. I just need to see what's happened."

"That door says no entry; you can't go in there," she says as my hand meets the metal.

I turn to face her, frustrated that I'm so close. "I know, but it's fine, it's to the locker rooms. We use it all the time and—"

"What is going on with you?" Her hands are gripping her waist as she shakes her head. "Is this why you aren't visiting? Hardly call anymore? Stopped showing any enthusiasm toward your real family and friends? Because you're busy with a new man? And what? You want to make Will jealous?"

I can name at least one hundred reasons why I do not want to have this conversation with my mother, but I can't think of any of them right now, because all I want to do is check that Henry is okay. "I don't care what Will feels, Mom. I'm so beyond worrying about what he's thinking, and I wish you were, too."

"I feel like you're not the same person you were the last time I saw you. What will the Ellingtons think? I don't know where my caring, loving daughter has gone!" she says, her voice getting louder with every word until she's shouting at me from six feet away.

"Good!" I yell back, the stress ricocheting around my body finally spilling over. I take a few steps toward her. "Because that Halle was *miserable*! And she was *lonely*! And she was stuck in a relationship with someone who pressured her to do things she wasn't ready to do and made her feel like there was something wrong with her! I'm tired of worrying about your reaction to decisions I make about my own life!"

My mom might be imperfect, but I know she'd never want that for me. "Honey . . ."

"I'm tired of having to think about everyone else before myself. I'm tired of putting everyone else's needs before my own. I'm tired of feeling like the only way I can make people like me is by doing something for them!"

"Halle, that isn't true. We love you so much," she says, her voice softer than before, but it's too late. I can't put a lid on it. "Unconditionally!"

"I stopped visiting because when *Will* broke up with *me*, we agreed that he could go home and I wouldn't, so you guys didn't pressure us to get back together! And I hardly call, because every time I do you put something on me. I have to speak to someone or organize something or tutor someone or listen to you talk about everyone else without asking how I'm doing. I'm trying to write a book for a competition, and you don't even know because you don't ask me about my aspirations! But you've never missed a second of Grayson holding a football!"

I can hear myself ranting but I can't make it stop. Even with Mom standing in front of me, stunned, I can't stop the words from tumbling out of my mouth. "I *hate* being the family manager. I *hate* that the only time anyone ever thinks of me is because they want something from me. I *hate* feeling like I'm everyone's mom when all I ever want when I call is my own mom. Being the eldest daughter is a curse and I'm *sick* of it."

Her face sinks. "Halle. You're understandably very emotional right now, and I think we should discuss how you're feeling back at the house."

"I am emotional because something bad has probably happened to someone I really care about, and instead of finding him we're arguing about Will freaking Ellington and the fact I haven't had a minute of peace since birth!"

"We are not arguing. I'm just trying to understand what's going on with my daughter! I want you to be happy, Halle. I hate that you've been keeping this 'friend' a secret from us. This is him then, the artist? I want to understand! I just need you to make things clear for me, honey."

"I love him! Is that clear enough for you?" Tears are running down my face and I don't know when they started, but there seems to be no sign of them slowing down. The reality of finally understanding my feelings for Henry at the same time as screaming my grievances at my mom is too much for a Friday evening. "Henry is my best friend and I fell in love with him when I wasn't supposed to and now I need to check that he's okay."

"I've always wanted Will for you, but *never* at the expense of your happiness, honey. Will has been your only true friend for so long, and I was scared if you guys broke up that you'd be lonely. I didn't mean to make you feel like you couldn't make your own choices." She looks like she's on the brink of tears and I feel awful. "Would you like me to help you find your friend? Henry, was it?"

The storm inside of me starts to subside. "No, I'll do it alone."

"Okay, we'll talk more in private later. I love you, Halle. All I want is for you to be happy." Closing the space between us she traps me in a tight hug. "I'm sorry I've put so much on you. I promise we'll fix it."

It's at that point I realize all I really wanted was a hug from my mom. "I'm sorry I just yelled at you."

"Shush now," she says, stroking the back of my head gently. "I can survive one outburst in twenty years."

After kissing me on the forehead, she heads back the way she came toward the seating. I don't move at first; I just watch her walk away while wiping the tears with the back of my hand. I jump when hands land on my shoulders, but immediately relax as soon as I hear him murmur my name.

Spinning around, I find Henry standing behind me dressed in his normal gym clothes, his bag slung over his shoulder. His face is calm, but there's something missing. A spark, I don't know. I know my instincts are right and something has happened.

"What happened? Why aren't you playing?" He hears the murmurs of people hanging around behind us at the same time I do.

He nods toward the rink exit. "Can we talk outside? Or in your car?"

"Do you want me to give you a ride somewhere?" I ask. "You're in your clothes and you're leaving with your bag, so I'm guessing something has happened? Right?"

"Do you not want to watch the game?" he says, voice steady in a way that makes me want to shake him and find out what's happened.

I feel like I'm losing my mind a little as I shake my head. "If you're not playing in it, absolutely not."

"Okay, let's go home."

I'd love to say that the car journey from the rink to Henry's house is filled with a very detailed and interesting conversation about what the hell happened, but the reality is Henry doesn't say one word until we're walking into his house.

"Do you want a drink?" he asks, dropping his bag next to the couch and walking toward the fridge.

"Do I want a drink? No! I want to know what the fuck is going on before I actually lose it."

He sighs, dropping onto the couch. I immediately take the spot beside him, not touching him, as much as I want to, because there's something about him that's off, and I don't want to do something to push him over. When I'm finally close to him I see the top of his cheekbone is starting to swell. "Is that *swelling*? Did you get into a fight?"

"Fighting is for fools, and I'm not a fool," he says, smiling at first then grimacing when he rubs his hand against the growing bruise. "He fought. I just got in the way of it."

My hand covers my mouth, because if I don't I feel like I'm going to scream this house down from frustration. Lowering my voice to a whisper, I give him a look that hopefully shows that I'm pleading with him. "Please give me a straight answer and just tell me what happened."

"There's a small area between the home and away hallways that meets before it goes into our respective tunnels. It's because they confused the designs when they were building the arenas because of the other rink and they'd already started constructing and—"

"Henry, *please*."

"Sorry. We call it no-man's-land, but it's basically just a short hallway that links us to the visitors. Under no circumstances do we stray into it and mess with the other team; Faulkner would have our heads. Will didn't get the memo and had some shit to say. I said some stuff, he said some stuff, I said some stuff back. He was being aggressive. I'm not playing."

"I feel like I'm a sim and someone is canceling the action where you give me a full explanation. *He was being aggressive, I'm not playing* doesn't help ease how sick with anxiety I feel right now. I'm sorry, I'm not trying to be hard work, but give me *something*. What's so bad that you're avoiding telling me?"

His face tells me I'm right immediately. He reaches for one of my hands and brings it to his mouth, kissing the back of it. "It isn't nice, Halle. I don't want to say it."

"If it was worth fighting over, I think I have the right to know."

"I didn't fight; he fought. I know you don't like fighting, so I didn't," he says seriously.

I'm confused beyond words. "So if you didn't fight, how come you're not playing?"

Henry rubs his jaw and looks everywhere but me. When I don't look away, he kisses the back of my hand again. "Because I wouldn't tell Faulkner what Will said. He said if I wasn't going to be honest with him then I wasn't going to play. I said fine. He said if I wasn't prepared to do things I didn't want to do for the sake of my team, maybe we needed to talk about if I have the right attitude to be captain."

My heart is breaking for him. I know how hard he's worked. "Oh, Henry."

"And then I walked out after he was gone."

"What can I do?" I ask, the desperation clear in my voice.

"I need to feel you. Can I?" I nod as he holds out his arms, and I've never needed to touch someone as much as I do right now. I think he feels the same because he tugs on my leg to pull it over his until I'm straddling his hips. He keeps my head to his chest, breathing deeply as he kisses my forehead.

His mouth works down the bridge of my nose gently, until he kisses my mouth, hesitant at first until it deepens. We don't talk as we begin to pull at each other's clothes. I have this frantic need to feel close to him, to keep him near me, almost like somehow deep down it feels like he's slipping away when he's right in front of me. I can't explain it, but I think he feels it too.

Henry holds me close as he lowers me onto the floor. Every touch serves a purpose to get us closer together until he sinks inside me. He's careful and tender, telling me everything and nothing in every kiss, every thrust. I cling to him tighter, and when stars burst behind my eyes, I still don't want to let him go. I want to believe that it's grounding to him, that it rids him of all the extra energy plaguing him. But it feels like an apology. Or maybe, it feels like a goodbye.

Henry rolls off me, pulling up his sweatpants and immediately helping me pull my panties back up. It's dirty and emotional, and yet neither of us is saying anything when we stare up at the ceiling of his living room. We're both breathing heavily, but it's the only sound.

"I need you to tell me what he said. Please, Henry. I'm going to create my own answers if you don't tell me, and it'll probably be far worse than the actual truth."

"Even though it's disgusting and will hurt you?" he asks quietly.

"If something is so bad you'll risk the thing you've been working hard for all year, then I feel like I need to know what it was. I know adjusting has been hard, but you're such a great leader. You can't throw it away. I'll only make you say it once, I promise."

He takes a breath and tells me as calmly as he can. My stomach twists as I hear how Will talked about my body. Henry pauses, which gives me a chance to apologize. "I'm so sorry, Henry. I know how hard you've been working to beat him fairly."

"He asked me if I liked the things he'd taught you," Henry adds, and everything that comes after makes tears fill my eyes, but I don't let them fall.

Will Ellington isn't worth crying over, and he never has been.

Henry is right, it is disgusting, and it's a weird moment where the anger and the upset fight against each other in my body. But as horrible as Will is, as embarrassed as I feel, I would never want Henry to lose something over me. "You should tell your coach what he said. I can drive you back to the rink right now, and you can tell him and all of this can be fixed so you can play tomorrow."

"I don't want to."

"Now isn't the time to be stubborn, Henry. We can fix this. I'm not worth getting in trouble over. I'll get over the embarrassment. Please let me help you. Don't make me watch you spiral."

"I felt relieved, Halle. When he said I might not get to be captain anymore, for the first time all year I was happy about hockey. And I don't know what to do with that information. I feel really lost about the things I have and the things I want. I think I might need a bit of time to sort my head and my feelings out."

I find his hand on the floor beside me and hold it tight. I make up my mind about what I'm going to say, then change it, then decide again. A lifetime passes before I speak. "I broke a rule, Henry. It's a big one; number four. Anastasia was right."

He brings the hand clutching his to his mouth, kissing my skin gently. "I know. When I feel better, I'll ask the board to forgive me for not doing number five." *He isn't going to break my heart.* "Can you give me time? I'm worried that if you're around when this all hits me that I'll push you away. I promise you and Joy can have me back when I feel better. I just don't deal with things well when everyone is around me. I feel a bit numb now, but I don't think that will last, so I'm going to go to my parents' house."

I want to beg him to let me help him, but he clearly doesn't want my help. As hard as it is to accept, especially when it comes to some-one I love, I can't fix everything. "Yes."

"This is the one thing you're allowed to say no to me about," he says, voice soft.

"I can give you time to get your head straight, Henry. As much time as you need. Just promise you'll come back to me as soon as you feel better."

"I promise."

Chapter Thirty-Seven

HALLE

THERE'S A PART OF ME that hopes that when I answer the knocking at my front door that it will be Henry with his shit together, but deep down I know that it isn't.

I don't get many visitors, so it's a surprise when I open my front door and find a woman I don't immediately recognize standing on the other side of it. I say don't recognize, but as she smiles at me and holds up her hand to wave awkwardly, I realize of course I know who she is.

"I'm so sorry to turn up like this, Halle," she says. "I'm Anastasia. Henry might have, well I hope he has, mentioned me before. He's talked about you so much I feel like I already know you."

"Oh my God, yes. Hi." I feel a little starstruck. Henry talks about Anastasia so much I feel like she's famous, but I've never met her in person because she's always so busy. Then my stomach drops, because why is she here?

"Everything is fine," she says quickly. "Sorry, you just looked panicked. I'm just looking for Henry. He isn't at home, and I guess I was just hoping he was with you. He hasn't been answering my calls, and I'm just worried about him."

"He isn't here. He told me he was going to his parents' house," I say, quickly putting her out of her misery. "We haven't talked, either. He said he wanted time to himself."

Anastasia nods, folding her arms to hug herself. "I've been really wrapped up in myself this year. I have a lot on my plate and my boyfriend moved to Vancouver, and I guess what I'm trying to say in a really long-winded way is I'm sorry I haven't found the time to meet you until now. I know you mean a lot to Henry. I'm really happy he has you, and I'd tell him that again if he would stop shutting me out."

In a way, hearing Henry isn't answering her calls makes me feel marginally better, even though I recognize that's a horrible way to feel. I think hearing that Henry is doing what he said he was going to do gives me the smallest bit of hope that things will work out.

"We kind of almost met last year. We were at the same party, and I saw you were talking to Henry, but we didn't really know each other then, so I thought you were his girlfriend."

Anastasia laughs in a way that would be better described as a cackle. "Girlfriend? He'd rather be celibate for the rest of his life. Henry only likes tall girls like, well, you. You're Henry's perfect type. He once told me I didn't have enough ass to be able to justify my attitude, and that he was going to invoice me for physiotherapy since he was getting a bad neck from always looking at the ground when he's forced to talk to me. So, definitely not girlfriend material."

"That's so harsh!" I say, but I can't help but laugh because I can hear him saying it. Aurora once said that Henry talks to me differently compared to how he talks to everyone else, but I didn't quite believe her until right now. "But to be fair, not unexpected. He told Lola she needed to finish growing if she wanted to be able to talk down to him, so it checks out."

"He once had a very serious conversation with Kris about the medical logistics of height enhancements. When I told them they were ridiculous, he asked me hypothetically, if it guaranteed I stopped falling on my ass during practice, would I do it? Because he counted, and he thinks I'm above average on the ass-to-ice ratio. Not gonna lie, thought about it for a hot second."

"That is . . . so random. Why would Kris be doing medical experiments?"

"Because he's premed," she says, looking at me funny. "Didn't you know? I'm not judging you. The idea of human life being in Kris's hands *terrifies* me. I thought everyone was pranking me when they first told me. I forced Kris to show me his class schedule."

"That is terrifying." Joy circles my feet, so I immediately pick her up to prevent her from escaping. "Sorry, do you want to come in?"

"I'm good. I'm sorry to randomly drop in on you. I'm just worried about him and I could trade ridiculous stories about all of them all day. I think I'm projecting, because I feel guilty about not spending a lot of time with people this year," she says. "If you speak to him could you get him to return my calls? I just want to know that he isn't spiraling."

"If you text him and tell him you're about to show up at his parents' house I'm sure he'll text you back."

Her hands go to her waist, her demeanor switching into something more awkward. "He'll know I'm lying. I've never been and I don't even know where it is. Do you have the address?"

I shake my head. "I only went once, and I slept in the car because I was sick. I'm sorry. Should I be more worried? Honestly? He promised me he'd get in touch with me when he felt better, and I've just kinda told myself that I'm not going to have a total emotional breakdown over a man who says he's coming back. Mainly because if he turns up here and I'm crying over him he'll call me dramatic. Has he done this before?"

She shakes her head frantically. "No, please don't stress yourself out because of me. Do you have siblings?"

"Yeah, I have three."

"I'm an only child, but Henry feels like what I imagine having a brother is like. He isn't great at working out *when* he's on a downward spiral, but he's learned that if he removes himself from the situation he can basically, like, process it all better. I'm still going to stress about him. I can't help it. But like I said, it's mostly guilt."

"I get the sister guilt, so I know exactly what you mean. I struggled with it a lot the first year living away from home. I'll make sure he checks in when I next hear from him."

"I really hope we get more chances to hang out properly before I graduate. I really want to know you, Halle."

I watch as Anastasia climbs into her car and drives off, leaving me analyzing if she meant what she said because she thinks I'll still be around, or if she was just being polite.

WHEN I WAS LEAVING HENRY'S house after agreeing to give him as much time as he needs, I told him there was no pressure to keep me updated.

I know that the simplest of tasks can feel like a heavy weight to him, and he will ruminate for hours over completing it when he isn't in a great frame of mind. I told him I'd rather he concentrates on feeling better than trying to keep me up to date with how he feels when he might not be able to explain it.

It was the right thing for me to say, but I still miss him. I'm wondering if Anastasia found him, and if I should have been the one trying to track him down instead of sticking to what I said.

I feel foolish more than anything. Maybe his other friends are what he needs right now and I'm not. I'm ashamed to admit that the idea that he could be out with his friends having dinner or something while I'm at home worrying makes me sad. Especially because I'm not supposed to be worrying.

Not sad because I don't want him to feel better, and a genuine part of that might be to get out with his hockey friends, but because Will's arrogant voice is playing on a loop in my head, and I can't get it to stop.

I promised myself I wasn't going to do this. I'm not going to sink the ship because the waters are rough. I am too good at fixing everyone else's problems to fail when I have my own. I'm making my own rule book, and the first thing on the list is that I'm not going to make myself upset over hypothetical situations.

Will told me that Henry would get bored of me. He told me that they were always going to be *his* friends, and I'd lose them, like I lost his, when Henry decided he didn't want me anymore. It's that thought that's been plaguing me, even though it went against rule number two, which was never thinking about Will, but it's the reason I'm so surprised when I answer the knock at my front door and Aurora, Emilia, Poppy, and Cami are standing on my doorstep.

I've had more unexpected visitors this week than I've had the entire time I've lived in Maple Hills. I take one look at Aurora and my heart drops. "Oh my God, Aurora, I'm so sorry I forgot about your group project."

She looks stunned. "What? No! I don't care about that! That's not why I'm here!"

"This is an ambush," Poppy says, immediately lunging forward to give me a hug.

I look at the rest of them through a face full of Poppy's curls. Cami holds up something behind Emilia's head. "But it's an ambush that comes with wine."

"And Kenny's wings," Emilia adds, holding up two paper bags with the familiar Kenny's branding. "Or some weird tofu vegan thing Aurora has if you're feeling especially masochistic today."

"You're the only lesbian I know who doesn't like tofu. Lesbians *love* tofu," Aurora says, holding up her own paper bag.

"I'm not sure you're qualified to make such sweeping statements, Ror," Emilia says, side-eyeing her. "Especially when your data pool is me and Poppy."

"If this is a safe space to speak my truth, love is too big a statement to make. I can tolerate tofu."

"Guys," Cami says. "The ambush."

"We want to check that you're okay, and make sure you're eating and drinking, and whatever else you like to do but might not be doing," Poppy says, almost like she's reciting something from memory, making me think it was pre-agreed. "We hope it's okay to just randomly show up, but we thought you might not be honest if we only texted. So here we are. Ambushing."

I realize I'm just observing from my doorstep like a weird out-of-body experience. The four of them look at me expectantly. "Do you want to come in?"

Closing the door behind them, I consider if there's some kind of visit-Halle memo that I didn't get as we all head into my living room. I follow them into the kitchen and watch like some kind of lingering ghost as they work to get five plates, five glasses, napkins, and ranch dressing.

"This is the cutest kitchen I've ever seen in my life," Aurora says. "I'm obsessed."

"So fun, right?" Cami says, running her hand along the window curtains.

I want to tell them that I've thought about changing it so many times but can't bring myself to say goodbye to something so quintessentially part of my nana and who she was. She would have loved the idea of the four of them plating up wings and pouring wine while admiring her handiwork. This is what she imagined when we planned for me to move in with her, and she was so excited to be one of the girls.

What wasn't part of her vision, or mine actually, was for me to start randomly crying because I have the thing I've always wanted but it feels like sand escaping through my fingers.

I'm not sure who is the first to hug me, or the last, but one by one the four of them wrap their arms around me. "Oh, Halle," Cami says softly. "I'm sorry things are weird right now."

They let go of me and take a step back, giving me space to wipe beneath my eyes. "Do you guys know something I don't?"

"No! But let's go sit down. Here, take your wine," she says, handing me a very full glass. We take seats in the living room, Aurora and me on chairs opposite each other, and the other three on the couch with Joy. "I saw Stassie in the library this morning and she said she stopped by yesterday. I won't sugarcoat it, Hals. She said that you looked really fucking sad. Henry told Russ and Robbie he was going to stay somewhere else for a while to feel better, so we all assumed he was here with you."

It's almost funny that Anastasia said I looked sad when I definitely thought I was holding it together.

"That's why we didn't check in sooner," Cami adds. "We thought you guys were just hiding out together."

"No, we agreed on a little bit of space," I explain. "I'm sorry for crying. Will just got into my head saying that I'd lose all of you as soon as Henry got bored with me, and that he *would* get bored with me, and—"

"Disrespectfully, fuck Will," Cami says harshly. "That guy is a jerk, and he has no idea what he's talking about."

"You know I adore Henry, Halle. He's Russ's closest friend and he's done so much for him. So you know when I say this it comes from a place of love—" My stomach sinks at Aurora's words because I feel the *but* coming. "But I'm *your* friend. I don't care if you guys are married or never going to talk again, I am in *your* corner. But Henry isn't bored with you. I don't even know what's going on with him because nobody tells me anything. I'm not in their inner circle and I'm cool with that. I have my own inner circle and so do you. It's us. We're the circle."

"If I bow out of having to listen to your problems, does the circle become a square?" Emilia asks Aurora.

"I bet the real Spice Girls never had to put up with this bullshit. Serious question: why do men?" Cami says, taking a long sip from her wineglass.

Emilia and Poppy fist bump, and their closeness makes me miss Henry even more.

"Why am I so bad at keeping the promises I make to myself? I swore I wasn't going to be upset over this. After my mom and step-dad left early, I cleaned this entire place. I did all my homework, and I did all the prep work for book club for the next two months. I was handling it. And now I'm being pathetic."

"You're not pathetic," Poppy says immediately. "You're just prob-ably a tiny little bit in love with him."

"I feel pathetic missing someone because of a few days without talking after this was only supposed to be a short-term arrangement anyway," I say, taking a sip from my own glass.

"As someone who misses someone they have no business missing, I feel qualified to tell you that you don't get to control how you feel about stuff like that," Cami says. "If you're pathetic, I'm pathetic. I honestly believe we're too hot to be considered pathetic, but who cares if we are. Maybe we're just cursed with big emotions. It's okay to feel things."

"What do you mean 'arrangement,'" Aurora says, and I have a split second to decide whether to trust my friends or lie. Given they've turned up here to look out for me, it feels unfair not to tell the truth.

"When Will broke up with me, I promised myself I'd put myself first because I had to sacrifice a lot of my time and happiness when we were together. There's this fiction competition I wanted to enter to win a place in a writing course during the summer, but because I've been so shel-tered, my lack of life experience was just so clear in everything I wrote."

"Oh, I saw that on the bulletin board. The one in New York, right?"

I nod. "Henry felt sorry for me, I guess, and he was struggling with Professor Thornton's class, so we agreed that I'd help him if he helped give me life experiences. It sounds so silly now when I say it out loud to other people."

"It isn't silly," Poppy says, trying to reassure me. "It kinda makes perfect sense. The only thing that doesn't is you thinking it was be-cause Henry felt sorry for you. He obviously liked you from the start."

"You wrote a book and didn't tell me? When you know I *love* reading?" Aurora says, practically jumping out of her seat. "Did you submit already? Can I read it?"

Emilia tsks and I watch her roll her eyes. "Way to not make this about you, Ror."

An uncomfortable heat prickles up my neck. "No and no. I haven't finished the third act, and the rest is basically a whole-ass mess that needs to be heavily edited. I didn't prioritize it; I got distracted with Henry, and you guys, and being unwell, and yeah. It wouldn't have won anyway, so no big deal."

"When does the competition close?" Poppy asks.

"Like, just over three weeks. It's the Sunday before spring break week starts, but I would need to be done the week before because there's an author bio and a cover letter I'd need to write. And I'd need to submit on Thursday because I fly back to Phoenix to go on vacation with my family and Will's family on Friday."

"You're still going on vacation with him?" It's like a cartoon as I watch all four of their jaws drop at the same time.

"I'm not going to talk to him. But I miss my family. I miss my little sisters so much, and the alternative is staying here and being lonely."

"It isn't." Aurora shakes her head, rubbing her temple with her fingers. "Let's deal with one blazing wildfire at a time."

"Halle, you have to submit this book. Even if it's totally rubbish, which it won't be because I don't believe you're capable of that," Cami says. "Even your system notes at work are beautifully crafted. But the point is, you owe it to yourself. You can finish this book; I believe in you."

"But I don't even know how to end it," I admit. "I've had an idea this whole time and now it just doesn't feel right, so I don't know what to do."

"Go with your heart," Aurora says. I want to tell her my heart is kind of busy being bruised at the moment. "Just start typing and see what happens. That'll be the story you want to tell. And send me what you have so far. I can start editing it while you finish the rest."

"Me, too," Emilia says. "I love being a grammar nerd."

"I am not a book or grammar girl, but I'll make sure you're fed and hydrated. I'm also fucking amazing at giving massages if your back and neck get sore," Cami adds.

"I've been writing emails for my mom since I learned to spell," Poppy says, laughing, and that task feels so familiar to me. "I can do the bones of your cover letter if you let me know what you want to say. Then you can just edit it to suit your style. We can do this, Halle."

"I don't want to waste anyone's time just for me not to win," I say honestly.

"Girl, shut up," Cami says, shooting me a look that tells me she's saying it with love. "We're finishing this book."

My instincts are telling me to say I don't need their help, that I'll do it all on my own. But in reality, that isn't what I want. I need help and I need support, and having a group of friends who offer that is what I've always wanted.

This whole time I've craved more superficial experiences like shopping and getting ready together. I've called it girlhood because to me it represented what I missed growing up. What younger Halle desperately wanted. But as we've grown closer and our lives have intertwined, I know I was so wrong. This is sisterhood. This is women supporting other women to meet their goals. This is what I've yearned for, and I didn't even know.

I nod enthusiastically, which somehow snowballs into me laughing kind of chaotically. "Okay, let's do it. But we're going to need more wine."

Chapter Thirty-Eight

HENRY

WHEN I LEFT MY HOUSE for my parents' house, I told myself when I got there I'd give myself a day to spiral and then I'd sort my shit out.

Like every other plan I've ever created, it didn't happen like that. I'm not sure how much further there is for me to fall mentally, because moving away and changing my name started to seem appealing for about five minutes last night.

It really took feeling like my entire life is falling apart for me to finally empty the clean laundry out of the basket from the holidays. Every task I've been putting off the past probably ten years has finally been completed. Basically, anything that didn't involve me leaving my bedroom.

For the first week, my parents gave me a pass when I told them I was overwhelmed and needed some peace. Now I'm into the second week and the pass has been shredded. They want answers, they want to support me, they're more people wanting something from me that I don't know how to give.

So I do what I do best: I copy their energy and tell them I'm fine. That I'm over it. And that I'm going home.

Russ and Robbie are their usual careful selves around me. Lola and Aurora don't visit. Nobody visits, actually. It stays quiet and calm. The emails from my professors are piling up, text messages even worse. There's only one person I want to text.

I look up why I'm such a bad procrastinator but get no answers that make sense to me. I look up why it feels like I'm frozen and get advertisements for winter coats. I look up how you know you're in love with someone but close the tab before I get more answers that I can't understand.

I know I owe everyone answers, but I don't know what the answer is.

I pull up Halle's name. Typing quickly before I can put it off, I tell her I'm going to keep my promise.

IT'S FRIDAY AND I SHOULD be prepping for the game, but Faulkner emails me, like he did last week when I didn't show up for practice, that I won't be playing, but he'd like to talk to me.

He actually uses the word *like*, and there aren't any curse words in the email. Maybe Robbie wrote it for him. I know he's avoiding the house by staying at Lola's. Russ told me he feels like he doesn't know how to be my friend and my coach when I won't accept help, and he'll be back the second I'll let him in. I'm not mad at him, or hurt, because I feel like I don't know how to be multiple things at once, too.

I text Halle and tell her I still don't feel great, but I'll get there.

THE FOG IS LIFTING, AND the realization of the mess I've caused almost gives me a panic attack. I could go to class tomorrow, but then I'd have to deal with it.

I missed Valentine's Day. I didn't even text Halle.

The guys won both games, which proves they don't need me, and it weirdly gives me a tiny bit of relief. I think that relief is what lifted the weight crushing me enough to feel the dread of my situation.

I sit with that thought for far too long when there's a knock on my bedroom door. I yell, "Come in," expecting to see Russ, but when the door beeps and opens the last person I expect to see standing in my doorway is Nate Hawkins.

"I can tell by the look on your face that you forgot I was around this week," he says, closing the door behind him. He sits on the end of my bed, and I scramble to understand what he's talking about. Right until I realize how long I've been hiding out and that his schedule has a cluster of games in and not too far from LA. We were supposed to make plans to hang out. "I don't know where to start with you."

"I couldn't be a captain like you. I'm sorry you put your faith in me and I let you down."

Nate stares at me like I have two heads. He scratches his jaw and shakes his head. "Hen, I was shitting myself the entire time. Literally before every single game Robbie would pull me aside and give me this wild pep talk to hype me up because I wanted to be sick. I just didn't let it get the better of me, and eventually I stopped worrying so much. You haven't let me or anyone else down."

"Faulkner isn't going to see it like that. I walked out on him. I've missed so many classes my grades are going to be ass. I've ruined everything, Nate."

"I know it feels like it. Honestly, I get it, and I'm not telling you that your feelings aren't valid, but you can fix it. Faulkner's the way he is because he loves the team, and he loves his players. He would not want you to hide away over fucking ice hockey."

"I don't know what to say to him . . . to say to everyone I've been avoiding. I feel like shit, and I can't even explain why I react the way I do. It's not fucking normal to just shut down like this, but I can't stop it."

Nate listens to me rant, saying nothing until I'm done. "Everyone knows that you haven't done anything to upset anyone. They want you to be okay, Hen. They miss you. Fuck, Stassie misses you, and I bet if I looked at my phone right now I'd have a thousand messages from her. But she's stayed away, like you wanted, because you know how to handle yourself the best. They just all want you back, feeling good, whatever that looks like."

"Do you practice giving speeches just in case you ever have an opportunity to give one?" Nate bursts out laughing, and it's the light in the dark of the past few weeks. I laugh, too, rubbing my palms against my eyes.

"Yeah, every morning before I leave my place." He drags his hand through his hair. "You don't need me to swoop in and fix things for you, I know that. But if you need a friend to be with you while you fix things yourself, I can do that."

"I want that. Thanks."

"Sasha is with Stas right now. She's decided to piss off my dad by claiming she wants to go to Maple Hills, so we've been tasked with keeping an eye on her until she goes on a college tour tomorrow. I have a game tomorrow night, but I can find an hour around lunch-time to see Faulkner with you. Even if I just sit quietly."

"Thanks, Nate."

"I think you need to get out of this room, buddy. Come for dinner with us tonight. The guys need to see you alive and kicking. Stassie needs to see you alive and kicking."

"I haven't been a good friend to her this year. I hardly see her any-more, and she never comes around, but I guess I never invite her and—"

"You know she cried and said the exact same thing about you? That she'd failed you by not being around. That somehow she could have prevented this if she'd seen you more. You'll both survive this. You've got that weird, pseudo-sibling thing going on. I always think I should call Sash more, and she only calls me when she wants some-thing. It's normal. Did you know Stas met Halle?"

That makes me sit up a little straighter. "No . . . when? What did she say?"

"Not a lot. She was at Halle's looking for you before she found out you were at your parents' house. She said Halle clearly missed you, and that she was very sweet and even prettier than she was expecting. Something about a type of cat someone else has that's apparently a big deal. I can't remember."

"I miss her, too. I want to call her, but I know that she'll drop everything to help me sort my mess out. She drops everything for everyone. She never puts herself first, and I know if she finds out I have assignments and studying to do, she'll prioritize me. I told her I needed space and I'd fix everything, and right now it doesn't feel like it could get worse."

"Come for dinner. The guys can help, but don't worry too much about it, Henry. You didn't ghost her; you didn't just disappear with no explanation. It sounds like you told her how you were feeling, and you set her expectations. Maybe don't feel like you need to apologize to her and feel more like you need to thank her for letting you take the time you need."

"I don't remember you being this wise when you lived here."

Nate laughs again and the cloud truly feels like it's lifting. "I don't remember your room being this tidy."

I FEEL LIKE THE WEIRD family member turning up at a wedding with the way everyone stares at me when I walk into the restaurant with Nate.

I take the seat next to Sasha, who is the least likely person to give me a headache, but then I remember that people can talk across tables. "It's giving *Nate is your favorite* energy," Mattie says as I put my napkin across my lap.

"I said I'd be able to coax you out of your depression pit, but Russ wouldn't let me try. Golden retriever to guard dog like *that*," Kris says, snapping his fingers.

Bobby is unusually quiet, but it doesn't last long. "Can't help but feel like I fucked your life up, dude. Sorry about that; he was just saying all that stuff and I could tell you were trying not to rise to it, but he went too far and I just thought fuck it."

"I'm glad you hit him."

Bobby smiles. "I'm glad I hit him, too. Faulkner knows and has been making my life hell as you would expect. Why didn't you tell him, Hen? You could have just blamed me and avoided this whole mess."

It's a question I've been asking myself for the past two weeks. It was only after I left, when the adrenaline had worn off and I was retracing every second of what happened, that I realized I hadn't told Faulkner that my swollen cheek was from me getting out of the way. That Halle hates fighting, and she would have been so disappointed. That I don't need to fight someone like Will because I've already beaten him in every way by getting to be loved by Halle. It was all too late, though, and rehashing the events with Faulkner felt like the least of my problems.

"I honestly don't know. I wouldn't tell him what Will said because I didn't want to embarrass Halle, and he said something about maybe I shouldn't be captain, and I felt relieved." I take a deep breath. "I don't like being captain."

A silence spreads across the guys and Russ is the first one to speak. I notice Aurora isn't beside him. "Then why do it? Why not just step down?"

I shrug. "I didn't want to let you all down. You all believed in me."

"Fucking hell, Henry," Kris groans, rubbing his forehead with his hand. "We believe in you because we love you, you fool. You could tell us you wanted to start, I don't know, fucking show jumping and we'd believe in you. You don't need to be something that makes you unhappy for us."

"What he said," Mattie says.

Bobby frowns a little, my eyebrows pinch together. "I'll be honest, I'd have my doubts about a future equestrian career because I've seen how much you fuck around on leg day, but yeah, don't do something just for us or whatever Kris said."

Anastasia is unusually quiet, and when I look to her she shakes her head. "I just love you and want you to be happy. Whatever that looks like."

The doors open and JJ walks in looking nothing like the weird relative at a wedding. "I heard we were holding an intervention. Has Nate made some corny speech yet?"

"Not yet," Robbie says. He's at the end of the table beside Lola, also staying quiet. "I'm sure it's coming. You're looking at me, Hen. But I don't have anything to say. I've got your back whatever you do. I've always got your back."

JJ takes the empty chair on the other side of Sasha and leans forward. "Let's talk about how you un–fuck up your relationship with the love of your life." Everyone groans, including me. "What? He's going to need something big."

I don't know who goes first, but at least three people say, "That's what she said."

ANASTASIA AND I HAVE ARGUED many times about the idea of manifesting.

I know for certain that it's absolute bullshit, because I ask the universe to give us flat tires so I can't get to Faulkner's office, and nothing happens.

"It's good to see you, Henry," he says when I sit in his office. He looks at Nate. "I thought I'd gotten rid of you, Hawkins."

I don't think Faulkner has ever called me by my first name, which is an immediate red flag. I think of the speech that Nate and I practiced on the way over here. I figured if I was going to make one I may as well run it by an expert.

"I'm sorry for going MIA, Coach. Sometimes I get really overwhelmed and it makes it difficult for me to process all my emotions, and I sort of shut down. I don't know why I do it. I don't know how to stop it, but I really want to. I love hockey, but I don't love being a leader.

"I feel responsible for everyone and everything, and I can't see outside of my own head sometimes. I didn't want to let down the people who believed I could do it, and I didn't want to let myself down. But I also need to admit when something isn't the right choice for me."

Faulkner doesn't interrupt, he doesn't yell, he doesn't slam his fist on the table. "You know we could have avoided all this upset if you'd just explained that you didn't hit anyone."

"I know."

"Why didn't you tell me that Ellington attacked you? You were the victim, Henry. I should have been looking out for you, not berating you."

"Your team's mistakes are your own when you're the leader."

Faulkner looks at Nate, his eyes narrowing. "Did you teach him this fall-on-your-sword bullshit? You're good at that, too."

"What?" Nate says, losing his cool slightly. "No!"

"I read it in a book by Harold Oscar. I was reading it to learn how to be a better captain. But it feels pointless now, because then you said maybe I shouldn't be captain and I felt relieved and I don't know. It's hard for me to remember."

Coach laughs, and I've never been more confused. I turn to Nate for guidance, but nope, he looks confused, too. "Harold Oscar? Have you ever looked up Harold Oscar? Or met him? Because I have. The guy is an asshole. He couldn't lead ducks to a pond. He was injured for most of the seasons his team won! Why the fuck would you listen to his advice?"

"I wanted to do a good job."

"You were, for what it's worth. We can fix this. No more though, Henry. I accept that you've had a rough time mentally, and your recent conduct is an exception. You pull this shit again and it's going to end very differently."

"I understand."

Coach grabs a pen from the pot on his desk and a piece of paper. "Here's what you're going to do: You're gonna make up every workout and every skate you missed while you were gone. You're gonna email all your professors and ask them what you need to do to catch up. Plus, you're going to talk to someone about shutting down when you're overwhelmed. When you've done that, and you're caught up and you've made up all your training, you can play. We can decide on a new captain."

"I can help," Nate says, nudging my shoulder.

Faulkner frowns at him. "Why would I want your help? I took your advice last year and look where it fucking got me." He gestures to me. "A captain who hates captaincy."

I accept the to-do list from Faulkner and tuck it into my pocket. "Yeah, he's got you there, Nate. You did drop the ball by believing in me."

Nate pinches his nose between his fingers. "I'm getting a migraine."

ONE HOUR LATER AND MY life feels like it's back on track.

It's ridiculous when I think about it like that. Russ is hanging out in the living room reading a textbook and working on his tablet when I get home. "All good?"

"I have a lot of work to catch up on, but yeah, all good. I think Coach was having a moment—he called me Henry."

Russ's nose scrunches. "That's weird."

"You can tell Aurora to stop avoiding the place now. It's

weirdly quiet without her here." It will also help me determine if she hates me.

"She isn't avoiding it. She's helping Halle with a writing project or something. She said it was a secret; she only told me because she needed to use my laptop when she left hers at home by accident."

I've been thinking of ways to show Halle how much she means to me since JJ brought it up last night. "I need you to show me."

He looks like I just asked him for a kidney. "Ror will kill me, Henry. I don't think I was even allowed to tell you."

"Please, Russ. I'll never ask for anything from you again. I need to make it up to Halle and I know how."

"Fine," he says, closing his book. "But you need to teach me how to be good at hiding out when Aurora inevitably tracks me down."

"You got it."

Pulling out my phone, I send Halle one more text. I tell her I'm working on fixing everything, and that I miss her.

Chapter Thirty-Nine

HALLE

"What about for ten million dollars?"

I frown at Aurora over my forkful of ravioli. "No."

"What about eleven million?" she continues.

Cami puts her glass back on the table and picks up her cutlery. "I'll cancel my plans and come with you for eleven million dollars."

"I only have the funds to bribe one friend today! You have a week with Briar and Summer," Aurora argues, absentmindedly moving plates around. She's separated the strawberries from her salad and is pushing them onto my empty side plate. "Halle has a week with the Antichrist."

The waiter is trying not to laugh as he refills the glasses of water on the table, and I can't blame him. Every time he's visited our table, Aurora has been calling Will something new in a bid to make me change my plans.

Aurora is upset I'm still going on vacation with my family instead of with her, Poppy, and Emilia. Considering how I don't want me to go on this trip, either, it's kind of nice to have someone be the dramatic one on your behalf. While she's definitely more creative than me, her outrage is enough for the both of us. "He's a jackass, but I wouldn't call him the Antichrist, Ror."

"He's *blond*!" she splutters.

Poppy looks up from her phone, visibly confused. "You're blond. Russ is blond."

"Russ is *light* brown," she argues, looking offended. "Will is *blond* blond. Sneaky blond. Untrustworthy blond."

"I know you've made looking like a Barbie doll one of your core identities, but normal people don't have personalities defined by their hair color," Emilia says, being the voice of reason. "Will is a jerk because he's a jerk, not because he's blond."

"Of course you'd say that. Your hair is brown," Aurora counters.

I finish the last of Aurora's strawberries and take the napkin from my lap, placing it next to my empty plate. "How about . . . I still go on my vacation because he won't be there the whole time because he needs to leave early for a game. *But*, if his head starts spinning or he starts speaking in tongues, I'll let you put me on a flight."

"Fine," she says, throwing her napkin onto her empty plate. "But your sister followed me, and she promised to keep me up to date because I don't trust you not to tell me what I want to hear. So just know, I'll be watching."

I think if I were a little stronger I'd have bowed out of this trip a month ago. Mom and I had a great chat after I arrived home from Henry's place. If I stank of sex and sadness, she didn't mention it as she cuddled me on the couch. I didn't tell her what Will had said, but I let her know that it was horrible enough that I was never speaking to him ever again.

She apologized for not realizing how much she put on me. She told me I was her rock, the one who kept her sane through all the stressful times, but that her dependence on me had robbed me of so much. She cried when she told me she worried that I'd matured too quickly and that's why I struggled to make friends. And that she thought maybe my reward for being so selfless was one of those once-in-a-lifetime kinds of love.

I told her I was never in love with Will, but maybe it could still be true.

She said she didn't expect me to come on the vacation anymore if I didn't want to, but I do really miss Gianna and Maisie. I already missed the holidays with them; I can cope with ignoring Will for a few days.

I know that Mom no longer feels any kind of allegiance to Will. In fact, I'd say she probably hates him now, knowing what she knows. She doesn't bring him up when she calls, and she only ever asks me how I'm doing and what I'm up to. Well, she tries, and I don't mind helping out with some things. Maybe next year she can plan the trip and I can go away with my friends.

When the five of us were desperately trying to edit my book, Mom sent a care package with snacks and candles, which showed me she heard what I said and is trying to be better.

"You're the only person worrying!" I lie, telling Aurora what she wants to hear. "I'm excited to hang out with my siblings. It's going to be great. And be careful, Gigi will extort you for race tickets. She's just gotten into Formula 1."

"You're going to have to get better at lying," Emilia says, waving her piece of pizza around as she talks. "I can't be surrounded by bad liars. I want to work in PR and it might rub off on me."

Romano's isn't as busy as I expected it to be on a Friday afternoon given I've never been able to get a reservation here. My spring break officially started yesterday since I have no Friday classes, but for everyone else, their break started an hour ago.

We agreed to meet for lunch before heading on our respective trips, to celebrate me finally submitting my novel to the competition. Poppy wanted me to do it here at the table in front of them all, but it felt like something I needed to do alone to fully absorb.

I finished a book.

I finished a freaking book, and I did something for myself.

I learned a lot in the process, and in the end, it wasn't about the knowledge I learned from the experiences I was given by Henry. The most important thing that this whole project has taught me is that putting myself first doesn't mean that I have to do it alone. Having people to help and cheer me on while I did this thing for myself is what made it actually enjoyable in the end.

Even if I don't win and I don't get to go to New York this summer, writing the book has given me more than I ever imagined it could anyway.

Lunch runs over, leaving me rushing to get back home to grab my bags in time for my scheduled Uber. The drive past Maple Avenue makes my heart ache; Henry's texts became less frequent as February passed, and I haven't heard from him since he texted me saying that he was working on fixing everything and he missed me.

I told him there was no pressure to keep me updated, so it was hard to battle mentally expecting no updates but also wanting them so, so much.

I'm happy he's fixing things, and I want him to feel better. I can't pretend it didn't sting to see him posted in pictures out for dinner with Nate and his other friends. The stunningly beautiful girl beside him in the picture made my stomach drop because I didn't recognize her, but Aurora immediately reassured me that she's Nate's younger sister.

Jealousy is a weird new emotion for me, especially because of the guilt it brought. I laughed in the end, because it resulted in my friends telling me all the times they've been jealous and unhinged. Cami was the clear winner, and after one story where everyone just stared in disbelief, she decided that she might be toxic.

In reality, I see how Henry spending time with his friends would be good for his well-being. In the alternative reality, the place where I get everything I want, Henry is with me.

I promised the girls I wasn't going to think about him or us while I was away, and I'd deal with my feelings when I'm home. But it's the

knowledge that I need to not think about it that's making me hallu-
cinate that Henry's sitting on my porch as I pull into my driveway.

Shutting off my engine, I stare. The hallucination holds up a
hand, mouthing hi. It moves toward my car until it's beside my door.
The door opens, and the hallucination talks.

"Are you having a moment? Why are you staring at me like that?"
I poke it in the stomach, and I'm met with the same hard surface
I've touched so many times. "Ow, Halle. Are you going to get out of
your car?"

I've spent the past month wondering how I'll react when Henry
finally shows back up in my life. I flipped between elation and anger,
depending on where I was in my menstrual cycle. I wasn't expecting
to feel so . . . guarded?

He crouches down beside me, hand shielding his eyes to block
out the LA sunshine. "You're not a hallucination. You changed your
hair. And you have a beard. You look different."

Henry's auburn curls are braided into cornrows. He nods, running his hand over the crown of his head. "Lower maintenance. It
isn't a beard; I just haven't shaved this week. Can we go inside, or do
you want to sit in your car forever?"

"I don't have a lot of time to talk because my ride to the airport
is coming soon."

"I want any time you have," he says softly.

Joy clearly doesn't have the same weird, unsettled apprehension I
have, because she makes a beeline for him like he's catnip. He looks
so much happier than the last time I saw him. Aurora and I enforced
a rule where she didn't offer information about Henry and I didn't
ask, with the promise that in an emergency she would update me.

It feels so silly now seeing him standing in front of me, perfectly
fine. Henry has always called me dramatic for various reasons, so I
guess it's on-brand.

Cami says that because I made prioritizing myself a goal but it always felt so unobtainable, it makes sense that I would be so accepting of someone else trying to do the same. Especially when, in her words, she would have been pounding her fist against his door after the first week. It made me wonder if I was selfish to leave him to deal with things on his own. I guess now that he's in front of me I could ask him, but I don't know if I'm ready to hear the answer.

"I missed you," he says, crossing the room to stand in front of me.

"I missed you, too," I respond, deciding not to move out of reach when his hands reach to cup my face. His warm grip soothes the anxiety that's been rumbling through me for weeks, and I fight the urge to cry.

His forehead rests against mine; his voice lowers. "Thank you for giving me space to work on myself."

I couldn't speak louder than a whisper even if I wanted to. "You're welcome."

He kisses my forehead tenderly, breathing in deeply before taking a step back. "We both know I'm not always the best person with words, and I know you have a vacation to go on, but I wanted to give you this." He hands me a small sealed bubble mailer. "It'll get through TSA. An email will come through soon, so don't open the envelope until you receive it."

"This is very mysterious and secretive," I say, shaking the mailer.

"It's a gift. To show you how much you mean to me, and that I'm sorry for needing so much time. I'm scared you think it's because you're not important to me, when in reality it took so long because you *do* mean so much to me."

"So it's my fault? That you couldn't feel better?"

"No," he says harshly. "Just that I wasn't in a good place and I wanted to get out of it so I didn't make you the anchor. I don't want to be a person who relies on you to fix everything. I can explain everything when you get home from vacation if you have questions. I'll tell you anything you want to know."

"Okay. I'd like that." The arrival notification on my phone rings, and looking out my living room window confirms my ride is here. "I have to go, I'm sorry. I don't want to miss my flight."

The driver beeps twice before I decide I need to touch Henry before I leave. His arms wrap around me tightly when I step toward him for a hug. His lips press against the crown of my head. "Bye, Cap. See you in a week."

To THE ABSOLUTE HORROR OF my Uber driver, I cry the whole way to LAX.

I don't even know why I'm crying, and neither does he, given he thinks the best thing to do is turn up the radio and blast rock music. I rate him five stars and leave him a nice tip as an apology, and drag my suitcase through the airport to the check-in counter while promising myself this will be the last time I cry this week.

If I turn up to this vacation emotional it'll be like blood in the water for the Ellingtons and I won't know a second of peace. They maintain that their beautiful baby boy was a victim in the *disagreement* that caused so much trouble for Henry. I maintain that they suck.

I decide to label the emotion causing my outburst in the car as relief. Relief he's okay, relief I've seen him with my own eyes, relief that he thinks he was gone too long as well, relief that he wants to see me when I'm home.

The check-in line is moving slowly, as the airport's normal busy nature is increased exponentially by the number of people leaving for the week. My phone buzzes in my hand to notify me of an email.

Even though Henry told me to expect it, it still catches me by surprise. Digging through my carry-on bag, I retrieve the mailer that's managed to sink its way to the bottom and click on the notification.

From: henry.m.turner@ucmh.ac.com
To: halle.n.jacobs@ucmh.ac.com
Subject: Put your headphones on.

I broke rule number 4 too.
Don't tell the board.
H

Henry Turner has sent you a file.
Click here to retrieve it!
Password: openthepackage

I fish my headphones out of my bag, slowly nudging forward closer to the front of the line, and slide them over my ears. I'm holding my breath when I click the link, not knowing what to expect when it takes me to an online folder with a huge audio file in it.

My hands shake while I enter the password and click play, then immediately reach for the mailer. Nothing happens at first, the sound of rustling and a bed frame squeak until I finally hear Henry's voice.

"Halle Jacobs knew she wanted to be an author the first time she attended a library-run author reading. Always daydreaming about people she imagined, Halle credits her mom for getting her her first library card and fueling her love of books, and a childhood obsession with The Sims *for her overactive imagination. Jacobs is an English major at the University of California, Maple Hills, and lives in Maple Hills with her beloved cat, Joy."*

My hands pull at the sealed flap, desperate to see what's inside. Henry just read the author biography I wrote for myself for the competition, word for word. I have no idea how he even got it. Then his voice starts again.

"Halle Jacobs is sweet and kind, always doing what she can to be a good person to others. She has a wide friend group of family, classmates, colleagues, and neighbors, who all agree that she's one of the most giving and loving people they know. Outside of reading and writ-

ing, Jacobs is an excellent baker, a skill she inherited from her beloved grandmother. She is funny, beautiful, and smart.

"Jacobs has a boyfriend, whom she has made a better man in every single way, and he hopes he'll be the love of her lifetime as they both evolve into the people they were always supposed to be together. It is also a widely known fact that Jacobs has the best ass in LA."

Maybe there can be a long list of complimentary adjectives when someone talks about me.

When Henry talks about me.

I have no choice but to step out of the line with my bags. My heart is pounding, hands shaking as I pull at the envelope, frantically trying to get past what is apparently the world's strongest adhesive.

It finally comes loose, just as Henry begins talking again.

"Chapter One . . ."

The book that comes out of the mailer isn't one I recognize. The cover is hand painted; two people are lying in a meadow full of daisies. The sky is the dreamiest purple and pink and my name is right there beside them.

Turning the first pages as Henry reads my words to me, I notice his tidy scribble on the title page.

This might be my favorite romance book, but we're my favorite love story.

Yours always,
Henry

Each page I turn has more and more Henry between it. His art is sketched onto the pages, over my words, binding us together. Every drawing fills me with more and more life, and I don't realize I'm crying until a tear drops onto the page and spreads across the ink.

As much as I don't want to, I pause the audio.

I have some calls to make.

Chapter Forty

HENRY

NATE TOLD ME TO TRUST the process and I'm trying to listen to him, but as it turns out, I'm not really a trust-the-process kind of guy.

I can be laid back, sure, but am I trusting that urge to just let shit play out? No.

I like predictability. I like routine. I like certainty.

Which is why when I sent Halle that email, I threw all those things I like into chaos, and I'm going to have to practice patience—something I'm not known for—to wait a week until she gets home to find out what she thought.

After only a handful of text messages to make sure she knew I was thinking about her during the month, I can hardly expect—okay, I've been told by the guys that I can hardly expect—her to contact me right away.

JJ said what I haven't learned from hooking up with whomever I want and then moving on is that when you do really like someone, it is inevitable that you will, at some point, cause a fucking mess that you need to fix.

All the guys agreed, so I'm taking this as one of those times JJ gives out okay advice.

According to him, followed by a team cosign, this is my "grand gesture" to make sure she knows how much she means to me.

After Russ finally caved and let me look at the book, I was immediately mad at myself for not insisting Halle let me read it sooner. I loved seeing her words on the page, recognizing her voice but seeing it tell someone else's story. It was magical, and maybe if I'd spent more time encouraging her and less time distracting her, we could have reached this point sooner.

Someone knocks on my door, and the beeping of the code being entered follows when I shout come in. Russ appears with a cup of tea for me, an unfortunate habit I've developed in the past month. As a rule, I hate listening to Aurora, but I'm going to let her have this win.

"Halle good?" Russ asks, putting the mug on my bedside table and sitting at the foot of my bed.

"I think I should have called her first. I caught her off guard; she poked me for some reason. I don't know how to describe it properly. She seemed . . . out of reach. Even though I could touch her. She seemed far away." Russ rubs his neck. "Go on. Say what you gotta say."

"It's hard saving someone from themselves," he says. Russ repositions himself to face me, leaning against his knee. "It might take her a minute to find her footing again. You guys went from spending every spare minute together to nothing, when you were still only just starting. Things were never going to be totally normal when you shut her out."

"But I didn't only shut her out, I shut everyone out. And in the end, I was trying to help her."

"It's hard for people to understand that other people sometimes just shut down; that not everyone's brain works in the same way when dealing with stress. I think she gets you better than anyone, though." I nod in agreement. "She knows that if you're left unchecked, the chances are you'll spiral and procrastinate and all the other shit, okay? But she also knows, like the rest of us do, that the more she forces you to try and do something, the longer it'll take for you to do it. You know that you'll hit a point and then you'll fix it. It's not the same thing, but with addicts it's called hitting rock bottom."

"The past month felt a lot like rock bottom."

"Yeah, exactly. For her, you know that she'll drop everything for you, even if it means putting herself last, which you obviously don't want. I don't mean this in a mean way, dude, but Halle wouldn't have finished her book if she'd helped you stop spiraling and get up to speed last month. You were keeping her away to help her help herself, while suffering because you missed her. And she was staying away because you asked her to, suffering because she missed you and probably believed that she could fix it. Am I making sense?"

This feels a lot like a riddle, but I think I'm following. "We both had to struggle for a while and do what we needed to do for ourselves, for everything to work out now?"

"Basically," Russ says, nodding.

"That was a really long-winded way to say what you meant. You spend too much time with Aurora."

Russ laughs, pinching the bridge of his nose. "I know. I'm sorry, I'll leave the motivational speeches to Nate."

"Is Aurora mad at me?" The question's been playing on my mind because Aurora, who normally spends a lot of time at this house, has hardly been here. "I'd understand if she was."

He thinks about it for a minute, mouth pinching while he considers what he wants to say. "No, is the easy answer. Rory gets that how we would deal with something together is not how everyone else would. I think she just feels very protective of Halle, and maybe a bit guilty? They've been in the same classes for two years, and it took you befriending her for her to realize that she called her a friend, but she wasn't really her friend, I guess?"

"Halle didn't think she had friends when we met. She told me," I say, thinking back to when I asked her why she lived alone.

"Yeah. Acquaintances was probably a better word, but Rory borrowed her notes and went to her book club and sat next to her in class, and that's as far as it went. So yeah, I don't know if guilt is the right word, but I think she thinks she could have done more before now. So she isn't mad at you; she just wants the best for Halle. And you, obviously."

"Is it weird that I miss her?"

"Who? Halle?"

I grimace. "No . . . Aurora."

Russ laughs so hard the bed shakes beneath him. "I'm not telling her you said that. She'll be unbearable. She's leaving for her girls' trip in an hour, but I'll get her to come over when she comes back next week."

As I reach for my cup of tea, Russ stands from the bed and heads toward the door. "I'm glad you're feeling better. Not sure what I'd do without you on the team."

"You made it weird."

He sighs. "Get over it. I'm going to watch TV downstairs if you want to hang out."

"I'll come down after I've finished this sketch. Hey, Russ . . ." Russ stops, holding my bedroom door open. "Not sure what I'd do without you, either."

"Am I interrupting a special moment?" We both look into the hallway outside my room. "I can leave if you two need privacy."

Halle's smiling face is the last thing I was expecting to see today. "I think we're all special-momented out, actually. It's really good to see you, Halle," Russ says, immediately moving out of her way so she can walk into my bedroom. The door closes behind her and I climb off the bed.

Her eyes are bright but puffy. I see the black marks beneath them where her eye makeup has smudged. "What are you doing here? Why do you look like a panda?"

Of all the things I want to say to her and to ask, that's the first one that comes out of my mouth.

"I'm here for the board meeting." Her hand reaches into her bag and pulls out the book that I spent hours working on. "I think we need to discuss all the rule breaking that's been happening. You read my book."

"There wasn't a rule about not reading your book," I say, taking a step toward her. "But I would have broken it if there was. I want to read every word you ever write from now on."

"There was a huge mistake in the book. Massive one, in fact."

My heart sinks. I checked it *so* many times. "What was it?"

She grins. "It said I have a boyfriend. And as far as I can remember, nobody has asked me to be their girlfriend."

"Hmm. You sure?"

"I can't believe you made my book a book, Henry." She holds up the bound novel, taking a small step in my direction. "And you made me an audiobook."

I nod because yeah, I fucking did, and it was hard as hell. It's given me a whole new appreciation for all the narrators Halle listens to. I remember the one thing I've been impatiently waiting to ask her. "You switched the ending. I knew my guy would come through. But why didn't you stick to what you planned?"

Halle holds the book to her chest, every emotion I felt reading the book written on her face. "I couldn't stomach the thought that two people in love might not get to live happily ever after. They deserved a chance."

I close the gap between us, pulling her mouth to mine. It's crazed and desperate, the excitement tainted by how long it's been since we last kissed. Breaking us apart, I rest my forehead against hers while she directs me backward toward the bed, climbing into my lap as my ass hits the mattress. "I love you, Halle."

"I love you, too. Please don't break my heart."

Relief is my dominant emotion right now, because after a month apart I worried if she'd still feel the same way about me. "Never."

I drag her mouth back to mine, slow and controlled. Patient, as much as I don't want to be anything close to patient. I want to enjoy that she's here with me when I thought I wouldn't see her for a week.

Wait.

Leaning back, I furrow my brows. "What about your flight?"

"I called my mom and told her I don't want to go. She thought something might have happened, but I was honest and said being there with the Ellingtons will really impact me negatively, and I'm choosing not to put myself through it just to make everyone else happy."

Pride. "And what did she say?"

Halle's beaming. "That she was of course disappointed she wouldn't get to spend time with me, but if I wanted to go on vacation with them next year, we could do it just as a family—no Ellingtons. She's glad I'm setting boundaries for my well-being, and she's going to bring my sisters to visit at Easter."

"That's incredible, Halle. I'm so happy for you."

She nods, and she's clearly happy for herself, too. "Yeah, she's been trying really hard."

Her arms loop around my neck as mine go around her waist, and we just hold each other. "Does this mean I get you this week?"

"Uh, no. I actually need to leave in, like, two minutes."

I move so quickly to look at her face to judge if she's joking that she almost falls off my lap. "Where are you going?"

She's smiling so hard, and I know whatever answer she gives me I'll be okay with just to see her this happy. "I'm going on my first girls' trip! I called Aurora when I left LAX and she said I could still go with them. I just need to hurry up and get there with my passport. I'm so nervous, but excited, although I have no clue about race cars, and Aurora said we have to support a team, and that their colors will really suit me, but I swear it's not her family's team . . . And I'm rambling because I'm excited, but I really do need to go."

"Yeah, it's a whole thing; I'm sure she'll tell you on the plane. Will you video call me while you're gone? I miss you when I don't see your face. I've spent a lot of time looking at pictures of you on my phone recently."

She kisses me once, twice. "Of course. I miss you, too. I'll be back in a week."

She climbs off me, and I really have to stop myself from clinging on to her. In reality, I'm happy she's doing something for herself. I guess I can cope with sharing her with Aurora occasionally. I watch her ass as she walks away, which reminds me of something else I need to say before she leaves. "Cap?"

Halle turns to look back at me. "Yeah?"

I clear my throat. "Can I be your boyfriend?"

I'll never get over being the person to make her smile so big. She moves toward me quickly, throwing herself into my open arms as I fall flat on the bed. She kisses me before answering. "Yes."

She rolls off me onto the bed beside me, cuddling into my side before sitting up, frowning. "You have a painting above your bed!" She gets to her feet to study the canvas properly and I stand to look at it next to her. "How the hell did I not notice that totally huge painting when I walked in here five minutes ago?"

"Too distracted by how good-looking I am, probably."

"What happened? What other art did I miss?" she asks, looking around the room. She won't find anything; there's only this one.

"Finally found something I wanted to look at every day."

She leans forward. "Wait, is this the, y'know. The one where we? On the canvas?"

"It's the canvas we fucked on, yeah."

Her mouth is wide open. "It looks so good! I was expecting it to be total trash if I'm honest. Like, I know you're talented, but there's only so much talent you can control in that kind of setting."

"You underestimate me." I can feel the seconds until she *has* to leave, even though I'm thankful she's here at all.

"What do you feel when you look at it?" she asks.

Wrapping my arm across her shoulders, I kiss her temple. "Love."

Epilogue

HALLE

Three Months Later

"This really feels like a *can I copy your homework if I change it a bit* moment. I have serious concerns that the contents of that letter are exactly the same as the contents of my letter."

Cami smiles in a way that tells me I'm absolutely right. "Has anyone ever told you you worry too much?"

"Yes, everyone, all the time. Pete's going to think we're bullying him if we both quit on the same day," I say. "Maybe we should space it out."

"Maybe Pete deserves to be bullied a little after he upgraded that woman who called you the bitch in the cardigan," she says, applying her lipstick clearly without a care in the world. "Have you considered that?"

I'm feeling a little sensitive when it comes to quitting on people. Sure, Pete has made me want to burn down the hotel on more than one occasion, but he isn't a bad guy. "You quit. I'll wait a week," I say.

"Halle Jacobs, we are quitting this shitty job and moving on to greener pastures. Those pastures being wine and books. Come on, let's rip the Band-Aid off together."

Climbing out of my car in the parking lot of The Huntington, Cami and I find Pete in his office and deliver what I imagine are identically worded letters after Cami asked to look at mine for "inspiration." By the time we're heading back to the car, unemployed with no notice period after Pete told us to never come back, I'm in agreement that maybe he deserved to be bullied a little.

Enchanted bookstore is thriving. So much so that Inayah needed to take on someone to help during the week. She asked me if I wanted the position before she advertised it to the general public. After being heavily influenced by all my friends, I said yes.

Tired of being verbally abused and hit on by snotty rich businessmen, sometimes in the same conversation, Cami decided that if I was jumping so was she. That jump happened to land in the wine bar next door.

I feel lighter now that I've lost some of the responsibilities that don't make me happy, and every time I put myself first, Henry treats me like I just saved the world. I kind of like that bit the most.

"I don't think it's normal for you all to be this invested in something that doesn't have anything to do with you."

"Henry," I mutter, refreshing the competition portal for what must be the millionth time in the past hour. "Don't be mean."

I look up from my screen at all the people watching with interest. The front door flies open and Russ and Aurora stumble through it wearing T-shirts with giant raccoons on them. "Did we miss it? We got stuck in traffic!"

"What are you wearing?" Henry asks, looking them both up and down.

"We're looking after the raccoon group this year," Russ explains, pulling at his Honey Acres summer camp T-shirt before closing the door behind them. He sits in the chair across from us and Aurora sits on the arm of it.

"Jenna is punishing us for lying last year by putting us with our last choice of age group. Teenagers are literally so mean; what is their problem?"

"You didn't miss it," I say, refreshing my screen again.

"There weren't this many people in the room when I got drafted," Grayson says, looking around at my friends.

"Halle, Bobby just texted me and asked when you become a famous author, will you go on their podcast?" Robbie says, looking up from his phone.

My eyebrows pinch together. "Their . . . hockey podcast?"

He types back, then nods. "Yeah. They're thinking of transitioning into books."

"Sure," I say, nodding slowly. "When I'm a famous author tell them just to let me know when to show up."

Henry leans in, his mouth millimeters from my ear, voice low. "Refresh it again."

"Hey!" Grayson snaps from the recliner on the opposite side of the room. "Get back onto your own seat cushion."

"Finally," JJ says, reclining the seat next to my brother. "Some code of conduct in this house. It's been a lawless land for years."

"Shut *up*, Jaiden," Emilia says. "You'd break any code of conduct for fun."

"You don't even live here anymore," Aurora adds. "You have no authority here."

"You've never lived here! *Oh*, I just gave myself déjà vu. Have we had this argument before?" he says. "Has someone else had this argument before?"

He thinks about it for a minute, looking at the other guys for them to weigh in. "Probably."

I'm about to tell the guys to shut up as well until I notice the warmth leave me as Henry shuffles away to his own designated cushion. "You can't be serious," I groan.

"He's huge, Halle. He looks like he doesn't think fighting is for fools anymore. I love you, but I also like having all my ribs intact, which is going to be my main focus when we play football tomorrow."

Grayson is in town for a meeting with a prospective team now that his contract is up. He's been trying to visit more before the season starts to ramp up, and he's back at training camp, whichever team that ends up being on. He says it's because he misses me, but in reality, he heard I have a new boyfriend and he wants to check him out. He thinks he's a good judge of character since he was the "OG Will hater."

So far, he has no complaint about Henry other than he stands too close to me and he's too affectionate.

"What if they actually hated my entry and it was so bad that they don't know how to tell me?"

It's the one thing that silences the room. Everyone looks at each other for someone else to answer.

"You got through to the final ten," Henry says, my forever voice of reason. "You're catastrophizing."

Cami taught Henry what catastrophizing was recently, and now he loves to point out when everyone else is blowing things slightly out of proportion. The irony is that she was explaining what it was to him because *he* was talking about how his natural response to conflict is to spiral.

"If it hasn't updated when I refresh one more time, I'm throwing my laptop out of the window," I say, silently seething. "They told me it would definitely be today."

"Maybe the system is just updating," Aurora adds. "Maybe their building got evacuated."

"Maybe Halle is just impatient," Henry says, causing every person in the room to stare at him. "Fine. Maybe we're all a little impatient sometimes. No big deal."

I click the refresh button one more time, and unlike all the other times, the screen turns white. "Something's happening! Something's happening!"

About ten people all jump onto our couch to get a look at my laptop screen. It's a ridiculous attempt to show support, and I know it's because Henry reminded them all to be supportive, but it makes my heart feel warm all the same.

The white screen lasts a lifetime.

Henry would tell me I'm exaggerating, but it feels like a lifetime.

The portal updates. The tiny box next to my entry that's read Pending since I found out I'd been short-listed a week ago has changed to Runner Up.

"Oh, I didn't win. That's okay; I wasn't expecting to anyway."

"Oh, Hals," Aurora says, and I feel someone's hand—maybe hers, maybe someone else from the pile of people surrounding me—pat my head softly like I'm a dog.

"You can't be hot and immediately successful," Cami says. "It'll make you too powerful. All hot people need to struggle first to make them likable."

"She's right, Hals," Poppy says somewhere among the pile. "You need humble origins so you can say you never saw it coming."

"Okay! You can all go back to your seats now. I'm over it. It's okay. It was a long shot and I still wrote a book, so . . ."

"Hallebear, can I talk to you outside?" Grayson says after being unusually quiet for the last two minutes. "You, too, lover boy."

"He can't ground us, right?" Henry asks as we follow Grayson into the garden.

"No, babe. He can't ground us." Grayson stops on the deck, putting his hands on his hips. "Can you not? You look like Dad right now, and you're freaking me out."

"Shut up. I'm sorry about your competition," is how he starts. "Anyway, I feel bad about low-key traumatizing you by calling you the family manager since you could talk, so, I spoke to Mom and Dad, and we agreed that if you didn't win the competition that we were going to pay for you to go on the course."

"Shut *up*! You're kidding." Henry doesn't say anything beside me, and I immediately panic that it's because I'll be gone for six weeks. We barely lasted a month not seeing each other, but this will be different and he can visit. "Are you sure? Thank you, Gray."

"Mmm. So, Mom and Dad don't know yet, but I'm moving to the West Coast. I don't know exactly which team right now, but I have offers on the table. My apartment lease isn't up so you can stay there while you go to class or whatever." He looks to Henry then back to me. "But I have cameras watching your every move, so no funny business. I'll know if my couch has been interfered with in any inappropriate way. And I'll be back at some point. You promise you'll look after her? The city is not for the weak."

"Why are you such a dinosaur? And I ca—wait, what?"

"I'm coming with you," Henry says calmly, like it isn't the most exciting thing I've heard all year. "I signed up for some summer art classes that looked cool."

"I"—would scream with excitement if it wouldn't make Henry banish me—"am so happy right now."

Russ appears at the French doors; he knocks before poking his head out, his raccoon T-shirt nowhere to be seen. "Sorry to interrupt, guys. We really need to go or we'll be late."

"Two minutes," Henry says to him.

I hug my brother and he reluctantly hugs me back like the pretend grump that he is. "Thank you, Grayson. Are you going to come to the party later? It's an open bar."

"No, Hals. Have fun with your friends. I'll see you tomorrow." He points to Henry. "No driving if you're drinking. Got it?"

"I don't even have a car," Henry says back.

"Good. Let's keep it that way."

As we walk back into the house, Henry looks at me. "I'm not going. I need to practice sprinting so I can get away from your brother."

"Yes you are, c'mon."

"I LOVE WHAT YOU'RE WEARING," Henry says to me loudly. "You look so beautiful."

About five people I don't know turn around and look at me with a mix of jealousy and appreciation. "Shhh," I say, laughing. "But thank you."

He leans in closer, nuzzling beneath my ear. "You're welcome."

"Can you two cool it?" Jaiden snaps. "Some of us are single and honestly don't appreciate this kind of treatment." He looks along the line of couples. "Never mind."

I try to cool myself with the paper fan I was given when we walked onto the hotel terrace. It was more gratefully received than the spritzy fruit drink they handed me.

"They're coming!" Aurora yells, followed by an apology when Henry asks if yelling was necessary.

A round of applause starts as the patio doors to the terrace open and Stassie, Lola, Mattie, Bobby, and Kris walk through in their graduation cap and gowns.

"Christ, that was long," Bobby groans, making a beeline for an ice bucket filled with beer bottles.

"Not doing that again," Mattie adds.

"That's what she said," Kris yells, following them closely toward the beer. "Both times."

"Will you three ever mature? Like, genuine question," Stassie says, putting her cap on the table. I can see the Long Story Short, I Graduated design we did together with a hot-glue gun and too much supervision from Henry stood the test of the day.

"No. Probably not," Robbie says as he appears with Nate.

More friends and family start to arrive, and the terrace fills up quickly. I keep myself stuck to Henry's side so I can run interference when it gets a bit too much for him. He said he has a face that parents like to talk to, and he needs me to make that stop.

Nate organized the event for everyone because he wanted to celebrate Anastasia and she said it was obnoxious to do it alone and to make it a group party. People moving on from college and starting new journeys is going to be a weird adjustment for me after making so many new friends this year. Henry promised it wouldn't be the end, and that he can almost guarantee that we won't be able to shake anyone. I cut him off when he started weighing the pros and cons of streamlining our friendship group anyway.

"Can we skip our graduation?" Henry asks. "I don't think I can do this amount of socializing two years in a row."

"At least finish your classes before you start trying to ditch your graduation, bro."

We both look to the person talking and I have no idea who it is. Henry hugs him immediately, something I don't see him do a lot with anyone other than me and his parents.

"Connecticut fucked your hair up," Henry says as he lets the man go. "You should move back to LA."

Then I realize the guy is Joe. "That's the plan. Give me another couple of years to survive law school, then I'll be back. Tell Damon I miss him, and I'll never cheat on him again I swear." They both laugh and look at me. "You must be Halle. I've heard a lot about you."

"I've heard a lot about your dates with Henry." He bursts out laughing. "It's really nice to meet you."

We chat about New York and promise that we'll all hang out when Henry and I are there next month. We talk about books, since Joe is a big reader, and when someone yells for a speech, he tries to convince Henry they're talking to him.

Nate stands at the top of the patio steps and fake-bows when someone wolf whistles at him. "Thank you, Colin, Stassie's dad, for that warm welcome." The crowd laughs and Henry wraps his arm around my shoulders, pulling me closer and kissing my temple. "I won't make this a long speech because I know everyone is eager to celebrate, and at some point, one of you will start booing me.

"I'm so proud to be here to celebrate all our friendship group has achieved. My best friend of far too long, Robert Hamlet, is the newest UCMH faculty member, and the owner of a shiny new master's in athletic coaching. Lola's heading back east to try to take over Broadway and continue her lifelong mission to be the scariest person in New York City. Mattie and Bobby are continuing their hockey careers . . ."

"God, he loves the sound of his own voice, doesn't he?" JJ says, coming up behind us and making me jump. "He didn't make a speech about me when I graduated."

Henry's eyebrow quirks. "He didn't make any speeches. You guys got really drunk and performed the *Mamma Mia!* soundtrack on the karaoke all night."

"Oh yeah," JJ says, sipping his beer. "Did anyone bring karaoke?"

Nate is still talking as JJ and Henry chatter behind me. "Kris is going to med school, which terrifies me, and should also terrify the rest of you."

"How many more people do we know? Surely it's nearly over," Henry says, looking at his watch.

"Shhhhhh," I hiss, silencing them both.

"And my beautiful Anastasia: I love you so much, baby. I am so proud of you and everything you've accomplished this year. You've worked so hard . . ."

"When can I start the booing?" Joe says, looking over his shoulder at Henry and JJ for guidance.

"Surely it's soon," JJ says.

"And I'm going to wrap it up there, folks. Enjoy the drinks, enjoy the music and the food. I'm so happy we get to celebrate here together tonight."

Everyone claps and cheers; Henry's arm leaves my shoulders, his hand slips into mine and tightens. "Do you want to go for a walk?" I ask, kissing his cheek.

"Yeah."

We ignore Jaiden's interrogation as we walk down the steps to a lower area of the outdoor hotel space. After walking for a couple of minutes hand in hand, we find a bench beneath a floral arch. I rest my head on his shoulder as we listen to the sound of a fountain running somewhere behind us.

"What are you thinking about?" I ask Henry, kissing the back of his hand.

"That we should get Joy a harness so she can come to places with us."

"I love you," I say, meaning every single syllable with my entire heart. "And how much you love my cat makes me love you even more."

"I love you, too, Cap."

"More than you love Joy?"

He grins wickedly, wrapping his arm around me to pull me in for a kiss. His hand travels down my back until it reaches my waist. He uses his grip on me to maneuver me onto his knee. "I was raised not to tell lies."

When I try to wrestle him off me so I can run away, he clings to me a bit tighter, laughing hard. "Fighting is for fools, Halle, and you're not a fool."

"We need a new rule book," I declare, wrapping my arms around his neck. "You're out of control without guidelines. Rule book entry number one: stop using that ridiculous saying against me."

His lips pull into a straight line as he shakes his head. "Sorry, the board said no."

"The board is biased, I fear."

"That might be true. They never punished me for all the times I thought about you naked."

My jaw drops. "That wasn't even a rule! It was that you weren't allowed to bring it up!"

"Oh, my bad." Henry kisses my shoulder, and in the distance, I can hear the start of a song that is almost definitely from *Mamma Mia!*

"Thank you for being on my team, Henry."

"Thank you for giving me the love I could never picture."

I take his face in my hands, kissing him deeply with every ounce of my love for him. "And how does it make you feel? Now that you can picture it?"

He's quiet while he thinks. "Like I'm living in my daydreams. So, pretty damn happy."

Acknowledgments

WOW. ANOTHER BOOK! LOOK AT US GO.

I have a long list of people I need to say thank you to for making *Daydream* happen:

To start, I want to say a big, fat thank-you to my agent, Kimberly Brower, because I wouldn't have gotten through writing this book without her and her patience. Submitting a book *very* late is a −12 out of 10 experience and I do not recommend, but taking the time I needed was a million times better knowing that I always have you in my corner, Kimberly.

My assistant, Lauren, who appropriately nicknamed this book NIGHTMARE. Thank you for letting me use your eldest-daughter trauma for my commercial gain, and I'm sorry I made you read it so many times. Thank you for listening to me talk about this book every day for a year and holding my hand every step of the way.

My entire publishing team at Simon & Schuster and beyond. Boy, I really made you wait for this one, didn't I? Thank you so much to everyone who changed their priorities, worked late, worked the weekend, did things in totally ridiculous time frames all so we could get Halle and Henry into people's hands on time. Thank you for your patience with me and your commitment to helping me find my groove in this weird traditional publishing landscape that I'm still adjusting to. I'm so grateful to each and every person who keeps the Hannah Grace wheel turning.

Johanie, thank you so much for your kind thoughts and input to make this book the best it can be.

My friends who have been so understanding and gracious when I ignored their messages for weeks at a time while working on this book. Thank you for telling me I *would* finish . . . repeatedly, because I've been super annoying for the past year and have needed so much reassurance. Thank you to everyone who answered my questions, read chapters, let me bounce a paragraph off them even with your own lives, projects, and deadlines looming.

Special mention to Nicole, Jess, Sarah, and Kimmy for reading the roughest drafts of this work. Then again, when I decided to start from scratch.

My husband and my dogs, for being my team.

My sister, because I couldn't write 125k words about Halle without mentioning the eldest daughter in my family. Thank you for shouldering all the weight so I didn't have to; I swear I'll make it up to you.

My readers, you're the best. I'm so lucky and I'm so excited/terrified to talk to you about *Daydream* now you've read it! I wouldn't be able to do all of this without you all.

Finally, thank you to Taylor Swift, Warburtons Potato Cakes, and my Stanley cup for all that you do for me.

(HALLE'S VERSION)

STAY BEAUTIFUL	3:56
OUR SONG	3:21
I'M ONLY ME WHEN I'M WITH YOU	3:33
YOU BELONG WITH ME (TAYLOR'S VERSION)	3:51
JUMP THEN FALL (TAYLOR'S VERSION)	3:58
BYE BYE BABY (TAYLOR'S VERSION)	4:02
ENCHANTED (TAYLOR'S VERSION)	5:53
HAUNTED (TAYLOR'S VERSION)	4:05
LONG LIVE (TAYLOR'S VERSION)	5:18
I KNEW YOU WERE TROUBLE (TAYLOR'S VERSION)	3:40
I ALMOST DO (TAYLOR'S VERSION)	4:05
HOLY GROUND (TAYLOR'S VERSION)	3:23
BLANK SPACE (TAYLOR'S VERSION)	3:52
STYLE (TAYLOR'S VERSION)	3:51
YOU ARE IN LOVE (TAYLOR'S VERSION)	4:27
KING OF MY HEART	3:43
DRESS	3:50
CALL IT WHAT YOU WANT	3:24
I THINK HE KNOWS	2:53
PAPER RINGS	3:42
FALSE GOD	3:20
CARDIGAN	4:00
MIRRORBALL	3:29

INVISIBLE STRING	4:13
WILLOW	3:36
NO BODY, NO CRIME (FEAT. HAIM)	3:36
LONG STORY SHORT	3:45
VIGILANTE SHIT	2:45
SWEET NOTHING	3:08
PARIS	3:16
I CAN DO IT WITH A BROKEN HEART	3:38
THE ALCHEMY	3:17
SO HIGH SCHOOL	3:49

About the Author

HANNAH GRACE IS AN ENGLISH author, writing adult contemporary romance between characters who all carry a tiny piece of her. When she's not describing everyone's eyes ten-thousand-times a chapter, accidentally giving multiple characters the same name, or googling American English spellings, you can find her oversharing online, or, occasionally, reading a book from her enormous TBR. Hannah is the #1 *Sunday Times* bestselling author of *Icebreaker* and *Wildfire* and a proud parent to two dogs.

Don't miss the
first two novels in
the *Maple Hills* series

Available now

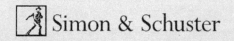